AMBER ROSE

A book of manners, magic and mayhem...and, perhaps, a tad too many scones

All Ambrose Fulton wants is to enjoy his idyllic life at Hatfield, helping his wife Milly raise their little son, tolerating Aunt Prudence and entertaining their friends.

What he gets is a ferocious assault from a violet-eyed automaton that devastates the estate and makes off with his enchanted clockwork arm, brutally ripped from his shoulder. To the rescue, barely in time to save his life, come friends Edward Huntington, gentleman magician, and his wife, the monster-slayer Jemima.

Whoever sent the machine can only have wanted one thing: to glean the secrets of Huntington's magical mechanical designs for purposes clearly nefarious. Now as well as wrangling an anxious innkeeper, a fake heir, interfering magistrates, odd magicians and some thoroughly unexpected visitors, they must uncover their mysterious enemy's identity and stop them or who knows what evil ends Huntington's inventions will be put to?

AMBER ROSE

Cry Havoc Book 3

DONNA MAREE HANSON

ISBN ebook 978-1-922360-19-9

ISBN Paperback 978-1-922360-24-3

ISBN Hardback 978-1-922360-20-5

ISBN Hardback Large Print Version 978-1-922360-21-2

Edited and proofread by Maxine McArthur

Cover by Croc Designs https://crocodesigns.com/

CHAPTER 1

Hatfield Estate, Near Kiddlington Oxfordshire, 1863

The noon sun shone through the drawing room's French windows, bathing the room in light. Cool, freshly painted blue walls refreshed Fulton's mind and heart, a result of his wife's redecorating. Her choice in furnishing was as tasteful as it was delightful. Fulton stepped closer to the windows to view the sweet prospect across the trim, green lawn to the woods beyond. In the distance, a light breeze bent a few boughs and branches rippled in the wind.

A fire crackled and popped in the hearth, making Fulton start. Why was he so jumpy? Giving a slight shake of his head, he turned his attention to the domestic scene. A sigh escaped as he smiled. On the sofa sat Milly with their new babe, Aloysius, in her arms. Brown ringlets escaped her lace cap and she wore a pale pink gown without flounces or elaborate trim and looked very fine. Their gazes met, her dark eyes glowed with joy. A joy he shared.

A few years ago, the idea of a family and owning this house was beyond his imaginings. Back then, he had longed for death, for release from the pain of his injuries and the pitiful existence that awaited him. All that had changed when he met Mr Edward Huntington, scientist and covert gentleman magician, and through his skill, Fulton's injuries were no longer a handicap but a blessing. He chuckled to himself and placed the newspaper, with its disturbing headlines, on the side table and rubbed his good hand over his shaved scalp, feeling the regrowth there. He still wore a white glove to hide his prosthetic hand, metal fingers covered in chamois to give the appearance of skin. Most of the time his good hand was gloveless, unless in company as the scars were unsightly.

He checked the time and cast his gaze out along the drive, hoping to see the Huntingtons a full hour before they were expected. He was keen to talk to Huntington of the things he read in the newspaper, and whether Huntingdon knew more. A series of strange attacks on factories with the papers stating that it was machines stealing parts. It was mind-boggling and odd. Thinking of Huntington brought Jemima Hardcastle as was, to mind. No one could be in her company and not be altered by it—for good or ill. Now Edward's wife, she had calmed somewhat. Although he would not underestimate her capacity for shenanigans, ever. Nor would he underestimate her loyalty to her friends and the lengths she would go to protect them from harm.

Fulton took a seat, hoping that this restlessness he was feeling would dissipate. Yet, he knew with this great gift of life and family came fear—fear that he could lose it all. Was that the reason he felt uneasy this morning? He was not generally given to fancy. A long sigh escaped him as he studied his companions.

On the other side of the room, Aunt Prudence sat with her generous behind on her favourite winged chair, and gestured feverishly to the footman who was bringing in a tray of refreshments. Her petticoats and flounces made her appear a lot larger than she actually was. Today's ensemble was a bright pink dress with dark purple trim. It ought to look horrible but for some reason it did not. Fulton was in such a good mood, he could tolerate her overbearing ways with equanimity.

"Over there!" Aunt Prudence said pointing vaguely in the direction of a trolley. "No, not there. On the table." The harassed footman delivered the tray, and Aunt Prudence wobbled over to fill the pot from the steaming kettle. Surveying the tray, she lifted the first cover to inspect a plate of sandwiches and sniffed, wrinkling her nose, not in distaste but rather in judgement as to which would be the better choice. Next she studied a large chocolate cake, lifting an appraising eyebrow before lifting another cover so that the scones suffered her scrutiny. Luckily, the fruit cake was already sliced and was saved from the sharpness of her stare.

The footman paused and bowed by the door before leaving the room. The key to the tea chest hung from the aunt's waist as she was the keeper of tea. Very soon, she busied herself with tea making and as she made a decent cup, Fulton had little to complain about. He wished she was kinder to his staff. Deep down, he knew she was a loyal, feeling woman. He had yet to penetrate the secrets of her past and was always on the lookout for clues.

"Would you like some tea, Fulton?" Aunt Prudence asked, as she looked up from the tray, tea pot aloft in one hand and a cup and saucer in the other. Her face was framed by a large, white linen bonnet, which emphasised the roundness of her cheeks.

"I would, thank you." Fulton leaned back in his chair.

A happy chuckle from Milly as she talked to their son drew his attention.

"What has happened?" he asked.

"Our son just smiled at me." She looked up at him, her face transformed by delight. "He is extremely clever."

"More likely wind," Aunt Prudence said as she walked over with a cup for Fulton. "I shall give his back a good rub and then review your diet. Bland food, my dear, if you want to reduce wind."

Milly's mouth opened. "Aunt, you have already forbidden my favourite foods from my plate. I cannot imagine my diet blander."

Fulton narrowed his gaze and nodded slightly. It was interesting that Aunt Prudence knew a lot about taking care of children and nursing mothers, though she was childless and thought to be a spinster. She called herself Mrs Wainwright even though no mention was ever made of a Mr Wainwright. It made him wonder and he filed that thought away for later study.

Milly had chosen to feed the child herself, insisting that it was healthier than any alternative. During the day, she kept him close and only allowed the nurse to assist during the night. Thank heavens, Milly dealt with the smelly, leaky incidents and Aloysius was thriving by all accounts.

"Nevertheless, we should have another look at what might be disagreeing with the young master."

Milly met Fulton's gaze and rolled her eyes, smiling all the while. They knew the aunt meant well.

It made him swell with pride as he watched Milly grow and bloom in her new role as mistress of Hatfield and as a wife and mother. Milly had grit and was nearly as fearless as Jemima. While he admired that trait, it made him chill to his bones at the thought of her facing danger. Aunt Prudence, also, showed amazing backbone when they were fighting off Geneck's minions. Both he and Edward had agreed they could not look at a hat pin, nor an umbrella, in the same way again. Who knew such items of feminine fashion could be used as deadly weapons. A slight shudder had him pushing the memory away. An errant heartbeat told him that he was still restless, still anxious.

He checked his watch and nodded to himself. Huntington and Jemima were expected soon. In her last missive, Jemima had written that she was now to be referred to as wife and monster slayer. Not that her occupation had anything to do with the visit, he hoped. Jemima's purpose was to come to see Milly and the baby and share in friendly discourse. They were a group who were at home together and bonded by events and mutual affection.

Aunt Prudence offered him a slice of fruit cake, smiling as she did so. The aunt gave the appearance of a cantankerous, small-minded old woman, but he knew better. She was smart and resourceful and he wanted to know more about her past because he suspected it was not as unexceptional as she liked everyone to believe.

The baby cried, a sort of low sound that had Milly cooing to him. Being six weeks old, he was still tiny, more wrapping than actual baby.

"How are you faring, sweet," he called to Milly. "Shall I take him for a while so you can enjoy your tea while it is still hot? You see, I have finished mine." He gulped the remainder and swallowed the last bite of cook's deliciously moist fruit cake.

"If you would like to, Ambrose," Milly said in her quiet way. "Perhaps you should have a sandwich to fortify you, for baby tending can be tiring."

"I will do as you suggest." Ambrose stood up, placed his cup on the side table and snaffled a neatly cut quarter of sandwich on his way over to the settee to collect his son. The heat of the mustard made his eyes water and his throat itch. He cleared his throat before bending down and kissing Milly's cheek as he took the small bundle into his arms. After he pressed his lips on the wee babe's slightly furred head, he rocked him gently. Walking back and forth, he held the baby until the child settled, its eyes closing in sleep.

Aunt Prudence jiggled her cup, making a clinking sound. Fulton looked up, wondering at the sudden noise. Eyes wide, she put her hand on top of it. "I beg ..." The cup tilted sideways, and she grabbed it and lifted her eyebrows in surprise. Fulton frowned, not quite sure what had happened. Suddenly, his gaze shifted to where the teapot bounced in the tray. A slight tremor shifted the floor under his feet. "What the devil!" He thought perhaps it was a quake, not unknown in these parts but they were usually mild. But when the vibrations increased and a low rumble grew in pitch, he knew it was something else. Something bad. Something dangerous. Something like the headlines in the newspaper.

"Prudence?" His voice was urgent.

"Yes," she said, coming to attention.

"Take Milly to the safe room now."

He passed the baby over to Milly, who had leaped from the settee. "What is it?" Milly asked, holding their now squirming baby to her chest. The vibration was growing into a roar as the ground and this house protested.

"I know not what, but I have a feeling it is not good."

Prudence threw her arm around Milly's shoulders. "Come now. We must hurry downstairs."

"But what about Ambrose? He must come too."

Dashing over to her, he kissed her forehead and gently touched his son's head. "I will wait to see what this is. I will come to you when all is clear."

Over her head, to Prudence he mouthed. *Lock the door!*

The rumble now was so loud it was hard to hear their voices. Milly turned her head over her shoulder to meet his gaze as Prudence led her away.

The butler, Discombe, came to the door. "Sir?"

He turned towards the thin man whose face was elongated with horror. "Take all the staff and flee out the back door. Do it now, man."

"Should I ring the alarm bell?"

"Yes!" He had installed the alarm bell for such a purpose, much to the amusement of the butler and his housekeeper. "Hurry!"

The bell tolled and Fulton nodded. He had done all he could to safeguard the lives of his family and servants. If it was nothing then no harm done. They would consider him a paranoid old fellow who needed to be humoured. The rumbling vibrations increased as if drawing closer, the sound low and heavy, making it hard to breathe. This was no mere earth tremor. Yet he had no idea what it could be.

Ambrose leaped to the window and peered out. Nothing was visible. Wait. In the distance, trees tops swayed, gently at first and then more violently. One aged ash tree toppled, pushing over another. In a screech of tortured wood and the crash of branches, it fell. Another tree screamed as it burst apart. Was the earth opening up to swallow them?

Fulton narrowed his gaze. "What on Earth!"

An enormous silver-grey contraption burst into the open, pushing thick oak trunks aside as if they were twigs. It was around twelve feet high, with a stumpy body and a crude square head. There were glowing violet orbs where the eyes would be if it was a living thing. Large wheels wrapped in metal straps drove it along at a lumbering pace. Huge arms, with two pincer claws punctured the ground, gouging out earth, tearing out shrubberies and smashing statues in its path. Already his replica of David had been swept into an arc, the head sailing away from the shattered body followed by the copy of the Thinker that crumpled when it was side-swiped, the small pieces flying away. The carefully tended lawn tore up as the wheels ground on. A groundsman who had not responded to the alarm bell screamed and ran, fleeing from its path.

It was heading straight for the house, straight for him.

"God almighty!" Nonplussed, Fulton did not know what the contraption was going to do and what he could do to counteract it. Those violet orbs locked onto him and the automated monster continued straight for him. Was it going to plough into his house to get to him?

Too soon that question was answered. The motor growled as the machine drew closer, swivelled as if it was preparing to ram the outer walls.

"None of that," he said and opened the French windows and ran out onto the lawn, waving his arms to get its attention. The machine looked much bigger close up. "Hey!" he called, and waved his arms, hoping to distract it from destroying his home. "I am over here!"

It kept barrelling forward and took no notice of him. He tried to get in front of it and if he had not jumped very high and very fast, he would have been trampled. The machine did not falter. Its engine growled loudly.

Boom! It crashed into the front of his house. Glass and bricks and plaster exploded outwards onto the lawn at the force of the impact. The concussion had him faltering. Thank goodness, his family were in the safe room, a steel reinforced space, stocked with supplies and a well, where they could remain safe for a week or more. He hoped Discombe had emptied the house of servants. As he heard no screams from within the house, he took comfort in this. Now he was angry. How dare this machine attack his home, his house and destroy his property? Before he could attack the machine, a loud concussion startled him.

Throwing his arms up, he protected his head from a cascade of stone and lead roofing, sprinkled with glass that rained down upon him. He bolted, diving out of the way of the bulk of the debris. From the ground, he gaped in amazement. The contraption had destroyed the front of his house without the slightest hint of damage to itself. It swivelled as if seeking something.

"Hey, over here!" Fulton yelled, struggling to be heard over the din of the machine and the destruction of his walls. He winced and his chest burned with outrage. How dare he be attacked in his own home —a man's house was his castle.

The brutish thing pivoted, violet eyes meshing with his own. It backed up suddenly, taking out an interior wall and causing part of the upper floor to collapse. Fulton sensed this was a deliberate provocation. It swung its upper torso, seemed to choose another target, pivoted on its wheels and rammed the next section of the outer wall.

Now Fulton was angry. "Stop! This is my home. Please!"

He ducked away as more debris flew in his direction. The portrait of his father whooshed past his nose. No great loss, he thought. His mother's porcelain collection shattered under a beam that dropped from the upper floor and he cringed. Milly had been fond of that particular set as had he, as it brought pleasant recollections of his sweet mother, who had endured a lot and died too young.

The contraption was so big and powerful he did not know where to strike. He picked up a beam, a heavy thing and threw it with all of his enhanced might. It hit the target but bounced off the outer casing harmlessly. One of its arms moved and Fulton concentrated, sprinted and leaped to latch onto it. The speed with which it threw him off surprised him. He tumbled through the air, a smear of green, blue and debris in his gaze. On landing, he lay stunned on the lawn, trying to draw breath as he assessed how far this thing had tossed him, like a leaf as they say.

He pulled himself to his feet and ran at the machine. Assessing the casing as best he could, he looked for a way to access its innards. He landed above the guarding that protected the wheels and studied the body. Ripping out the heart of the mechanism appeared the only way to stop it. Yet he could see no ready access. All the panels were welded shut.

If only Huntington and Jemima had arrived already. He was sure his clever magician friend would know what to do. Huntington could throw a spell and smash it to pieces. All he had was brute force in one arm and a leg. These had served him well in the past, but against this monstrosity he feared he might come off second best. A daunting prospect that put him at odds with his former contentment. He could lose it all. The house could be repaired but lives were not replaceable.

The mechanical beast travelled further into the house, heading for the library. Ambrose wondered how Milly and the baby were doing and he prayed that the safe room held up to the total destruction of his house. Even though the safe room was nigh on impenetrable, he wondered whether the weight of the machine could cause it to drop through the floor and crush the heavy steel. This attack was beyond anything he had envisioned, and he hoped the preparations he had made would withstand the onslaught.

Fulton took a running jump and caught hold of the machine's mechanical arm. He tried wrenching it off but it was futile. Not soft flesh and bone that could be ripped apart. This machine was reinforced, made to withstand heavy impacts. He was about to let go when the machine's other arm reached for him, its pincer hands grabbing him around the waist. Sensing danger, the machine had finally taken notice of him. He tried to push off the carapace to leverage his body free, but the pincer holding him moved him out of reach and left him dangling foolishly. His heart fluttered as he sensed some intelligence behind this new move.

Using both fists, he smashed against the pincer gripping him and nothing would budge it. His organic hand bled, leaving red smears on the grey metal. Desperate to break free, he pivoted and kicked and bashed against the metal prongs that held him. It dawned on him too late that he was held fast.

The other pincer hand drew close. At first he was puzzled. What was the thing trying to do, bash him against the ground, tear him apart? With finer precision than he supposed the machine to have, it gripped his mechanical arm. Fulton tried to pull away but he was held fast. Panic seized him. The automaton tugged, twisted and ripped his arm off. Fulton screamed. The pain rushed into his brain like a punch to the head. He may have blacked out. Blood pumped out of the raw stump of his arm where his artificial arm had been attached.

Fighting nausea and fear and regret, he tried to stay conscious as the machine lifted him to its face. The last thing he saw was the violet glow like a fire burning in dark pits. Fulton struggled to maintain consciousness as blood pumped from the stump of his arm. He wrapped a hand around his wound, trying to stop the blood from flowing. He felt weakness wash over him. The arm was more than an appliance, it suffused him with Huntington's magic. They had discovered that previously when the gem powering his arm was drained. So too had Fulton been drained near to death. He could survive this. Had to. He had so much to live for. Blackness crept in from the side of his field of vision. He struggled to stay conscious. He had the leg still. He prayed that the machine did not take that as well as the sense of his surroundings faded.

The pincer fingers released. He dropped from a height, felt the passing of the air. The debris field of his house rushed up. He could not even use his legs to cushion the landing. The ground smashed him in the face. The world went into a dark spiral of agony and senselessness.

CHAPTER 2

The carriage travelled at a quick pace, jostling them on their jolly way. Jemima was excited and happy. After a lovely snuggly time with Edward in bed that morning, she grinned from ear to ear. That was followed by a delightful and nourishing breakfast prepared at the inn. She peered out the window at the green of the countryside, fields of corn, a few bare fields with fluffy white sheep. A number of black cows lifted their head as they trotted by. "We should be arriving soon," Jemima said to Edward. "I am so excited to see the baby."

Edward chuckled and his intense blue eyes regarded her with amusement. His curly brown hair swept around his forehead and ears in a Brutus style. He was overdue for a haircut so it was not a deliberate affectation. "Not Fulton or Milly or even Aunt Prudence?"

Jemima smoothed out the creases on the skirt of her burgundy silk gown. Her high-neck blouse was lightly frilled around her neck and the cuffs were embroidered in white statin. Her short jacket needed to be buttoned up before she alighted. She noticed the affectionate twinkle in her husband's eye. "You are trying to tease me."

Her reflection showed a small black pillbox hat cocked on her head, with a fine lace veil and burgundy silk flowers attached to the crown. She had spent a good deal of thought on her wardrobe, wishing to impress Aunt Prudence with her taste and to please Milly that she looked so well.

"I would not dare tease you. I am just trying to gauge your level of anticipation. You will be pleased to see Fulton, I am sure." Edward glanced away to the window and his Adam's apple lifted and fell. Jemima narrowed her gaze. Her fondness for and closeness to Ambrose Fulton was not quite a bone of contention between them. Fulton had looked after her when Edward had been kidnapped and her friend knew her well. And they liked each other. They were not in love with each other but they loved each other. At least Jemima knew she loved Fulton as well as trusting him with her life and that of her husband's. Also, he was so easy to tease that he gave her much sport. She had hoped that now Geneck had been laid to rest and she had had time to know and love her husband more, that his envy of Fulton might be less. She reached for his hand and squeezed.

"My love, of course I want to see them all. Just as I would be pleased to meet little Aly's nurse. God forbid I was left with the baby to tend on my own without knowing who to call on."

He studied her and she smiled at him easily, no longer shy. He was her life as well as her love. She owed him the very air that she breathed. To top that off, he was a remarkably good and compassionate man. Generous to a fault. Although he would not agree, given his treatment of those closest to him. But that was all to be forgot, now that he had made amends to Milly and Aunt Prudence. "How logical of you, Jem."

She could have taken that comment as a compliment or a tease. As Edward's clear blue eyes were entirely shining with love, she decided it was a compliment. She smiled and batted her eyelids. "I have not had much to do with babies, in general. I have seen them being wheeled through the park when I was living in London. And our under gardener just had a little girl, called Mary Jane. I saw her in her mother's arms. The mother, Margaret, asked me if I wanted to hold her, but I pretended to sneeze and said I ought not."

"What you have said goes against this desire to see the baby."

Jemima laughed. "Yes, well it is Fulton and Milly's baby so is bound to be perfect and well behaved."

He took her hand in his and squeezed it gently. "Are you sad you do not have a child, my love?" He lifted her hand to kiss her knuckles. The reasons for not being able to conceive were due to her operation to install her Ruby Heart, a device implanted in her chest to keep her heart beating. The ruby that powered it was filled with Edward's magic and caused such a bright glow, he had to fashion a metal casing to close it up and dampen down the light. In the dark, the ruby glow would infuse her skin. When Edward had operated on her she had been technically dead and Edward theorised that she would not be able to have children. Later, when she appeared to be absorbing magic from the ruby itself, that was further evidence that she was not normal, that she had her own inherent magic from birth. When the savage vampire beast, Geneck, had come for her at the Priory, where the Brotherhood had taken her, something even more extraordinary occurred. In her effort to defeat Geneck and save her soul, she drew all of the emerald fire from Geneck, thus killing him. Afterwards, she had absolutely reeked with power and it had taken long months to tame it, and longer to hide it. She had accepted her lot was to be infertile and as there had been no conception to gainsay Edward's theory.

She leaned into him companionably. "Well ... yes ... sometimes. I am sad for you too, as would not you like a son to carry on after you?"

Edward rested his head against the seat and looked straight ahead, as if he was picturing something in his mind. "To be honest, I have not given it much thought. You have brought me such happiness so I have not had time to think of such things. I am just now twenty-five, mind."

"Well, yes, still young, I suppose. When I think about it, I consider it would be hard to be a monster slayer with a babe in arms."

Edward chortled. "You destroyed Geneck and now you think you are a monster slayer?"

She slid her gaze sideways at him. "It might end up being a career choice. We know more danger lurks. We just do not know where or what. I imagine there will be monsters involved. I am a dangerous weapon and I do not like monsters." Serious, Jemima turned to peer out the window and frowned. White and grey haze, no, smoke, funnelled into the sky. "Ohh there is smoke rising over there. Is that not near Hatfield?"

Edward leaned over her to take a look himself. Dark brows settled over his eyes. "I think you are right. The farmer burning off, perhaps?"

"Perhaps not," she demurred, getting an uneasy feeling in her belly.

They shared a look. "Surely they are safe. It has been so quiet since Geneck was destroyed." She grabbed hold of his hand. "Do not leave me behind." He had been practising translocation and was good at it now. The first time he had tried it was when she was trapped at the Priory with evil magical brothers and the monster Geneck. The situation had been dire. Diligently, Edward had practised translocation with tutelage from Uncle Ferdy and he was a dab hand at it now. She interpreted the look of concern and the decision in his eyes in a second. She had come to have an intimate knowledge of his much-loved face, this last year.

Edward gave her a sharp nod and bashed on the roof. "Faster if you can, driver!"

Immediately, the driver called out and cracked the whip, urging the horses faster. The carriage jolted and then picked up pace. It was an agonising wait as they sped along, the column of smoke spewing thicker and faster. After twenty minutes, they turned into the drive at Hatfield. The smoke did not increase further from its initial display, which was a good sign, but did little to ease their worry for it definitely did originate at Hatfield. She clung to Edward's hand, fearful for their friends.

While the monster Geneck had been destroyed, one or more of those who had tried to take her Ruby Heart was at large. Uncle Ferdy had identified the culprits and theorised about the cadre being more widespread than those who had been killed in the attack on the Priory. And they had been expecting something. That the evil sorcerer was after Edward's machines, that was all they knew. They had tried to take her heart. If not for Geneck's attack, she might very well be dead. The only other devices resided in Fulton.

Utter chaos spilled across the landscape as they rounded the curb on the gravel drivel and the house came into view. The building had been demolished as if by some earthquake. Piles of brick lay in mounds and parts of the upper floor hung precariously as if waiting for a wind to assist in their final collapse. The sight that met their eyes had them speechless. Jemima covered her mouth, eyes wide. The driver pulled up short of the house as the drive was gouged up and tumbled with debris. Pushing open the carriage door, Edward stumbled out, his features composed in utter disbelief.

"How?" she cried as she joined Edward on the drive. What could have razed Hatfield to the ground?

"Nothing good. I cannot detect magic."

Jemima blinked as she tried to take it in. If not magic, not an earthquake, then what?

"Fulton! Milly!" Edward yelled as he ran toward the ruin.

Jemima tumbled out of the carriage, still stumped by the scene before her. "Mr Coarchman, quick as you can. Get help from the village."

The driver gaped at the destruction, then called on his mounts, reversing and turning them in the drive.

Following, her maid Beth shared a smaller carriage with Roderick Seaward, Edward's valet. Jemima ran over and waved them to a stop. "Go with our carriage to the village. Bespeak rooms at the inn if you can."

"Yes, ma'am," Beth said. "Cor, what do you think happened?"

"I have no idea but it is not good."

Jemima gathered her skirts in one hand, her other on her hat, as she raced after Edward. She scanned the wreckage as she ran. Edward searched for Fulton amongst such a jumble of roof parts, sections of walls and broken furniture. It seemed an impossible task. Jemima wished she had a connection to Fulton as she had with Geneck, because then she could have located him and sensed if he was alive or not. Alas, no such connection existed and her emotions, her fears overwhelmed her. Tears ran down her face. Her hat had fallen off in her mad dash after her husband.

As she neared where the front of the house had been she saw dual tracks where something had gouged its way across the lawn. Narrowing her gaze, she paused to study them, wiping her eyes with her handkerchief. It was not time for tears, she had to concentrate.

Huge ruts dug a path through the grass and the woods beyond. It must have been a machine of some kind. A huge machine, given the destruction of the kitchen garden walls and trees broken off, leaving jagged stumps. A machine she had never encountered or even imagined. An enormous train engine, perhaps? But the railway was not close. Besides, train engines ran on tracks and this machine had eaten up the lawn and knocked over tall trees that had stood for a hundred years. She pivoted to look around her. The machine had barrelled into the house, smashing through walls as if they were butter until it had levelled the whole building. Whatever the contraption was, it had not run amok and ploughed through the house and on its way again. It was a deliberate and calculated attack. From what she could see, the machine had not returned from whence it came but had continued on through the house and into the fields and woods beyond.

It was too quiet. No-one had answered Edward's cry.

"Fulton!" she screamed as well. "Fulton!"

Edward's voice reached her as he too called to his friend. Tears threatened. What a tragedy! The beautiful house, his and Milly's belongings destroyed. Such devastation. What of Milly and the baby and Aunt Prudence? Had they escaped? They had been waiting for her and Edward to arrive so they must have been here in the main reception room. "Fulton!" She called again, desperate for a sign.

A sob escaped her, and she put her fist to her mouth as her feelings started to get the better of her. All kinds of horrible fates flooded into her mind. For her friends' sake she had to hold herself together and not give in to the sheer horror and desperation this scene excited.

She was certain Fulton had acted to protect his house, his family. He would have tried to prevent the attack. She remembered his letter, telling her about the safe room he was building in case there was an emergency. He would have faced the threat outside in the front of the house and he would have sent his family to safety. She was sure. Fulton had such a clear head when faced with danger.

She followed along the path the machine had taken, stepped around gouged earth, fallen bricks, broken furniture and splinters of floorboards. Casting her gaze around, she saw Edward climbing over chunks of the outer wall. Calling for his friend and digging around to search.

Jemima focussed her mind, assessing where Fulton had fought. Here the creature changed direction. Her mind conjured up Fulton fighting and distracting the thing from harming his family. She continued on in that direction. Books lay in piles, destroyed and crushed. A small fire burned, a spill from what used to be the fireplace.

"Fulton?" she checked the ground, behind overturned furniture, under pieces of wood, flinging a section of wall away using her magical strength. Overhead, parts of the upper floor creaked and swayed. There were remains of floor boards and support beams and carpets. Jemima thought the creaking sounded ominous, as if a section was about to fall.

It was the blood that caught her eye. A pool of blood, bright crimson among the pages of books. "Fulton!" She turned to call to Edward. "Over here."

Edward's head jerked up. With a nod, he headed to where she stood. In a pile of debris, she saw Fulton's leg. "Oh please, be alive, Fulton!" He was her best friend, the closest person to her other than her husband. He was strong and solid and she could not imagine him not being alive. Could not imagine a life without him in it.

His real leg was warm, despite cuts and his bloodied trousers. "Help me, I need to lift this. Is it safe to do so?" she called to Edward.

Soon he was there, checking where Fulton's body was in relation to the furniture pinning him. "You can lift it away now."

Jemima carefully hoisted the heavy oak bookshelf and tossed it away. There were benefits to having a vampire's strength.

At first glimpse, Fulton appeared dead. A wail of despair escaped her throat. "No, Fulton!" Tears fell down her cheeks. "Please Fulton!"

Edward knelt next to his body, flicking away the smaller debris clinging to Fulton's clothes and face.

Fulton let out a low moan. Despair leaped to hope. Jemima knelt next to Edward.

"Oh my God!" she saw his bleeding stump. "His arm!"

She searched around for the prosthesis but instinctively knew it had been taken, not lost in the battle.

Edward pulled out a handkerchief and scrambled to tie a tourniquet. Fulton's flesh was ash grey. He had lost a lot of blood. His forehead had a massive bruise and she could picture the machine dropping him there as it tore off its prize.

Edward's face showed it all. One of his precious devices had been stolen. Memories of the evil personages surfaced. Cold-hearted humans who had wanted knowledge no matter the cost. They had nearly ended her and had been thwarted and then fled. Some were killed outright but others had scarpered.

Fulton roused slightly and mumbled, his usually bright amber eyes dulled with pain and delirium. Jemima leaned in closer to listen to his words as Edward was trying to staunch the blood flow. "Miilllyyyy. Safe … roooom." Mercifully, Fulton passed out.

Her gaze passed over the remains of the house. Milly was buried under all that along with her baby and Aunt Prudence.

She drove to her feet. "Milly!"

Edward, intent on saving Fulton, did not look up. "You go," he said. "I cannot leave him like this. The danger has passed, I think. Be careful, though, you do not have proper control of your magic or your strength."

He and Uncle Ferdy had been training her, only it was taking time and she had not grasped all the essentials.

"I will do what I can," she replied to her husband. Given her strength it was logical that she do the heavy lifting. Edward knew how to keep Fulton in life. "Help will arrive soon from the village."

Fighting panic, Jemima assessed the ruin, trying to decide which way to go to retrieve her friends. She glanced down at the skirts of her beautiful dress and sighed. There was no hope for it as her skirts were already covered in dirt and soot. There were ragged tears where the fabric had snagged on sharp bits, revealing her petticoats beneath. There was no time to change into something else, even if she had something with her. "Goodbye, lovely new dress. I give you up for a good cause."

Closing her eyes, Jemima focussed and gently teased the power that dwelt inside her forward. The green of Geneck's emerald magic infused her body, muscle and bone and at its centre was the gentle ruby glow from her heart. The essence that she had drawn from Geneck fused with her own natural magic and also with what Edward had fused into the gem that powered her Ruby Heart. While the magic had come from different sources, it was all hers now.

Thus infused in sinew and in blood, she ran, building up speed as she leaped over a chunk of wall, tore through the remains of plaster and pushed and shoved roof beams and collapsed wainscotting out of her way. She tore off the shreds of her once beautiful day dress, so they did not impede her progress. Smoke from the untended fire licked around wood and carpet, and smoke billowed. This reunion had been intended to be a joyous occasion, a celebration of life and happiness. Now it was a desperate act to save life and limb. She turned back to where Edward tended Fulton and her heart clenched. She feared the worst but had to trust that Edward could hold Fulton in life as he had her in the past. Images of the blood haloing his body made her shudder.

"Milly!" she cried out, knowing her friend could not hear her but using the cry as a focus for her determination. Trying to orient herself in the ruin, she assessed where the stairs to the basement in this section of the house might have been. Fulton had written that stairs had been added close to where the family gathered as it was in the best position to access the safe room. Fulton was meticulous so she tried to figure it out. If this was the drawing room, and they were gathered there for tea, then the stairs to the basement specially excavated for the purpose would be about there. She pointed to what appeared to be the mid-point of the house. It was also away from the kitchen, which was at the other end of the house. Near the kitchen were basement rooms, left over from previous eras, where dry goods had been stored, a meat larder kept things cool, a cheese room a buttery, a place for barrels of ale and wine. No, those rooms were at the rear of the building.

She recalled the letter Fulton had sent to her describing how his staff were curious about the construction and thought him eccentric. Why did he not use the existing subterranean rooms? Because they were too far away and had way too much accessibility. Nodding, she narrowed her gaze at the destruction around her and thanked God he had the foresight to build a safe room. "Milly?" she called and was pleased there was no answer. If she had answered it would have meant they did not make the safe room in time. It was silly to be optimistic as dead bodies usually did not respond to queries. She checked as best she could for signs of limbs and blood and there was none visible. That gave her hope that they had indeed made it.

Jemima assessed her hands, which looked too delicate for heavy work. Her arms also belied the strength hidden in them. Again she set to, lifting away broken furniture, pushing bookcases to the side, parts of an old oak bed from the upstairs bedrooms tossed to the right. Chests and cabinets she threw aside, not caring where they fell or if they shattered on impact. She heaved fallen roof beams and tossed them to clear a path, brushing aside the masonry and plaster that showered over her as a result.

Coughing from the dust, she broke through smashed wood and a collapsed ceiling and sent the pieces sideways. Lighter fragments she swept out of the way until she came to another pile of brick which held down a heavy beam. It was taking too long. She checked her surroundings. No one had arrived to help them yet. Haste was important for when help did arrive, she would need to be circumspect about her abilities. She would have to pass herself off as having lesser strength.

Edward still tended to Fulton and she could only imagine what Milly and Aunt Prudence must be feeling, trapped below and not knowing what had happened, for surely they had heard the destruction taking place upstairs. The bricks she tossed behind her, working as fast as she could to uncover the beam. Then she bent down and heaved it up. It would not budge. There was more work to be done to release it. Moving along the beam, she found the problem. It was still attached to a cross beam that was buried in a hole in the wall that sloped over it. With a punch, she created a crack. Her knuckles smarted and as she blew on them, the pain soon receded. She kicked at the wall and the fracture grew. Another three kicks and she could then push and shove and peel off the remains of the wall from the cross beam. Then she yanked it away, making further inroads to clearing a path.

She was still a fair distance from where she thought the doorway was. Checking over her shoulder, she ensured no one was around, then she bent down and tossed debris left and right as she cut a path to the door. Under a collapsed section of the upper floor, she found an area free of debris and crawled through it, catching her petticoat under her knees every time she moved. If only she was wearing Milly's leather corset and breeches, this rescue would not have been as tiresome. Better still, she would have rescued them long before now. Ahead the door frame was intact, a solid frame holding up the floor above. She had not realised that Fulton had reinforced it as well. How clever of him.

Climbing to her feet, she tried the handle. It did not budge. She checked around it for where it was stuck and there was nothing. Surely they had not locked it. Oh well. Nothing for it but to kick it open. She backed up and shoved her feet at it, and rebounded. The door shuddered in the frame. This time she used her shoulder and the resistance threw her back as she fell into the pile of debris. That was not good. Perhaps debris was blocking it from the other side. What else could possibly go wrong? She worried for her friends and how afraid they must be. She was afraid also. *What if the machine came back? What if Fulton...* She shook her head. *You must not think like that.*

"Milly? Aunt Prudence?" she shouted. "Can you hear me?"

She listened with her ear to the door. Nothing. Her heartbeat kicked up. Surely they made it down there before the machine attacked. She blocked out the image of them on the stairwell, buried in debris, crushed by large wooden beams. *Stop thinking like that.* She shook herself. There was nothing for it but to break the door to pieces and as the rest of the house was already in a similar state, she supposed no one would object or even notice.

There was not sufficient room to have a run at it. Since the draining of Geneck, Jemima had not tested out the full limit of her strength. Focusing with all her might, she punched the centre of the door. The surface appeared to flex inward and then straighten. The impact of her punch rebounded to her own fist. "Oww!" She blew on her knuckles and thrust her hand between her knees. That smarted. The door was reinforced. She was not like Fulton. A steel reinforced door was not something she could rip apart.

"Damn and blast!"

Why did Fulton have to be so thorough? Because that is what he was like, she muttered under her breath. So intent was he on keeping them safe, he had not considered the rescue part.

She had to find another way. Crouching down, she edged around to the left of the doorway and met a wall of debris. Edging around to the right, there was more debris, but less jammed in than the rest. Assessing what was above her, she chose a few pieces to remove. Nothing came crashing down on her. Breathing out slowly, she continued. Once a sufficient amount of the obstructions were gone, she saw there was light coming through from the sky that revealed next to the door a hole in the floor, which was large enough for her to pass through. She could bypass the door. She picked up a piece of marble and tossed it through the gap. It bounced, and bounced and bounced. The were stairs below.

"Milly? Can you hear me? Aunt Prudence?"

She held her breath, waiting for a response. Still nothing. Her hands shook. "Oh lord let them be safe."

The remains of her petticoat were cumbersome so she tore off some more, leaving the ragged remains of her undershift to cover her legs. Thank goodness, she had not worn her new crinoline cage petticoat. What a performance that would have been. As her clothing was now less bulky, she hoped it was enough for her to pass through the gap in the floor. Carefully, she manoeuvred her body to slide feet first into the gap. Swinging her booted feet to check the way was clear, she lowered herself down. There was nothing there to use as a foothold, just empty space. Reconsidering her approach, she was left without a choice as the remains of the floor she was holding onto began to give under her weight. "Damnation!"

If she was not careful, she would be the one buried under the debris. She pushed herself away from the floor before it collapsed and slid into the open space through to the basement. She fell and had time to wonder just how down far this safe room actually was. Her boots connected with fallen timber and gravel, making her ankle twist. Losing balance she ended up sprawled, a sharp spike of wood jutting out of the partially collapsed wall narrowly missing her face. Recoiling, she shifted to hands and knees. Her body ached in places, her back, her knees, her ankle and her head throbbed. Even though she was strong, she could be hurt. Not badly hurt as yet. However, it was a reminder to take care.

The visibility was poor. Shafts of sunlight lit up the remains of the ceiling but barely penetrated through the dust and smoke wafting through the air. Coughing, she waved the haze away and squinted into the dark corners. There looming out of the shadows was a dark grey box, resembling a large safe. Jemima had finally found the safe room. Fulton had not been original in his thinking. It did not look comfortable or romantic at all. If she was going to take refuge in a safe room, she wanted it to look pretty and be filled with nice things, good food, soft sofas and so on. Why could he not have painted it yellow with butterflies?

With a glance overhead to check if any debris looked likely to fall, she half crawled over to the hatch. Rapping her knuckles vigorously, "Milly? Milly!" she called, using her best loud voice.

No response. She checked over her shoulder just in case she had missed their bodies in the dim light. Nothing that she could see. That meant they were inside and if it really was thick steel, how on Earth were they going to hear anything?

Using her fists, she thumped on the door. The noise was muffled but if they were inside they would have heard it. She banged and banged and slapped the metal door with an open hand. "Milly!" she yelled.

Leaning her head against the cold surface of the door, she tried to think. She was certain they must have heard her so what was the problem? They did not know what had occurred. They could not be sure if it was safe. She tried thinking like Fulton, with his flashing amber eyes and lips tight: *Do not open the door until I give the all clear!* She nodded absently. Yes, that was definitely something he would do. That meant they were not going to open up because someone knocked on the door.

It was a safe room, meant to keep them secure in the event of an attack. She tried to think it through and then tried to think it through from Fulton's point of view. There had to be a code or some way to signal that all was clear. Had Fulton ever mentioned it? Possibly, but she could not remember, as her mind was in disarray. Fulton was injured, his house destroyed and all that tied up her mind in emotional knots. "Come on think! What would he do?"

What sort of code would a man like Fulton use? One that Milly or Aunt Prudence would understand. Not Morse code, surely?

She tried tapping out a rhythm, feeling stupid as she did so as she did not know Morse Code, just that it was dots and dashes. Surely Milly and Aunt Prudence would ignore it. Ear pressed up close to the cool metal wall, she listened. The door did not open. There was not a sound from inside.

Frowning at the door, she knew there was no way she could wrench it off with her bare hands or any other implements. Squatting down, she peered through the gloom into the remainder of the room. Maybe there was a lever or something to release the door. Would that make sense? What kind of things was Fulton protecting his family from? She sighed. *Well, let me see—murderers, monsters, vampires and their minions, evil sorcerers, a cranky brotherhood of magicians and Aunt Prudence's hat pins. Add huge machines to that list.* As she crept around, she found a small cupboard down low to the floor. The door to this opened easily. Inside was a small device. Luckily, next to it, folded into a corner was a small piece of paper. It had the Morse code alphabet on it. "Thank you, Fulton!" Slowly, she began to tap on the lever. *Unlock the door. It's me. Jemima.*

She peered toward the metal door and nothing happened. A terrible thought struck her: what if they did not know how to open it? She shook her head. Fulton was not that stupid. He would have shown them. Perhaps they did not believe it was her sending them a message.

She tried again. A low blow this time, but she was desperate. *Fulton is hurt.*

A few breaths later, the door unlocked with a series of metal clunks. Jemima raced over, thinking she and Edward should invest in a similar device in their own home. It must have cost Fulton a fortune, and the tradesmen and the servants must have thought he had lost his mind. Oh well, they would change their mind about that smart-like after this.

Milly pushed the door open and Jemima slid inside. They embraced. "Oh Jemima? I was so scared. Ambrose said not to open the door, except when he keyed in the code."

"Not helpful, when other people come to the rescue," Jemima observed.

"The sound. It was incredibly loud, even in here and I was so frightened." She paused to look out the door and around at the debris filling the basement. "What happened?" She grabbed Jemima's hand and squeezed.

Jemima glanced over her shoulder. "Well, it is a bit of a mess, actually." Jemima bit her lip. She needed to do better than that. Milly had lost her home and her husband had been left for dead. "Prepare yourself. It is bad. The house is badly damaged."

Milly opened her mouth, her skin went white and her eyes rolled up. "Milly! Milly!"

Jemima darted to support her friend. Luckily, Milly did not faint dead away. She gathered her strength. "I am well." She took her own weight. "How?"

"I think it was a large machine, the way things are smashed up. We will not know for sure until ... um."

"A large machine? How big is large?" Milly shook her head, eyes hollow with disbelief. She clung to Jemima as if she were her only anchor with reality. Her grip tightened on Jemima's forearm. "Tell me."

"As large as one could imagine and then bigger than that." Milly swallowed and her head shook slightly, a hasty denial of Jemima's words and their seeming unreality. "And Ambrose?"

"Alive but injured. Edward is with him."

Milly let out a cry and tried to push past Jemima. "Wait."

A pale Aunt Prudence stood, bonnet ribbons trailing the remains of a hat down her back, plaits half hanging down, a sleeping Aloysius in her arms. "Heaven protect us. Are we safe?"

Assuming the aunt had overheard, Jemima stepped further into the safe room, bringing a distraught Milly with her. Taking in her state of dress, Aunt Prudence sat down, holding the baby close to her chest. "You look to have battled at the gates of hell, my dear."

Jemima looked down at herself. She had lost the sleeves and bodice of her gown somewhere and was dressed solely in a bloodstained, smoke smeared corset, the shreds of a shift and ripped bloomers. She still had her boots but her stockings were torn and stained. Her hair was a right tangle. "I am not fit to be seen," Jemima said before the aunt could.

As if conscious of her own appearance, Aunt Prudence tried to order her hair one-handed but stopped after she gaped at the vista of destruction visible through the open door. She patted Aloysius and made soothing noises, clearly upset herself. Jemima lifted her eyebrows. Who knew Aunt Prudence could be calm in a crisis? That women was layered in mystery.

Milly made to step around her again. "Wait," she said, putting her arm on her friend's forearm. Jemima's hands were bloody and torn but did not pain her. Milly's mouth gaped open at the sight of it. "You need to prepare yourself. The house ... it is completely destroyed ..."

Aunt Prudence exclaimed, throwing off all pretence at calm. "What, all of it? Destroyed?"

"I am so sorry." Jemima fixed her gaze on Milly, concerned her friend might lose her reason for surely it had not sunk in, the extent of her loss, the ramifications.

Milly looked down at the hand holding her still and then pressed a hard gaze at Jemima. "Let me leave," Milly said in a voice full of command. "I care nothing about the house. I must see to my husband."

"I know how you feel, Milly. Edward is with him and doing his best."

Milly's mouth hung open, and she covered it with a handkerchief, not exactly in time to stifle a sob. "I must go to him," her voice emotion-clogged.

Jemima pressed Milly to her shoulder. "I know, dear heart. But the staircase is blocked. We have to wait. We need help to get up to ground level." She gestured to her current state of undress. "As you can see, I had issues getting through."

Milly stood back and gazed down at Jemima, finally registering the state of her clothes. "But," Milly said. Her head lifted up and she gazed around, taking it in and then finally believed. Her chest rose and fell rapidly and her hands curled into fists.

Jemima patted her on the back, lowering her voice and speaking calmly. "Help is coming. Fulton is in the best of hands. You know this."

Milly burst into tears, finally giving way to despair-filled sobs. Jemima held her close, stroked her back and mumbled vague words of comfort.

Aunt Prudence looked on, shock and the need to care for the infant keeping her quiet for the moment. "It must have been frightful," Jemima said. "Did you hear much from in here?" Milly howled in response. Naturally curious and possibly insensitive, Jemima rolled her eyes at her own faux pas.

The poor woman was beside herself with worry. Not only was her home destroyed but her life could be irrevocably changed if Fulton ... god she dared not think it ... died.

Luckily, Aunt Prudence was ready to enlighten her. "We felt vibrations, deep ones. Will you not tell us what has happened? We were sent below before ..."

Jemima considered after all they had been through it was right to be straight with them. "Well, I did not witness it, so I can only tell you what I deduced from the evidence left behind. It was a monstrous machine as big as the house that has methodically and completely destroyed Hatfield, from the kitchen garden to the house itself. Nothing is left standing."

Aunt Prudence nodded slowly. "Right then. Hard to imagine that. As we are not leaving just now, do you think we could stay here in the safe room and make ourselves comfortable? There are some amenities within, and I think the baby needs changing."

Jemima looked about her. "Yes, that is a jolly good notion."

After Jemima led Milly further into the safe room, she was immediately impressed. While the exterior looked like a large safe, the interior had been decorated like the morning room, with cupboards full of supplies and a small area behind a privacy screen for necessities. A settee sat against one wall. Aunt Prudence proceeded to change the child's soiled clothing and Jemima put her hand over her nose and looked away, lest she lose her breakfast. Who knew babies were so odoriferous? Once the baby had his clothing sorted, the aunt comforted him as she sat on the settee. Milly calmed by the time she took a seat next to Aunt Prudence. The child cried, and she took her son in her arms. "He needs nursing. Forgive me. Do continue, please. What is the precise nature of Fulton's injury?"

Jemima let out a big sigh, pulled out a chair from the small table and could not think of a nice way to put it. "The machine ripped off his arm."

Aunt Prudence gasped. Milly paled. Milly knew of the arm, of course, but Aunt Prudence, Jemima was unsure if she knew.

"Did he lose a lot of blood?" Milly asked as she stroked her son's head as he fed from her. Jemima tried to keep her eyes on the ceiling lest she be accused of ogling Milly while she nursed.

"I am not sure. There was a lot of blood when we arrived." Why could she not find a way to lie to Milly? If she was in Milly's position, she would like the unvarnished truth.

Milly sighed and tears slid silently down her cheek.

"The poor man," lamented Aunt Prudence. "Why on earth would anyone harm him in such a way?"

Milly met Jemima's gaze, knowing the truth of it.

The baby nursed, his slurps audible in the confined space. A little soothing required after all the upset.

"Tea?" Aunt Prudence asked.

Jemima had a chance to notice the adequate provisioning. There was a kettle and a teapot, but she did not see how they could heat the water. "Why, yes, I would like a tea, thank you. Is there any of cook's fruit cake?"

Aunt Prudence busied herself in making tea. A makeshift stand with a lantern underneath served to heat water. It took an awfully long time, but it did distract from the situation. A watched pot never boils, but a kettle eventually lets out a small stream of steam and, eventually, boils once you look away for long enough.

They were just finishing off a good strong cup, when voices reached them.

"Hallo? Anyone there?" It was faint, but Jemima had been listening for help to arrive. "Excuse me, will you Aunt, Milly."

Jemima slipped out the door and stepped beneath the hole she had come down. "Down here," she called.

"Ahoy, Miss," the voice called again.

Jemima turned in a circle and then tilted her head to throw her voice up. "Hallo, we have a mother and a baby down here. And our old Aunt Prudence. The stairs are destroyed so we need assistance to get them out."

In a pinch, Jemima could get herself out. Although she was not about to leave the others and now there were people in the ruins, questions would be asked if she did. Avoiding undue scrutiny had to be a consideration in all this. The Fultons had to live in the neighbourhood and they wanted as normal a life as they could. She pulled a face as she considered the ruins. Maybe, a show of strength would go unnoticed.

"Don't you worry, Miss. Don't worry your little head about it. We'll handle it."

Jemima rolled her eyes and muttered under her breath. "I will handle you if you are not careful."

"Did you say something?" the voice asked.

"No, all is fine. Just be quick if you can."

There were a couple of men treading through the ruins, hopefully with enough sense to assess the damage and work out how to successfully get them out. There was no point standing there when she could be comfortable with the others. There might be some tea left in the pot after all. She went back into the safe room. "Is there any more cake, Aunt Prudence? Rescue is here, but I fear it will take a while for them to think of a way to get us out."

Aunt Prudence drew herself out of her chair and went to one of the cupboards. She drew out some fabric and brought it over. "You had best use this robe to cover yourself. You will not be fit for proper society but at least the workmen will not ogle your naked flesh."

Jemima was not naked but she was showing more flesh than what was thought proper. "That is thoughtful of you, thank you." Jemima replied, unravelling the cloth, which was a red silk Japanese robe. She slipped it on and tied the sash. It was better than nothing and it concealed all her pertinent bits.

Jemima was completely bored by the time their rescuers bellowed that they had devised a way to get them out. For herself, she could have managed to climb out but had to suffer herself to be rescued as well.

Their rescuers had devised a makeshift lift—a sort of swing, where one by one they sat on a bit of wood, which was tied to the ropes. Once secure, they were pulled up to the ground level by sheer brute strength. The simplicity of the solution annoyed Jemima because she could have thought of it first and rescued them ages ago. Milly went first, then Prudence with the baby and then herself. They gathered outside in a cleared space. Milly and Aunt Prudence gaped at the ruins, the shattered ornaments and crushed portraits. A half-burned sheet of music fluttered around their feet before disappearing into the stand of wall beams that remained upright. A cloud of misery hung around them. Milly muttered under her breath and Aunt Prudence prayed quietly.

In the waning light, as clouds obscured the sun, she could see that some of the debris had been shifted and stacked. Carriages and carts and horses and men milled around. It was apparent there had been much industry in trying to make order of the chaos. From where they were brought to the surface, a path had been made to the lawn, the part of the lawn undisturbed by the wheel tracks of the giant machine.

Edward and Fulton were nowhere to be seen. Jemima frowned. She stopped someone. "Excuse me, can you tell me where Mr Huntington and Mr Fulton are?"

Milly came up behind her. "Yes, tell me where is my husband?"

The man took off his hat and Jemima shivered in case it was bad news. "Excuse me. My name is Bright. I am a builder from up Yarnton way. I happened to be visiting a site nearby when the alarm came so I came here to volunteer my service to oversee the conservation of the building and rescue of survivors."

"We are grateful for your efforts." Jemima inclined her head.

The man continued. "The local magistrate is due to arrive in the morning to investigate this incident, ma'am. He will be in charge then."

"And my husband and Mr Fulton?"

"Mr Fulton's been taken to the inn in Kiddlington. You're to be taken there as soon as the carriage is ready. They had been resting the horses, ma'am. They are being harnessed back up to the carriage as we speak."

Jemima fretted. The survivors had no belongings. She had hers in the carriage, whereas Milly, the baby and Aunt Prudence had nothing but what they were standing up in. She turned on her heel and assessed the house. In daylight, they might be able to retrieve some items, but it was too late now as the sun was dropping rapidly to the horizon. They had been below for hours after the attack and Milly sagged against her, exhaustion caving in her cheeks like a chisel. Jemima hugged her across the upper arms. "You will see him soon, Milly."

The sky did not look like rain. She had to hope it would stay that way so that some personal items could be salvaged in the morning.

"But the baby, Mr Bright," Jemima said. "We have nothing."

Mr Bright nodded and bowed to Milly. "Your plight is well understood, Mrs Fulton. I believe the village has asked around, ma'am. There's a cradle and wrappings and whatnot at the inn already." He turned and indicated with his arm. "Come this way and I'll take you to the carriage. It looks to me that they have almost finished hooking up the horses."

With her arm around Milly, Jemima guided her to the carriage door. Aunt Prudence walked slowly, as if she was tired, but carried the baby effortlessly. Jemima tried to take the burden herself, only the aunt refused. Aly was Prudence's responsibility it seemed. That was a good thing, thought Jemima, as Milly was not up to much. Milly wept some more and buried her face in Jemima's side.

"He will be well, Milly. He cannot leave you now that he has found such happiness."

Those words of comfort were received with an increase in the volume of wailing. Through weeping words, Milly brokenly advised that it was what Fulton feared most. Having achieved such happiness, he feared, nay expected, to lose it all.

"Oh dear!" Jemima said as she assisted Milly into the carriage with the aid of the footman.

Aunt Prudence passed little Aly to her so she could climb into the carriage. Jemima took a moment to enjoy a cuddle. "Hello there, handsome boy. I am your Aunty Jem." The child did not reciprocate her greeting as he was still in the arms of Morpheus. A quick assessment of his features revealed no amazing resemblance to either parent. Time would tell, she supposed.

Aunt Prudence's eager hands reached down for the baby bundle. Jemima handed Aly over and hoisted herself inside to join them. Milly she took immediately back into her arms, making soothing sounds instead of talking, because all she did was make things worse when she opened her mouth.

Jemima peered through the window for a last glimpse of the smoking ruin of Fulton and Milly's beautiful home. Heads were going to roll if Jemima had anything to do with it. She was going to slay the monster machine that did this, and find who created it and give them the comeuppance they deserved. No matter what argument or obstacle her husband may toss her way, that was her vow.

CHAPTER 3

At the inn, she found that Edward had commandeered all the rooms. As the news of the disaster had already spread, the innkeeper had obliged. Jemima was met by Mr Copperwraith, the innkeeper, who advised that Fulton was settled in the best room and that Mr Huntington was attending on him.

Nursery furniture and supplies were arriving by cartloads and the ostler was sending them upstairs to the rooms set aside for Milly and the baby. Aunt Prudence was to reside in an adjoining room. "A room for yourself and your husband has been prepared," the innkeeper advised. "I have also taken the liberty of creating an upstairs parlour so you can gather and receive guests in style."

"Guests?" Jemima retorted. "We shall not be entertaining guests as far as I know."

The innkeeper smirked and touched the side of his nose with a forefinger. "You will find that the Fulton's neighbours will want to pay their respects to the family. The vicar too and others I am sure."

Jemima wrinkled her brow. "I suppose you are right. We will need another bedchamber, too, for I believe we will need to send for a doctor from London."

The innkeeper frowned. "That will take up all the available rooms."

She could see the calculations taking place in that distant but slightly greedy look in his eye. "I suppose I could rearrange my family to accommodate things." He met her gaze. "Leave it to me. The servants can be housed in the converted barn. It is absolutely comfortable. Mr Discombe, Hatfield's butler, is organising the staff as we speak."

"Excellent." A maid led them up the stairs with Aunt Prudence spouting orders: a meal, hot water, a tub, and if there were any robes they could use so their clothing could be laundered.

"At once, ma'am," the maid said as she opened the door to Milly's room and then the adjoining one for Aunt Prudence. She was a young girl, hair tied up in a bun, with a little cap perched on it. She wore a clean white apron that draped down the front of the dark brown dress.

The maid curtseyed. "Mrs Huntington ma'am. If you will follow me, your room is around the back."

Jemima blinked. "The back?"

"Yes, it is one of our best rooms."

The maid led the way and Jemima followed, thinking that all the rooms appeared to be the best room. It was a small inn and she supposed they were doing their best in the middle of an emergency. Let us get through the day before we think on long-term plans. There was no point in talking to Milly at this point in time and inviting her to Willow Park. The Fultons had a small townhouse and there were various well-to-do neighbours that might invite them to stay while their house was ... rebuilt? Abandoned? She had no idea and it was none of her business, even though she would offer what assistance and accommodation she could.

Jemima stood on the threshold of a perfectly adequate bedroom. There was some space for a chair by the fire and some hooks for clothes and a chest of drawers with a mirror for her toilette.

"Is the room to your liking ma'am?" the maid asked. "There is a dressing room over there, with a trundle bed if required."

"Yes, thank you. Pray what is your name?" Jemima asked.

"It is Martha. Martha Copperwraith."

"Thank you, Martha."

She was still standing there when the innkeeper strode up the hall. "Will you not enter?"

Jemima started. "I am terribly sorry. I did not mean to linger in the hall. There is so much going on my head is in a spin."

Martha received a nod from her relative and curtseyed before heading out.

"Indeed, Mrs Huntington, a most calamitous day. Is there any news from Hatfield about what happened?" He blinked hopefully at her. "I heard it was a quake of some kind but we felt nothing here. Perhaps there was some instability in the land."

"I cannot enlighten you, sir. We arrived after the ... er ... incident."

The innkeeper waited and then nodded when he realised she was not going to elaborate. "We haven't heard of such devastation since the floods of 1833."

"We are much obliged to you and the village for all your support."

"This inn was built in 1815. This town has witnessed many great happenings. Withstood a civil war. We were on the side of the King here, ma'am. Hence the name. We can withstand anything."

"Of course." Jemima prayed that the inn did not need to survive anything. God forbid that the machine was sent again. As she could not or would not entertain such a possibility she swept it from her mind.

Narrowing her gaze, she stepped into the room and could find nothing amiss. The innkeeper had been modest in his description. The accommodation was neat and well-appointed. She opened a door to the dressing room and a small trundle. Room for a maid or a valet. Perhaps Mrs Copper wraith had good taste. "It is a sweet room. I am sure we will be most comfortable."

"You are so gracious, ma'am." He bowed and backed out of the room. Not long after, a couple of men lugged their trunks up the stairs and plonked them at the foot of the bed. After she counted their trunks and hat boxes, she tipped the ostler and was alone.

On looking at her reflection, she gasped. Her face was dirty, her eyes darkened with soot. Her hair stood on end. Heavens, she had been having a conversation with the innkeeper looking like she was a destitute chimney sweep. Opening her robe revealed strips of shift and bloomers, blackened with soot and her bodice barely doing the work of hiding her breasts. "Heavens. How did Mr Copperwraith keep his countenance?"

She opened the door and called out for assistance. "Beth?" All was silent. "Yoohoo! Hot water and a bath, if you please?"

Martha appeared, panting as she arrived, having run up the stairs. "I'm sorry ma'am, we only have a hip bath. Will that do?"

Jemima blinked, as she calculated this disappointment. "It will have to, I am afraid. Have you seen my maid, Miss Street?"

Martha curtsied. "Yes, ma'am. She is in the kitchen. Shall I fetch her?"

"If you will let her know I am in need of a bath and her assistance."

"Right away, ma'am." Martha scurried back down the stairs.

Back in her room, Jemima stripped off her ruined things and drew on one of her dressing gowns and slid her feet into some soft slippers. While she waited for her tub and hot water, she rummaged around her things to find some items for Milly. A nightgown, undergarments, a petticoat and a dress that might suit. Gathering these up, she sauntered down the hall to deliver them and check in on how the other women were settling in. Aunt Prudence was holding the sleeping Aly and there was no sign of her friend.

"Gone to see Fulton. Poor fellow. Such devastating news."

"What news?" Jemima did not stay to hear the answer. She flung the clothing on the bed and darted out of the room. Fearing the worst, she bustled down the hall and burst into Fulton's room. Milly was crying into her handkerchief and Edward was leaning over Fulton's inert form. "Is he all right? Please tell me he is not dead!"

Edward straightened, dark shadows haloed his eyes. His clothes were stained, his shirt was covered in blood and his hair was a ruin, standing on end.. "He is not dead, but he is in a bad way. I must fetch Heaton and my equipment so we can repair him."

It was Heaton who had operated on Fulton the first time and often consulted with Edward on his experiments. She had met him at the house party where she had met Edward again after four years and Heaton had proposed to her dear friend, Sylvia.

Milly gasped and gaped at Edward. Jemima coughed.

Edward met her gaze, then looked to Milly. "Heal him," he corrected. "Set him to rights."

Jemima raced over to Milly and took her into her arms. "There. You see, Edward will look after him. I will help nurse him. You must look after yourself, rest and be easy so you can care for little Aly."

As Fulton was perfectly senseless, there was little either of them could do. "I wish to stay with him."

"Of course, you do." Jemima turned her gently toward the door. "Edward will take excellent care of him. He brought me ..." She was going to say he brought her back from death, but that was so close to the absolute truth that it could not be spoken of. Because she had really died. What was she now, but some creature powered by her husband's magic? A cruel fairy tale, to be sure, and she would not accept that. "Well, he took good care of me."

Milly nodded and the sounds of little Aly wanting to be fed echoed up the hall. "I will feed Aloysius and then I will return."

"Very good. I have left a few things for you to change into in your room."

Milly's head jerked up and she put her hand on Jemima's and squeezed.

"No, do not thank me. It is the least I can do," Jemima said quickly. "I am afraid I have nothing that will fit Aunt Prudence so you might bear the brunt of her complaints. Hopefully, someone can supply something ample ... I mean suitable."

Drawn by her child's distressed cries, Milly left, gazing over her shoulder as Jemima smiled reassuringly until she left the room. Not long after, the door to Milly's room shut, cutting off Aly's cries.

Jemima learned her back against the door, feeling ready to sag. "How bad is he?"

Edward shook his head. "Not good. He has lost a lot of blood. I am using the stasis stone to keep him in life, but I must dart off to alert Heaton and to request his presence. Then, I must fetch my equipment. Can you stay here with him?"

"Surely I can. Are you going to use your translocation spell?" Her bath would have to wait.

"Yes."

"Are you confident you can travel so far? To London and then to Sussex?"

"Only to London. Heaton has a store of the equipment I need, so it is only one trip."

Jemima frowned. "Will you pop right back or travel with Heaton?" She wanted to estimate how long Fulton had to linger in this way and how long she had to wrangle Milly and Aunt Prudence. Also, there was the contraption, the monster machine, to track down. Although she was certain it was not going to lead them to the culprit. No one as clever as the maker of that machine would be stupid enough to leave a gouged-out track back to their lair.

"You make a good point. I need Heaton to assist with the surgery so there is no point in starting without him and again, I need to prepare a replacement arm." His blue eyes, now shrouded with worry and concern, met her own. "I will come back directly, with what equipment I can carry. Heaton will have to bring the rest. I hope he can come straight away. At least there is a reliable train service." He frowned as if mentally calculating. "I believe if he catches the morning train and comes direct via carriage he will arrive by tomorrow afternoon, earlier if I hurry. He might make the night train."

She nodded slowly, as she thought things through. "If there is an opportunity do give my love to Sylvia and pass on my wishes for her health and that of her family. I will watch over Fulton."

Edward drew closer, embraced her and kissed her soundly. "You are a rock, my love. I will be as fast as I can."

She hugged him back and kept the worry and concern from her face. He had not mentioned the risk of further attacks, such as the person behind the destruction of Hatfield and the theft of Fulton's arm might come again for his leg or her heart. She hoped that the evil person had taken all that he needed and that they would be prepared when he was found, for she was sure it was a 'he'. Her dearest wish was that the stolen device could not be replicated. Not without its maker. What Edward did with magic and machines was unique to him.

Edward took himself off to their room to prepare himself for travel. She did not worry because he had translocated before, and had been practising it often. He had played tricks on her, popping in behind her when she was busy sorting books in the library. Once she had hidden in a downstairs closet only to have him grope her in the dark. They had to explain it was a joke to the housekeeper, who had come running at the sound of her screams. Poor Mrs Eddington, Eddie, had smiled and rolled her eyes when she realised they were playing games. The old housekeeper was pleased they were living at the house and that they were married and happy now. Poor Eddie had been the one who had to deal with her tantrums and tears when Edward had sent her away to school all those years ago.

Jemima took up a seat beside Fulton and took his good hand in hers. Gloveless, it was a strong hand, scarred, with shortish fingers. She gazed upon his face and sighed. He had helped her and cared for her. To see him so pale, with dark shadows around his eyes, his chest barely moving, scared her. There was nothing she could do to fix him. The only thing she could do was find the person responsible and stop them. Take revenge even.

A candle flickered, and the fire crackled as she sat there holding his hand. "You know Fulton. It has been good to see you so happy. A wife, a child. So lucky to have so much. I know you have Aunt Prudence, and I do thank you for taking her on as she can be a prickly old melon when she wants to be. As you know, she is so in awe of your wealth and station that there is no risk of her crossing you."

A knock at the door silenced her idle banter. "Come in," she called softly.

Milly slipped inside the room. She was wearing the gown that Jemima had given her and had washed and changed. Her hair was pushed into a cap. "Any change?" Milly crushed a handkerchief in her hands as she neared the bed. "He looks as still as death. Are you sure ..."

"He is alive." Jemima stood up. "You can take up station here if you like. I have just been blathering on about nothing to him. I am not sure he can hear me. It does not hurt to try." She sidestepped out of the way. "I do believe I ordered a bath." She sniffed. "I am in desperate need of one. Do you mind if I leave you alone with him for about twenty minutes?"

Milly took the proffered seat. She reached out and placed her hand on Fulton's chest. With a gasp, she sat back up. "He is not breathing."

Jemima waved a hand in dismissal. "He is but slowly. You do know Edward has special talents? He has placed Fulton in a state of limbo, I suppose you must call it. The stones he uses are holding Fulton in life until he can repair the damage. He has gone to get the doctor who helped him before with Fulton's injuries."

Milly stared soulfully at her husband. "Doctor Heaton, if I remember. Oh Jemima I am so frightened. I do not understand any of this. Why destroy our home? Why take his arm?"

Jemima stood by Milly and patted her on the back, gently. "I do not know or understand the why of destroying the house. I think to make a point. Revenge perhaps. Taking Fulton's arm ... well, that was to discover the secret of it."

Milly sucked in a breath. "They could come again. He has a leg as well." Milly stood up suddenly. "Or they could come for you."

Milly might be quiet, unassuming and quick to tears, but she was no fool. Jemima had thought the same thing, but somehow she doubted it. Or maybe she hoped it would not happen. Surely there were going to be repercussions when the device could not be replicated. But had not the attacker set a machine on them? Already they had some ability to create an automaton, unless they were piloting it themselves, which she doubted. However, she would investigate once Edward returned ... well maybe after a good night's sleep and a decent breakfast. She was tired and thought a breakfast of kippers in the morning would go down nicely.

"That is a slight possibility I do own. However, the thing that destroyed Hatfield was large and I cannot imagine it is just sitting there waiting to attack again. Farmers and people hereabouts would have noticed it. It has either returned to whence it came or has been destroyed. I will put money on it."

"Jemima you cannot be serious. Ladies do not place bets."

Jemima laughed. "Indeed they do, just not ones we know. Famous ladies in history have been rolled up for their debts. The Duchess of Devonshire is a famous case."

Milly blinked at her. "The current Duchess? I thought she had passed on."

"No, she has passed on. A relative from the hurly burly days. But I digress. I think we are safe for now. Besides, I am capable of protecting us, if required."

Milly took up Fulton's hand. "I pray that now is forever." She let out a sigh. "Truly, Jemima, I think you overestimate your abilities. If Fulton was injured after fighting this machine, I do not think you could do better."

Jemima smiled and nodded in agreement. However, in the back of her mind, she was not so sure. Other factors were at play. She had the emerald fire and it filled her veins. Her strength and ability had not been fully tested. She sniffed theatrically. "I must wash. I shall return in a while. Call me if you need anything."

❧

BETH WAS WAITING FOR HER WHEN SHE RETURNED, BESIDE A STEAMY tub inviting her to get clean. Jemima washed her hands in the basin first. After the dried blood dissipated, her skin had fresh pink scars. The damage she had done to them searching through the wreckage had healed. The rest of her person was very dirty. Beth managed to hold her tongue as she scrubbed Jemima's body and washed her hair. Another two kettles helped to rinse the last of the dirt away.

"I have not seen bathwater this colour in a while," Beth commented. "Not since you went into the London sewers."

"Do not remind me. Let us hope to never see such again. However, I do not promise you for you know I get into regular scrapes."

"Aye you do, Mrs Huntington."

Once dry, Jemima stood in a robe. "I do not know what to do."

"Are you going to sleep now or staying up?"

"As much as I want to take my rest, I fear I must stay up. Nothing fancy though. That day dress will do for now."

Beth gathered up the yellow dress, with fine white trim and lifted it over her head. "I do not think I need the second petticoat this evening."

Beth cinched in Jemima's waist with a belt to complete the ensemble. Soft slippers graced her feet. Jemima was fit to be seen. Recollecting her conversation with the innkeeper, Jemima shuddered. What must he think of her? Would he even recognise her?

"That shall be all tonight, Beth. I can put myself to bed."

"I can stay up and help. I am not so tired. You must be sore for you have so many bruises and scrapes."

A sigh escaped. "I cannot tell you how late I will be. I must tend Fulton for a time."

"Nevertheless, I will wait for you."

Jemima smiled and sighed. "Thank you then."

Milly left her station by the bed when Jemima slipped into the room. Edward was not back as yet and Jemima should keep up her vigil, even if only to stop someone dislodging the stasis stone. Milly clasped Jemima's hand as she passed before pausing at the door. "I must tend to Aly again. Please wake me if there is a change."

"Of course, I will," Jemima said and gave Milly a hug.

Jemima took her seat, reached for Fulton's hand and squeezed. "It is Jemima here now, Fulton."

Bored, she gazed at Fulton, at the wallpaper, at the ceiling and at the window in turn and then repeated the exercise. She wished Edward would return soon. She must have dozed off because a knock woke her.

"Yes?" Jemima struggled to sit up straight.

"I am sorry to startle you," Milly said. "I wanted to let you know that Aunt Prudence will sit with Fulton for half an hour if you need a break."

"Thank you for letting me know." Milly shut the door and Jemima groaned. Milly was exhausted and had sensibly decided to rest. Aunt Prudence would have to be accommodated, although Jemima would have to stay in case the older woman touched the stone or something else. Jemima slipped out to refresh herself and when she returned to Fulton's room, the aunt was moaning and crying over Fulton as if he was a corpse. She was in danger of dislodging the stasis stones.

"How now Aunt Prudence. You will scare Fulton to death with all that racket."

Aunt Prudence sat up straight and wiped her eyes. "My Milly's husband lies dying and you call it a racket?"

Jemima tried to soften her expression. "I hope he is not dying. You will see, Edward and Dr Heaton will put him to rights. Perhaps you should go to bed. I can stay with Fulton for now."

Taking the hint, Aunt Prudence stood, puffed out her chest and skirted around the edge of the bed. "I will do as you ask. But you must look to your own rest, Jemima. You are looking positively haggard."

Jemima grinned. "Indeed, I must look like a witch."

Aunt Prudence scoffed, stuck her nose in the air and waddled toward the door. She opened it and paused. "By the way, Jemima. I heard your maid has been quartered with the Hatfield servants. I am sure you are in dire need of her services."

"Oh that's a relief. What would I do without my maid? Who would fix my hair and keep my dresses in good condition? Beth wanted to wait up for me, even though I told her to go to bed."

"Indeed," Aunt Prudence did not pick up on Jemima's irony. It was past midnight and she had already been tended to by Beth. "I shall be off to my bed. Please let me know if there is any change." She gazed upon Fulton and shook her head solemnly as if he was dead.

"Rest well, Aunt. I shall go to bed too, when Edward comes to relieve me. He is resting just now. The ordeal quite overwhelmed him." Jemima was pleased she was able to lie so glibly. A necessity when one's husband was a gentleman magician.

"Indeed it might," Aunt Prudence replied. "You have more fortitude than the rest of us. While you may be an unnatural woman, you have a good heart. Good night."

Jemima's mouth fell open. What did she mean unnatural woman? Did she mean because she did not embroider cushions and arrange flowers or was there some deeper meaning? That because Jemima had a Ruby Heart that she was not a real person. Or that she could not become a mother? Her breath caught in her throat. What did the aunt know and was she being deliberately cruel? Jemima screwed up her mouth and clenched her fist. "I will not let that old battleaxe upset me. She means well ... in her way ..."

About an hour after the aunt went to bed, Edward came through the door. He looked tired, his complexion was pale and he had bags under his eyes and his posture sagged around the shoulders. "Any change?" he asked, although his gaze was already on Fulton.

"None. Both Milly and Aunt Prudence have been in. I think they will sleep now. Milly is wrung out with the stress and the baby. Aunt Prudence is well ... normal for Aunt Prudence."

He gave her a quick glance. "You go rest now. Heaton will be here in a few hours. I will finish off the work on Fulton's new arm." He pulled out a metal appliance from under his coat and drew out a large piece of amber from his pocket. "I need to prepare this gemstone. The gem that powers Fulton's leg is a piece of amber so I thought another for the arm, only slightly bigger this time."

"That will match the one in his leg. What did you use in the arm previously?" Jemima had never seen the inner workings of the arm. It had been a mystery to her that Fulton had a fake arm until he had used it to rip out monster vampire hearts. Prior to that she had only known about and seen closely the inner workings of the leg. His arm had been a powerful weapon. Very useful for slaying vampire minions. No wonder some wayward magician wanted to steal it.

"It was a piece of amber as well. However, this new arm is a better design and can hold a bigger gem. I have also decided on a new way to anchor it to Fulton. Instead of meshing it with his flesh, I want to build a scaffolding to hold it. That will also have a ring of gem embedded in it and a way to join up the mechanism to his body so that he can move his arm."

"How will it mesh with his flesh?"

"The scaffolding will, of course. The arm will not need to, not like my original designs. This means he can detach it if he wants without harm to himself."

Jemima nodded. "Oh I see. You are doing this so that it will not be ripped off again."

"In part."

She reached up and cupped his chin. "You are a considerate man and a clever one."

"If only I had been cleverer before, Fulton would not be injured like this."

"You could not know this would happen."

Edward dropped his gaze. "What?" she asked, realising he had been keeping something from her.

"There have been a few smaller scale attacks over the last six weeks. Mostly on warehouses that store items used in the construction of my devices. I should have guessed it was leading to something larger."

Jemima shook her head. "No. How could you? And Fulton is strong. He is able to take care of himself. I read those reports too. Small-scale machines barging through walls and carrying things off is nothing compared to what happened at Hatfield. I did not put it together in my mind that it was in any way connected with you. Do not take this guilt on."

Edward drew her close and kissed the top of her head. "I will try not to blame myself. I only hope Heaton is able to help me meld the scaffolding device to the flesh. There is some serious damage there."

"Can you use your magic to help him with the blood loss, make him stronger?"

Edward stared down at his friend. "I might, but for the moment he is without pain or sensation. It will serve us in the end because there is nothing easy about Heaton's surgery and allowing him some respite will do him good."

Jemima leaned in to kiss him full on the lips. "I will go to bed. Remember to wake me if there is any change or if you need me."

He kissed her back and smiled wanly. "Sleep well."

Jemima laughed at this. She would not sleep well, but, if she was lucky, she might doze long enough to restore her energy. It had been a strenuous and emotional day.

He took up station by Fulton's bed. She paused at the door and turned back. "And thank you for everything," he said with much tenderness then picked up Fulton's hand and held it.

Jemima blinked away tears. Thank heavens she had Edward in her life.

Beth sat just inside the door and was rubbing her eyes when she walked in. She stood when Jemima approached. "The master said you'd be along soon."

Jemima started. Had Beth witnessed Edward winking back into existence? Surely he had used the dressing room. Her maid seemed calm enough so she imagined she had not been startled by her master appearing suddenly in the room.

"You did not heed my urging that you go to bed and not wait for me."

"No, Mrs Huntington. I wanted to see you off to bed before I head to my own."

Jemima smiled. "You are very considerate, Beth. Have you somewhere comfortable to stay?" Jemima asked as she undid the belt of her dress.

"Yes, ma'am. I'm with the Hatfield servants, in a converted stable. It's been made into rooms apparently for a while now."

Beth lifted a nightgown that she had selected from the clothes chest and Jemima nodded in silent agreement. Beth laid it on the bed and began to unhook Jemima's dress. When undone, the gown dropped to the floor and Jemima stepped out of it. Next, Beth unlaced her corset. "Such a terrible thing to happen. We've been talking of nothing else." The maid said as she efficiently disrobed Jemima.

"Indeed. I hope none of the servants were hurt," Jemima replied, as she was not averse to hearing what Beth could tell her.

Beth lifted her shift off over her head. "No. Apparently Mr Fulton had an alarm bell installed and everyone got away. Do you think he was expecting an attack?"

Jemima frowned. "He is a cautious man generally so perhaps he wanted to be prepared if something did happen. I am certain he did not know calamity would visit today. Not when he was expecting house guests to stay."

Jemima stepped to the basin to wash. The servants knew more than what was in the general report. She guessed that everyone would know it was an attack and not an earthquake by morning. What would the magistrate make of it and of them? After towelling off, Jemima took a seat in front of the dressing table. Beth let down Jemima's hair and brushed it. She assisted Jemima into her nightgown. Then went to pick up the discarded clothing from the floor. "Oh ma'am, I suppose you know that other corset is ruined. It's not fit to be darned and no amount of scrubbing is going to get that black stuff out."

"Yes, I was fond of that corset. My new burgundy silk gown was also ruined."

Beth turned, shock evident in her stance and the gape of her mouth. She shut it and exclaimed. "Never, ma'am! Those shreds of clothing I picked up was your dress? It was quite the thing. And your cute little hat?"

Jemima shook her head, pursing her mouth with regret. "I cannot even account for its whereabouts. Somewhere in the ruin of Hatfield I suspect."

Beth's eyes widened. "But you so loved that hat. You must be so upset."

Jemima thought Beth was more woebegone at the loss of her new outfit than Jemima was. Her maid had an excellent eye and had accompanied her to the dressmaker to choose the fabric.

"I mourn its loss and have moved on to other concerns."

Beth shook herself. "Pfah! That dress is no more. You can always have another made."

"Very true, believe me, Beth, I do not mean to deprive you of one of my future cast-off gowns so I will find another to pass on to you. I have a pretty dark blue damask one that I no longer wear."

"That's kind of you." A smile lit her face as she finished tidying the room. "Shall I bank up the fire?" Beth asked.

"Yes, thank you and then you may go. Have a pleasant sleep, Beth." Jemima was too tried to do anything more. She pulled back the covers and climbed in. When the maid finished, she left the room, wishing Jemima a good night.

Jemima lay against the pillow and stared up at the ceiling. What a mess they were in. They had suspected that the escapee from the brotherhood would raise his ugly head one day. However, she had not expected machine monsters. To see her good friend hovering near death was beyond all imagining. Edward did not turn in and as that was to be expected, she tried to sleep without him beside her. It took an hour or so of tossing and turning, where she tangled the bed covers, until finally she fell to dreaming.

When a cock's crow woke her in the early hours, she saw that Edward had not come to bed. The dreams that had plagued her fell away, leaving a vague aftertaste. She lay there trying to recall at least the subject of her dreams but was thwarted. Her gaze rested on the pillow where Edward should have laid his head. However, she was not surprised he had stayed to tend Fulton, given how driven he was and the work he had to do to build a new arm.

Sitting up, Jemima slid her legs over the side of the bed, feeling the kiss of the carpet as she stepped to the window. The horizon was obscured by cloud and sunrise was some twenty minutes away. Looking down into the yard, already work had begun. In the dim light, ostlers and stable hands moved about, bringing feed for the horses and rubbing them down. A carriage had arrived. The occupants had alighted and now the inn's workers were taking care of the carriage, the driver and the postilions. The murmur of voices reached her and soon the inn would wake.

She was in a quandary. There was a task she needed to do while Edward was occupied and she wondered if sneaking out before light would arouse the suspicion of her maid. If she had been more aware, she could have told Beth to come to her late in the morning. If she sought her services now then she would be waking the poor girl up in the wee hours. As it was not yet light, she had better wait. There was no point in going on foot and she was not a good horsewoman so would need to seek to rent a gig or something.

A knock at the door had her turning. It was Milly. "Oh you are up already. Doctor Heaton has arrived. He is examining Ambrose as we speak. He told me not to worry and that Ambrose was in good hands. He said Ambrose was an excellent patient."

Jemima came up and took Milly's hands. "You see, he will be well." She frowned though, because Heaton must have travelled on the night train to get here so early and would have had a most uncomfortable journey. The carriage that had arrived must have been his, hired from the station.

Milly pulled Jemima into an embrace and cried into her shoulder. Jemima was left to pat her on the back and soothe her. "I am so sorry this has happened. We will get through this."

Milly nodded and pulled back, wiping her eyes with the backs of her hands. "Forgive me. I seem to be weeping a lot of late."

Jemima lifted her lips in a half smile. "Nothing to forgive. I love him too, you know, as I do you and little Aly and even Aunt Prudence."

Milly sniffed and chuckled. "Thank you."

"Now, if you have a minute, I was hoping you could do me a favour."

"A favour?" Milly replied in what seemed to be a voice that waited for the bad news.

"Yes, I need to go out and I wondered if you could help me dress. If I do not return before Beth comes to tend me let Beth know that I am out."

"Of course. Are you going on horseback?"

"Not if I can help it. I was hoping to rent a gig of some kind."

Milly nodded. "Right then. If you get your clothes together, I will go ask the innkeeper about a gig or a cart for hire. He is up already due to the doctor arriving."

In no time at all, Jemima was dressed in a skirt, blouse and little jacket, a smart outfit that she preferred. Her bonnet was tied under her chin and a map of the surrounds mostly etched into her brain. Milly had helped her arrange her hair, and she was all set. She climbed into the gig and as she flicked the reins, the sun spilt over the distant hills to light her way. As she careened out of the drive, she settled the horse into a brisk pace and followed the road to Fulton's house. When she bowled up the drive a little while later she saw workmen crawling over the debris and making order out of the chaos. Bricks were being stacked to one side. Paintings and furnishings were being sorted, some to be carried to the chapel or the stables and those that were damaged stacked under the part of the house that still had a roof.

Jemima approved of these arrangements. Best to let Fulton and Milly decide what could be repaired. It also warmed her heart that these workmen, servants and villagers, were honest enough to care for his belongings rather than pilfer them. He was an excellent master, with good servants and there was mutual respect. She hoped they were able to salvage some clothes for the ladies and the baby.

A workman waved and she pulled up on the drive. "Morning, ma'am, can I help ye?" He held onto her horse's bridle.

"Oh good morning. I was wondering if you could assist me. I was to be a guest here before the disaster. I was wondering if you could find some of Mr Fulton's servants and ask them to look for clothes for the ladies and the baby. They have nothing suitable to wear. If nothing is found that is wearable, could they send a message to the family at the King's Arms? As they will need to make immediate arrangements for new clothes."

He doffed his cap. "Will do as you instruct, ma'am." He let go of the horse and stepped out of the way.

"Thank you," she said, and flicked the reins to get the horse moving again. She tooled the gig around to the back of the house and then pulled up and applied the brake so she could climb out. It did not take long for her to find what she was looking for. The trail of the machine was clear as day and continued on, right through the kitchen garden, the walls of which were partially collapsed with broken bricks and mortar now scattered inside and outside of the ruins. A path ran around the outside of the garden. Reins in hand, she led the horse and gig over to the other side, where the machine continued on regardless of what was in its path. Some of the leisure gardens remained intact but the small wilderness and temple were destroyed. She climbed back into the gig and followed the path of destruction.

It cut through the home farm, destroying a few hedgerows and dry stone walls. It headed for the woods and then the lake beyond. "Where are you going?" she said to herself as she flicked the reins, keen to find the answers.

It was there she found what had become of it. In a clearing, a pile of rubble in a burnt ring of grass met her gaze. The leaves on the trees were singed and the scent of smoke lingered in the air. Metal parts, cogs, gears and random bits lay in a rough round pattern. She edged around it and then dissected the debris, using her keen gaze to assess the mess. She inhaled and something sharp and burnt teased her nostrils. Blown up, she thought. She widened her promenade, seeking all the pieces of the contraption so she could mentally reconstruct it. Part train engine, she thought, but also like bits of a factory device.

Beyond the centre of the debris field, she found what looked to be a head. It was nearly as big as her and lay on its side. There were dark holes where the eyes would have been. Whoever made it had destroyed it. Why though? Had it served its purpose? Was it to thwart pursuit, to dull the trail back to the perpetrator?

They were clever despite their evil intent and the harm they caused. It was a truly remarkable construction. Surely it could have been put to better use than destruction.

A shaft of sunlight burst into the clearing and she studied the debris closely and could not see Fulton's arm. It had been retrieved, she surmised. Mission accomplished. She wondered if the machine had been driven by a person or operated by other means, magic or something else. It would take Edward to figure that out. Alas, he was busy and his inspection would have to wait. As far as she could tell there was no mechanism for steering and no seat for someone to sit in.

Turning in a circle, she realised there was no obvious hint of who had sent it. Destroying it must have been the plan all along, she had suspected as much. There was no point with something so large and heavy leaving a trail to its owner. No, they were not that stupid. Why such a large machine? Surely, something more compact would have achieved the same outcome. So the goal was more than the taking of Fulton's arm and destroying Hatfield. A statement. A schoolboy bully making himself known, making himself appear bigger. Was he a small man then? A giggle escaped her. Then a laugh and another until she was wiping the tears, picturing a little man with his big machine making people pay attention. She sobered. It was not a clue she could share, as it was so random and unscientific.

After calming her mirth and completing her survey of the site she had more to do. Now she had to see from where it had come. From her review of the map, she suspected the railway lines that ran on the other side of Kiddlington towards Thrupp. She hopped back into the gig and set out along the trail. She avoided the house as best she could, not wanting to delay by speaking to anyone. Casting a glance over her shoulder, she saw another carriage had arrived and a number of men in sober coats had alighted. Perhaps this was the magistrate. That investigation was going to be interesting, to say the least.

It did not take more than an hour or so to find the point of origin. It had been dropped from the railway line. Nothing was left to show from which direction, but the tread marks from the wheels started there and cut a path in a beeline for Hatfield. Fulton had not stood a chance. She followed the trail and saw that it had been slow at first and had built up speed over time and distance. The change in the tracks showed deep gouges and churned-up turf where the machine had reached its maximum speed.

Squinting into the distance, she could see the last stream of smoke where the house had stood. This had been planned perfectly. Whoever it was had calculated exactly from the initial drop off, the warm-up of the machine, the increase in pace and the distance required for maximum effect. They must have also known the train timetable so that the line would be clear. They had provided enough power for the machine to clear Hatfield and continue to the woods where its demise could be disguised. As there had been no sign of Fulton's arm, the perpetrator had arranged for it to be collected or the villain had been lying in wait to retrieve it. There had been no footprints, only her own.

The sun beat down, warming the air. It was getting late, and she knew she would be missed. Taking off her jacket, she sat under a tree in the shade so the horse could rest for another five minutes before turning the gig back toward the inn. At least when she returned, Heaton would have completed his examination and hopefully would have some good news regarding Fulton. She also hoped her husband was too busy to notice her absence or suspect her errand before they met again. When she knew she was in the wrong, she found it difficult to counter an argument. After all, she was knowingly taking risks.

The journey home was spent with a frown on her forehead as she imagined what he would say and how she would respond. As it was, Edward was fast asleep in the dressing room, which allowed Beth to help her with her toilette and to dress in a demure gown of dark green, with a sash of sage green. Matching ribbons adorned her detestable lace cap. As a married woman, wearing one was expected, but as a young woman it was not. She turned in the mirror looking this way and that. Adjusted the cap so that it sat way back on her head, leaving her ringlets and curls to frame her face. Edward would like that feminine look. Right now she needed all the good feeling from him as she could get.

Jemima entered the parlour, where Aunt Prudence sat, with Aly in her arms. Milly greeted her, with bright eyes and a pale complexion. "Edward was asking after you."

Jemima paused, swallowed. "Truly?"

Milly frowned. "Yes, I would not say if it was not so?"

"I was not accusing you of lying." Jemima sat down on the settee next to Milly.

Milly folded her arms, lifted her chin. "I had to say I did not know where you had gone exactly."

Jemima met her eye, realising that the refinement was too close to a fib for Milly's comfort. "I am so sorry to put you in a difficult position."

The aunt put the baby in a small crib in the corner and sat down in a chair by the dining table. "So you should be," Aunt Prudence said. "Gallivanting about when you are needed here."

Jemima shifted her attention to the aunt and narrowed her eyes. She was about to respond ever so impolitely when the aunt continued. "A man came, one of the magistrate's men. We have been giving statements all morning. He wants yours."

"That was quick. I best go find him." She rose from the settee.

Heaton entered the room and flashed a grin. A surge of gratitude swept into Jemima's chest at the sight of Edward's trusted friend. "Patient is doing well under the circumstances." He moved further into the room, rubbing his hands together. "Any chance of some breakfast?"

As Jemima was on her way out, she said, "I will speak to the innkeeper."

When she found Mr Copperwraith he was at his desk writing notes in a log. "Ma'am, good morning. You missed Mr Cousins, the magistrate's deputy. He said the magistrate himself will come later after he has finished inspecting the site."

"I see. Thank you. Is it possible to have some breakfast brought up? Dr Heaton is famished."

"It shall be delivered directly, ma'am."

The innkeeper smiled at her but had a funny look in his eyes.

"What is the matter?" Jemima refrained from looking down at her clothing, fairly certain nothing was amiss with her attire.

"Mr Cousins asked me some questions as well."

"Really? But you were not there."

"Exactly."

"What did he want to know?" she asked, frustrated by his hints instead of being given information directly.

"He wanted to know what you were wearing when you arrived."

"What I was wearing? Whatever for?"

He shrugged. "I do not know. It was a strange question and I am afraid I answered it truthfully. He also enquired where you were this morning and, as I didn't know, he asked me where I thought you were going."

Jemima swallowed, not able to understand the direction of the questions but grateful to have been given a hint. "Thank you. No problem at all. Truth is always the best policy."

CHAPTER 4

Fulton was in a dark space. It was strange, he thought, as he floated there in blackness. "Am I dead?" he asked himself. Emotion hit: sadness, fear, loss. The face of his beloved, Milly, and their son. He would not see her again. He would not see his son grow. If he were dead.

Should not there be light? A tunnel? A path to heaven or a slippery slope to hell? Neither of these options appeared. Maybe he was not dead after all, and the emotions he experienced were wasted. No need to mourn for what he had lost because he was still alive. It was more of a torment than comfort. Were Milly and Aly even alive? Had he saved them? He fought for the memory.

Recollection hit like a smack in the head. His arm being torn off, the fountains of blood. The machine so ruthless, destroying all to get to him. No, that was not right. He had put himself front and centre and the machine had wanted him, but whoever was behind it wanted to hurt him too, wanted to take everything from him. Wanted to grind him to the ground and destroyed his home to do so.

Violet eyes. Glowing violet eyes in the machine—malevolent and fierce. Yes, now he recalled that automaton. The eyes were not alive but there was something there, something peering out at him. It could not have been idle fancy. Something or someone with intent had driven that machine.

A sharp pain radiated from his shoulder and a cry burst out of him. It was so intense, his chest heaved as he sucked in breath. This was life. Life was pain.

Still dark surrounded him. Thick and impenetrable at first until it grew grey, like after a storm when a shaft of sunlight broke through heavy clouds. Another sharp pain. A moan. His own. Dull aches resolved into fingers pressing into his flesh. A buzz in his ears became voices. He wanted to open his eyes, but it was if heavy weights were upon his eyelids and his lashes were gummed together. He wanted sit up and to tell whoever it was prodding him to stop, to stop the pain. He wanted to scream as the forks of hurt increased to a peak that he did not think he could bear. He was held motionless, unable to cry out, unable to scream his pain and unable to escape from it.

Time drifted on. Immeasurable. He lingered there, one foot in hell and the other trying to step back to the earth, to keep all he held dear. If only he could push through.

"Fulton?" Edward's familiar voice called. At first Fulton thought he imagined it until it sounded again, closer, right by his ear. "Fulton? Can you hear me?"

It was definitely his friend, his lifeline. Fulton eyelids flickered and as he tried to focus, he came fully awake to the state of his body. While he was battered and bruised everywhere, his damaged arm was a dull, heavy weight, and he was so weak it took all his energy to breathe. A thumping in his head made him blink a few times and gasp. Awareness of his surroundings flooding in, the bed beneath his body, light coming from a window, the scent of wood burning, the pressure of the bed coverings. He turned his head slightly to the right. Dr Heaton came into focus, smiling but lines of weariness cut into the skin around his eyes and mouth. Blood painted his apron in clumsy strokes. His blood.

Edward touched his fingers lightly to his good hand. "You are safe now, my friend."

"How ... bbbads?" he croaked, his throat so dry he was not able to speak normally.

Edward knelt by the bed so his head was near level with his. "You were seriously injured, Fulton. You have lost a lot of blood and you are weak. Heaton has cleaned your arm wound as best he could. We have a new arm ready to attach. I wanted to check with you. Do you want a new arm Fulton? We could let the stump heal if you wish."

Fulton fluttered his eyelids, trying to make sense of the situation. Stump? New arm? The machine. It had been real. Images flashed in his memory. The absolute terror as the machine picked him up, ripped the arm from his body. The long fall to smash on the ground to join the ruins of his house. He wanted to turn his head and look at where his arm had been but Edward held his gaze. Trustworthy Edward.

Trying to focus, he breathed in deep as the world span around him. This was important and he had to fight to keep his train of thought. What would his life be without his arm? He had fought so hard to make the prosthesis work. All that sewing to get the fingers moving, make him dexterous and the strength in it had saved lives. His memory returned to his flesh arm that was sawn off as the boat rocked about him. The surgery so brutal he lingered for weeks not knowing if he would live or whether he wanted to. The essence that was him sank, as if he was once again on that ship, then it rose up again as if on a wave. He closed his eyes and pulled all his strength together. "New ..." he breathed it out on the exhale. "New arm, please."

Edward squeezed and then patted his hand. "Very well. I warn you there will be more pain, Fulton. Heaton can dose you up with laudanum but you are so weak and have lost so much blood we fear the syrup may carry you off and not even my talent could keep you in life."

Fulton blinked, shifted his gaze to Heaton and then back to Edward. "Do what you must ..."

Edward let go his hand and stood up. Facing Heaton he said, "We must do more to help with the pain levels. The stress on his body could kill him, just as readily as too much laudanum. My stones help, but he will still feel the intrusion of the mechanism."

"A small dose but enough to help him sleep. However, I cannot watch his breathing while I am operating and you will be too busy as well. We need someone in here to help monitor him."

"You are right." Edward ruffled his hair and tilted his head. "Mmm

I wonder if Jemima could watch Fulton. She will not like it but she is strong and not likely to keel over."

"A good choice. Your wife is an unnatural woman. No insult intended."

Edward chuckled lightly. "She owns it so it is no insult to her. Fulton enjoys telling her so."

"While you fetch her, I shall prepare for the operation. We need more water to boil the instruments."

"I will see to it."

Existence seemed to wink out. He was in that dark place again. Body clasped in the grip of pain, every breath like a thousand knives stabbing his skin. Some time later, he opened his eyes, surprised that he was alive and that he had not dreamed the previous interactions with Edward and Heaton.

"Hello, Fulton," Jemima said quietly and squeezed his hand. He saw the pity in her eyes. Their positions had been reversed. He once stood by her deathbed. He tried to smile and she brushed a finger along his cheek. "Someone wants to see you before they start operating."

He nodded vaguely and closed his eyes and when he opened them again it was Milly. "Ambrose?"

He nodded slightly, as much as he could without moving overmuch.

A sob escaped her and she covered her mouth with a handkerchief. Controlling herself, she picked up his hand. "You can do this, my love. You will come out of this stronger than ever. We will be here waiting for you. Me and Aloysius. We are both extremely well. Your son is feeding more than ever. Never fear for us."

He returned the pressure on his hand and inclined his head, too emotional to say anything.

Milly stood up and then leaned in to kiss him on the forehead. He inhaled the scent of her, savouring her light perfume. "I must go now. They are going to begin. Remember be strong. I love you."

Fulton closed his eyes. He heard the snick of the door as it shut. Next moment, a small glass was held to his lips. "Drink this, Fulton," Heaton said. "It will help a bit. We will try to be quick, so hold on and we will get through this."

Fulton was no stranger to pain. He had endured much when he had first been injured and when Heaton and Edward had repaired him. There were long months of recuperation, rehabilitation where he learned that needlework was soothing to the mind as well as therapy for the body. He knew he could survive this and as he inhaled the fragrance that Milly left behind, he knew he had much to live for.

Jemima sat down beside him, taking his hand and squeezing it gently. "Never fear, Fulton. I am here to watch over you. Remember that, Ambrose. You are my friend and I will not let you falter."

Fulton started to drift off until hot pain stoked him awake. His eyes opened and he stared at the ceiling. Jemima clung to his good hand, hard. Her eyes averted, then returned to his surgery and then averted again. A growl leaked out of his lips. "Ambrose! Squeeze my hand."

Ambrose did and it did not help with the pain but Jemima's grip told him he was not alone.

"He needs more laudanum," Jemima said. "He feels every cut you make."

A mumble of voices through the pain haze registered. Next he knew Jemima lifted his head, holding a small glass to his lips. "Here, drink this."

He took what she offered, felt it slide down to the pit of his stomach. The pain told him he was not dead. Yet, some relief was needed. The drug numbed him. Not like when he had awoken in that dark limbo, unable to discern if he was alive or dead. Sharp bits jabbed into his arm. Oh how he remembered that pain when Heaton needed to soothe the muscles into place.

Ambrose faded, his sense of self and of life dissipated. "Edward?" He heard Jemima say. "He is not breathing!" Jemima called to him, shook him. He wanted to come back to her, wanted to reach out but he sank lower, beneath the waves, into the dark, still waters, to the depths of the ocean.

He was not sure how long he was absent for. His chest hurt, like he had been hit by a train. Jemima leaned over him, sponging his forehead with pungent vinegar. "There you go, Ambrose. Nearly done."

He faded again, feeling numbness in his arm. "No, Fulton. Stay. Please."

Her hand clasped his. It was as if she reached down into depths where only the drowned and their gods dwelled and heaved him up, as if she breathed air into his lungs, as if she squeezed his heart with her small white hand, as if she willed him to live with all of her life force and he complied.

LIGHT SPILT IN THROUGH THE WINDOW NEXT MORNING, BURNING A path across his eyes that had him wincing. As he blinked away sleep, the room gradually came into focus. It was the room he remembered. Yet it was different somehow. The walls had more colour, the fire more warmth. His gaze shifted to where Edward sat slumped in a chair by the window. Heaton was nowhere to be seen. Jemima was absent.

"Is it over?" he rasped, wincing as his chest hurt.

Edward sprung up, arms and legs jerking before he focussed on him. "Ambrose?"

Fulton nodded slowly. Edward dashed to his bedside. Immediately placing a hand on his forehead. "How are you feeling?"

Fulton licked his dry lips. "Like someone ..." He licked his lips again and Edward poured a glass of water and held it to his mouth. He drank and was surprised how delicious the water was. "I feel like someone kicked me down the road like a useless, broken-bottomed coal bucket."

Edward grinned. "That bad. You have a few more buckets of coal to haul before you go down that road."

Fulton eased a crick out of his neck. "Tell me."

Edward drew the chair closer to the bed. "We did it. You have a new type of arm prosthesis, stronger, detachable, which makes maintenance easier. We can go over the differences when you are feeling better. Now you just have to heal."

"My chest?" Fulton lifted his good hand to his heart.

A crease developed between Edward's eyes and he licked his lips. "We nearly lost you. Jemima noticed straight away that your breathing had faltered and that your heart stopped beating. Jemima grew savage when she pounded on your chest to get you going again. My wife's resilience amazes me." He frowned. "Some of the names she called you gave me pause. I did not know they were part of her vocabulary. Very unladylike. Although as they did the trick, I cannot complain about her language, but I do wonder about the standards of education at the school I sent her to."

Fulton closed his eyes. Once again, he owed his life to Edward, Jemima and Heaton. "Milly?"

Edward nodded. "Yes, she is fine and wanting to see you. I think you should rest now, though."

Fulton shook his head. "I want to see her."

"Very well, old chap." Edward went to the door, opened it and Milly rushed in.

Rushing to his side, she began to blather. "Ambrose! Oh Ambrose, I did not believe them when they said you were awake. I thought I would never speak to you again."

Taking up the chair Edward had vacated, she then buried her face in the bedcovers. Fulton rested his hand on her shoulder, feeling her convulse with tears. "I am well. I will be up and out of bed in no time." Fulton closed his eyes. "So tired now."

Milly sat back. "Oh my love," she whispered, stood and kissed him on the forehead. "I will let you rest now."

Milly left the room and Edward came back in.

Raised voices echoed out in the hall. Ambrose frowned as he wanted to sleep but the disturbance prevented him. "What is going on?"

"Ah ... yes well there is a bit of a hullabaloo this morning. Nothing terrible I assure you. Anyway, Jemima is sorting it." Edward handed Fulton a bell. "Ring this if you need anything. I am for bed."

The sounds of a ruckus increased. Voices raised. Too many voices. Steps rushing up stairs and up and down the hall. Fulton's lips twitched, but he let out a miserable moan. It hurt to smile. He was curious as to what was going on, but he was left to imagine the fracas Jemima Hardcastle Huntington presided over. It sounded entertaining.

CHAPTER 5

Jemima had a few moments of quiet in the parlour as Aunt Prudence had gone to see if she could be of service to Fulton, while Edward slept and Milly attended to her toilette and that of her baby. A teapot stood on the table, a faint spume of steam wafting to the ceiling. Still warm enough to drink, she thought as the door opened. Martha the maid stepped through.

"Excuse me, ma'am, Sir Giles has arrived. He and his deputy Mr Jenkins are here to interview you."

"Me?"

Martha eyes grew wide as a step sounded behind her. The door flung open and in stepped a middle-aged man, dressed in tan breeches and a coat of blue. He had long sideburns that reached to his jowls and eyes so dark they appeared black. "Mrs Huntington I presume?"

Jemima stood. "Yes, you must be Sir Giles and Mr Jenkins." She curtseyed and inclined her head to Deputy Jenkins. "I am indeed Mrs Huntington. Do come in." She turned to the maid, who appeared to be distressed. "Martha, perhaps, you could alert Mrs Fulton as to our visitor."

Sir Giles turned and spoke to the quivering maid in a heavy, ponderous voice. "Do not trouble Mrs Fulton on my account. I have her statement in writing and it was sufficient for my purposes."

Jemima grimaced and then gave a nod to Martha. "Please take a seat. I would offer you some tea but I fear this pot is either empty or cold."

Resuming her seat, she smiled at her guests. Sir Giles drew out a chair as if he was making way for the queen and sat down, flicking his coattails out as he did so. "I have not come for tea, Mrs Huntington, but to ask you some questions." Mr Jenkins put a saddle bag on the table and took a seat himself. He took out a notebook and pencil, and waited.

"Me? Questions? But I was not there during the event. I arrived subsequent and can hardly elucidate you."

"Humour me, please, Mrs Huntington. I must be allowed to direct my enquiry where I see fit." She gave him a slight bow of her head in acknowledgment.

He continued. "I have surveyed the ruin of the house, the scene of the accident, and the safe room where the females of the house and yourself were rescued."

"And?"

"And there are certain inconsistencies that I was hoping you could explain for me."

Jemima frowned, not sure where this interview was leading. "I will do my best." She batted her eyelids, hoping to dazzle her interlocutor with an appearance of stupidity.

"Can you tell me how some heavy beams and furniture were moved after the collapse of the main part of the house?"

Jemima froze. He wanted to know about that? She had moved heavy beams and such but did not think anyone would ask about them. She had to think quickly. Licking her lips, she thought up the first thing that popped into her head. "I am not sure. I saw workman there this morning and I am certain they had already commenced when we were brought out from below."

"Not the beams I saw. Those will require heavy equipment and a lot more men to shift, yet they were moved."

Jemima tugged her ear and stared at the teapot. Her gaze flicked to the magistrate. "That seems interesting, indeed. I fail to see why you are asking me about it."

The deputy unstrapped the saddle bag and drew out several strips of burgundy silk. "We found these, one was even under the beam that had been moved."

Jemima eyed the fabric and licked her lips again. "I had to rip some of my skirts to get through to the staircase that led to the safe room. Perhaps, that particular piece worked its way under the beam."

"You did not lift the beam yourself?"

Jemima's cheeks grew hot. "I did try. It was too heavy. But alas I am just a woman and as my husband was tending to the injured Mr Fulton, I left it."

Sir Giles studied her through narrowed eyes for what seemed like an age. Jemima swallowed and tried not to appear guilty, and waited. Why she felt guilty she did not know. She had only tried to help. It was important, she knew, not to advertise her talents if she wanted to live close to a normal life. Being different in this world was not an easy thing. She neither wanted to be an object of pity nor one of curiosity.

"How did you get into the safe room?" He asked after a while.

Jemima frowned. "It is such a blur really. How is this relevant to the attack on the house and Fulton?"

"Just answer the question."

Jemima nodded. "I am embarrassed to say that I fell. There was a hole in the floor and I tried to be careful but it gave way under my feet."

Sir Giles sat up straighter. "You fell?"

"Yes. And I was lucky I landed on my feet for I fear I could have done myself an injury."

"You did not punch your way through a wall?" he asked, eyes lidded, watching her.

"That would be most unladylike."

His assistant, Jenkins, snickered. A flick of the magistrate's dark gaze and all signs of emotion disappeared from the deputy's face. "And how did you gain entry to the safe room? My examination revealed that it was not easily breached."

Jemima lifted a hand as if to wave the problem away. "Oh that is easy. Fulton wrote to me about building it. I used morse code to signal Mrs Fulton to open the door."

Sir Giles was sitting upright in his chair as if a string had pulled his spine taut. Jemima thought he was not amused. "I see. Most ingenious."

Jemima sighed, feeling suddenly tired. "What makes you ask these questions?"

"I am investigating a crime."

"What crime?"

Sir Giles rolled his eyes. "Attempted murder for one and destruction of property."

Jemima narrowed her eyes. "Oh yes, I see. It could be seen as attempted murder. If we did not arrive when we did, Fulton could have died. But then, what would have happened to Milly, Aunt Prudence and the baby?" Jemima thought she was thinking but was actually speaking aloud. "But they would have let themselves out in that case so that is all right, I suppose."

Sir Giles gave a sound of exasperation. "This is a serious crime and if you are concealing facts from me, you will feel the full weight of the law."

"But I was not even there."

A growl escaped Sir Giles's clenched teeth. "I have heard reports of you, your husband and Mr Fulton through official channels," he barked. "It appears you are connected with some strange events in London and in Kent." He pulled out a piece of paper from inside his jacket pocket and opened it. "It reads, 'Mrs Huntington is possessed of some unusual abilities'."

Jemima brightened. "Oh how wonderful. It is so good that the London Metropolitan police are able to appreciate my intellect. I am afraid that they sadly underestimated me a number of times."

Sir Giles lifted an eyebrow. "You think they are speaking of your mind?"

"Why, yes. What else could they be speaking of?"

Sir Giles tapped his forefinger on the table, bouncing some crumbs on the tablecloth. "Have you any idea then why Mr Fulton and his home were attacked? It was not by any natural means, such as a earth tremor and nor does it seem that there was any subsidence to cause the house to collapse. It is my considered opinion that Mr Fulton was attacked by persons unknown, perhaps driving a machine of some kind that was capable of ramming the walls."

Jemima pursed her lips. He was skimming close to the truth of it. "I can only guess. Perhaps, it would be better to speak to Mr Fulton when he has recovered."

"Mr Fulton is still alive and conscious?" Sir Giles leaned forward in his chair, studying her face with his curious black eyes.

"Most definitely alive and on the mend I believe."

"Right. One more question before I release you. Is this incident connected to the events in Kent and in London approximately a year ago now?"

Jemima considered her answer. She did not know what information the man had. What she knew was not known to the police, well not in its entirety. "I have not spoken to Fulton so I do not know the full of it. My husband would be the better person to ask. I can say that the threat that faced London and Kent last year was dealt with."

Sir Giles 's chest deflated as if all his breath had left his body. He breathed in again through his nose. "Thank providence for that. I had to be sure."

"However, according to the newspapers there have been some similar happenings in two other places. The scale of this attack is much more considerable so I am not sure there is a connection."

"Ah thank you. I have not had the opportunity to read the paper in the last day or so."

He lifted a hand when she was about to speak. "Never fear, I will interview your husband as soon as I can." He stood and nodded to his deputy. "Thank you for your time. I will endeavour to return the fragments of your clothing in due course."

Jemima's face dropped. "I assure you, Sir Giles, that will not be necessary, in fact I would be embarrassed if you did so as it would be a shocking reminder of my state of distress at the time."

He inclined his head. "As you wish." He turned to his subordinate. "Jenkins?"

They let themselves out. Jemima sat there going over the interview and wondering what the magistrate suspected. That she had supernatural strength? Would it be so bad if he did? Absolutely! She could not let such a report begin to circulate. It was hard enough to get by in society without gossip making one a figure of contempt. Also, there was the Fultons to consider; they would be tainted by association.

Aunt Prudence strode into the room, a bustle of skirts, lace and frills. Her bonnet was poked to within an inch of its life. "There you are. You were missed at breakfast." She smiled. "I must say the beef stock I just spoon-fed to Fulton is working a charm. I swear he grew stronger with each mouthful."

"I am sure your ministrations are appreciated and helpful. How is Fulton now?"

"Asleep. He did not wish me to read to him."

A knock heralded the arrival of Martha with a tray. "More tea, ma'am, as requested and some griddle cakes."

Jemima flicked her gaze to Aunt Prudence, for she herself did not order anything, but perhaps Martha overheard her say to the magistrate that there was none on offer.

"Thank you, girl," Aunt Prudence responded, pronouncing girl like 'gel'. "Just put it on the table, we shall serve ourselves."

Martha gave a quick nod and hurried to obey. As Jemima had missed breakfast, she eyed the griddle cakes and licked her lips. There was already jam and butter on the table so she pulled a clean plate over and fished around for a knife.

Aunt Prudence did the honours and poured her some tea and with a knowing smile slid the plate of griddle cakes her way.

"Thank you, Aunt. Most kind of you to think of some morning tea."

Jemima tried not to snatch as that would show a lack of decorum and being lectured by Aunt Prudence about her manners or lack thereof was not her favourite pastime. However, the cakes were hot and she juggled one onto her plate, with both of Aunt Prudence's eyebrows raised in disdain.

Not half an hour later, after the demise of three griddle cakes with butter and jam, a carriage swept into the inn's drive. Noisy ostlers and grooms called to each other as they raced to attend the new arrival. As Aunt Prudence was on her feet walking about the room in an attempt at exercise, she moved to the window and shifted the curtains so she could give a running commentary. "They seem in a hurry. Horses are in a sweat. Oh some young women, it seems."

Jemima stuffed a fourth griddle cake with marmalade into her mouth, washed it down with a mouthful of tea, and went to peer out of the window. There was no law against being curious. As the inn was full with the Hatfield family, their friends and servants, she hoped the newcomers' disappointment at being turned away was not too extreme.

The footman stepped around to open the door of the carriage. A woman alighted. She was dressed in a sensible maroon coat dress and beret with trailing white feather. Jemima sighed and looked again and near choked. "Sylvia?"

Another woman alighted and stood next to her friend. This woman was not the maid, as that lady climbed out the far side of the carriage and went to the rear to see to the disposition of the luggage. This lady was taller than Sylvia, thinner and bonier. She towered over Sylvia and clutched a carpet bag to her body with long, thin fingers.

"What in the world!" Jemima exclaimed and wiped her mouth with a napkin. She needed to get outside fast. Not only was Sylvia unexpected and a complication, bringing a friend along as well was a disaster. What was Heaton thinking?

The innkeeper nearly collided with her as she raced to the front door. He was coming in, wringing his hands. "Oh dear me. Where shall I put them? No one mentioned more visitors."

He did not stay to hear her response, which was probably a good thing, as it was not ladylike. Pulling up short, she checked her visage in the mirror, tidied her lace cap and then hastened out into the yard of the inn.

"Sylvia!" she cried as she neared the carriage and the growing pile of luggage next to it. Her friend turned, face full of smiles, her golden locks falling nicely from beneath her beret. "I was not expecting you."

They kissed each other's cheeks while Jemima tried to think up something nice to say. "I know. A last-minute decision."

"I see. You look wonderful as always. But I am afraid the inn is full at the moment."

Sylvia waved a hand dismissively. "That should not be a problem, I shall share with Heaton. When he told me he was coming here and that you would be here, well, I could not resist. I just had to see you." Sylvia slid her arm through her companion's elbow and drew her forward. "This is my cousin, Miss Amabel Horton-Sprigge. She was staying with us and I could not abandon her. Miss Horton-Sprigge please meet my old school friend Mrs Huntington."

Jemima curtseyed, smile not quite reaching her eyes. "How pleased I am to meet you."

The cousin laughed, a strange guttural sound combined with a wheezy breath. "Hahahahuh! The pleasure is all mine, I am sure, Mrs Huntington." She flapped a limp hand by way of greeting. "Cousin Sylvia did not stop talking of you the whole time and the journey was so fatiguing. I am in desperate need of refreshment and then I will need to lie down for an hour or two in peace and quiet to recover my spirits."

Jemima blinked and kept hold of her tongue. Had this woman meant to imply that Sylvia speaking of her was tedious? Jemima decided that could not be the case and that she needed to rely on her patience—a dangerous course of action as she had no patience whatsoever. "Perhaps, if you come into the main parlour upstairs we can organise some tea."

"And sandwiches?" Miss Horton-Sprigge suggested. "Cake too. Oh and scones. I am absolutely famished."

As she was a thin woman, with stick arms and a narrow neck, Jemima could understand the need for food.

Sylvia laughed nervously and battered her eyelids at Jemima. In their school days, she might have understood such as a secret message but as they were no longer at school and there was so much chaos in her life, she could not give five seconds to even try to understand the silent code her friend was trying to send. If Sylvia had brought her cousin out of duress, Jemima had little sympathy for her. All her sympathy was for Milly and Fulton and the wreck of their home.

Jemima fixed a smile on her face and stopped herself from

shaking her dear friend and yelling into her face 'What were you thinking?' Of all the times to spring a surprise visit, this was the worst. Now the women were here, they would have to muddle through. Somehow. She flashed a grin at the cousin. "I am sure we can only ask."

"I have not been to this part of the country before," Sylvia said, looking around her at the yard. "The journey was picturesque. We saw hills, caught a glimpse of canals and quaint villages. With Heaton working all the time, we do not go on journeys much."

Jemima nodded in agreement. "As an important and talented surgeon, I am sure he is always busy."

Sylvia turned to her and grasped her hand. "Oh yes, he is forever in demand. Always, so tired."

Jemima frowned, detecting the discontent in her friend's comments. Sylvia released her hand, allowing Jemima to lead the way. At the base of the stairs, she turned and beckoned them. "Come on up."

At the top of the stairs, Mr Copperwraith's eyes widened in alarm. Jemima waved and got his attention as she grew closer to the landing. "Forgive me, Mr Copperwraith, is it possible to have a tray sent in with tea, sandwiches and some other comestibles your wonderful cook may have in her larder?" He stepped back into the corner as the entourage passed him. "We will be in the parlour. My friends will rest there while we sort out the arrangements."

Sylvia and her cousin headed down the hall to the parlour door that Jemima directed them to.

Mr Copperwraith's complexion had turned a dark red. He took out his handkerchief and wiped his forehead. "I will see what can be done, ma'am. They are not expecting to stay, are they?"

Her guests entered the parlour but still she lowered her voice. "Mrs Heaton will share with Mr Heaton. The other lady? Is there a closet big enough for her?"

The innkeeper paled rapidly. "I cannot put a lady in a closet. But I can move my daughter out of her room. It is small but at least there is a bed."

"You are too kind. I am so sorry for the inconvenience."

"Are we to expect more persons to join your party?" the innkeeper said in a tight voice.

"I hope not."

Leaving him to digest that comment, she followed Sylvia and her cousin into the parlour. As she entered the room, Aunt Prudence was cuddling young Aly and talking in baby tongue, some gibberish that sounded deranged. To a stranger she would sound like an idiot. Just inside the door, Sylvia and Miss Horton-Sprigge stood waiting to be acknowledged.

Milly was nowhere to be seen. She coughed to warn the aunt and announced, "Aunt Prudence, we have visitors."

Usually quick on the uptake, Aunt Prudence turned and gaped at her. "Visitors?" she repeated stupidly. Her gaze shifted from Sylvia and her cousin back and forth in rapid succession.

"Yes," Jemima performed the introductions. "Oh, you are that aunt," Sylvia said with a lack of aplomb. Jemima fixed a grin on her face and hoped she did not look like a loon.

Under lowered eyebrows, Aunt Prudence shot her a knowing look. It was true she had corresponded with Sylvia about the odious aunt, but Sylvia should have more tact. Perhaps she had lost her society polish now she was married to a physician.

"May I present Mrs Heaton's cousin, Miss Amabel Horton-Sprigge?"

Aunt Prudence stood up, placed the baby in its cradle, taking a moment to tuck a blanket around him and turned to face Amabel. "You are not related to Colonel Brinkton-Sprigge are you?"

Jemima rolled her eyes and hoped not.

"Why, yes, he is my great uncle Brinky! Are you acquainted with him, Mrs Wainwright?" Miss Horton-Sprigge was wearing a dress with way too many layers and frills on her skirt which on her narrow frame made her resemble a maypole. Her throat was adorned in lace so stiff it might cause a rash.

Aunt Prudence's eyes narrowed and her expression grew decidedly grim. "In former times. A pleasure to make your acquaintance, I am sure."

To break the tension, Jemima invited the visitors to sit. "I am afraid Milly, I mean Mrs Fulton, is resting. I will see if Heaton is awake yet. I think it was near dawn when he finally found his bed."

Aunt Prudence glared at Jemima, the silent signal begging not to be left with the visitors evident. "I will not take long, Aunt. I have ordered some refreshments."

Jemima heard Amabel exclaim just as she was closing the door. "Oh my, is that a wee baby over there? What is it doing out of the nursery? It is not sickening or contagious is it? Will the nurse not come and take it away? The noise of mewling infants is an anathema to me."

Aunt Prudence responded and, fortunately, what she said was muffled even though her words were delivered in harsh tones. Jemima ran up the hall to Fulton's sick room. With a quiet knock, she poked her head in and saw Edward looking on while Milly wiped Fulton's forehead. Clearing her throat to gain attention, she beckoned him when he finally noticed her.

Joining her in the hall, he planted a kiss on her cheek. "Good morning. You look lovely. I hope—"

She squeezed his hand affectionately.

"It is not a good morning, I am afraid. I was interrogated by the local magistrate. Beware he has you in his sights next. He asked a lot of questions about the business with Geneck and my special talents. I will fill you in later. Also, Sylvia just arrived, and she has brought a cousin. The innkeeper is going to pass out in a moment, and I have left them with Aunt Prudence, who is not amused."

Edward's delicious blue eyes widened as he listened to her list. "The magistrate I can worry about later. But great god, what was Heaton thinking bringing his wife here and without a word to anyone?" He ran his hand over his head, ruffling his already disordered curls further. She sniffed and noticed that as well as not having slept much, he had also not washed as yet.

Jemima shook her head. "I do not think he was consulted, but you might enquire gently before there is a great rupture between husband and wife. Either way, he must move them on to another village or something. They cannot stay here. It is like Christmas. There is no room at the inn."

Edward's complexion had greyed during Jemima's recital of events.

"Quite so." He rubbed his chin. "Nothing for it. I will have to wake Heaton, even though he is exhausted. Poor man."

Jemima stepped back to allow him passage. He grasped her hand and squeezed it affectionately. Their intended visit was not going to plan and a silent accord to do their best in the situation existed between them.

Popping her head back in through the gap in the door, she smiled lovingly at Milly and waved to her. No use in upsetting her with the burden of additional people at this time. Fulton was asleep and the angry-looking flesh contrasted with the shiny, new apparatus which lay on top of the covers. Between the bright metal prongs that mimicked the bones of the arm, sat the amber gem about the size of a duck egg that glowed like a captured piece of sunshine. It lit up the room, bathing Milly's pale face in a golden glow. His prosthetic hand looked almost real, the fine chamois like skin with even finger nails etched on the tips of his digits with Edward's magic. Despite the poor state Fulton was in, she admired the genius of her husband and was in awe of his skill.

Ducking back out of the room, she followed Edward. She did not enter Heaton's room, as that would not be decent or delicate. She suffered from neither of these afflictions but had no wish to see Heaton undressed. Besides, she could hear clearly Heaton's reaction to the news. "Sylvia did what? Brought that odious cousin of hers, here?" A slam followed this, so she imagined he had banged his fist on a table or thrown a book. She shrugged. While she was not pleased that Sylvia was in the black book with her husband, it was good to know that Heaton had not encouraged this folly.

So she would not be caught listening at the door, she made haste to the parlour. The maid with the tray was before her and Jemima said, "Do let me get the door for you."

The maid smiled and stepped through after the door was opened. The people in the room, besides the baby, stopped talking, all with gaping mouths and words cut off. What a pity Jemima had not been in the room, for the discussion appeared to be interesting.

"What took you so long?" Aunt Prudence said to Jemima, with no attempt at disguising the complaint. She took no umbrage at the aunt as they were technically her acquaintances that she had thrust on the old woman to entertain. An old woman who only wanted to sit quietly with the baby and dote. Jemima narrowed her gaze and wished she had time to pursue why Aunt Prudence was so attached to the baby. Was it because she had none of her own? Jemima gave a mental shrug. A puzzle for another time, perhaps.

The maid jiggled the tray nervously and curtseyed. "I'm sorry ma'am but we had to boil the kettle as it is not yet ..."

Aunt Prudence waved a hand. "I was not talking to you, Martha. Thank you for bringing the tray. Awfully quick of you, given the circumstances. Please thank the kitchen staff for their efforts."

The maid backed up, obviously confused. She curtseyed again by the door. "Thank you ma'am." She beat a hasty retreat.

After Martha left, Jemima smiled at them all in turn. "Is this not lovely?" she said with such false sunshine, she thought she should be struck down by lightning for such an obvious falsehood. How she wished she could find an excuse to take to her bed with some obscure and highly contagious illness until the situation had blown over. However, that would be grossly unfair to Milly, Fulton, her aunt and her husband.

Aunt Prudence harrumphed and inspected the tray's contents—a large teapot with steam uncurling from the sprout, a tiered tray packed with sandwiches, a plate of sliced dark fruit cake and cups and saucers. Another knock and Jemima went to open it, thinking it was Heaton on a rampage. It was the other maid, Daisy, with a smaller tray. "These are fresh out of the oven, ma'am. Compliments of the cook."

Jemima took the tray. "Thank you, these smell delicious. If you could get another two cups and saucers for us, that would be lovely. The gentlemen will be joining us."

The tray was placed next to Aunt Prudence as she had seniority and a bursting passion for fresh scones. On the tray, curls of fresh butter glowed yellow in a fancy dish, next to a big bowl of whipped cream and another of strawberry jam. It was like Christmas. Jemima stifled a giggle. A smile graced Aunt Prudence's face as the soothing aroma caressed her into a gentler demeanour. "They smell good," Aunt Prudence said.

"Will you do the honours, Aunt?" Jemima asked. "Or would you like me to pour?"

"I will pour and you will deliver if that is all right with you, dear." Aunt Prudence responded with a genuine sincerity. The scones had worked their charm and whatever had passed between them all while she was out of the room appeared to be forgotten.

Jemima delivered the tea to their guests and then took them around a portion of their preferred treats. Despite the cousin Amabel requesting sandwiches, she partook of none and honed in on the scones, taking two of them and piling them high with jam and cream. Jemima spied the aunt's eyebrows quivering in alarm at the younger woman's gluttony. This was despite the fact that Aunt Prudence was already on her second helping.

A knock at the door and before Jemima could answer, the innkeeper came in. "Excuse me for interrupting, Mrs Huntington. There's a gentlemen here who calls himself Fulton."

"Fulton?" Jemima parroted.

"Yes," he replied and handed her a calling card. 'Bertrand Fulton Esq' it said. Jemima had no idea who this was. With a shrug, she said, "May as well show him up."

Honestly, what else could go wrong at this moment? "And what of his luggage?" Mr Copperwraith asked.

"His luggage?" Jemima swallowed noisily. Surely he did not wish to stay at the inn too. The innkeeper obviously thought so because he looked ready to faint.

"I cannot speak to his intentions as this man is a stranger. But if he does want accommodation, you must do your best." Catching his look, she smiled archly. "You have very well-kept stables, sir."

That brought out a smile as he nodded and turned to go. Within a minute or two, another knock sounded at the door. This time she prayed it was Heaton and Edward but alas it was not. Why did she have to do this on her own? She rolled her eyes, realising that her husband needed to wash and dress before appearing in company, and likely Heaton as well. She sighed. Men took so long to get dressed

A short man, balding with a thick moustache and long fussy sideburns, stepped in. "Bertrand Fulton Esquire at your service." He gave a brief bow, as his beady eyes flitted around the room. He was shorter than Jemima she found, as she studied the few wisps of hair on his head.

"I am Mrs Huntington. This is my friend Mrs Heaton, her cousin Miss Horton-Sprigge and Mrs Wainwright, my aunt." She indicated a chair for him to seat himself. "You are a relation of Mr Fulton, I expect?"

He was wearing trousers and hitched them up to sit. "Yes, I am the heir. And how are you connected to him?"

"Mrs Wainwright is Mrs Fulton's aunt. My husband and I are dear friends."

"And are the remains of my cousin Fulton here as well? I wish to see them immediately."

"Remains?" Jemima blinked as she sat opposite him. Aunt Prudence sent him a withering glare, but as he paid no attention to the older woman, the look was not appreciated as it should have been. Jemima was tempted to leave them alone in a room together and see who gained the upper hand. Her money was on Aunt Prudence.

"Yes, I heard of his accident and that he was ... deceased."

"I fear you are precipitous." Calmly, she took a sip of her tea. "Mr Fulton is wounded only. Not dead."

"Not dead," he repeated dumbly. Then as the words sunk in. "Wounded?"

"Yes, he is recovering from his ordeal in his room. I had assumed that is why are you here to enquire after his health. But never mind that. You can help celebrate his good fortune in surviving." Perhaps her comment was going a bit too far, but she found she did not like Fulton's odious cousin.

"Not dead?" he said again as if he did not believe her. "But I heard reports. I will have to see him with my own eyes."

Jemima's mouth grew tight and decided she did not have to be nice to Fulton's heir and Fulton could tell her off when he was recovered. "You might have a bit of a wait on your hands, as the doctor will decide if and when he can have visitors." Jemima glared at him, but he took no notice.

Sylvia giggled inanely. "That is my husband, the renowned London surgeon, Mr Heaton."

Bertrand Fulton Esquire inclined his head, his lips thinning.

Her cousin Amabel smiled. "This is an extremely delicious repast. Who would have thought you could get food like this outside of London?"

Jemima fixed a smile on her face. "Quite shocking to think it possible, I am sure."

She turned to the new visitor, wondering when she would be rid of her earlier two guests, but expecting 'never' would be the answer. "Would you care to take ...?" she began. She wanted to say, take yourself off, but Aunt Prudence was before her.

"May we offer you some tea and light refreshments, sir?" Aunt Prudence offered in a tone reserved for simpletons. Jemima locked gazes with her. The old aunt let a hint of a smile embellish her lips before they firmed up again.

Bertrand Fulton Esquire brightened his countenance at the mention of comestibles. "Indeed, I am parched. I would be delighted to partake. Very kind, I'm sure." He stood to receive his cup and then piled up an empty plate with sandwiches and cakes, then resumed his seat across from Jemima.

Behind his back, she rolled her eyes and asked the heavens how such a fool could be related to the excellent Fulton and be his heir apparent. Next, she hoped no one had seen her expression.

"You said you heard reports of Fulton's accident?" Jemima asked politely, hiding the gnashing of her teeth. She had never wanted to smack someone so strongly and on first acquaintance before. If only there was a dead fish close to hand, she could have employed it for such a purpose. She gripped her skirt instead as she did not want to cause a ruckus, no matter how tempted.

He met her eye, appeared to try to show some compassion but failed. "Yes, that my cousin had been killed, or near death in the post office yesterday. As the heir, it was my duty to come as soon as I may."

Jemima fixed a smile on her face. *Wanted to come and lay claim to the property, I am sure.* Fulton had never mentioned the next heir, but she supposed as his estate was entailed on the male line she should not be surprised. But Fulton was not dead. Fulton had a son, so this man seated before her, eating their delicious food and sipping their excellent tea deserved their contempt entirely. "I am sorry to inform you, sir, that you cannot possibly be the heir. Mr Ambrose Fulton has a son."

The fussy man lifted his nose. She detected a tremor in him, so perhaps it was a surprise and he deserved sympathy after all. "An infant is hardly a barrier to me being the heir. An adult son would be, of course. But with child mortality so high." He shrugged. "I will bide my time."

Jemima gasped at the totally crass comment. Before she could give him a good set down, Aly took that moment to let out a lusty wail, advertising his good health. Aunt Prudence put down her plate, wiped her hands, and stood to lift him out of the cradle. "There, there it is all right, young Master Fulton ..."

Bertrand Fulton Esquire stood up suddenly, sending his plate clattering to the floor. "Is that the brat?"

Jemima rolled her eyes. "No, sir. That is not the brat. He is the heir to Hatfield, and he has a good pair of lungs and a healthy appetite."

He sat back down and shook himself. The day, Jemima thought, could not get any worse.

"Can I bring you a scone, Mr Fulton?" Amabel asked, batting her eyelashes and gushing at the Hatfield heir.

He met her smile as if suddenly noticing her. "No, thank you. I am not fond of scones. Another piece of fruit cake, though, would certainly be a treat. I could certainly eat some more of that."

Jemima watched in fascination at how Amabel reacted to his words, her enthusiasm quieted when he disavowed the scones, her smile dropped only to become alive again when he requested fruit cake. She busied herself cutting him a slice and taking it over to him as if it was a pantomime.

Just then Edward and Heaton walked in, looking freshly washed, shaved and dressed. "What in the world!" Heaton exclaimed, turning towards his wife as if he had no knowledge of her arrival. "Sylvia? What are you doing here?"

The room went quiet, eyes and ears alert. "Is that all the welcome I am to receive?" Sylvia replied, hot spots of red on her cheeks, eyes flashing with heat.

"How vexing," Heaton replied, turning slightly to glance at Edward and failing to step further into the room and greet his wife. "I was not expecting you."

Just then, Sylvia erupted out of her seat, spilling her cup and saucer onto the rug, and let out a screech of outrage then burst into tears. Jemima gaped, taken aback. Surely Sylvia knew better than to make a scene but no, Sylvia began to howl like a wounded cow, making Jemima cringe and worry about what the inn's servants would think. Aly, startled by the noise, began to cry.

Eyes wide, Heaton blanched, gave a helpless shrug and silently appealed to Edward.

Milly came in at a run. "What is it? Is there something wrong with the baby?"

Oblivious, Sylvia kept on wailing, although less vigorously as Heaton had made no step toward her.

Aunt Prudence rose, gave them all a glare and handed Aly over to his mother. "No, dear. He is fine. Just startled by the noise." Aunt Prudence narrowed her gaze at Sylvia, who had now subsided to hiccups and sunk onto the couch.

Meanwhile, giving the room a slightly alarmed once-over, Milly took the baby, whispering soothing words before retreating to her own room to nurse him. Jemima thought it was good as far as tactical retreats went. Nothing to fault there. Pity she did not have an infant to care for.

Jemima waved to Edward, catching his eye. "Perhaps Heaton and Sylvia should discuss things downstairs?"

If the room had not been so full, they could have quietly departed and left them alone to discuss things.

Edward nodded, whispered to Heaton. "Good notion," Heaton said. "Come Sylvia. Let us talk about this elsewhere." He beckoned to his wife as one would a recalcitrant cat. Sylvia, handkerchief to her face, turned her head away.

"It will be fine, Sylvia," Jemima said softly to her friend. "Go on. It will be fine. You will see. We will keep your cousin entertained."

With a nod, Sylvia averted her face, gathered her reticule and followed her husband out of the room.

Amabel giggled. "Oh my, that is not good is it? He seemed very put out." She gripped her hands together in her lap. "I hope it is not because of me."

Before Jemima could assure their unwanted visitor that it was no such thing, Bertrand Fulton Esquire moved to sit next to Amabel. "Such bad manners," he said in disgusted tones. "I do hope your sensibilities are not offended Miss Horton-Sprigge. Indeed, the rudeness of some people, venting their feelings in public."

Edward stood behind the couch and leaned down to talk to her. "Who is that chap?" Edward said crossly. "What is going on, Jemima?"

"Err ... um ..." Flustered, she was not quick enough to respond to her husband's inquiry as Bertrand Fulton Esquire stood up and repeated his assertion that he was Fulton's heir.

Drawing his head back, Edward looked the man up and down. "Heir?" Edward replied in a tone that indicated the heir was a simpleton. "Nonsense."

Jemima blinked. Trust her husband to sort everything out. The heir presumptive turned bulging eyes on Edward, as ripples of outrage stained his features. It was an intense look and despite Edward's rudeness and disregard of his claims, the glare gave Jemima pause.

By then Edward had spotted the tea things and asked Aunt Prudence for a cup. "Scone, jam and cream?" Aunt Prudence asked, her eyes darting around the room for the next explosion.

"You cannot speak that way to me, sir," Bertrand Fulton Esquire said, puffing out his chest. "I am a pugilist and I will land you a facer so hard you will land in next week."

Jemima's ears perked up. That was witty.

From the courtyard, Heaton's voice could be heard. "What the devil! I told you this was an emergency. We can take a leisure trip some other time."

"You always say that and we never go anywhere. Jemima is my friend and you would deny me friendship with her."

An inarticulate sound of outrage echoed up the wall and into the window.

Jemima rolled her eyes up and then tensed. Edward was focussing on food and had not responded to the threat of physical violence.

"I am your husband," Heaton bellowed in the tone of one who must be obeyed.

"And I am your wife. You said you adored me but you just ignore me. I need a life of my own."

Jemima winced and then shook herself. Perhaps if she closed the window? Doing that discreetly was not possible as everyone was looking and listening.

Edward took a bite out of a scone, cream sticking to his chin. Aunt Prudence sighed loudly and rolled her eyes. Amabel chose that moment to swoon dramatically, thereby securing to her the said pugilist's attention.

He put his arm around her to stop her falling to the floor. "There, there Miss Horton-Sprigge."

Amabel made a slight noise, a cross between a sigh and a groan. "Oh forgive my weakness."

The Fulton heir levelled an angry glare at them all, sent a particularly pointed look at Edward before returning once again to the dishevelled young lady beside him. "Please, let me escort you from this most disagreeable situation. The innkeeper must have a private room for you to repose in."

Jemima sat forward in her seat. "I am afraid there are no rooms at the inn," Jemima said, inclining her head in the direction of the window and arguing couple. "With the destruction of Hatfield, the inn is at capacity." Jemima frowned, grasping for ideas. "The next village will have some accommodation, I am sure."

Bertrand Fulton Esquire turned a beetroot red. "You impugn this lady's honour with such a suggestion. I have never encountered such ill-mannered people purporting to be of the upper class."

"I do not. I appeal to your sense of chivalry as Sylvia's maid can accompany her to preserve her modesty. Sylvia can make do without, for I dare say there is no room for extra servants as it stands. The stables are full up. Unless you suggest we move the servants along to make room for you there."

"The stables?" he replied. "You expect this young lady to sleep in a stable? Or is it me you wish to house there?"

"They are well kept. I suppose you could be made comfortable."

"Me? You cannot be suggesting I sleep in a stable."

Somewhat revived, Amabel grasped Bertrand's sleeve. "Oh do take me away from here, Mr Fulton. It will be dreadfully uncomfortable to remain here with my cousin at odds with her husband, and I have never stepped foot in a stable in my life."

The horrible man took this in his stride. He cast a look at Edward, who was stuffing his face with a second scone, cream on the end of his nose. His complexion still heightened, he addressed Jemima. "Very well, Mrs Huntington, we shall seek a room at an inn in the next village. I will return on the morrow and expect to see my cousin in health and life. Miss Horton-Sprigge can return with me and reunite with her kin."

He held out his arm to Miss Horton-Sprigge, who smiled ever so delightfully. "You are so gallant, sir," she said as she rose from the couch, looking fit and ready for a journey. No trace of faintness in her posture. That her willowy figure towered over him did not seem to distress her or him.

Pausing at the door, Bertrand Fulton Esquire turned to address Edward. "I take no leave of you, sir. You deserve no such attention."

Edward turned his head, whipped cream now scoured from his nose and chin. "My name is Huntington and I wager you are not Fulton's heir." He narrowed his gaze at the departing man with a thoughtful expression on his face. She wondered what was troubling him, if anything. He was often distracted by his thoughts, ruminating some spell or some such, yet there was something. Jemima wondered, because she herself took Fulton's heir in dislike before he opined odious statements. Perhaps it was her magic sense that was responding to him. Later she would speak to her husband about it.

Perplexed, but sympathetic to her husband's feelings, Jemima followed the couple out to bespeak the maid. Once that was done, she charged the maid to oversee the transfer of luggage to Bertrand's small carriage. Jemima found some coins in the pocket of her apron and handed them to the maid. It was enough to cover a room and food.

Fulton and Miss Horton-Sprigge made their way down the staircase with all the sombreness of a funeral procession. As the Fulton heir was in high dudgeon, he did not ask after her health or leave his best wishes for the patient. Miss Horton-Sprigge clung to his arm as if wild horses were attempting to drag her away. Jemima thought the couple were in a fair way to becoming engaged. As they finally climbed on board, she let out a huge sigh. Within a minute, the carriage was hurtling out of the drive as if it too had been insulted.

What a tedious man! Jemima put her hands on her hips, and tried to decide what to do next, when she heard Sylvia crying somewhere. Her conscience would not allow her to ignore her friend's plight so she set off in search of her.

Jemima found her in the downstairs entry, face to wall. "Sylvia?"

Her friend turned and threw herself onto Jemima's shoulder. "It is so horrid having Heaton cross with me."

Jemima smiled and patted her friend on the back. "Dry your tears. He will get over it and so will you. You love each other."

Sylvia drew back, an incredulous expression on her face. "Oh no. He cannot love me now. I have ruined everything."

"Really? How?"

Rolling her eyes, she replied, "I brought my odious cousin with me."

That was typical of Heaton to give an epithet to Amabel. She wondered idly what he called her behind her back. "You did indeed. What were you thinking? However, she has gone off with the equally odious Bertrand Fulton Esquire."

Sylvia's red eyes widened. "You are joking. That is not possible. You could not have done such a thing."

Jemima tilted her head, studying her friend as if she was barking mad. "Indeed, I could and did. There is no room here and my offer of the stables was categorically rejected so I suggested they take themselves off to the next village. I am afraid I sent your maid with her for appearance's sake so you will have to do without."

"Oh Jemima!" Sylvia's eyes were wide, and she put a hand over her mouth. Her friend's complexion paled. "How could you?" Sylvia said weakly, fanning her face now with her hand. "The scandal?"

"I will not speak of it to anyone and I imagine you will not either. If there is to be a scandal let it be the result of their own behaviour alone."

"I am shocked, awed." Sylvia's expression altered from misery to shock to a smile in rapid succession.

"No need. I can share Beth with you so you should not be inconvenienced too much without your maid. A night off from Amabel and her preening, weasel ways should do you and Heaton a world of good."

"Jemima!" Sylvia threw her arms around her and squeezed. "You are the best friend. I can share with Heaton and I do not have to worry about her."

"They will come back tomorrow though, I am sorry to say."

"But I have tonight. She has been staying with us these six months. We were both driven out of our minds but could not move her on. None of our relations would take her as she had already overstayed her welcome with all of them."

Jemima was not surprised. "I think she has a fancy for Bertrand Fulton Esquire, next heir. With any luck, she might get him to propose overnight. Poor thing if he does propose. He is awful."

Sylvia laughed again as if a weight had been lifted from her shoulders. "You have not changed one bit from school."

Jemima grinned and rubbed her hands. "Of course not." She drew Sylvia along by placing her hand through the crook in her elbow. Patting her hand, she said, "Perhaps you should go upstairs and wash your face, rest for a bit until your complexion settles. I think by then Heaton should be over his ... um ... surprise at your arrival and you can exert yourself to making him comfortable."

"Oh yes, that is a brilliant plan. Thank you." Sylvia ran up the stairs to do as she was bid.

After all the shenanigans upstairs, Jemima thought it was a good time to take a walk in the country to soothe her mind. However, that would be cowardly and she was no coward so she headed back upstairs to deal with the aftermath in the parlour, stopping to check on Fulton on the way. The invalid was asleep so Jemima puffed out her breath and made her way back to the parlour.

When she entered the parlour, Aunt Prudence was taking a large bite of some kind of bun. Jemima was fond of buns and she wondered how the aunt had come by it, as the platter was empty. She guessed that Edward had eaten all the food while she was dealing with their visitors.

White powdered sugar coated the older woman's lips. "I went to visit the kitchen," she said, seeing the direction of Jemima's gaze. "The cook gave me a bun to soothe my wounded spirits."

She turned to Edward who reclined in a chair, dusting crumbs from his fingers. "Did you say you wanted to set off to investigate the scene at Hatfield?"

Edward eased his neck and adjusted his collar. "Yes, urgent work. Have you got rid of that odious fellow? Something not right about him."

"Yes, he is gone for now. What do you mean not right, love?" She moved closer to him so his response was hers alone.

He met her gaze. "Just some strange vibrations."

"Oh really?" she whispered and nodded her head. For Edward strange vibrations was code for a person with magic. Surely, Bertrand was no magician. Perhaps he had residual talent that Edward detected. However, that strange vibration accorded with her feelings on meeting the man.

Edward eased out of the chair and started for the door with determination. Jemima's eyes widened. It was time for her to confess, maybe it was better to hint. She cast a glance at the aunt and then cleared her throat. "Ahem ... No need go to Hatfield just now. You must be so tired. Perhaps you should rest," she began. "It has been a long night following a stressful day."

Turning, Edward's brow furrowed while he studied her. She tried not to squirm and failed.

"You have not!" he erupted.

Jemima winced at the force of his words. She took in a breath. "Not what?" she replied, all innocence. She blinked a few times to add effect to her honest endeavours.

"Are you out of your mind?" Edward's voice rose an octave and Jemima tried not to cringe. Aunt Prudence mis-swallowed the last of her bun and began to cough, choking on a doughy morsel. Jemima raced over and thumped her on the back. "There, there aunt. All will be well."

She flashed a look at Edward, as if it was his fault the aunt was choking. "I was in no danger," Jemima said across the aunt as the older woman tried to breathe.

With fist clenched by his side, Edward growled out, "You are completely, utterly—"

"Wonderful?"

Aunt Prudence dislodged the offending crumb and sent it flying across the room. Jemima tracked it and gathered up a napkin to scoop it up before there was more bother. That task achieved, she stood and lifted her chin and flicked her eyes in the direction of Aunt Prudence.

Edward screwed up his mouth and swallowed what he was going to say as he had finally noticed the aunt. "Jemima, if you could step outside the room for a moment, I have something I want to say."

Wise to the direction of his thoughts, she shook her head. "I would rather not. I think I will pop to the kitchen to see if I can beg for a freshly baked bun."

She stepped to the door, but with two lengthy strides, Edward blocked her. Hand on the door, he leaned down to speak to her. "You overestimate your ..." He glanced at the aunt who stared with large eyes. "Robustness."

Jemima squinted at his blue gaze. She was readying for a response when the maid knocked on the door. They stepped out of the way as she opened it. The baby's cries echoed up the hall. Aunt Prudence drew to her feet. "I must see how poor Aly is getting on. If you will excuse me." Luckily or unluckily, the aunt took that opportunity to flee. They stepped back to get out of the way of her skirts.

The maid was still there, hands held together in front of her apron.

"Yes?" Jemima asked the maid.

The maid curtseyed. "The cook wants to know if you would like more tea and some fresh buns. And if I could clear away these things so we can set up a new lot."

Jemima smiled. "Delightful. Yes, please to all."

Brooding Edward loomed. However, he did grin at the mention of buns. Where did he put all that food? As he was distracted by the maid leaving, she said, "I need to refresh myself." She slid out the gap in the door and made it to their room.

A few minutes later, she was towelling dry her face when Edward walked in, his brow as thunderous as she had ever seen it. It appeared it was the morning for domestic spats. Next thing, Milly would begin upbraiding Fulton for being torn apart trying to save her, her child and the aunt.

"Tell me," he said, surprisingly calm.

Jemima tossed the towel onto the chair and walked to the window. "Early this morning, I set out to see where the contraption had gone."

With a sigh, he came up behind her, rested his chin on her shoulder. "How in the blazes did you get there?"

"Gig. I managed it just fine. I followed the path of the machine, through the ruins of Hatfield and beyond. The automaton had been destroyed, pieces of it all over the field. No clues that I could see about how that had been accomplished. However, I think the whole attack was meticulously planned and timed. That being said, it could have been a timed explosive."

"It was definitely destroyed?" he asked.

"Yes, there were no tracks leading away from the point of demise. I followed the path of destruction back to the point of origin, which was the railway. When you are better rested, you can look for yourself."

His hands slipped around her waist and drew her close, back against his chest. "Darling Jemima. I am sorry I spoke harshly just now but it could have taken your heart."

"The machine was in pieces." She turned in his arms, put her hands around his neck.

He pressed his nose to hers and leaned back to study her face. "There could easily be another. Whoever is behind it wants my work. You, lovely one, have a contraption of mine within you. One you cannot live without."

"Yes, and we know that I can withstand much. Geneck's magic is part of me. The Ruby Heart is not the only thing that keeps me alive."

He shook his head. "I know you have a notion that you are indestructible, but that is bollocks!"

Jemima gasped, overacting the shock. "Did you just use a profanity in front of your wife?" She tried to keep the smile off her face, even though she had considered the danger to herself but had discounted it. He had a right to be worried for her as far as he was concerned.

"I would do more than that if I thought it would make a dent in that thick skull of yours. I would like to spank you, but I fear you would probably enjoy that. Glutton for punishment."

She took in a huge breath. "Edward!" He had never been violent toward her, or ever threatened such. The image of him spanking her was titillating, though. She hid her response lest he suspect she had been reading ribald literature on the sly.

He shook his head and cupped her chin gently, lifting her face as if to kiss her. "You must take care. I cannot lose you." The light in his eyes caressed her soul. "You are my life."

The soulful look of hurt in her husband's gaze swept away any lingering anger. He loved her and she him.

"I did not mean to be reckless. Besides, I do not have a thick skull, I am just determined." She stood on tiptoes and he kissed her deeply.

He eased her away from him so he could look her in the eye. "Determined to sell your life cheap, I will wager. If Fulton could not defeat that contraption, what makes you think you could?"

Jemima lowered her chin and gazed up at him. "You are right but I was not convinced that the machine would be after me. I will try to think more strategically in future. However, I have the emerald fire, and that trumps a magical arm and leg of extraordinary power. "

Edward sagged. She had scored a hit. Her control over any magical aspects of the emerald fire was still lacking, despite tutoring from him and Uncle Ferdy. Her physical strength had been proven, though not the full extent of it. Any aspirations that the emerald fire would contribute to unusual longevity were theoretical, to say the least. Time would tell or a great battle with some evil being, living, dead or mechanical would prove the theory either way. She did not call herself wife and monster slayer for nothing.

Edward dragged her to him by the shoulders, mashed her face to his chest and kissed the top of her head. "If I was a mean-hearted fellow I would say you are a blessing and a curse. However, I am not.

You are my delight and any angst I feel and express is because I am afraid of losing you. I do not mean to cosset you or deny you agency. I just want to keep you safe."

Jemima detected some moisture in the corners of her eyes. That had been a pretty speech that had achieved the desired outcome. She was not angry at her husband, and he was not angry with her. They were once again on a footing of mutual respect and affection. She smiled up at him and he kissed her. "Did you draw a map of where you found the wreckage?" he asked, after he had mussed her hair and dislodged her lace cap.

"No need. It is straightforward." She gave him verbal directions and waved him off, following him out onto the landing. No need to share the buns then. Her grin was self-satisfied.

As he reached the top of the stairs, he stopped and looked back at her. "Save me a bun, will you?"

Jemima deflated. Edward could murder a trio of buns in a second. Beth chose that opportune moment to climb up the stairs. "Oh thank providence. Can you assist me, Beth? I'm afraid I need to repair my hair."

By the time she made it back into the parlour, Milly was sitting on the sofa cuddling Aly. She smiled at Jemima, looking tired but happy. "Aunt Prudence is sitting with Fulton. He has asked after you."

Jemima came over and inspected the depleted tray of buns. She took a plate and added three to it. "For Edward," she said to Milly, whose eyes had widened. She covered the plate with a napkin and put it on the shelf behind Milly. "Guard them with your life." Milly laughed and it was good to see that she could in the circumstances. "How is Fulton?"

"He has slept most of the morning. I fear the various raised voices woke him and he was curious."

"You described to him all the various contretemps." Jemima picked up a bun after pouring a cup of dark tea, and eyed it with anticipation.

"I did. Although, I am sorry to say I could not bring myself to mention that odious Mr Bertrand and why he was there."

Jemima bit into the bun, closed her eyes and chewed. What a delight. So soft, so sweet, so doughy. She swallowed. "It would not help his recovery if he leaped from his sick bed to throttle the poor fellow. He is not worth the effort."

"Jemima!"

"What?" she asked as she contemplated the next bite and whether a smidgen of butter would improve the bun experience.

"Fulton would not throttle someone without cause."

Jemima let out a chuckle. "Yes, I know. Believe me, you were out of the room when that odious man made the most contemptible remarks. If you had been here, I fear you would have been the one we would have to restrain from said throttling."

"I would do no such thing!" Milly moved the baby to lay him over her shoulder and rubbed his back. A large belch filled the gap in the conversation. Jemima's eyes widened at the sound. Milly giggled. "Just like his father."

That broke the mood. Jemima laughed so hard, she forgot about her bun for a full minute. She finished it off, but soon began to wonder when they could have a proper meal. Thinking of proper meals, Jemima excused herself. "I will talk to the innkeeper about dinner and then take my turn at Fulton's bedside. I must find something to read him. I know he is fond of Tom Jones, but I fear I find it irksome. I shall fill up his head with Dickens. There is an old copy of The Pickwick Papers in our room."

Milly was staring into the face of Aly and looked up. "You know his chin is very Fulton. I fear there is nothing of me in there at all."

As Jemima could see no resemblance to either parent, she quipped. "He is all you."

As if realising that Jemima had spoken, Milly said, "Whatever you read Fulton will be a salve. He is a poor patient and is so bored, as well as being in pain."

Jemima took her leave. The innkeeper promised to convey her dinner order to the cook and grinned when she conveyed the news that two of the visitors and a maid had left to find accommodation elsewhere. Dusting her hands, she decided it was time to see Fulton. As she entered the sick room, Aunt Prudence drew to her feet. She smiled fondly down at Fulton. "You should rest. I will instruct the cook to bring you more gruel."

Jemima's stomach curdled at the thought.. She thought Fulton would much prefer a freshly baked bun but, as she was not in the mood for a fight with Aunt Prudence or sharing buns with anyone, she kept mum. Aunt Prudence angled around her, her wide skirts colliding with Jemima's. "Try to soothe the poor fellow and do not excite him," the aunt said quietly as she left the room.

As soon as the door was shut, Jemima held up the tome in her hands. "Up for some amusing reading? I brought some Dickens."

Fulton groaned. Jemima loved a captive audience and knew he hated Dickens. She was not going to let Fulton's grey complexion and red-rimmed eyes or the angry flesh around his newly reattached arm to get in her way.

"Forget that tripe, I want to know what has been the cause of all that ruckus? Milly mentioned uninvited guests."

Jemima smiled and patted his good hand. "First you must listen to me read. Too much excitement is not good for you."

CHAPTER 6

Fulton closed his eyes, relaxed his body as best he could, hoping to convince Jemima that he had fallen asleep. Not too hard, given he was exhausted and hazy from pain and drugs. The sound of rustling skirts advertised that Jemima had taken a seat by the bed and the flick of pages that she had opened the book. She began to read:

Posthumous Papers of the Pickwick Club, Chapter 1. The Pickwickians, The first ray of light which illumines the gloom, and converts into a dazzling brilliancy that obscurity in which the earlier history of a public career of the immortal Pickwick would appear to be involved...

"Stop!" he begged in a gasping voice. Eyes snapped open, full with his best glare aimed at his would-be nurse. He could take no more. He hated Dickens with a passion. Too many words. Too long to get to the point. And the characters, so terrible that they haunted his dreams.

Jemima shut the book with a snap. "I see my efforts are in vain. Being tiresome must run in your family."

Fulton tried to make himself comfortable. He could not disagree, his father and his brother were indeed tiresome. "I am not that bad. Why do you make such a remark to an invalid?"

Jemima stood up, tugged on the bed covers, smoothing non-existence creases from the counterpane. "Oh just your awful relative, your next heir."

Fulton's mouth dropped open and then snapped shut as blood ran into his neck and cheek. "What in the devil are you talking about? My next heir? Have you lost your mind?"

Jemima lifted her chin, looking down on him as if he had lost his senses. "Of course I have not lost my mind. I did not invent him. He claimed to be your heir."

Startled, Fulton widened his eyes. "Who did?" Fulton had a terrible feeling in his gut.

Blinking as if she was ordering her thoughts, Jemima adjusted her cap, tucking away a stray golden ringlet. "Bertrand Fulton Esquire arrived and demanded to see your remains. Odious man."

That twisty feeling in his gut sank to his toes and then rushed up to the back of his throat. It would be terribly inconvenient to be sick at this time. He closed his lips, holding back the bile and when he had his body under control, he growled out, "There is no next heir in this country. I have no idea who this Bertrand person is but he is definitely no relative of mine."

Jemima's face froze, and leaning forward, searched his face. "That makes no logical sense. Why would anyone claim to be your relative? Why it is ridiculous! I must put this reaction down to your illness." She put a hand on his head. "Do you have a fever?" She leaned closer, studying his face with rapid flicks of her blue eyes. "Are you delirious? Should I fetch Heaton?"

"No. No. NO!" he rasped, for a yell was quite beyond him. She leaned back, giving him space. The explosive movement of his denial made his arm tug and he winced. Controlling himself yet again, he added reasonably, "Leave Heaton alone. He pokes me too often as it is."

Book in hand, Jemima sat back down in her chair as if all her energy had dissipated. He watched her warily in case she did something unpredictable. Next, she lifted her eyes from the book and met his gaze. "But how can you know who your next heir is?"

Fulton rolled his eyes and grumbled to himself. Only his affection for Jemima made him keep any nasty remarks to himself. He was out of patience with everything. "Because it was all laid out by the solicitors when I inherited the estate. The heir after Aloysius is someone living in Boston in the Americas, called Frank Baxter Fulton and he is at least ninety years old, if he is still living. The one after that is his son, who is seventy, and then his son and so on."

Suddenly, Jemima stood up, the book falling to the floor. Flustered, she panted, as if she found it hard to breathe. "Oh dear," she said, putting a hand over her heart as if to quell its rapid beating. "Oh my, what have I done?"

Fulton watched this display with some dismay. Had she invited the fellow to stay? If so he could be easily got rid of. "For God's sake, Jemima. Surely you sent this man on his way."

She turned to face him, face pale, eyes darkened with worry. "I did," she said in a high voice. "I sent him away with Sylvia's cousin, Miss Amabel Horton-Sprigge."

Fulton's mind had to speed up to keep up with Jemima's rapid disclosures. Milly had told him that Sylvia Heaton had arrived with a cousin. "Dear God!" Fulton crossed his eyes, confused. "You did what? But he must be an imposter, a sinister fellow, and you sent this poor, innocent relative of Heaton's into his power."

Jemima's nodded vigorously, hands clenching and unclenching. "I did not know that! And I certainly did not even entertain the idea." Jemima paced up and down, tossing the book she had onto the end of the bed and rubbing her chin as if it was a magic coin. Fulton wanted to kick the offending book off, only he was still trying to comprehend what was going on and open his mind to the potential ramifications. His body and mind had been hard used after all, and he was no longer a young man. With a sigh, he closed his eyes. He was in no mood to deal with Jemima in one of her flights. "Please fetch Edward. He will make more sense of the situation."

Jemima's eyes widened. "I make perfectly good sense." She came to his side and gripped his good hand. It still hurt. He hurt everywhere.

"Oh Fulton. Edward is not here. He has gone to look at the wreckage of the machine that attacked you."

Fulton groaned and squeezed her hand back with some urgency. "Not by himself?"

"Of course." She wriggled her hand and he let go. Rubbing it, she added, "He was not happy that I went by myself early this morning."

Fulton cursed and did not care if Jemima heard him. "Of course he was not happy. The attack was about Edward and his machines. Are you daft? You have a machine inside you." He hissed as the movements of his fist jolted him.

Jemima pursed her lips and then glowered. "No need to be rude. How was I to know he was lying about who he was? But why would someone impersonate your heir and demand to see your remains?" She covered her mouth, and he nodded as he saw the realisation dawning there. "He was after your arm?"

"What else could it be?"

"To make sure you were dead and out of the picture!" she exclaimed.

Fulton nodded. "That too."

He had tried to protect his family, had nearly died doing so, if Heaton and Huntington were to be believed. Still after all that effort, they were not safe. Someone had dared to enter the inn where his family stayed, where he lay near death. But the arm was taken. His brain grew hot as he tried to think of the why. If he was dead, what would this imposter gain? His other apparatus. His leg. Fulton liked to think he was a man, a man who was more than the sum of his parts, but, obviously to those with envy and evil intentions, he was only parts and the man inside did not matter. His view of the world dimmed. He had seen much in his time, but this savage attack, this single-minded focus on the gifts of life, movement and strength given to him by Huntington, dear Edward, shocked him. Had they no mercy, no care for who he was and what he valued?

"No," Jemima countered. "Your leg." She had come to the same conclusion as he had.

Fulton rolled his eyes and groaned again. Why did everything have to hurt? Why could he not heal quickly? "Give me more of the laudanum will you? Just a bit to take the edge off this pain. I need a clear head because obviously none of you can think rationally."

Shakily Jemima poured the dark liquid and helped him to sip. "I am so sorry to have distressed you, Fulton. But why are you so angry? He did not see you and he did not take your leg or your new arm for that matter."

Fulton calmed himself, realising that ranting at Jemima would get him nowhere and would probably be deleterious to his continuing mental health. As the medication took hold, Fulton relaxed against his pillows and let out a slow breath. "You entertained a man, pretending to be my heir. A person with unknown motives who now knows who is here and what our weaknesses are." With a sniff, Jemima nodded and was about to speak, but he shook his head. "Then you let Edward go out there." He nodded to the outside with his chin and winced. "Where he could be snatched."

Fulton should not have put so much on Jemima. He knew it as soon as he spoke the words. Frustration at being bedridden drove him to say more than he ought, more than he truly meant.

Jemima drew back, streaks of red climbing up her white neck, her delicate hands clenched into fists. "What? I am Edward's wife and I can no more stop him from what he wants to do than hold up the moon." Jemima exclaimed. "If I told him not to go, do you think he would listen? I suppose I could have tied him up, held him against his will. Only that is against the law, I think. He certainly did not think that Bertrand Fulton Esquire was any danger." She paused, screwed up her face, and stared over his head as if remembering something. "Oh? Oh dear."

"What?"

Her cheeks grew pink, the angry streaks staining the flesh of her neck fading fast. "Edward said he felt vibrations from him. Although he did not say outright but it was like he would if the person had magic. Do you think that stupid fellow could be the one behind all this?"

"Destroying Hatfield was a brazen attack so why would he stop at coming here to collect my parts in the aftermath?"

Jemima paced and her chest heaved. "This is a terrible situation I own. He was such a small, insignificant sort of person and full of his own importance that really annoyed me. A good disguise, I suppose, because I dropped my guard. I felt so superior and indignant on your behalf. Your device was their goal and we know they succeeded ... although it seems they want more. We could surmise they thought you dead and your leg would be for the taking." She tapped her chin and pivoted to head back toward the head of the bed. She gazed down at him. "Edward did say my heart could be a target too. You are right, as now he knows who is here and where we are situated. But why would Edward be in danger?"

Fulton rolled his eyes. "Because he created these devices. What better way to get what they want than to take him?"

"Oh! Like before when they forced him to make that emerald heart for Geneck? I did not think that nightmare could reoccur." She patted his good hand gently, trying, he thought, to reassure him. The truth of the matter had not sunk in yet. "I could not bear it if he was kidnapped again."

Fulton gloomed at the room, the bed and at Jemima. If only he could get up and do something. "I am with you there."

Jemima sighed as she sat back down, fluffing out her skirts to arrange them nicely. "Do you think this Bertrand chap is the evil person behind all this? Surely he could not be a threat to Edward. He is a magician after all, growing in knowledge and power daily. Besides, Bertrand has gone in the opposite direction, accompanying Miss Horton-Sprigge to the next town and does not know Edward has gone to inspect the wreckage."

"It could be this Bertrand fellow is an associate of the perpetrator. You said Edward felt something, perhaps magic from this Bertrand fellow."

Jemima dimpled her right cheek as she clenched her jaw in thought. "I thought the perpetrator would be taller, maybe more menacing ... wearing a dark cloak. Bertrand was just odious and annoying. I cannot see him directing anything, except a servant to pour tea."

"I cannot know for certain, but given the circumstances it is suspicious. He claimed to be my heir, demanded to see my body."

"But then you were not dead so he could not."

Fulton rolled his eyes again. "Where did you send this imposter again?"

"The next village, but I expect them back tomorrow, with him possibly engaged to Miss Horton-Sprigge."

Fulton growled. "Do not behave like a simpleton." It was highly unlikely the imposter would return pretending to be his heir. He knew Fulton was alive as Jemima had no reason to lie about that and while Milly was upset and distressed, she was not mourning him.

"Do not call me names. How was I supposed to know he was a fake? We will not know for sure until they come back in the morning."

"If he comes back at all."

"Fulton do not make me angry. Of course he will bring Miss Horton-Sprigge back. He cannot take her because that is abduction. Besides she is as odious as he is." She frowned as she considered this. "Well suited then. Oh dear, the woman has Sylvia's maid with her and how will Sylvia manage without her?" She put her hand to her mouth as his words sank in. "I did not think it through at all. Heavens, what am I going to say to Sylvia if he does not bring them back? "

"Nothing for now."

Jemima turned and looked out the window. "There is no sign of Edward either but he has not been absent for long."

"When did he leave?" Fulton asked, trying to estimate how long before his friend returned.

"Perhaps an hour or so. As I do not expect him back for another two, at least, I will not worry about him until this evening."

"I do wish you knew how to heal me, Jemima. All that power and you cannot fix this." He inclined his chin to his wound.

Jemima turned back, brow furrowed. "I could try. I have been learning how to use this magic after all. It would be best if Edward were here, though, to direct me."

"And if he does not come back?" Fulton studied her. He knew she was strong and he knew if she could help she would, no matter the circumstance.

"You are very maudlin today, Fulton. 'Tis not like you. If Edward does not come back, I will try to heal you."

"But have you any idea about healing?" He wished, more than believed, she could help him. He had to do his best on his own to heal. Getting out of this bed was the first step, except he was still as weak as a new-born kitten.

"I have not undertaken any healing. I have been practising how to direct my power, fine-tune it so to speak. I many not know how to heal, but Heaton does and he could direct me."

Fulton mulled this over. He was recuperating well, faster than normal because of Edward's magic and his device. Yet, if Edward did not come back, Fulton needed to be completely healed and ready to go in pursuit. It was risky. Jemima could kill him instead of heal him. If they had no choice, though, they would have to try. Jemima was strong, but she needed Edward's guidance to use the power she had. Way more power than Edward had, to be sure. With Edward at her side, Jemima could be indestructible. Whereas Fulton had proven to be otherwise. He had thought he was resistant to harm and had been proven wrong. He lifted his good arm to poke at the damaged one. The new arm was sleek and the glow of the amber warmed him body and soul.

"Right then," Fulton said before tiredness gripped him. "You will not tell the others about Bertrand, yet. We shall wait and see if Edward returns before we shift to a more dramatic footing."

"Yes, agreed." She hoisted up a watch on a chain to view the time. "It is Milly's turn."

Jemima leaned over and kissed his brow. "Sleep now and I will return this evening."

He must have drifted off, because a small warm hand holding his drew him up through the layers of sleep to wakefulness.

"Hello, Ambrose." His wife leaned down and kissed his forehead. "Your colour has improved. I thought you might like a wash. We can get some of that blood off you."

With a wan smile, he let her minister to him. He hated being helpless but confessed that the bed bath did make him feel so much better.

He dared not tell his wife about the true situation with the fake heir or his concerns for Edward. His plan to have Jemima to try to heal him was also not to be mentioned. He decided to be docile and sleepy and enjoy her company. Dealing with all her questions would tire him out in any case and arguing with her when she was already so distressed by his injured state and having to care for their child on her own would be entirely bad form. Besides, Jemima had completely scrambled his brain.

A knock at the door and Heaton came in. "May I have a moment with Fulton, Mrs Fulton."

Milly stood up, straightened her skirts. "Of course. Let me know when I should come back."

"Take a rest, Milly," Fulton suggested. She looked haggard, and he hated being the cause of it.

"I will try."

Heaton walked up, inspected his arm, felt his forehead and then took his pulse. "I see Mrs Wainwright's gruel is doing you good."

Fulton flashed him a look and pouted. "Do not jest as it does not become you. I am quite able to eat something else more substantial. I am wasting away here. Edward has not returned, has he?"

Rubbing the back of his neck as if he had slept badly, Heaton shook his head. "Not yet." He poured a fresh glass of water from the jug and placed it on the side table and nodded to Fulton to take it. Fulton was not up to holding the glass himself so he ignored the drink. Heaton let out a long breath as if he had let go of some great burden. "Mrs Huntington spoke to me about your request. I hope you understand that I do not comprehend how Huntington's magic works, and I will be a poor substitute to guide her if you are serious about attempting such a thing."

Fulton met his eye. "I am serious. The situation is too dangerous for me to linger in this fashion. Useless and a magnet for trouble. I cannot be that, not to the people I love. You can guide Jemima I am sure of it. Try, that is all I ask, all I can hope for." Fulton licked his lips suddenly thirsty for that glass of water he could not hold. "You understand the body, and healing better than either of us. You know where the hurt is and what she would need to do to repair me. Will you help me?"

"I will."

Fulton nodded, like a salute. "Thank you." Fulton let himself relax again and Heaton, seeing he had not taken the water, lifted the glass and assisted Fulton to drink. "Thank you again for that. I hate being this weak."

"So say all my patients." Heaton returned the half-empty glass to the side table.

Fulton licked his lips, satisfied now that he was no longer thirsty. "Did Jemima tell you about that fellow pretending to be my heir?"

Heaton folded his hands in front and nodded solemnly. "Yes, I met him just briefly. Hard to believe he might be the mastermind behind the attack. He seemed so ineffectual. I thought you were hunting for a monk or something."

Fulton puffed out his cheeks. "Indeed," he agreed. "But what is a monk without his robes and the trappings of office? He is just a man."

Heaton bit his lip. "Or a wizard."

"Quite." Fulton tried not to grin, for surely to do so would set some part of him hurting. All this talking made him tired, and he needed to build up strength. "When shall you begin?" Perhaps he could fit in a nap.

"We must wait until we are certain that Huntington has not or cannot return this evening. He would be powerfully angry with me if I went along with your plan when it was unnecessary."

"All right then," Fulton agreed. "I might rest. See if you can keep them away for an hour or two."

Heaton nodded as he headed for the door. "I will do my best but your womenfolk are determined."

Fulton closed his eyes, felt the drugs and sleep woo him down in the dark of dreams. He thought of Milly and his son and of sunlight and happiness. Each time his thoughts turned nasty, he would force them back into the sunshine.

WHEN NEXT HE WOKE, IT WAS DARK OUT AND SOMEONE HAD CLOSED the window to keep out the damp of night. His sheets were tucked high. Someone had come in while he slept. Heaton was right, he could not make them stay away.

When Jemima slipped through the door some five minutes later, he did not need to ask her, only look at her face. Edward had not returned. He saw the tears in her eyes and understood her concern. She raced over and grabbed his hand. "Oh Fulton. 'Tis all my fault. He has not come back. I have sent a couple of the ostlers to the wreckage to search for him. Although it is too late and they will not see much with only a lantern to light the way."

He squeezed her hand. "Edward is strong. He can look after himself."

She returned the pressure on his fingers. "Yes. I must keep positive."

"Indeed you must. What are the others doing?"

"Aunt Prudence is organising the parlour for dinner. Milly is taking a nap while Aly is also asleep. Sylvia is sewing up a delicate little bonnet for the baby. She bears Aunt Prudence's instruction better than I ever did. We have some time."

"I am ready. Can you fetch Heaton?"

She let out a sigh. "No need as he is on his way in. You do not ask if I am ready."

Fulton looked her in the eye. "You are always ready for anything. I trust you."

She took in a breath. "I do not know whether to be worried about your trust in me. I fear I am not so confident. Heaton suggested I look at your wound and study it so I might see the workings of Edward's magic on you."

Fulton tucked the sheet down so she had unrestricted access to the site. "Hand me the mirror please, I want to see."

Jemima took the small hand mirror off the dressing table by the window and handed it over. He moved it so he could see his wound from as many angles as he could manage. Considering what he had been through, he was remarkably healed. While he could not feel it, Jemima was right, Edward's magic continued to work in his absence. The pain was not as acute and that meant he was more clear-headed and needed less pain relief.

Jemima studied his arm, moving her face close to the device and where it joined the metal ring at the shoulder. "Why did he do it that way?" she asked, sounding intrigued.

"So I could detach it easily."

"Detach it? Why would you need to do that?" Her eyebrows knotted together and she nodded. "So no one tears you apart. I see." With Jemima staring so intently, he kept his mouth shut so as to not disturb her concentration. When he looked again, she had her eyes closed. "I can sense rather than see the flow of Edward's magic." Awe was evident in her hushed tones. "I think if I sped up the flow that might hasten your healing." She pointed to the shoulder ring. "This is where your body must mesh with the device. The arm looks mostly self-contained, although I imagine there is a connection there so you can use it."

The door shutting alerted them to Heaton entering. "Let me see how we get on." Heaton stepped up and took Jemima's place. As he studied the wound and the arm, he spoke to Jemima. "I think what you suggest is a good place to start. Edward did say he just tells the flesh to heal."

Jemima started, as if surprised that Heaton had spoken to her. The innocent blue of her eyes met his. He nodded and hopefully conveyed confidence in her abilities.

Shifting, Fulton tried to sense what Jemima sensed but could not. Heaton stood by her side, pointing with a thin metal instrument. "There," Heaton said. "See if you can speed the mending there."

Quiet, Jemima lifted only an eyebrow as she studied the wound. Heaton picked up a magnifying glass and leaned in close. "Yes, that is it. Do more of that."

Given Jemima talked so much all of the time, her quiet concentration made Fulton uneasy. Heaton pointed again, directing her to focus on another spot. He could detect nothing. It was all pain and throbbing and aches. "I need to shift your arm, Fulton," Heaton said. "It might pain you."

Fulton cried out. He must have fainted. His arm was a heavy weight but his shoulder by contrast felt lighter. "Sorry about that. Huntington fashioned a join between the arm device and your shoulder and Jemima needs to apply herself to that so you can move it. It may take time for you to use your arm as well as you did before."

Fulton blinked and a tear leaked out of his eye. He was not weeping, he was not so weak. Jemima looked over to him. "I am sorry for hurting you, Fulton. A necessity it seems." She moved his arm again and he cried out. "Can you open your hand?" she asked.

Fulton felt nothing. Just numbness. "Again," she urged.

Heaton looked on as she shifted his arm, bit by bit, and every time the movement hurt until he thought he would scream in a most ungentlemanly manner.

"I think the connection is working now. Fulton just has to find his way."

Heaton wiped Fulton's face with a cool cloth, washing away tears and perspiration. "There you go, Fulton. We have done what we could. It is now up to you and Huntington's magic. Sleep now, for that is the best thing."

Jemima touched his cheek, a weary smile on her lips. "You did well, Fulton."

Unable to utter a word, Fulton closed his eyes, forgot the memory of pain and drifted off to sleep.

GREY MORNING LIGHT FILTERED IN THROUGH THE CURTAINS. HE was alone and that had him blinking. Usually there was someone to keep him company, ply him with liquids, make him comfortable. He shifted in the bed and it did not hurt as much as it should have. Reaching for the small mirror on the side table, he looked at his shoulder and gaped. No longer bloody and raw, the healed flesh was healthy and pink around his shoulder. The edges that met the metal were less puckered. He moved his arm gingerly and it moved, no longer the lump of wood it had felt like yesterday. And he did not scream in pain. A whir escaped from the shoulder join. Using his good arm, he edged up the bed and then he opened and shut the metal fingers of his other arm. Jemima had done it. She had sped up the healing, just like he thought she could. What a wonder!

Noise filtered up from below. A disturbance of some kind. He could hear voices, Jemima's of course. Had Edward returned? The mysterious Bertrand?

He edged along the bed using his good arm for leverage. Swinging his legs over, he sat still for a few minutes as the room spun and he felt as weak as a kitten. He was better, but not back to normal. At least, he could take himself to the pot to piss for the first time in days. With his foot, he hooked the chamber pot from under the bed and drew it out. It felt so good to be capable of something besides passive resistance. Using his foot he pushed it in gently back after he was done.

He shifted on the bed so that he could see his reflection in the mirror on the dresser. A gasp escaped his dry lips. Grey flesh sagged on his cheeks, a mottled beard clung to his jaw and black circles surrounded his eyes. A light fuzz on his scalp from where he needed to shave. He really had been close to death. Once again he owed his life to Huntington and Heaton ... and now Jemima. Would she ever let him forget it.

Best not to waste this second chance.

He drank some water from a glass by his bed and stood up. The room spun ridiculously and his stomach was a hollow space that needed to be filled. In the courtyard below, the noise grew louder. Curiosity meant he wanted to see, to know what was going on, only his body had other plans. He sighed and lay back down, flicking a sheet over himself as he shifted on the mattress to get comfortable. God he wished the room would stop its slow spin. It was important to conserve his strength and he would find out soon enough. A nap before he rang the bell for food was a good idea and he let his eyes close and sighed into repose.

❦

JEMIMA HAD BARELY SLEPT WITH WORRY AS EDWARD HAD NOT COME home. She had assisted Heaton with Fulton with more competence than she thought possible. It was Edward's magic, his application of science and soul that she had encouraged along by seeing what it was doing. It was unique, she thought, because she detected Edward in there, in the machine, in the gem and even in Fulton's flesh. It was like a familiar hum attuned to her own life force, her own love for him.

The commotion in the yard could not be good news. Edward did not screech like a girl. Or was that the sound of a horse protesting. From this distance she could not tell.

"Jemima?" Milly called to her. "Come quickly. I will wake Mrs Heaton."

Jemima had little to do to repair her appearance. Not being able to do more than doze, Jemima had dressed early and Beth had fixed her hair and set her lace cap on her head. Trundling down the stairs to investigate, she came to a stop on the stoop. She could not believe what she was seeing. Two bedraggled women stood there: Miss Horton-Sprigge and Sylvia's maid, Jane Cosgrove. Miss Horton-Sprigge's frills drooped on her dress that might now only be good for the fire. Her face was smudged and tears had left a clear path in the grime on her cheeks. "What happened?" She looked for the carriage they had left in and no such conveyance was evident. "How did you get here and where is your escort?" Jemima asked, fearing the answer.

"That man is no escort of mine!" Miss Horton-Sprigge shrieked and then commenced some noisy hysterics, which she had been doing before Jemima arrived. Ostlers gave them a good distance, mouths agape and eyes wide. As Jemima had been to a girls' school, she was familiar with such tantrums. "There, there," Jemima said. "You are here now. You are safe." That comment only made it worse and the woman began to waver, to totter in an ever-broadening circle. Quick as she could, Jemima timed her move precisely and grasped the girl under both arms just as her legs buckled. Miss Cosgrove stood still and stoic. If anything, it was perhaps she that was more perturbed by events than Miss Horton-Sprigge. Jemima had to call on her supernatural strength to keep the young woman from dropping into the mud as it had rained during the night, leaving glossy brown puddles in the forecourt.

The maid gave an exasperated sigh and took to chewing at her inner cheeks as if that would help her keep her outrage in. Delicately as she could and still be hurrying Sylvia came down the stairs in her dressing gown, and enthusiastically drew her maid into her embrace, despite the dirt and the audience. "Thank the heavens you are back. I missed you so."

This act of welcome was witnessed by Miss Horton-Sprigge in quiet rage. All of a sudden instead of fainting, the woman stood up straight. "How dare you insult me like this. I am your kin."

Sylvia gaped and Jemima could see the cogs turning in her friend's mind. "Forgive me, Amabel. I did not recognise you."

Jemima winced and could feel the outrage gathering in Amabel. Soon she would have enough breath for one last scream to announce her arrival in the bosom of her friends. Miss Horton-Sprigge did not disappoint. Even Sylvia winced as the loud ululation coming from that thin throat.

If she was to screen the next part of this play from the various onlookers, Jemima had to act fast and made her voice the most sincere and welcoming as she could. "Come inside, Miss Horton-Sprigge. There is fresh tea and warm baps and butter," Jemima said with an arm around the shoulder of Amabel, gently urging her inside. "You can tell us what happened when you are more comfortable. I am sure we can find some clean clothes." By then all the fight and outrage had left Amabel weak and compliant. Sylvia took up station on the other side of her cousin and together they helped her up the stairs.

"Oh Martha?" Jemima said, when she saw her maid had come to witness the commotion. "Come take Miss Cosgrove to where the servants are quartered and help her settle."

Martha bobbed and gently ushered Sylvia's maid into the hallway and beyond.

She and Sylvia half dragged their charge into the entry hall. "Excuse me, Mr Copperwraith?" Jemima said as the innkeeper approached. He should not be surprised, she thought, as their group had done nothing but cause a hullabaloo and upheaval from sunup to sunset.

"Yes, Mrs Huntington," he said in a deceptively calm voice. They would have to tip him considerably when they departed.

Jemima made a vague gesture along the road. "I fear there has been some kind of accident on the road from Thrupp. Would it be possible to dispatch a cart and two capable fellows to find Miss Horton-Sprigge's luggage? She will need her things to go on a journey home."

At the mention of his unwanted guest's imminent departure, he stood up straighter. "At once, madam."

Touché, thought Jemima. She deserved the 'madam' she supposed. However, not yet being one and twenty, such an epithet annoyed her. The term 'madam' aged one so.

She joined Sylvia and her cousin in the upstairs parlour. Hot water had been ordered and a hip bath set up in Sylvia's room after Heaton had been moved to Edward's dressing room so there was not much left to do in a practical sense, except to listen to the story. As the tale had begun by the time she arrived, Jemima had to take a seat, pour some tea for herself and snaffle a bap and butter while the story unfolded.

"He was quite the beast once we set out. I did not know what to do. He drove like a mad thing."

Sylvia leaned in, eye wide, mouth agape. "And what did he do then?"

"He said I was of little use to him and that I was excess baggage. Before we came near the next village, he halted the carriage in the middle of nowhere and ordered us to get out. Then he went to the back of the carriage himself, unstrapped my traveling chest and my band boxes and threw them to the ground."

"Not a gentleman then," Sylvia replied. "I am so sorry you had to endure such a thing. Heaton will call him out. You will see."

Her cousin's eyes widened and tears began to flow anew. "Why did you let me go with him?"

Nonplussed, Sylvia met Jemima's eye. Jemima cleared her throat as it had been her doing. "You were so taken with him," Jemima said before Sylvia could reply. "And much offended on his behalf. I feared there was no stopping you. You were decisive."

"But he was a relation of Mr Fulton. His heir. Not that I have met Mr Fulton but I deemed him an acquaintance due to his relationship with dear Heaton. Why would he behave so abominably?"

Jemima shook her head and looked to the floor. She would have to own up to everything. "Sadly, we were mistaken in him. Mr Fulton tells me he has no such relation. We have been harbouring an imposter and by the sounds of it, not a gentlemanly one."

"Oh!" Miss Horton-Sprigge looked near to fainting.

As Jemima had not caught the earlier exchange of confidences, she did not know if Bertrand had behaved in other non-gentlemanly ways. And if he did, it should not be spoken of as it would forever stain the young lady's reputation.

After another cup of tea and several hot baps with melted butter, the young woman was encouraged to take a bath and have a rest in Sylvia's bed.

Jemima was enjoying the last of her tea when Sylvia returned. "I have let the innkeeper know we will stay another day."

"How did he take it?" Jemima asked archly.

Sylvia frowned as she took a seat. "What do you mean? He was perfectly polite. He says he can fit a trundle bed in our room."

Jemima replaced her cup in the saucer. "I meant nothing by it. We are just creating such a fuss and bother I assume he must be keen to see the back of us. It is good that you are willing to share."

"You are so droll sometimes." Distracted, she stood up and went to move away. "I must look after Amabel and see how Miss Cosgrove is settling in as she was shocked by what occurred." Adjusting her skirts, she fingered a flounce and furrowed her forehead and Jemima could see there was a lot on her mind, particularly after the argument with her husband. "Heaton is resigned to staying another day, although it chafes him as his locum is nowhere as proficient as he is."

Jemima tried to offer an encouraging smile, but failed. "At least he has someone to care for his patients. You will take the train I expect and be home by tomorrow afternoon."

"Yes." Sylvia sighed. "I had wished for a nice visit with you and not all this hullabaloo"

Jemima cleared her throat meaningly and lifted her eyebrows.

Sylvia blushed and nodded quickly. "Yes, so sorry to have foisted my cousin on you." She took a few steps to the door, finally taking her leave. She paused and looked back to Jemima with a cheeky smile on her face. "Look, when things settle down, do come for a visit. Heaton will love to drink his wine with Huntington and I want to show you the shops and our house. You could make it a stay of a week or two or even a month."

Jemima was warmed by Sylvia's invitation. "I would love to once we deal with the situation at the moment and I am sure Edward will be amenable to such a proposal."

"I shall be back in a minute." Sylvia left the room and Jemima had some time to sit in the relative quiet of the parlour considering their situation. She knew Fulton would be dying to know what was going on and was pleased to make him wait. The result of her magic healing was not clear as yet and while the waiting was driving her to distraction, she knew Fulton needed time to heal.

The maid had cleared most things away and clean plates and silverware had been brought up. A few meagre morsels remained on plates in the centre of the table.

Jemima noticed one in particular and was about to reach for it, when Sylvia bustled in. "Amabel is sleeping and I have given Miss Cosgrove the day off."

Jemima grinned. "Great news. She could do with a good nap too, I suspect."

Sylvia's gaze focussed beyond her to the table. "Is that the last bap?"

With a laugh, Jemima lifted the plate in offering.

Sylvia snatched up and placed it on a plate. "Thank you. I am starving." With a critical eye, she surveyed the table. "We need something more substantial than bread. I can smell bacon cooking. Do you think they are preparing breakfast for us?"

"I certainly hope so." Jemima slid out of her seat. "Look, I best fill Fulton in on what has occurred. But I will first inform Aunt Prudence and Milly so they can be delicate around Miss Horton-Sprigge, just in case she joins us after her nap. They were resting but I hear Aly crying so they must be awake now."

"You think of everything. I will wait here and let everyone know when the food arrives. I think a full belly will make Heaton a bit more amenable generally."

CHAPTER 7

Fulton had to wait to find out what had caused the ruckus below. And nothing irked him more that to have to lie in bed waiting for others to provide information. After a good deal of commotion, screaming and a lapse of time, footsteps thundered along the hallway. He knew Jemima's step anywhere. He took a breath, arranged the blankets and waited with an air of boredom. It would not do to let on that he was anxious to hear all.

The door flung open with a crash. "Fulton! It's Miss Horton-Sprigge and Sylvia's maid. It is quite shocking! They have returned alone," Jemima said in a rush.

Fulton twitched and winced. Damn this pain. She came over to the bed, wringing her hands as the words poured out of her. "They said your odious relative threw them out of the carriage and left them by the side of the road."

"Not my relative," Fulton growled, the fist of his good hand landing on the bed covers.

In her excited voice, Jemima continued. "Not even a bed for the night in the next village. They have slept rough by the side of the road and walked back here. They walked all night and it rained."

Fulton blinked. "Damn the man and his impertinence." This

phoney Fulton was not a relative and he resented the disgrace his pretence had caused his good name.

"Is that all you can say?"

Fulton opened his mouth and then thought better of it. There was a merry sparkle in her eyes and she missed nothing.

Heaton had brought him hot water earlier and he had shaved and was sitting up in bed, rather than lying on it and Jemima failed to comment on his improvement.

Jemima stepped to the side of his bed, tucking the sheet in absently. "Do you need some gruel or something? I am sure Aunt Prudence will see to it once the fuss and bother has settled. I thought you would want to know all as soon as may be."

At the mention of gruel, he erupted. "Keep that gruel away from me. I want something more ... give me meat and eggs and bread and cheese and ale. And, of course, I want to discuss things but you have not drawn breath since you burst in here."

Jemima frowned. "But ..." Her lips tightened, and she looked him over quickly. He had fallen asleep after her ministrations and they had not met since. Did she not see his improved energy, his increased vigour, was she not curious if her first healing attempt succeeded?

"Jemima, I am much improved thanks to you."

Her response was to blush and look away. "Without Heaton I would be useless."

"No, no. Not useless, maybe dangerous."

Her blush disappeared and she laughed. "Well then, I shall order some breakfast for you." She headed to the door, pausing before flinging the final little titbit bit at him. "The men I sent last night found nothing and Edward is still not back. Only Heaton knows and the others with the Miss Horton-Sprigge incident have failed to notice his absence. But they will before long. After you eat, if you are up for it, can we go looking for him?"

He lifted his good arm and stretched, slightly shrugging the bad arm. It twinged, but he kept his face composed. "Yes, food, then hot water. Is my valet about?" He rubbed his chin. "I have shaved but I need a better hand." He rubbed his good hand over his scalp.

Jemima nodded, her eyes dark with worry but a smile playing

around her lips. "I am glad it helped, Fulton. Thank you for agreeing to come with me."

"Do not mention it. I shall be ready."

Jemima went to shut the door behind her and then paused before it shut. She pushed it open and again and leaned in. "What shall I tell Milly?" Jemima narrowed her gaze. "Or should I leave that to you?"

Fulton considered this. He could not leap from his death bed and embark on another exploit with Jemima and not incur the wrath of his loving wife. She might appear meek and mild but he had experienced the steel in her, her resolve, and she loved him fiercely. "Tell her, I am much improved but to give me some more time before she comes to see me. For God's sake make her rest."

Leaning her head on the doorframe, she sighed. "I see. You will not tell her what we are about. I will hold off getting ready then to avoid suspicion."

A sharp pang in his middle snagged his attention. A hunger he had rarely experienced plagued him. "Food!" Fulton said in a gruff voice. He needed food before anything else. "Now!"

He did not hide things from his wife. It was a matter of timing, knowing when to reveal unpleasant news. Contemplating the arguments he would have with Milly if he did advise her before the time was right, held his tongue. Best to surprise her with his miraculous recovery. Jemima was right. To avoid upsetting his wife, he would have to speak to her. One could only hope that his recovery would make such a good impression that this latest venture would be overlooked. Somewhat.

❦

Two trays arrived, full of food hot from the kitchen. Fulton blinked when he saw it, for it was enough to feed three men. The aroma of cooked bacon, fried chops, eggs and fresh muffins made his mouth water. The lamb chops he managed to put away along with the scrambled eggs, bacon, sausages and a chunk of bread. Fulton ate as much as he could, disconcerted to find that his stomach would not hold so much food, even though he had only been an invalid for two days. A large draw of ale had tipped him to the edge. He lay there, tray half full, belching and wavering between feeling bilious to feeling satiated. He liked satiated better.

True to her word, Jemima sent Hampton, his valet, to assist him to shave and wash and dress. Hampton was a new hire as his old valet had sought another situation, and while he was not accustomed to the man, his skill was undeniable. After going through his valet's ministrations the room began to spin. To disguise his weakness, he sent the man away and stayed sitting in the chair until the feeling waned.

Experimentally, he flexed his legs, his good arm and tried lifting the damaged one. Nothing too untoward happened, no sharp pain or teeth-twisting agony. Despite being foggy headed, he was hale if a little lacking in energy. If only he could ask Jemima to share hers as she always seemed to have so much, what with her emerald fire, Huntington's magic and her own, if he understood correctly.

If only he had been the one to drain the beast, Geneck, then he would not be in this predicament. Mentally, he chastised himself for such a piteous thought. It was beneath him to envy Jemima. Besides, he would not have even thought of such a ploy to drain Geneck nor had the courage to almost die to save them all. He loved Jemima, as a friend, and would put his life on the line for her and he did not envy her power, not really. He just hated feeling like this, like he was a useless lump of flesh unable to assist, unable to fight and worst of all unable to protect. This line of thinking had him clenching his good fist and tapping it on his knee. No point in getting tense. Jemima had helped him, more than he thought possible.

From memory, Jemima healing him had been the first practical use of that power. Although she was generally strong, much stronger than a lady should be, this was its first positive magical application he had witnessed. Edward and he had discussed the ramifications of the combinations of magics within Jemima on many a night over a glass of port and in their correspondence. The most chilling of which was that Jemima might outlive Edward, and perhaps himself. He had his own share of Edward's magic and even now he could feel it tingling through his flesh. In repairing him, it appeared that Edward had given him even more power than previously. He had said he had used a bigger and better quality gem that powered his devices but it was something more, he was sure of it. A machine is a machine, but Huntington's devices were more than machines, they had a life. Yes, that was it—a life of their own. Without Huntington's devices, Fulton did not have a life, not a full life. A flash of what might have been came into his mind. Him alone, in a room somewhere, peg-legged and a stump for an arm, with nothing to live for and drinking away the misery of his existence. Huntington had saved him from that. With his magic and his life force combined, Edward had given him a gift. He shook his head in amazement. The gift of life had strings attached, although he was sure they had been unintentional. Fulton might be dependent on magic to live and he did not care a jot.

Jemima's magic though, had that augmented him more? Would it be enough to fight the villain who had tried to destroy him? With the expertise of their opponent and the size of the gargantuan automaton — a large country house could be demolished by one alone—with no way to stop them, he would need this new boost to his power and more. They would need Jemima's too. Although Huntington would oppose his wife facing danger, they needed as much as they could get on their side. Combined, the three of them could do it. They had to do it or all was lost. Not only their lives but the rest of the world. A brief flash of a future held to ransom by a maniac with giant machines made him shudder.

Breathing deep and gathering his strength, it was time to prove to himself and the others that he could conquer this injury. He knew this inn and had stayed here or visited often in the past. His room was on the same floor as the parlour and not too far down the hall. If he did not make an effort now, he may as well go back to bed. With a push of his good arm, he shoved out of the chair, wavered slightly and breathed slowly until his balance returned. He was not himself, but on the road to recovery. It was time.

Along the hall carpet, he took careful steps, now and then steadying himself against the wall. There were murmurs echoing, evidence of a discussion so he knew that was where they all were. When he reached the parlour, he pushed open the door. Aly was in the arms of Prudence. Milly sat on the lounge turned to Jemima and talking animatedly.

"Good morning," he said. His voice came out gravelly and weak. He swallowed and then cleared his throat.

"Fulton!" Aunt Prudence exclaimed, jolting the baby out of a doze. She bent to sooth him, blinking wet tears that threatened to dampen her cheeks. He was moved by her display of surprise and emotion. He inclined his head.

Eyes wide with shock, Milly bolted upright and let out a scream. "Ambrose?" He blinked, stepped further into the room and used the back of an upholstered wing chair to support himself. Next, he knew he was being hugged by his wife, who being a smart woman, avoided his injury. She leaned back to stare into his face. "Oh Ambrose! You are walking around. Jemima told me you were much improved, only I could not believe it. How is such a thing possible?"

He smiled dotingly on her, ran his good hand over her head, careful not to dislodge her lace cap. Tears streamed down her cheeks, and he wiped at them with his thumb. Her nose was red and bringing a lace handkerchief to her face, she blew her nose and sniffed.

He had never been so happy to see anyone. Yet he saw the toll his illness had taken on his wife. Dark smudges under eyes, the pale complexion, the thinness of her wrists. "Milly, my love. I am well, much improved. But you must take better care of yourself."

She leaned in to kiss him on the lips. "I will take better care of me now that you are up and about. Aly is well you see. Aunt Prudence has been most helpful."

He nodded to the aunt. He wanted to hold his son but felt it was best not to. Not only could he not trust his grip, he did not trust that he could then leave them all to go in search of Huntington.

As he was busy romancing his wife, the rest of the room faded from his notice until he heard Jemima go to the window, as if she was trying to pretend she was not in the room by whistling no particular tune badly. His gaze shifted, drawn to where Aly fussed and Aunt Prudence crooned.

"Come let us sit," he urged, guiding Milly back to the settee where she had been not five minutes before. He stayed standing, not completely sure he could get up again without betraying that he was not as hale and hearty as he made out.

He faced the window. "Are you ready, Jemima?"

Drawing back inside from her place on the window sill, Jemima replied, "No. But I will be soon. There is tea and your son to cuddle so you will not miss me."

Jemima made her escape just as Milly stood and confronted him. "Ready? What do you mean ready?" Hands on hips, she glared at him. "You are not going anywhere."

Fulton met her gaze, blinked before turning to the aunt. His wife had not spoken to him in such a way before but as he had been near to death, he did not take umbrage at her tone. He had expected a scene and he had to weather it calmly.

"May I have some tea, Aunt. I will hold my son if you do not mind."

She passed the baby to him. "Certainly. Will you take a sandwich, some fruit cake?" she asked, indicating the plates on the table.

Fulton was full of breakfast and should not partake further. But the fruit cake looked so moist and the piece so small. "A touch of fruitcake if you please. I am afraid I ate well this morning." He turned to Milly. "Please sit and we can discuss things."

Milly narrowed her dark eyes, nodded with mouth pursed and sat. Lifting his son in his good arm, he gazed upon him. The child was awake, moving his arms and smiling. "Hello, little one," he said, voice catching. All at once he felt overwhelmed. They were alive. He had saved them from harm. He blinked before the tears fell.

"Fulton?" Milly said in a quiet voice. "Are you all right? We are all fine you see. You were the only casualty."

He nodded, sat gingerly on the settee next to her and exchanged the baby for tea and cake. "I had a moment to realise that you are all safe. It made what happened worthwhile."

"Worthwhile?" Milly's eyes widened. "It should not have been necessary." She swallowed as if changing the direction of her thoughts. "Your planning saved us. Your bravery gave us time." Tears trickled down her cheek. "I wish your actions had been unnecessary only we have no control over that. We must live our best lives." She wiped at her eyes.

Fulton sniffed, nose running as tears stung his eyes. "Our best lives." He lifted his lips in an attempt to smile, but could not quite manage it. He was sad, sad that those he loved were not free from whatever pursued him. It was a quandary. The reason their lives were at risk was because of a gift that gave him this life to share with them.

His wife sat next to him, tension rolling off her. It was not anger, it was fear. "Jemima has told you Edward did not return yesterday," he began.

She nodded. "She said she must go look for him." Milly looked away as if knowing what he was going to say and not wanting to hear it.

"Yes, that is her plan."

"Silvia's cousin and her maid arrived back on foot after going away with your pretend heir. They are in a terrible state and are just now being cared for by Doctor Heaton and Sylvia. Surely you must stay and hear what they have to say."

"I know enough, Milly. I have to look for Edward. Edward is my immediate concern. I am not going after the imposter heir just yet."

Damped eyelashes framed her sad eyes. "They could be connected. Surely, you need to know."

He shook his head, smiled a small smile, trying not to trivialise her concerns. "Jemima has told me some of it. She may fill me in on the rest as we travel."

Milly held a handkerchief to her face. "But you are not strong enough. What if there is another machine there?"

Fulton's instinct was to shrug, but to do so would cause pain. "I am in no condition to fight a machine and I have no intention of doing so. If there is a large machine there I will turn back as quick as may be. You can count on it. However, there was a wreckage and Edward went to look at it. Edward may be lying there, injured, or there might be some clue as to his whereabouts if we cannot locate him. You would not have Jemima go off on her own, would you?" That was a low blow, he knew. Milly loved and admired Jemima and it must be hard to challenge her loyalties against her love.

"But Jemima has already been off on her own, yesterday." Milly's expression grew defiant and angry. It was the first time he had seen these emotions from his wife. Hands gripping his, she said, "There is no stopping her from doing anything. You are not duty bound to protect her."

Fulton blinked. "Milly?"

"I do not mean that how it sounded. She does not have a baby to look after and, therefore, she has little to constrain her."

Understanding, Fulton nodded. "You wish you were free to come with us, guard us, help us?"

Milly met his gaze. "I do, even though I am not brave at all. I hate that you are gone from my sight, that I have this hole inside of me where you are meant to be and losing sight of you makes me think it will be empty forever." She buried her face into his shoulder and took a shuddering breath, as if to hold in her emotions.

He stroked her back and spoke softly. "I am bound by friendship to look for Edward. I owe him my life." He was going to add that she owed Edward his life too, but his wife was well aware.

"Yes, I know. We all owe him so much."

He rubbed her back some more, feeling her relax. "Jemima is capable of protecting me, you know. She rescued you all from the ruins of our house. She is strong and smart. Do not underestimate her." He wanted to add that she helped heal me, helped me sit next to you now, except that in her current mood Milly might resent Jemima for that, for readying Fulton once again for battle.

At last, she nodded her acquiescence. "I understand why you must go. Do not ask me to be happy about it or ask me not to fret until you walk back in the door."

He shook his head. "Of course not. I will fret until I see you again and us out of this situation."

At least she did not ask or insist that she come along too. She had chosen to feed their son herself and would not abandon him, no matter her protective instincts for him. Fulton was certain Aunt Prudence could protect them as she had proven herself to be inventive and brave. He had not discovered the mystery of the aunt but there was something different about her, as somehow she took all that was strange about their lives in her stride. He hoped to find out one day but for now just had to be content that Aunt Prudence would not baulk at anything. Jemima had that effect on people he supposed.

Jemima strode back in, dressed in a leather corset, a long leather coat, which she was still buttoning up, leather trousers, a gorget and a fetching leather boater. She tugged and a plain brown skirt dropped over her trousers to disguise them. It was the most outrageous and unladylike outfit, yet it was so Jemima and there was no point in commenting positively or negatively. "Is that Milly's handiwork?"

Jemima made a gesture with her hand, inviting Milly to speak. "The design, yes. The leatherwork was commissioned and it was my idea about the skirt to hide it all. It is easily removed if required."

Milly blinked innocently and smiled at him. "I apologise for my objections. You are right. Jemima will look out for you."

"Come along, Fulton. Do not dally." Jemima said, looking toward the open door. "As much as I am shocked by what happened with Miss Horton-Sprigge and Sylvia's maid, I do not wish to delay to hear more of their complaints and their conjectures about the odious Bertrand Fulton Esquire. I had a full accounting at breakfast. Judging by the sound emerging from Heaton's room, I fear they are headed this way." She quirked her head as if listening. "We shall leave by the back stairs. I shall ask the kitchen to bring morning tea on my way out. Come along Fulton."

Fulton stood slowly and walked gingerly to the door, his lack of verve and vigour evident for all to see. Fulton hated that feeling and wanted to be back to his old self straight away. Only he had to be patient and that was not a strong character trait of his. Jemima spoke directly to Milly. "I will have him back and in one piece as soon as I can."

Fulton did not catch Milly's response exactly, just the tone and she no longer sounded angry and upset which soothed him greatly. He kept walking as he needed a head start on the stairs. Even then, Jemima grumbled as she walked behind him as he took each stair carefully. His injured arm hung like a dead weight. He tried clenching his fist and felt nothing.

True to her word, Jemima ordered morning tea for the upstairs parlour. "As you wish, Mrs Huntington. The cook has anticipated you and nearly has everything prepared." The landlord inclined his head at Fulton and acted if it was no small thing that a fatally wounded man was now walking around. "Good to see you on your feet, Mr Fulton," Mr Copperwraith said.

"Indeed, rumours of my demise are unfounded."

"It would seem so and much joy does it give me." Mr Copperwraith tapped the side of his nose. "I should mention that the magistrate has asked me to let him know as soon as you were fit for visitors. May I inform him that you are improved?"

Fulton inclined his head. "You may. We are just going to take a look at Hatfield, what is left of it."

"A very sad business, indeed sir." The innkeeper bowed as they passed through the hall to head into the courtyard.

Jemima touched her hand to his arm and he gazed into her earnest blue eyes and saw the concern in them. "I took the liberty of hiring a gig. I hope it will not be too uncomfortable for you, Fulton." She knew exactly how healed he was and he felt transparent to her eyes. Probably, Milly saw through him in the same way and it was only his fragile masculine ego that thought he could fool them and himself.

The russet-coated horse pulling the gig was led up to them by a young stable lad.

"Thank you," she said as she studied the traces and patted the horse. Fulton had observed that the creature appeared sound as it was walked up to them. "I shall drive," Jemima said turning to him. "If that is all right with you."

"Fine by me," he replied, as he did not think his shoulder up to holding the reins and holding the whip at the same time. She climbed onto the seat, took the reins from the stable lad, who still held the bridle, and looked down at him. "Do you need help to get on?"

He eyed the gig. It looked way too flimsy for two, but it had a tray at the back sufficient for Edward to sit, stand or even lie down.

"I can manage." As it was, she pulled him up by his good arm and helped guide him into the seat. Next, she nodded to the boy to release the bridle, cracked the whip and steered the gig toward the road. They cleared the yard and headed off at a trot toward Hatfield.

"I think you need to be careful or you will be the subject of gossip."

She turned briefly taking her eyes off the road. "What do you mean?"

"When you heaved me up, the boy's eyes nearly fell out of his head. Even being ill as I have been I am still a large man."

"Oh I did not think about it. You are right. Speaking of gossip, Miss Horton-Sprigge is extremely distressed about her mishap with your heir."

Fulton let out an explosive sound. "He is not my heir, and if you say so again to my face, I shall clip your ear."

Jemima laughed. "You would no more do that than set a bad stitch in your embroidery. I fear she harboured feelings towards Bertrand."

Fulton scoffed. "I am in no doubt that the whole escapade was very frightening for her and the maid. That man behaved in a brutish way, leaving them abandoned on the side of the road, without protection. I can hardly think about it without wanting to pop him one on the nose. But feelings? She just met the man. Foolish girl for departing with him in the first place. She is lucky to be alive." He coughed and sat up straight. "Hang on. Why is she alive? Surely, he would want to cover his tracks."

Jemima kept her eyes on the road and flicked the whip gently. "Mmm, well, I did give her little choice and while she is an irksome creature, I would not wish what happened to her on anyone. As to why he left her alive, I have no idea but thank providence that he did. Think of the explaining we would have to do, and with that magistrate sniffing around. All kinds of bother there."

Fulton turned to her. "What did happen besides being dumped by the side of the road with her baggage?" Was he really going to have this conversation? He had known for a while that Jemima liked playing with his brain, often throwing inanities at him while keeping the pertinent points until last.

Jemima frowned. "He was very rude, apparently."

Fulton grunted. "Just rude? That is strange. Is he sending us a message?"

Jemima blinked, licked her lips. "I cannot for the life of me think of what message he was trying to send other than I have pierced your soft bits and I can do worse?"

"That is a strong message if you ask me. Anything else we need to know? Any clues from either the young woman or the maid?"

Jemima bit her lip and nodded. "Apparently, he quizzed them on what they knew about you, Edward and me."

"And?"

"Miss Horton-Sprigge knew nothing, of course. She is Sylvia's odious cousin and the maid is new to Sylvia and was not at Primrose Manor when those terrible murders took place and Edward was under suspicion. If Bertrand, if that is really is his name, wanted information, he absconded with the wrong woman. Sylvia would have been a better prize."

A sigh escaped his lips. "Then what happened?" He guessed there was more and he would have to wheedle it out of Jemima before he lost all his patience.

"He abused them soundly, accused them of being a waste of space and put them to sleep."

"What? How?" He replied.

Jemima waved her fingers in a vague way that might have mimicked Edward.

"He is a magician?"

Sighing, Jemima shrugged. "Of some kind. They did not drink anything or eat anything from his hand so it must have been a spell. Unless, of course, they were so fatigued they fell asleep naturally."

Fulton scoffed. "Do not try to bamboozle me. Tell me the whole of it."

"Miss Horton-Sprigge and the maid do not know what happened while they were asleep. They woke up some hours later in a field beside the road. None of their baggage was deposited with them."

"Did they make the next village?"

"Not straight away. They woke up in some distress in the dark and walked down the road until they found a small hamlet. There, they were given some tea and a ride to the next village. Eventually, they made their way here, mostly on foot as the village had no equipage to spare and they had no money. He had taken all the coin they had."

"Devilishly dastardly of the fellow." Fulton was sympathetic. Both women were innocent and had no inkling of the trouble their association with the Fultons and the Huntingtons was going to cause them. Luckily, the Heatons escaped the worst of it. "I take it someone went to look for their luggage?"

"Yes, they found it up the road aways from where he dumped them and what has not been damaged by being scattered to the four winds has been returned to them." Jemima glanced his way. "I have to tell you I did not like him," Jemima said. "Even when I thought he was your relation."

Fulton did not bite at the relation comment. "I am of the opinion that he is not nice, but at least they are alive. He could have done away with them and we would have been none the wiser until their bodies were found or we went looking for them, which we probably would not have done given they are Sylvia's and Heaton's responsibility."

"I did not think of that." Jemima gave a little shudder. "It does put a different perspective on things." Jemima flicked the reins and tooled the horse into the drive leading up to Hatfield. "It does seem like this Bertrand is working with our nemesis, but possibly he is not the one we seek, for would he not have attacked us when you were so low?"

"I agree. But he may be the one to lead us to the culprit. He will have to be tracked down and made to speak of what he knows." Fulton did his best to put a bridle on his anger. There was no object for him to direct it at other than himself. However, he dashed well was not going to take the blame for some diabolical plan to attack him or a pretend relative. The ache he felt was for those he loved and cared about. Not a religious man generally, he still thanked the maker that his household had suffered no fatalities.

The gig skirted the curve in the drive, bringing them within view of the house. Fulton's mouth fell open at the sight of his demolished house. It was hard to take in, bold as day as it was. He hardly recollected the scene, taken as he was with fighting the automaton. Nothing much left, the destruction was near total. He would have to rebuild, if funds allowed. He could not engage with that just yet, the shock was too recent, his injuries too new. He could see that some effort had been made to salvage their belongings. Even now he saw some people carrying long beams and stacking them under cover.

Jemima put her hand on his arm gently. "You can rebuild, Fulton, and do it in such a way that all those annoying things like drafts and awkward layout can be fixed."

It was not easy to hold all he felt in. The stiff upper lip was hard-fought for. He nodded and tried not to think on his past, on the bad memories from his childhood and the happier more recent ones. "Quite right," was all he could manage. He dared not say more lest he weep. At least they had another small house in Chelsea. It was not commodious but they would not be homeless.

"You can stay with us at Willow Park as long as you need. I would love to have Milly there and Aly and you, of course."

He lifted an eyebrow, touched by her generosity. "And Aunt Prudence?"

A laugh trickled out of her. "Of course, if forced." The grin on her face belied any ill feeling.

"Is that Edward's horse in the stable yard?" Fulton asked.

Jemima peered into the distance. "It must be as his mount did not return to the inn."

Setting the gig in motion again, Jemima explained where she thought the machine had been dropped off on the railway line, which followed the line of destruction to his house. They continued behind the house to where she had discovered the wreckage and where Edward had supposedly gone to investigate. They followed the track gouged into the soft earth until they reached the debris. Jemima slowed and applied the brake before getting down to secure the horse. Next, she held out her hands to help him down. He accepted her help and landed gently on his feet. His shoulder twinged with the impact and he hissed out a breath.

Meanwhile Jemima looked around, forehead wrinkled in puzzlement. "There are fewer bits of debris than before. Someone has taken parts."

"Not Edward surely," Fulton opined.

"Possibly but I doubt it. He did not bring anything to carry them away again. I am certain he came on horseback. We will need to check your stables for his horse. I imagine he came to the house, dismounted and walked the track, looking for clues."

"Is someone stealing them?" He hated to think that one of his neighbours or servants would try to profit from his misfortune.

Jemima looked askance. "On your land? No, I do not believe it. I think the farmers and workers around here would not steal from you or have a use for the parts."

Fulton let out a pent-up breath and nodded, for her thoughts accorded with his.

They approached the pile of metal that remained with caution, passing by a hedge that had been ploughed through. Clearly, there had been heavier objects that had been removed for there were indentations in the soft ground.

There was no sign of Edward. "Nothing to say he was even here," he whispered to Jemima.

"He did not bring the horse here for there are no hoof prints on the ground. No horse leavings." She studied the ground further, bending down to examine the disturbed soil. "Footprints here."

Walking in a wider circle, Fulton looked around and found evidence that a cart or wagon had been there. There were also some stranger imprints, deep gouges in the ground, like someone had repeatedly shoved a pike in the ground looking for a soft spot.

The hairs on his neck rose. He looked to Jemima and saw movement behind her. "Watch out!"

A metal creature stomped along. Slightly larger than a dog, it had six legs and two front arms that ended in pincers. At his words, the two front arms lifted as if ready to attack. He looked along the path it had made and gasped. Hidden by the trees, there was a wagon, which had some of the metal pieces stacked in it. This clearly was what it had been sent to do, recover the remains of the machine to take back to its owner.

Jemima spun, and kicked the machine. It stopped its forward movement, jerked its head and continued on. Jemima stepped into the machine's path. "Stop there, little beastie." She kicked out, harder this time, and the machine fell back, not quite falling over. She had given it a mighty kick, and it had not fazed the beast. With her level of strength, it should have broken apart. A solid little thing then.

Jemima leaned down and picked up a thick strip of metal. It had some heft. This time she swung it hard at the upper body and the machine fell sideways with a thunk. Its legs kept moving, but it was not going anywhere, unless it had the dexterity to twist its torso.

Fulton came up to examine it. "Nice work." He met her eye. "Do you play cricket? I could use you on our local team."

Jemima cast him a sideways glance, with a touch of loathing. "Only if I can be captain. I thought you preferred needlework to sport."

Fulton nodded. "I do, but one does have to try to blend in socially. A gentleman cannot be caught pulling needle and thread. It would be a terrible assault on his masculinity. "

Jemima laughed as she bent her knee to get a closer look. "It does not look too menacing. Edward could not have been harmed by it."

Fulton rubbed his chin. "Perhaps it took him unawares. Let us look around."

Together they closed on the cart. No sign of Edward amongst the debris stacked on the boards. He had thought perhaps Edward's body had been placed like the metal rods and casing. Jemima began to circle out from the cart and in among the undergrowth from the destroyed hedge.

"Here," she called an urgent note in her voice.

He rushed over as fast as his weakened body allowed. Edward's booted foot stuck out from underneath the bush. Jemima squatted down and moved a branch and nudged his foot. The foot moved but the leg did not retract. Moving some leaves, they could see it was attached to the rest of Edward. Holding his breath, Fulton waited and then relaxed when Edward's chest moved up and then down. Not dead. Thankfully. It was his secret dread. That they would be too late. That he would be too late. He was not normally this uncertain in his abilities. He guessed the attack on his house, on his person, had taught him the measure of himself, something he had not had cause to do for many a year. Edward's apparatus had made him near invincible. That is, until it had been ripped away.

He studied Jemima as she leaned forward and patted her husband's cheeks. "Edward? Edward? Wake up."

She rapidly ran her hands over his body and the back of his head. Her hands came back with blood on them. "A head injury."

His heart skipped a beat when he saw the dark red stain on her fingers.

Jemima wiped the blood on the leaves and stood. "I will bring the trap closer so we can take him back to the inn. Thank providence that Heaton had to delay his departure. Can you stay with him while I go?"

Fulton spluttered. "Of course I can bloody well stay with him. You are not going that far." Her eyebrows creased and he could tell she wanted to ask him what was wrong. Concern for Edward took precedence so she shook her head and ran off, lifting her fake skirt, the tail of her coat flapping behind her. Soon she was out of view.

The machine moving its legs made an irregular click, clicking sound. It was still moving, still trying to right itself. From his vantage point, he tried to peer at its insides, wondering if it held something more sinister within its carapace. Obviously, it was deadlier than they thought, or someone else or something else had been here and taken Edward unawares. An accomplice perhaps. He kept a lookout. Was this where Bertrand had returned to once he had got rid of the women? If so, there was no sign of him now.

Jemima pulled up in the gig. Closer but not close enough to easily lift Edward into the back. "I will carry him," he called out.

"No, you will not. I can manage."

She was right, of course. He might have his new arm healed, but he was not sure if he could lift his friend yet. His prosthesis still felt like a dead weight. He needed to train it to respond to his commands.

"Can you drive the gig?" she asked. "I will stay on the back to make sure he does not fall off and bang his head."

"I think I can manage that."

And he did.

❦

HEATON STOOD AT THE FRONT DOOR, SMOKING A CHEROOT. "MR Heaton! Thank goodness you are still here," Jemima called. "Edward is injured."

Heaton tossed his lit cheroot into the mud and then bounded down the steps into the yard to meet them.

"Thank heavens you found him." Heaton did a quick survey. "Mmm, I do not think his skull is cracked, though I will not know for sure until I have examined him."

He called for assistance, and two of the ostlers put down the chest they were carrying and raced over. They gathered up Edward and carried him inside.

Heaton paused in front of Fulton. "You are looking remarkably well old chap, but as a favour to me, please no more excursions until you are completely healed."

Fulton inclined his head. "I will do my best. Circumstances and all that."

To Jemima Heaton said, "Perhaps you can assist me, Mrs Huntington. I may be in use of your talents."

Fulton followed after them and before he could ascend the stairs, his wife threw herself into his arms, not actually weeping for joy but there were tears. "Ambrose! I am so glad you are back. It is wonderful that you found Edward. What will become of us all?"

"We shall relocate soon, my love. Perhaps we should rent a house by the sea. Whatever you decide. I am afraid it will be a while before our house is rebuilt."

Milly pulled back. "You are going to rebuild?"

He smiled back at her, never forgetting how lucky he was to have her. "Do you not wish me to?"

"Yes, of course I do but I thought ... well I have not seen ... I thought it destroyed."

He cupped her chin in his hand. "It is pretty destroyed but it can be rebuilt. Our servants and neighbours saved our chattels so once repaired it will be as before."

"Could we not repair the chimney so it does not smoke? And perhaps we could adjust some rooms so we can access the nursery more easily. And the kitchens are too far away."

His smile became a laugh. "Why Milly I do believe you want to try your hand at design. Of course we can make some changes. We will consult an architect immediately, well, after we have dealt with this current business. Perhaps you can make up a list of candidates. I will make sure the steward consults you on which architect to hire when we have put this bit of wrongness to right."

She smiled, wiped her tears and took his hand. "Come and see how little Aly is doing. I swear he smiled at me this morning. He is growing so fast."

Fulton smiled but inside fear twisted his innards. All he cherished in the world was at risk for they were not out of the woods yet. Danger lurked, and he had to do his utmost to protect them.

CHAPTER 8

Edward lying motionless on the bed and his cold clammy skin made fear climb into Jemima's throat. She could not lose him. They could not lose him. But spiralling out of control and being over-emotional was not to be borne. She had to be brave. Jemima held her breath, relaxed her clenched fist and pushed her thoughts in a positive direction.

Taking his time in his examination, Dr Heaton performed a thorough review, returning to Edward's head and eyes more than once. Impatient to have his assessment, Jemima shifted her feet and managed to stand on Fulton's toes. "Sorry," she said, not really paying attention. "I did not see you there."

Fulton squeezed her elbow. "I just came in. He will be fine, I am sure," he said in a soft voice. She turned to him and saw the worry in his expression.

Edward looked so pale, so still. Mr Seaward was there, removing Edward's cravat and deftly slipping him out of his coat. The boots he had earlier removed when they first laid Edward on the bed. At the ready, Mr Seaward had a night gown and some warm socks to make Edward more comfortable. Jemima felt superfluous, standing around wringing her hands. She wanted to punch something but that would be considered unladylike in company.

"Perhaps you can see to hot water," Heaton said, looking up and meeting her eye.

With a nod, she ducked out of the room, her feet pummelling the stairs as she descended to the kitchen. Martha had just walked into the hall. "Oh Martha. Can you bring a jug of hot water to my room, please. Hurry. I think we will need more wood for the fire."

"Straight away, Mrs Huntington." After a quick curtsey, the maid swivelled on her heel and raced back to the kitchen.

Jemima took a moment on the stairs, mentally preparing herself to return to her husband's side. He looked so fragile and wan that she found it hard to bear. Thoughts of losing him drove up into her mind, like spears poking into prey. He could not be close to death. Not her Edward. While she had worried all night about where he was, this was the first time she had faced his mortality. It gave her a glimpse into his state of mind when he saved her from David Longhurst and why he made the bargain to raise Geneck. The anguish felt like it was pushing out of the pores of her skin. *Oh Edward, please be well.*

With a big lungful of air, she turned to go back up the stairs and face what she did not want to face. As she returned to the room, Heaton stood up straight and rubbed his chin. "That will be all thank you, Seaward. We can manage from here."

"Very well, sir." The valet bent to gather up the soiled clothing. "I shall see to these." Seaward paused by the door and turned to her. "Please let me know when you have news."

Jemima's eyes widened. Seaward did not have much cause to speak to her and at times she felt like she did not exist when the valet was around. Beth said he could be a real stickler and put on airs. Jemima inclined her head. "I will, thank you for your concern."

However, it was the act of Heaton's dismissal of the valet that really caught her attention. He had something to say that could not be said in front of the servants.

When the door shut behind the valet, she turned to Heaton. "What is it?" Her husband looked the same, unmoving, skin like milk. Nothing had changed for good or ill.

Heaton turned to her and then encompassed Fulton in his look. "'Tis a small wound and I do not think that is the cause of his unconsciousness. It is something else."

Fulton shook his head. "Something else?"

Jemima could tell Heaton felt uncomfortable talking about it so that meant it was magical and outside of his medical expertise. "You think it is magical in origin? Like a hex perchance?"

Fulton ran his good hand over his scalp and shook his head. "That is all we need."

Heaton lifted both shoulders and dropped them. "I have cleaned him up. I have tried the traditional means of arousal and he does not respond. It is not simply a head wound. No bone is depressed and there are no other signs of serious injury. If he does not come around soon, you might need 'other' assistance."

Jemima nodded slowly and stepped up to the bed. She studied her husband and her senses were not acute enough to sense any magic on him. He did say that a finely tuned spell could escape notice, particularly if it was crafted to fit a person, sort of like a bespoke glove.

"What do you think, Fulton?"

Fulton shook his head. "If he does not wake up on his own we are in a right pickle."

"Agreed," she said solemnly. She tried pushing magic into him, calling his name through the connection but it was as if she had hit a brick wall. It required more skill than she possessed at this moment in time. If she could not help him with all the magic she had then there was no help for it. She knew who to call.

"Jemima?" Fulton asked after she sighed. She gave a shrug and turned to Heaton.

"Thank you for all you have done. I will see what I can do. I have an idea. I just hope the innkeeper does not have apoplexy when we add another person to our retinue."

Heaton sighed. "You know we had already put off our departure, which is lucky as I was here to treat Huntington's injury. As I can offer you nothing further, I will leave in the morning with Sylvia and her cousin. I think the local doctor can handle this wound if it gives you any further trouble. As for the rest, you are a better person to organise that assistance."

"I see." She reached out a hand and he clasped it. "Thank you so much and I apologise for the chaos."

Heaton smiled. "Chaos? That is such a good word to describe Huntington and his shenanigans. However, I would not begrudge him a little disorder for he has helped me understand the human body more than anyone. Please send me word of how is he doing." He packed up his equipment and when he closed up his bag, he lifted his hand for Fulton to shake. Then he turned to her. "You must come visit us, when you can. You and Huntington are most welcome at any time. I want Sylvia to be happy, but I have my work and it does take up a lot of time and my attention. Perhaps if you visited more she would be content."

"I will do my best. Perhaps Sylvia can come visit us while you are busy."

Heaton sighed and creased his forehead. "I like having her at home and her travelling alone requires planning. Someone must accompany her and I have found that her mother rubs Sylvia the wrong way, so too many days with them spent together can lead to tiresome arguments. Yet, I will talk to her and see if you can organise something." He frowned. "However, it will not be long before she may be too occupied to travel around the country."

Jemima blinked. "Occupied how?"

Heaton flashed her a quick grin and his eyes sparkled. It made him look mischievous and brought back memories of his courtship at Primrose Manor. She caught a glimpse of why Sylvia liked him so well. "I will let my wife tell you."

Fulton stepped forward, face a pale grey. He must be done in. "Fulton, you must rest."

"As I am no use to here, I intend to. But first I must see my wife and son and bring them news of Edward. Please excuse me." He then bowed his head quickly and left the room.

Following Fulton's exit, Heaton moved toward the door and then paused, his face losing the smile and taking on a thoughtful pose.

Jemima had stepped to Edward's bedside and then looked back to the physician, who smiled at her. "Huntington is an unusual man, but an excellently talented one. I value his friendship greatly and wish you both well."

Jemima parted her lips, wondering at this heartfelt comment. Did he think Edward might die? She shook herself. He would not leave if he thought that. "I thank you for the sentiment. I know Edward values you highly. I also appreciate your skill and I am glad we were able to work together."

With a nod, he turned and exited.

After he shut the door behind him, Jemima tried to reach Edward. She called to him, put her hands on him and again tried to use her power, but nothing worked.

Standing back from the bed, she closed her eyes and focussed. "Uncle Ferdy? Uncle Ferdy! We need you. I need you!"

She had no idea if her call would work as she had not tried to call him with power before. Her skill was much improved from when she first garnered Geneck's emerald fire to herself. However, she knew Uncle Ferdy kept an eye on them even when he was not there, so suspected there was some tracking spell that alerted him in certain circumstances. Edward called them probability spells because they used a mathematical formula such as if this happens then do this. Apparently it was a basic spell and as long as one used logic when formulating them they did not go astray. The opportunity to use one herself had not arisen as yet. There was a knock at the door. She started, thinking it was awfully quick of Uncle Ferdy, when the maid came through with a bucket of coals for the fire. These were already alight and giving off warmth. She had forgotten that she ordered them.

"I'm sorry they took so long."

"Thank you. They will warm the room soon enough."

When the maid left, she took off her battle dress and put on a gown, apron and lace cap, then she hopped onto the bed to snuggle her husband. His skin was pale and cold and she tried to rub some warmth into his hands and feet to no avail. He was as still and pale as death, yet breathed. It looked like a hex. She tried to nap, but thoughts of Uncle

Ferdy intruded. How would she explain him? What if he just popped in? He could translocate. She sat up suddenly. Uncle Ferdy could teach her that trick and more. She closed her eyes, put her power behind the call for her uncle, erstwhile magical monk, and sent a stream of words out and aiming them at her Uncle, not uncle. He had been her father's dear friend and she had been used to call him Uncle Ferdy since she was a child. Aunt Prudence would be pleased to see him. The older woman had a soft spot for the old monk. After waiting for an hour, fatigue got the better of her and she fell asleep.

THERE WAS NO CHANGE IN EDWARD COME MORNING AND JEMIMA was beside herself with worry. If he could not wake, he could not eat and though he had a healthy appetite generally, he was lean. She could not imagine him going without food for long before he became skin and bone. Beth knocked on the dressing room door and helped Jemima dress in there for the day. She did not want the maid to see her husband like this. After Beth left, Jemima looked down upon her husband, so pale and still, and fretted.

Uncle Ferdy had not yet answered her call. She had not given up hope, nor had she mentioned her summons to the rest of her party. The Heatons and Miss Horton-Sprigge were at breakfast, their coach packed and waiting for the horses to be brought around.

Reaching down, she cupped his face in her hand. "Dearest? Heaton and Sylvia are leaving now. He has a busy practice to return to and they need to take Miss Horton-Sprigge home. The poor woman is in need of repose. I shall return soon after I have seen them off and perhaps had a spot of breakfast."

Her words flowed over him and did not penetrate. Lifting her hands, her brows knitted in consternation as she studied them. Why did she have this power and insufficient skill to use it? Why was she such a slow learner? Edward and, even Uncle Ferdy, had been teaching her and she was useless. It was taking too long and she felt that she would never learn. As she passed the threshold of the door, she paused, recalling that she had managed to speed up Fulton's healing. "That is something I suppose." That thought put a spring in her step.

Fulton came out of his room, a tune on his lips. "Jemima? Any change?"

"Not as yet, no."

Fulton nodded and pursed his lips. "He will get better. I am sure."

"I agree, I just wish it was soon."

CHAPTER 9

Fulton and Milly had spent their first night together since the attack. Jemima could tell Fulton's mood was much improved and other than letting Milly snuggle up to him, there was no doubt it was a platonic reunion. Aly had slept with Aunt Prudence, who only fetched Milly at feed times. This arrangement had apparently suited all parties. The old aunt revelled in assisting with the baby, not only because she was doing something useful, she doted on the little bundle of arms and legs. Jemima would dote too, given half the chance, but needs must.

She turned to head down the hall. "Jemima! We must talk." Fulton grabbed her wrist and drew her inside.

"I am in a hurry. I wish to say my farewells to the Heatons."

Fulton nodded. "I will not keep you long. I have been thinking," he began, voice edged in a serious tone. "We need to take action. Now I am healed, we must find this Bertrand fellow and force him to tell us what he knows."

"That sounds like a great plan, Fulton. We cannot go without Edward."

Fulton shook his head. "But the delay?"

"There has been no improvement. Not a moan or a groan or a

wiggly toe. He is as still as ...” she trailed off, not wanting to mention the worth 'death' and 'Edward' in the same sentence. One could not tempt fate, particularly when one knew there were forces such as magic, spells and hexes alive in the world. Jemima looked him up and down. “Your complexion has improved and I can see you are in less pain. However, you are by no means healed.”

“I feel so much better after your ministrations.”

“Are you trying to flatter me? Ha! It will not work.” She took his prosthetic hand in hers. “You need to get this working and fast. If we cannot get Edward conscious by the end of tomorrow, we will do it your way. Although I doubt Milly would like it if we both depart on a perilous journey leaving her to mind Edward in my stead. She has her hands full as it is.”

“Ah yes, perhaps we should keep mum about our plan until closer to the time.”

It was apparent that Fulton hated arguing with his wife, almost as much as he hated arguing with her.

Jemima shook her head. “It will not do, Fulton. You must discuss this proposed venture with your wife and what are they do to while we gallivant around the country with no clues as to where our destination will be. How will they contact us in an emergency? Where can they live and be comfortable and safe?”

Fulton swallowed and nodded his head slowly. “You are right.” Twin spots of colours grew on his cheeks. “I am ashamed to say that I did not think clearly about the matter. I will consider your counsel. May I look in on him?”

“Yes, of course. I shall return shortly.”

Jemima frowned as she thought over the conversation. Fulton was right that the trail would go cold if they did not depart soon. That much was true. Her own thoughts had been elsewhere, and she had not envisaged pursuit even though it made perfect sense. It was the best place to start. They had the man's description and the general direction of travel so it was likely they could track him down. Yet the idea of leaving her husband in such a vulnerable state did not sit well and, while Fulton was walking around, he was by no means the powerhouse of might that he was previously. There might be more machines lying in wait.

The sound of horses' hooves on the cobbles and the cry of the ostlers advertised that the Heatons were soon to be on their way.

Her friend waited at the top of the stairs. "Sylvia!"

Sylvia rushed forward, putting out her hands to grasp Jemima's. "We are leaving now. I wanted to say goodbye."

They kissed each other's cheek, while squeezing each other's hands. "Have a safe journey. I hope to see you again soon. Heaton says we can organise something. Me to you or you to us."

Sylvia blushed and Jemima drew back. "What is it? What is wrong?"

Sylvia shook her head and bit her lip. Then she leaned in to whisper. "I am with child."

Jemima's heart thudded and she tried not to gape. Her mind busily tried to muster the correct response. "Con ... congratulations!" This changed everything, Jemima knew. Travel would be out of the question and visiting the Heatons would take on a new aspect. Much like Milly and Fulton, she supposed. "I am excited for you."

Heaton called from by the carriage. "Sylvia!"

Arm in arm they hastened down the stairs. Heaton held the door open and beckoned to Sylvia. "The horses are hitched and we cannot keep them standing. We do not want to miss our train." To prove his concern, he pulled out his watch and studied it. "As it is, we may have to shorten our luncheon so we can board in good time."

With one last embrace, Sylvia ran and took her husband's hand to climb aboard. Jemima followed at a sedate place. Heaton surprised her by leaning in to kiss her cheek. "Keep well, Mrs Huntington and do let me know how Edward goes on. I really hate to leave you like this."

She smiled up at him. "Thank you and we will send word. Look after yourself and Sylvia and my best wishes to Miss Horton-Sprigge." He gave her a swift nod and climbed in after his wife. The doors were shut and the coachman called the horses, got them moving and heading for the gate. Sylvia fluttered her handkerchief out the window. Jemima waved back in response.

Miss Horton-Sprigge sat back against the squabs, looking at nothing. A twinge of sympathy uncurled in Jemima's chest. The woman had had an awful time, one beyond her usual experience. Perhaps, she would learn from it and be less irksome. Jemima rolled her eyes. She doubted it.

As the carriage moved on its way, Jemima tried not to be sad. It was hard to part with one's friends and there had been so much chaos, she did not know how it would all end and when she would see her friend again. Sylvia was to be a mother. Jemima silently wished her friend well and tried not to feel sorrow that she could not join in on the motherhood journey.

Heaton leaned out the window, lifted a hand in farewell, a happy smile on his face. The carriage entered the road and was soon out of sight. Heaton was going to be a father and Sylvia would have a baby to focus on and less time to complain of his neglect. A sigh escaped her, tinged with something like regret. Did she envy them their normal lives and the expectation of children? Yes, she damn well did. They did not have to fight monsters and giant machines or learn how to unhex their spouses.

With a low mood, she made her way to the upstairs parlour to partake of some breakfast. Aunt Prudence was at table when she entered. "Good morning, Aunt. I hope you slept well."

"Good morning. I had a passing night. Aly woke three times to be fed. Otherwise he caused no trouble. Have your friends set out?"

"Yes," Jemima replied taking a seat. She reached for some bacon, which was most likely cold and eyed the scrambled eggs. Perhaps her stomach was not up to cold eggs. She cut into the bacon and nodded when the aunt lifted the tea pot.

"Thank you. I am starving."

"You mean are hungry, dear. You are certainly not starving. That is a state of being you might never experience."

"I stand corrected. I am very hungry. Is that a bread roll peeking out of the napkin?"

"Yes." She passed it over.

Jemima buttered it quickly and cut it in halves.

"Why did you not say that your Uncle Ferdinand was coming to visit? I would have taken greater care with my hair and my toilette this morning."

Jemima dropped a spoon of jam on the tablecloth. "Uncle Ferdy? He is here?" She grabbed a napkin to clean off the offending stain.

"Yes, that is what I said. I bumped into him in the hall and he complimented me on my gown and complexion before he went to see my nephew." She preened as she conveyed this. "I am so pleased I chose this particular gown as it does wonders for my complexion." The gown in question was a deep maroon and did look well on her. With only fine lace at the collar and cuffs, it was remarkably unadorned. Her curls looped nicely around her ears, offset by a lace cap with trailing ribbons.

"That is good news, Aunt. I was hoping he could come. I must have missed him in all the noise of departure. Thank you for telling me."

Jemima thought Uncle Ferdy must have popped in. The innkeeper was wily so she did not know how she was going to explain the new arrival, who was likely not seen arriving in a conventional fashion. Had he walked up plain as day, she would have noticed him. She did some mental calculations. If they consolidated Fulton and Milly, the sick room would accommodate him or there was the room the Heatons had vacated. She frowned as she thought it through. Or he could just pop off again and go home but the questions, the questions. No, he would have to play the part of guest.

Standing up suddenly, she gulped the last of her tea. "Forgive me, I must see Uncle Ferdy and check on Edward."

"Has there been no improvement?" The aunt asked, turning in her chair as Jemima made for the door.

"Not just yet, Aunt."

"Very concerning. Do tell Mr White that I can procure fresh tea for him if he is in need."

Aunt Prudence inclined her head, turned back to the table, and as if she was the queen, lifted the teapot to pour herself another cup of tea.

Bursting into her room and rubbing the crumbs from her lips, she found Uncle Ferdy bent over her husband. "Thank heavens you heard me."

Uncle Ferdy stood up straight and turned to her. "There you are. I was wondering what you were about. Sorry to not come sooner but I was in the middle of something." He peered at her. "Have I interrupted your breakfast?"

She waved him off. "No, but Aunt Prudence is keeping the kettle warm for you."

He lifted his eyebrows. "I see, how thoughtful of her."

Hands clasping each other in turn, she asked, "How is he? Can you help him? Is it a hex?"

Uncle Ferdy met her gaze. He had stripped off the bedcovers, leaving Edward in a night shirt, and sock-adorned feet. "The same. Perhaps and, yes, I believe so. A nasty one."

Jemima went to the other side of the bed, not sure whether to be relieved or not about Uncle Ferdy's answer. At least he was better equipped to help. "He looks so pale. He is breathing, but it is slow and shallow."

A sharp knock on the door interrupted their conversation. "Mrs Huntington? It is Sir Giles, the Magistrate. I need to speak with you urgently."

Alarmed, Jemima stared at Uncle Ferdy. How was she going to explain him to the magistrate on top of the innkeeper. "Go away now," she hissed under her breath.

"It is not that easy to pop in and out," he whispered back. "I need to rest between."

"Mrs Huntington?" The magistrate repeated.

"Coming!" She turned to Uncle Ferdy. "Hide then."

CHAPTER 10

Uncle Ferdy gave a nod and stood by the door. When Jemima was certain he would not be spotted easily, she called out. "Come in."

The magistrate walked in, flanked by his deputies, Mr Jenkins and Mr Cousins. "So it is true. He has been struck down in another dastardly attack."

Jemima faced him calmly, hoping they did not turn around to see a magician behind the door. "Yes, I am afraid so."

"How do you account for it?" The magistrate demanded.

"Sir Giles, I understand my husband went to investigate the remains of the machine we think attacked Mr Fulton and his house. When he did not return, Mr Fulton and I went looking for him and found him like this."

"And what did that physician say about it?" he said, moving closer to Edward's bed.

"A head injury. We should allow him to rest and he would recover soon enough."

The magistrate drilled her with his fierce black eyes. "Until you came into this county we did not have such despicable crimes, Mrs Huntington. What do you say to that?"

She shrugged. "Your meaning is unclear, Sir Giles. Do you mean to accuse me of these crimes?"

Sir Giles blinked and then cleared his throat. "No, of course not. It is just that trouble appears to follow you around."

"Indeed. How did you hear of my husband's situation?"

"The innkeeper keeps me informed. I am put up with my sister at her estate on the other side of the village."

"That explains why you were so close to hand. Perhaps, we can discuss the situation at a later time and not by my unconscious husband."

Sir Giles fingered his white cravat. "Why yes. I still need to obtain Mr Huntington's statement about the attack at Hatfield, and given the situation another one on this latest incident."

The door to the hall had remained opened, successfully hiding Uncle Ferdy, unless he had rallied enough to translocate out of the room. It was imperative that he remain undetected until they could concoct a reasonable excuse for his presence.

She carefully stepped toward the door. "I will make sure he sees to it as a priority when he recovers. Will you be staying in the county long, Sir Giles?"

He took a step to follow her to the door, his deputies falling in behind him. "As long as it takes to find the answers, Mrs Huntington and to apprehend those responsible."

"That is reassuring." They had reached the hallway. Sir Giles stood there as if he wanted to say more. Further along the hallway, the door to the parlour opened and Aunt Prudence called out. "Oh it is you, Sir Giles? I thought perhaps it was ..." Jemima shook her head, hoping the aunt picked up the clue. "Would you like some tea, gentlemen?"

Sir Giles bowed his head. "I will certainly, Mrs Wainwright. My deputies have other duties." He turned to Jemima. "If you will excuse me, ma'am."

He walked down the hall and was welcomed by Aunt Prudence, who smiled, touched her hair and batted her eyelids. Jemima blinked. Was she flirting? Again? Shaking her head, she stepped back and shut the door.

Uncle Ferdy breathed out slowly. "What on earth is going on?" He stepped forward.

"I will fill you in once you fix Edward. You said it was a hex."

Uncle Ferdy nodded slowly and moved back to Edward's bedside. "It is a repressive hex. Whoever cast it is skilled. They have created an invisible magic blanket that weighs him down. I believe he can hear us but cannot respond. If we do not lift it then he will starve to death."

Jemima covered her mouth. "That will not do. Can you help him, Uncle? If it is power you need then you can have some of mine. Or could you teach me? If you show me perhaps I could lift it."

Uncle Ferdy looked up from his examination of Edward. "I am happy to instruct you as I go. Do not be upset if you do not catch on straight away. You need a lot of practice detecting magic, differentiating the layers before you can attempt such."

"Oh, I see ... my power is not much help then."

Uncle Ferdy looked between Edward and herself. "Of course you are a help. If your husband approves, I will agree to instruct you further. However, it takes time to practise and I am not sure time is on your side at the moment."

"So you know what has happened?" she asked, thinking that was useful as explaining it again would be tiresome.

"I read it in the papers, my dear and put two and two together. Now, let me begin."

"I feel so frustrated. So angry. If only I knew how to use magic, I would not have to rely on others and I could have fixed this already."

Uncle Ferdy spluttered. "I do not like the thought of you being angry. There is no need to for that. Anger just clouds your judgement. Now clear your mind." He moved around the bed where Edward lay, rubbing his chin and frowning. "Can you see the hex, by any chance?"

Jemima studied her husband and then what was on top of him. She could not see anything. "I cannot."

Uncle Ferdy ran his hand just above Edward's form. "What about now?"

Jemima folded her arms and pouted. "Not a thing."

Uncle Ferdy then ran his hand along the edges of the space above Edward and Jemima could almost imagine it was there. It was like an invisible blanket. She closed her eyes and reached out a hand to an equivalent spot on the other side of the bed. She felt a tingle, a slight vibration. She slid her fingers along it and could feel the pressure of the hex. When she opened her eyes she could not see it.

Uncle Ferdy titled his head in query. "Well?"

"I cannot see it, although I can feel it. Does that make sense?"

"Perfect sense. It takes time to see clearly with the eyes. Using your senses is always best in any case as our eyes can be deceived. You sensed the hex, which is good. Now can you sense the layers? Try with your fingers."

Her fingers rested on the hex. It felt like greasy air at first. "I feel two layers."

"Good, good." She glanced up at him and could not tell if he was pleased with her success as his expression was solemn. He met her gaze. "Ready? When I say pull, I want you to tug the hex away."

Jemima stood up straight, eyes wide and almost losing contact with the hex. "Just like that?"

"I need to make an incantation first to loosen its hold. I will then get you to tug it away on my mark."

"What do I do with the hex once I have done that?"

"Oh, good question." Ferdy nodded and looked about the room. "Ah!" He pointed. "Throw it in the fire."

That seemed a bit simple. Jemima pursed her lips as she studied the potential passage of the hex from Edward to the fire. She had no idea if it would be heavy or light. With her strength she could take out the chimney if she threw too hard. "What will it feel like? A sheet, a blanket or a bit of metal?"

His eyebrows lifted from studying the hex. He put his fingers along the edge and ran them along as if considering. "I had not thought about it in those terms." He lifted his gaze to her, as if remembering her power. "I think perhaps for you it will be like a woollen blanket. One that is living and might fight you." She nodded, preparing herself as Uncle Ferdy made several intricate gestures and spoke words like a prayer. Jemima could not quite grasp them. "Pull!"

Jemima grabbed the edges of the hex, it had the heft of a bed sheet more than a blanket, and tugged with all her might. It was not how she imagined it. Slowly, ever so slowly the fabric of the hex released. Heavy in her hands, it draped like a blanket until it started to move, like it was going to wrap around her. It tried to go back to Edward then shifted direction to cover her.

"Toss it now," Ferdy instructed. "Quickly!"

With great dexterity, she aimed the hex at the fire place. The chimney made a thump sound and the coals hesitated for the briefest of moments before leaping up, sending huge flames up and a waft of dark smoke into the room.

Jemima coughed and waved a hand. Uncle Ferdy went to the window, flung it up and said another incantation to which the smoke condensed, reshaped into a triangle shape and arrowed out the window, leaving the room with just a hint of smoke in the air. Like a simpleton, she gaped. That had been impressive and not for one minute did she feel threatened. Uncle Ferdy was full of surprises.

"Shut your mouth, Jemima before a bug flies in it. I am a magician and a magician always seeks to expand their skills. That, perhaps, was a bit showy, but necessary I assure you." Jemima's mouth clicked shut. "Let us see to your husband."

Dropping her gaze to Edward, she held her breath until she saw his chest rise and fall. It did so again, a bigger breath. His eyelids fluttered.

"Edward!"

Edward's eyes shot open and he sat up straight like he had been folded in half. "Damnation!"

"Edward?" Jemima said, not certain she should lay her hands on him at this moment. He was confused and a confused magician, no matter how gentlemanly, might do some unwanted magic. Her own magic seemed to be flowing under her skin as if seeking a way out. Her fingers tingled and her toes and the tip of her nose as well.

"Calm yourselves, both of you." Uncle Ferdy put a hand on Jemima's forearm and her attention centred on him. She could feel his magic, like a pulse from his hand. His eyes widened as if he felt it too. He flashed a smile and then looked to Edward. "You are safe, now. The danger has passed. Breathe deeply. Both of you."

Jemima listened to Uncle Ferdy and so did Edward as she slowed her breathing and the magic under her skin dissipated. The wonder of her assisting in dealing with the hex filled her up. She could do this. One day, she could be a magician too. She had magic and she could feel it.

Confused, her husband shook his head once, sharply, and looked around the room. "Jemima? What am I ... Mr White?"

Uncle Ferdy nodded and lifted his lips in a smile.

His gaze returned to her. "Jemima! Thank god." He sat up and winced.

Given the commotion, it was not a surprise that Fulton chose that moment to put his head through the door. "Everything all right in here?" Seeing Edward awake, his eyes widened and then he stepped carefully inside and shut the door with a snap. "Thank the heavens for small mercies." He approached, gaze assessing the room to then focus only on Edward. "I am glad you are back. Does your head hurt?"

"My head?" Edward reached up to the back of his head and felt the bandage. "I must have hit it when he ... he hexed me."

There had been someone there besides the mechanical hound.

"Did you see who it was?" Fulton asked, leaning forward in anticipation. "Did you recognise him?"

Jemima and Uncle Ferdy drew closer to hear his answer.

"No, I only felt the vibration of him just before he hexed me. I got the impression he was tall and thin." He lifted his blue eyes to Jemima, and cocked a sideways grin. "Taller than me, thinner than me. To be clearer."

Jemima grimaced and was unable to hide her disappointment. "No cloak? No distinguishing clothing? Beard?"

Edward bit his lip and shook his head before wincing. "No, nothing but a fleeting glimpse and now a terrible headache." He rubbed the back of his head.

"Pity," Ferdy commented. "I can think of at least three of the brotherhood who are tall and skinny and skilled at hexes."

"So we have no clue whether this person is from the brotherhood? What about Bertrand?" She filled Ferdy in on the fake heir.

"A shortish, ineffectual fellow, with a balding head and a mean demeanour." Uncle Ferdy rubbed his chin, lifted his lips sideways in a grin. "I am afraid we have about ten of them in the brotherhood just off the top of my head. Bertrand could be a false name too."

Edward moved his legs to the side of the bed, ripped the bandage off his head and rubbed the spot. "I sensed something about that fake heir. It did not occur to me at the time that he had magic. He must have been disguising it. A neat trick to be sure."

Uncle Ferdy nodded. "Indeed. Difficult to accomplish as well. That narrows it down to about five fellows. When you find him, give me a call and I might be able to track down his accomplice. Many of my brothers work together in groups. Find one and identify the rest."

Fulton gave them all a hard look. "Well?" he asked.

"Well what?" Jemima answered.

"Do you not agree? It is imperative now that we hasten away after that fake heir of mine. Now." Fulton said.

"No, not right now," Jemima replied hotly. "We have things to organise first."

Uncle Ferdy tsked. "We have only just revived the poor fellow," he said, gesturing at Edward, who was lacking complexion and wearing a nightgown. "Give him at least five minutes to rest."

"Rest?" Fulton said. "We have been waiting for him to wake up for over a day. Surely he is sick of lying around."

Rounding on Fulton, Jemima put her hands on her hips. "Listen, Fulton, I have not had a chance to even say hello, yet." With a harrumph, she turned to Edward. "Hello." She leaned in and kissed the top of his head.

Edward smiled at her, a twinkle in his eyes. "Hello yourself." He glanced around the room. "Heaton?" he asked, eyebrows scrunched in puzzlement.

"Gone," Jemima supplied. "Once he realised your injury was magical in nature, he returned home. He passed on his best wishes for your recovery and looks forward to seeing you again." Edward's eyebrows inched higher. "They have taken the poor Miss Horton-Sprigge home. And Heaton has a busy practice. Did you not hear me tell you?"

Edward shook his head. "I do not remember much. Poor Miss Horton-Sprigge?"

Fulton slipped his response in before Jemima could open her mouth. "You recall, the rascal Bertrand Fulton Esquire abandoned her on the side of the road. We are certain he is in league with whoever hexed you."

Edward put his feet on the floor and stood to face them. "I see. It is coming back to me now. He was never your heir, Fulton. I did not believe that for a minute. We must make plans. However, I am terribly hungry."

"You are not dressed," Jemima reminded him. "I will ring for Seaward and he can help you while I organise some food."

"Ah! Quite right," he agreed, rubbing a hand through his curls and wincing when he connected with the sore spot at the back. Jemima rang for the maid. Martha arrived and said she would fetch the valet right away as he was currently in the kitchen cleaning his master's boots.

"Let us head to the parlour as there might be some breakfast and we can order whatever you wish," Jemima said. "Is that agreeable to you?"

"Of course, I do not wish an audience while I dress."

"The magistrate is in there," Fulton advised. "Perhaps a tray?"

Jemima waved a hand. "The magistrate wants Edward's statement so best do that now while he eats. You never know but the magistrate might be useful."

Fulton coughed into his hand. "What?" Jemima said, distracted by Edward, who poured water in the wash bowl and threw some on his face. He peered in the small mirror attached to the wall and screwed up his face. She met Fulton's gaze, lifting her eyebrow in question.

"I fear Aunt Prudence has taken a liking to Sir Giles."

"Oh," Jemima said, flicking a glance at Uncle Ferdy, whom she thought was a favourite of the aunt. "That should prove entertaining. After a rocky few days I am due some fun."

Uncle Ferdy snorted. "Really, Jemima, your taste in amusements needs to expand, to the theatre or a recital."

Jemima sucked in a breath. She did not mean for Uncle Ferdy to overhear her conversation. Heat rose up into her cheeks and she sighed. Fulton opened the door and held it for her. Gathering her skirts, she replied before leaving the room. "I only go to the theatre when I am not monster hunting. Now if you please, let us see to food."

Lifting his nose, Uncle Ferdy sniffed as the aroma of bacon cooking was in the air. "I see, well you did say we could eat so let us at it. I am suddenly ravenous."

Once last glance at Edward saw him gazing into the mirror and running his fingers through his curls, organising them into something resembling a Brutus. A knock at the dressing room door heralded the arrival of the valet. Edward flashed her a smile. "I will not be long. Please order me a large, hot breakfast and plenty of toast."

"Yes, indeed," Jemima replied, not able to wipe the grin off her face. Edward was safe, he was awake and appeared unharmed by the hex. She felt extraordinarily lucky.

"Wait." Edward hesitated joining his valet. He came forward, some drops of water flecking his night gown.

Jemima stopped and turned, Uncle Ferdy flanking her. "Yes?"

"We must think carefully, as we cannot in all good conscience take Aunt Prudence, Milly and the baby with us."

Jemima covered her open mouth with a hand. "Indeed, it would complicate our journey and possibly place them in danger."

She sent a questioning gaze at Uncle Ferdy. "I can stay here and look after them," he offered, a smile playing around his mouth. She thought he enjoyed being patronised by Aunt Prudence but was not sure if the pleasure was real or feigned as she did not know Uncle Ferdy or Mr Ferdinand White, Brother of the Societas Magical, that intimately at all. Their intimacy was a fragile lace of childhood association and the experience of working together to destroy Geneck. He had proved brave and loyal but whether he was married or not was a fact she had not gleaned. He could be an old bachelor, living in an old castle with one faithful servant or have a cosy home with a wife and a nest of children. Her guess was the former, though she had never sought such information. The conversation never came up. However, if his attentions to Aunt Prudence continued, or better put, if he continued to receive Aunt Prudence's attentions, then she must have that conversation. As irritating as the old aunt was, she would not stand by and let her heart be broken, her reputation ruined or even be dealt a heavy dose of disappointed hopes.

Both Fulton and Edward gaped at him. "We could use you with us," Fulton said, cheeks turning red, a sure sign he was about to start ranting.

However, Uncle Ferdy was not to be denied. "Get Jemima here to call me if you are in need and I will pop right where you are." He opened his hands out. "It worked this time as I am here, am I not?"

Fulton and Edward turned their astounded gazes on her. Jemima smiled and shrugged. Had they not realised it was she who had summoned magical help? Honestly, those two could be dim at times. Well, she could not blame Edward as he had been unconscious. That she did not know if it would work, she would not own. That the power within her had been put to good use these last few days had put her in a good mood. The destruction of Hatfield put a dampener on that good mood though. The sooner they could deal with the continuing threat of the evil magician who stole Fulton's arm, the better. Maybe then they could settle and have some semblance of a normal life, a quasi-normal life perhaps: she was a monster slayer after all.

"If you will excuse me, I will join the ladies in the parlour." Uncle Ferdy bowed and left her there with Fulton. He must be hungry indeed or eager to meet his competition.

Edward shook his head and backed towards the dressing room. "Will you wait for me to join you or are you brave enough to break the news to Milly and Aunt Prudence yourself?"

Fulton scowled and nailed Jemima with a hard glare, daring that she add insult to injury, she guessed. In a mild voice, a counter to his raised colour, Fulton answered. "We will order your breakfast and see if we can raise the prospect during the meal. There is the question of the magistrate."

"Oh yes, Sir Giles," Jemima replied. "I do not think he can stop us leaving, and chasing after this fake heir is a reasonable proposition. It would only be awkward if he wanted to join us."

Fulton shook his head slightly and then shrugged. They left Edward to his valet and went into the parlour.

The parlour appeared full to brimming with Milly, Aunt Prudence, Sir Giles at the dining table and a maid bringing in dishes.

"Oh Jemima, good morning. How good it is to see you again, Mr White," Aunt Prudence was all smiles as Uncle Ferdy bowed over her hand. Uncle Ferdy stepped away and Aunt Prudence's smile widened and Jemima did not think she had seen so many teeth in her smile before. "May I introduce Sir Giles to you Mr White? He is the magistrate who is investigating the terrible events at Hatfield and telling us about his investigation over breakfast."

Uncle Ferdy shook hands with the magistrate and then addressed Aunt Prudence. "I have heard of the tragic events and came as soon as I heard the news. May I say how pleased I am to see you in good health." He paused and his gaze encompassed Milly, who was cuddling her baby. "You are all in good health."

Aunt Prudence gushed and then seeing her in-law. "I am afraid that Fulton is still recovering himself. He was sorely injured but somehow has miraculous healing abilities for he is here to share in our repast."

Uncle Ferdy went to bow over Milly's hand. "That must be a comfort to you, Mrs Fulton, to know your husband is on the mend."

Milly only had eyes for Fulton and managed a polite. "It is a great comfort."

When Martha appeared Jemima requested a large hot meal for Edward as she could see that food was already brought up.

Aunt Prudence offered the gentlemen tea and both of her admirers pulled out a chair and sat either side of her. Perhaps Aunt Prudence would not mind being left behind if she was satisfactorily entertained. Contemplating this happy scenario gave Jemima comfort. Milly would be the more difficult of the two to reconcile to a separation from Fulton.

Taking a seat, Jemima poured herself a cup. She was beginning to feel like she was full of tea and if she moved too quickly it would swish around inside her. The scent of bacon was enticing but she had to wait until all the dishes had been set out on the sideboard.

Martha stood by the door. "Breakfast is served, Mrs Wainwright."

Jemima did not decline the invitation to eat before the gentlemen and filled her plate with all kinds of good things. They were all served and eating when Edward joined them. Martha had just brought up a plate, already stacked high, and to this he added what he liked from the sideboard and found a seat at table. "Excuse me, terribly famished." As no one gainsaid him, he focused on the food. Inspecting the sideboard herself, Jemima took another rasher of bacon and some scrambled egg, rationalising that she did not know if her next meal would be warm or as good.

When everyone except Edward had finished eating, the magistrate stood, and Jemima could tell he wanted to interrogate Edward at that moment. Not even lifting his head, Edward drew out a sheet of paper from inside his jacket pocket and waved it. "My, um, statement." He shoved a large chunk of pork sausage into his mouth. The magistrate took it from his hand and walked to the window to read it. Jemima's gaze switched from watching Edward demolish the food to the expression on the magistrate's face as he read the statement. Would it be enough?

The magistrate came back to the table and declined more tea. "Your statement is thorough, Mr Huntington. I thank you and I cannot think of more questions at this stage. Will you be staying in the area?"

"About that," Fulton said. "We wish to depart as soon as maybe to pursue this fake heir, who we think is involved in the destruction of Hatfield. You aunt, and you Milly with Aly can stay here or relocate to Willow Park as Huntington has offered his home for the duration. It will be some time before we can reside at Hatfield again."

The magistrate's eyebrows rose.

"No, you cannot," blurted Milly, her cheeks colouring. "You are barely out of your sick bed."

"I am well, Milly." He went to where she sat on the settee and took her hand. "We can discuss this in private in a few minutes."

Aunt Prudence looked sombre at the announcement of their departure. " I did not expect you all to dash off at the drop of a hat but I should not be surprised by your shenanigans. I suppose this is one of Jemima's harebrained schemes."

Jemima smiled and tried not to blush.

"Indeed it was Fulton's idea and we agree," Edward replied, after a big swallow.

Fulton started and Jemima frowned as she did not mind being blamed and she could not rightly collect who had thought it was a good idea. Edward swallowed another mouthful. "It is something we have decided must be done." He waved his fork vigorously.

With a nod, Fulton continued. "It only remains for you to decide whether to wait here for our return or decide to take up Edward's offer of Willow Park."

Milly placed Aly in the small crib. Her eyes flashed as she cast her gaze around the room. She did not cry, nor did she look at Fulton. It was worse than tears as it seemed to be a silent anger that rippled under her friend's skin. If one was to prick her, all the rage would spill forth. Jemima could understand the sentiment as Fulton had been at death's door and now he was to leave again, barely healed. It was folly, indeed, but she was not going to gainsay Fulton, as he was far too useful to leave behind.

The magistrate stepped forward and cleared his throat. "I have something to add to your deliberations. Firstly, as I will be staying in the district until my investigation is complete, I will also be available to keep an eye on the ladies and the young gent for a few weeks at least. Secondly, I have found the site where the machine that destroyed your house, Mr Fulton, was winched onto the railway tracks. It was near Thrupp. From there it had followed a direct line to arrive at your property."

"Could that be near where this person lives?" Edward asked. "In Oxfordshire, not far from here?"

Fulton leaned forward. "There are neighbouring counties, Buckinghamshire, Warwickshire, Northamptonshire and Gloucestershire and that is not even considering those to the south like Berkshire." He tapped his fingers and nodded to himself. "If they are not from Oxfordshire my guess is Gloucestershire."

"It is possible. There was a witness, a local farmer who spotted the large cart that had its large load covered. He deduced that the load was heavy as it was drawn by four oxen. It is possible to estimate how far those oxen travelled as they are slow and steady creatures but it also depends on whether they were changed over, and when they started. However, loosely within a range of twenty miles."

"Description?" Fulton prompted.

Sir Giles shook his head. "The driver had a hat and a smock on, nothing to be seen. The second cart had two men driving it."

"Two carts?" Jemima asked. "But does that mean they assembled it on site?"

Sir Giles met her gaze and lifted his eyebrows. "That could be an explanation." He cleared his throat and looked at them in turn to ensure he had their attention. "These men were seen. One was a tall, thin man with a shock of dark hair. The other was a shorter, balder man."

Fulton nodded. "The shorter man could be Bertrand." He looked to Uncle Ferdy and lifted a questioning eyebrow.

Uncle Ferdy frowned and shrugged. Jemima thought he was troubled, that he had suspicions.

"Will you not come with us, Uncle Ferdy, now that the magistrate has offered to keep an eye on our kin?" Jemima asked.

Uncle Ferdy leaned back in his chair and lifted his lips in a not quite smile. "I am afraid that I prefer to stay and keep an eye on the family."

Jemima met his gaze. There was a serious glint in his eyes and this made Jemima think Uncle Ferdy feared further magical attacks so he must stay. She dared not voice this thought to Fulton. Edward nodded in an absent way as if only half listening.

Uncle Ferdy lifted his hand to attract attention. "While I may not accompany you, I expect my assistant, Frank, will be able to join you and can go in my stead. He is a trustworthy fellow and can assist you while I stay here in this pleasant company." He smiled at Aunt Prudence, winked at Jemima and cast a pleasant gaze in Milly's direction.

Aunt Prudence tittered and batted her eyelids. "You are too kind, Mr White. To have two distinguished gentleman keep danger at bay and to dine with us is a treat indeed. Do you not think, Milly?"

Milly stood up, bowed her head and reached for the baby. "I am glad you find this situation agreeable, aunt." She headed to the door, baby nestled to her chest and aimed a significant look at Fulton. "I must put Aly to bed now."

Fulton appeared to take the hint. He stood, adjusted his trouser legs and cast them a look. "You must excuse me. I shall return soon and we can discuss our plans further."

CHAPTER 11

Fulton shook to his bones and closed his eyes before joining his wife in their room. He knew what was coming, knew the complaints and his answers. Yet it wounded him to hurt Milly, to cause her pain, to be far from her and their son. But what was a man to do in a situation like this? He had to protect them and himself, and the only way he considered he could do that was go hunt the threat down and neutralise it.

He cracked open the door quietly, not wishing to disturb Aly. Straight away he saw that his son was awake, arms and legs waving as he cooed to his mother. "I dislike this, Ambrose." And then to his consternation, she covered her face with her hands and burst into tears. His heart lurched and his stomach plummeted. How he hated to cause her pain. On the bed, he drew her into his embrace. "I am sorry, so sorry." He rubbed her back and she turned and threw herself upon his neck, where the sobs became louder. Aly paused, arms and legs suspended in the air. He met his son's surprised gaze and waited for him to wail too. The child smiled at him and tears welled into his eyes. "You know I must go. You know if we are to be safe this threat must be removed."

She nodded as she sobbed. "I wish you had confided in me instead of Jemima."

Fulton's head jerked up. "Jemima?" Confused, he wondered what this was really about.

"Yes, she knew before me."

Fulton had the urge to scratch his head. "I would like to think it was her idea and she confided in me."

"But Edward said it was your idea."

Fulton chuckled. "If Edward knows whose idea it was then he is a better man than me for he has been unconscious for a day."

Milly drew back, wiped her eyes with the back of her hands until he passed her a clean handkerchief. She blew her nose. "I feel so silly and it sounds as if I was jealous." She looked him straight in the eye. "I was not jealous in the way it seems. I know Jemima cares for you and trusts you. I just wish I had been involved in the conversation. Even though I know the outcome would not be any different."

Fulton sighed. "You would have been but it happened so fast. Jemima summoned Mr White and then they woke Edward up and then the plan happened before I knew it. I confess. I had been keen to go after this Bertrand fellow and had voiced that desire more than once. We came straight away to tell you." He saw the disappointment in her face. "I promise I will endeavour to make sure decisions do not happen when you are not there. I realise I should have asked for the discussion to include you. It would have been but a moment to fetch you."

Milly smiled through her tears. "You really are the most amazing man I have ever met or imagined could be. Thank you for understanding."

Fulton nodded, a grin on his face. "You are the most amazing woman I have ever met."

"Now, I have one other objection."

"Just one?" He grinned.

Milly sniffed. "Yes, what if this person takes your new arm? You have barely started to use it."

"Ah, well, Huntington devised a detachable arm. It can come off without being ripped from my flesh. I cannot tell you in detail but somehow he uses magnetism to hold it in place and the bits of me that tell my arm what to do separate also." He tilted his head and gave a wry grin. "It is why I am having difficulty using it just now. I have to train my arm to respond to the commands of my brain."

He reached out his gloved hand to pick up the handkerchief. It took a few tries for his pincer grip to snag the fabric.

"That is good news all around, Ambrose. You will not be so hurt if you lose your arm." Taking the white cotton from his fingers, she nodded and wiped her nose again. "That has eased my mind somewhat. I cannot say that I do not want you to go, I do not, but I am much reconciled to you going and the risks."

Fulton gaped at her in wonder and with much love. "Coming back to you, Milly, is all the incentive I need to stay alive and well. Keeping you and our son safe is my main motivation."

Milly lifted her lips in a smile. "And ridding the world of evil comes a close second."

"Indeed it does."

"And must you leave straight away? It is late in the day. We have just had breakfast but it is after noon already. I would love to have you hold me for a night before you leave."

He drew her to him and kissed the top of her head. "You talk perfect sense. It is late in the day and I want to hold you in my arms all night long. I will talk to the others."

It did not take him long to track down Edward, who was sleeping off his large meal. "It is perhaps, a twelve-hour difference. I will let Jemima know," Edward replied after hearing Fulton's plans.

Mr White was ensconced in Fulton's old sick room. He put down the book he was reading when Edward entered.

"Good. It gives Frank some more time to prepare."

"Who is this Frank anyway?" Fulton asked as he was leaving, hand on the side of the door as it stood ajar.

"My apprentice, I suppose you could call him. I am training him up. His name is Francis Octavo, but I just call him Frank. He is a bit young and wet behind the ears but he is a good far caller."

"Far caller?" Fulton frowned, not having heard the term before.

"He can call me over long distances, much more reliable than

Jemima. I had been listening out for her summons. I tend to keep an eye on her. Whereas Frank can reach right into my brain and snag my attention."

Fulton was pleased with this explanation and grinned because Jemima was not as clever as she thought she was.

JEMIMA PACED UP AND DOWN, SAT DOWN AND STOOD UP AGAIN. Despite stating their intention to leave immediately, they did not venture on their travels until the next day. Jemima was not completely happy with the decision but her husband laid out the reasons. He needed to recuperate his strength and Fulton had agreed with Milly to stay another night, given the lateness of the hour. The time of day excuse was thin. It was midsummer and it remained light until late. However, she understood Fulton's desire to appease his wife. Milly had been through a lot.

Putting her hands around Bertrand Fulton Esquire's neck would have to be delayed. It had been her intention to argue the point, detail the reasons they should leave immediately, when Aunt Prudence weighed in, when the discussion resumed in the parlour. Before she had opened her mouth, Aunt Prudence ordered a good hearty dinner. Edward's eyes widened at the thought of roast beef, gravy and all the trimmings. "You can leave early in the morning after a light breakfast. And I shall request the cook to prepare a good hearty hamper to sustain you on the road." She clapped her hands together. "It is all in train."

"Thank you, Aunt," Jemima had said, biting back on her annoyance. "Perhaps request a pudding as well."

To save the innkeeper's nerves, Jemima had prevailed upon Uncle Ferdy to sneak out and then knock at the inn's door so that his presence could be explained, rationally. The old magician had the wherewithal to invent a story about his horse being stolen by thieves and complained of sore feet. Once the innkeeper ascertained he was one of their party, he ordered a mustard footbath and Mr White sat on the settee, wrapped in a shawl, sipping tea with his feet in the small basin. Jemima rolled her eyes. He had only walked around the corner. "Appearances, Jemima. You insisted on it." Mr White picked up a newspaper that had been placed on the side table and buried his face in it.

Bertrand Fulton Esquire had more than two day's head start. "We will never catch him," Jemima complained.

"I think we might," Uncle Ferdy said. "He will note the lack of pursuit and take false comfort. And then there is the chance that he could have disguised himself, you know." He shook out the paper.

Jemima grimaced and went to her room to get ready for dinner. When she entered the room, Edward was stretched on the bed, fast asleep. She checked her watch. Plenty of time to dress for dinner. "Could you help me get undressed, my love."

Edward's eyes snapped open and he sat up. "Get undressed?"

"Yes," she said with a smile. "I am glad you have recovered yourself." She turned her back and Edward scooted over to stand behind her. He helped her take off her top and stood back as she stepped out of her skirts.

He leaned down and kissed her shoulder. "How long do we have before dinner?"

"Enough time," she said and turned in his arms. His lips came down and met hers, light at first until a hunger awoke in him and her. The inn was quiet as they enjoyed each other and by the time they were done and getting dressed, Jemima was no longer annoyed at their delayed departure. Her stomach rumbled. She put her hand on her middle. "Oh dear. I have worked up an appetite."

Edward kissed her forehead and then her mouth, a slightly hungry kiss after what they had shared. "I think Seaward is waiting for me. I hazard a guess that Beth is right outside our door."

A knock at the door followed this statement. "Indeed, you are a clever man."

He slipped into the dressing room and Jemima called out. "Yes?"

"It is time to dress, Mrs Huntington."

"Come in."

Beth came in. "Oh you started without me."

"Not really. I undressed to take a nap. Please help me choose what to wear and then we will need to pack some things because I am leaving in the morning."

"I heard that, Mrs Huntington. I have a list all sorted and your trunk shall be packed right away."

As she dressed, Jemima thought through what items were necessary and, what could be left behind. Bess crossed things off the list and added things and then crossed some more items out. "At this rate you will only need your large carpet bag. Two dresses and one nightgown?"

"Oh, my leather corset set." The maid did not raise an eyebrow as she was used to her mistress's wayward ways. "Right then. A band box too, I think."

When she entered the parlour where they were to eat their meal, conversation was in full swing. "I say we wait here for Ambrose to return. If we go to Willow Park we will be in Sussex and too far away."

Aunt Prudence nodded sagely. "Very well thought out. I have no complaints. The innkeeper has been attentive and the bed is only marginally lumpy. I can suffer through my bad back if that is what is required."

"Perhaps you can change rooms, now that the Heatons have left."

Aunt Prudence inclined her head, a large feather bobbing about with her movement. A dark blue dress, with ivory lace frills adorned the neck and the wide skirts of her gown. Some of their clothing had been retrieved from Hatfield, thus expanding the aunt's wardrobe choices.

"Jemima, that green silk certainly becomes you, dear," Aunt Prudence said. "Will you take some wine?"

"I will, thank you. You look nice Aunt." She turned to Milly who was wearing a pale blue gown and her cheeks glowed pink. She suspected Milly of indulging with her husband as she had done herself. "That colour looks lovely on you, Milly."

Fulton walked in like he was on a mission. He was dressed finely, crisp white cravat at his neck, blue coat and cream trousers. His amber coloured eyes were alight with a gleam. Jemima smiled and inclined her head to acknowledge him. He was well on the way to recovery.

Edward came in and Jemima sighed at the sight of him. His coat was dark green and hugged him to show off his physique. He came up to her and kissed her cheek. "You look beautiful in that gown, my love."

Jemima smiled back. "You look pretty good yourself."

Lastly, Sir Giles and Uncle Ferdy joined them. Uncle Ferdy was dressed in a weird coat that resembled a carpet, a red silk cravat at his neck and white shirt with frills at the end of his sleeves. He looked like a Nabob. He wore what appeared to be dark velvet trousers and red slippers embroidered with gold. They had an oriental feel. Jemima frowned at the sight of Sir Giles who was dressed in a black coat, black trousers, with a white shirt and a black cravat. It was a very stark outfit but one befitting a magistrate she supposed. But who had invited the magistrate?

"I am so glad you accepted my invitation, Sir Giles," Aunt Prudence cooed, as the magistrate bowed and kissed her knuckles.

That answered that question. They took their seats after the gentlemen had greeted one another.

"It has been decided that we will await our gentlemen here. You, too, Jemima. We will wait for you as well. Milly has a preference to be close to home."

"I do, thank you Aunt," Milly said.

Fulton nodded decisively. "I will speak to Mr Copperwraith after dinner and ensure there are adequate funds to disperse our current tariff and the future one."

Sir Giles stood and cleared his throat. "If I may venture a better solution to your housing needs ..."

Fulton blinked. "Why yes, what do you suggest?"

"My cousin, Mrs Brinkwood, has a house to let in the village. Not up to the standards of Hatfield to be sure, but more efficacious for a longer-term stay. Your servants could be accommodated in the attics, instead of them sitting idle here at the inn. Also, it is an easy distance to supervise the reconstruction of Hatfield, if that is what you wish to do."

Aunt Prudence adjusted her cap. "What an excellent idea. What do you think Milly? Fulton?"

Fulton stood up and shook Sir Giles's hand. "That is an excellent solution, sir. I wonder why I did not think of it."

"Under the circumstances one would not expect that it had occurred to you."

"Milly?" Fulton asked.

"It is an excellent notion. We shall go see the property tomorrow and if all is well settle the terms and move in."

"I shall write to my agent directly so he can assist you. If you do not like it then you can stay here, unless Sir Giles has other properties in mind."

Sir Giles blushed. "Indeed I do not. The idea only just came to me."

"Very good," Aunt Prudence said and then grew quiet as the servants brought the platters with the meal. The aroma nearly made Jemima keel over. She was hungry and the amount of food could have supplied a regiment. A large joint of beef, crusted on the outside, bright red on the inside, partially sliced into thin pieces. A platter of roast vegetables piled like a pyramid, Yorkshire pudding, little jars of mustard and horseradish, and a huge jug of gravy. Next came Frenched beans, minted peas and what appeared to be creamed spinach.

"Thank you," Aunt Prudence said to Martha when all the food was arrayed in the centre of the table, which had been extended to accommodate the diners and the meal. "Please send our compliments to the cook."

Martha curtseyed. "I shall return with the pudding, anon, Mrs Wainwright."

Sir Giles coughed as their hands darted to the dishes. "May we, perhaps, say grace?"

Aunt Prudence lit an enormous smile. "You honour us with such observance. Would you be so kind as to lead the prayer?"

Jemima bit her lip, thinking do not ask him! And she was right to be concerned, for Sir Giles gave a rambling, five-minute prayer before even getting to the part where they were thankful for the food. "Amen," Jemima chimed in at the end.

For the next few minutes, the party kept themselves busy piling up their plates and asking for things to be passed along the table.

Aunt Prudence found time to ask Uncle Ferdy about his dress for the evening.

"This old thing? I had to cobble together something for dinner." He waved at his coat. "These are mostly garnered from my travels. I am a tad eccentric and I hope my dress sense has not given offence."

Aunt Prudence chuckled. "You could not ever give offence, Mr White."

Jemima blinked. Was not Aunt Prudence taking offence every other minute? Or was that just in reaction to Jemima's presence?

With a nod of acknowledgement, Uncle Ferdy reached for the gravy and poured a copious amount onto his thinly sliced roast beef. It was a stark brown against the dark pink of the rare meat. After replacing the gravy boat, he reached for the mustard and layered it on the meat.

Edward inclined his head. "A nice trick if that is so." Edward cut into a roast potato with gusto. "You should teach me that one, old man."

Jemima kicked him under the table as Uncle Ferdy looked at him blankly. He did not understand that the nice trick was not giving offence to Aunt Prudence.

With his plate piled so high, Jemima could barely see Fulton over the food. He was definitely out to replenish his lost strength. "Can I pass you anything, Ambrose?" Milly asked, in a voice that held no angst. Jemima admired her fortitude.

"The gravy if you please."

Milly reached for the gravy boat and peered inside. She smiled and then turned to a server who stood by the door. "I fear we need more gravy." She cast her eye around the table. "And bread and cheese, too, I think."

"Very well ma'am." The server, a thin youth with a bad case of pimples, bowed his head and left the room. Fulton continued to eat around the edges of his plate, cutting green beans with vigour. About five minutes later, the new gravy boat arrived and with a sigh of satisfaction, Fulton poured it over the pile of meat on his plate.

Jemima was uneasy and while she was hungry, her appetite was weak. Her plate was sparsely arrayed with vegetables and one thin slice of beef. This she cut into tiny pieces and ate. By the time she had finished her small portion, Fulton was asking for seconds.

Edward ate well so she had no cause to worry that the hex had any lasting affect or that the blow to his head made him dizzy. Other than sleeping off the huge lunch, he had no repercussions and appeared ravenous for his dinner too.

Manners meant she needed to sit a little longer at table and listen to Aunt Prudence chat to Uncle Ferdy when all she wanted to do was see that her packing was complete.

"To celebrate the return to health of my nephew, I have arranged for us to have a syllabub for dessert."

Fulton smiled. "Indeed, an excellent choice."

"If I may be excused, aunt. I must pack for our journey."

"Nonsense, Jemima. You must eat more as your maid can fret about your packing. You need not bother yourself. Who knows when you will get such a fine meal again. If ever!"

Jemima blinked. "Ever?"

Aunt Prudence waved her hand. "You know what I mean. Please do justice to the meal."

Jemima ground her teeth and took another slice of beef, more vegetables and side dishes and a few spoons of gravy. If it was going to be her last good meal she should enjoy it. When she had eaten the additional food urged on her by the aunt, she felt queasy and unsociable. Arising from her chair, she announced, "I must retire now."

"Very well, if a syllabub cannot tempt you, I do not know what would."

Jemima thanked the aunt, said goodnight to their guests and as she left the table, she whispered in Edward's ear. "Bring me some syllabub, please."

He smiled and nodded.

Jemima left the room and entered her own where Beth was busy sorting through her belongings. "Really Mrs Huntington, I can manage," Beth said.

"I know but I think I have a headache." She was being truthful about that as the headache arrived to keep the mild feelings of nausea company. Jemima was unused to feeling unwell and had no patience with herself. It must be the aunt and her flirting and nerves about the journey and, possibly, a reaction to all that had happened that day. She had removed a hex and had taken her first real step into using magic. She had felt the layers of magic. Worry for Milly and the baby plagued her too. She had to ensure that Fulton returned to them whole. Only how was she to do that when she had no control over any of this?

"I have finished for the evening. Are you able to help me prepare for bed?"

Beth left off packing. "Of course, Mrs Huntington."

Her preparations for bed took half an hour and she was yawning by the time Beth went off for the night. Jemima sprawled on the bed and put a hand to her head as all her worries came crashing into her mind. They were heading into the unknown, not knowing where they were going or for how long. The situation discomfited her more than fighting off the beast Geneck. In her imagination she once again pictured Geneck, physically huge and rippled with decay, the glow of his green heart, the subtle sound of the heart machine beating, and the corruption that oozed through his mind into hers. It had touched her and that part of her mind had recoiled. The beast had been capable of heinous crimes, murderous and mindless in its need for blood and destruction. She would never forget the connection and the rot that was inside him.

Had her adventures in fighting the vampiric beast caused her to be cautious now? A magician was not such a beast as Geneck had been. A flash of memory came out of nowhere, of the blood on the ground and the near-dead form of Fulton in the rubble. This was serious and it was personal. That was what made her wary. Whoever they were dealing with did not care who lived or died. But unlike the beast Geneck, there was a deep intelligence there and a knowledge of her and those closest to her. Her hand fluttered to her belly where she felt her dinner sitting heavy and the room spun so much she had to close her eyes. Sick with worry. That is what I am and I have to stop, she told herself. Be brave. Be smart. Be strong.

CHAPTER 12

Later when Edward entered the room bearing a glass of the creamy dessert and a spoon for Jemima, he commented. "You broke up the party, you know."

Jemima perked up at the sight of the syllabub. It was one of her favourites and perhaps the sweetness would enliven her spirits. "Me! Not possible." She took the proffered dish and ate a spoonful. "Maybe the party broke up because Aunt Prudence ate her bonnet and choked and had to be saved from her own millinery."

Edward chuckled. "She is rather enjoying the situation. I had not noticed her enjoyment of male company before."

"Not the situation itself. Uncle Ferdy and Sir Giles together. Two men in competition. What a boon that must be for her. Who knew you can be old and still need to flirt?"

Edward drew off his jacket, untied his cravat and went to the dressing room to hand them to his valet. He dismissed Seaborne for the night and then he lay down on the bed next to her, letting out a light moan.

"Are you not well?" she asked.

"Just a headache and a stomach full of anxiety."

"Oh, I know all about that," she replied, taking another spoonful and then another until the dessert was finished. "General anxiety or specific anxiety?"

He flicked his blue gaze in her direction. "Both, I suppose. It has been a hectic few days. I worry for Fulton as he is not hale, but he is so determined to go there is no stopping him."

Jemima sighed. "We need him. I need him. You need him as well and it is best to have him with us, under our eye, do you not think?"

"Still, he must heal." He met her eye. "I know you did great work speeding up his recovery. He told me. However, he still does not have full use of his arm. The new connections need to be worked on, trained."

Jemima frowned. "You worry for him. I worry for you. You were hexed, Edward. You could have died. Surely, there is something we can do to protect from such hexes."

Edward cupped her chin and kissed the tip of her nose. "Thank you for the worry. Uncle Ferdy has undertaken to make us charms by morning. He said he can catch up on sleep after we leave. He told me he taught you how to remove the hex and that your magical ability and training were coming on well. However did I manage my life before I married you?"

Jemima smiled and kept mum. No point in ruining the moment with the bald truth.

The kiss on the nose changed to a kiss on the mouth and then another more serious kiss, longer, luxurious and demanding. By the time they had divested themselves of their clothes, blown out the candles and enjoyed each other for a time, it was near midnight. Jemima yawned widely. "We should sleep now, as we have to get up early."

There was no response. A soft snore greeted her. As she had sent Beth to bed and Edward had handed his coat off to Seaborne, there was not much for her to do but to roll over and fall asleep herself.

❧

UNCLE FERDY WAS UP EARLY TO SEE THEM OFF AND JOINED THEM for a light repast of hot baps, butter and jam, followed by tea and hot chocolate. Jemima had both tea and hot chocolate for fortifying purposes. As they were finishing up, the old magician handed them each a leather thong with a blue stone attached. "Put this on for protection. Smaller hexes will be deflected. A personalised hefty one might stick, but not for long or not as hard."

Edward slid his over his head. "Thank you. We will try to keep moving if we are in a magical battle."

"Indeed you should."

Jemima took hers and watched as Fulton put his on and tucked it out of sight. He wore his cravat loose so was able to hide it nicely.

Martha knocked on the door. "Excuse me, ma'am, the cook has a hamper prepared for you and I have put it in the carriage."

"That is kind of you, Martha. We shall miss the great service we have received at the King's Arms."

Martha curtseyed and left the room.

"I suppose that is the hint that the carriage is waiting," Fulton said.

"Yes, but Mr White," Edward began. "What about this assistant of yours, this Frank? When shall he arrive?"

Uncle Ferdy waved a hand in dismissal. "Do not concern yourself. He will catch you up."

Edward's eyebrows rose in surprise. Jemima smiled, hiding her gritted teeth. The idea of someone being able to catch them up was sobering indeed.

Once they were all aboard, they set off at a quick pace and through the town they went, along narrow streets to get them out onto the main road. The carriage rocked and they lurched about. Fulton winced and hugged the hamper to his chest. Edward glowered as he peered out the window and pursed his lips. "How much farther to this next village?"

Fulton sighed loudly and shook his head, not able to hide his ill temper. "Can you not magic yourself a headache cure? We must first stop where that rascal chap dropped Miss Horton-Sprigge and see if you can pick up a magical trail."

Edward's expression fell. "You know I have a headache? How?"

Jemima sighed. "Nothing could be more obvious," she replied. "We have not yet been in the carriage for twenty minutes and," she glanced out the window. "We are technically still in Kiddlington." It was a spread-out town. Edward, who had been monosyllabic since their departure, pouted as he glared out of the window.

"Oh," he replied, adjusting his cravat.

She softened her tone. "We could ask for a cold press at the next inn if that will help."

Edward glared at her.

Leaning back in his seat. "Very well." He waved his fingers in front of his nose and muttered under his breath. Instantly, the lines creasing his forehead smoothed out. He turned his head left and then right. A slight grin touched his lips before they firmed again. He did not like to be so transparent, Jemima thought.

"Better?" Edward asked Fulton.

"Yes, now if you could do the same for me, I would be much obliged." Jemima blinked. She was so used to Fulton being circumspect about any ailment that she did not think that he was in pain. But of course he was. Not yet healed, his hurt must be greater than a mere headache.

"Ah ... I see. Apologies." To ease Fulton's many pains took a bit more time, a lot more gestures and a full verse of some spell that Jemima wished she could put to memory. It looked to be a handy thing to have in one's magical repertoire. After Edward finished his magical ministrations, he asked, "Is that better?"

Fulton grinned and lifted his eyebrows over shining amber eyes. "Indeed it is. Thank you. It is ddd ... very inconvenient not to be in the peak of health."

Jemima rolled her eyes. Fulton was far from being at his normal self. She saw, out of the corner of her eye, his attempts to open and close his hand. He was practising and it took effort, which is why he was feeling poorly. He still clung to the picnic basket and she realised it was to work his arm as there was room on the seat next him and on the floor besides. Fulton always worked hard at improvement.

Now as Jemima peered out the window, her companions began to converse instead of snarling at each other and she smiled. They were on the main road now and the landscape was devoted to pastures of ripening grain. Not more than an hour later, she turned to them. "I think this is it."

Fulton banged on the roof of the carriage. "Stop here."

The wheels rolled before the driver engaged the brake fully. The footman opened the door and lowered the stair. Edward and Fulton alighted and Edward stayed to assist her from the carriage. As there was some sun peeping through clouds, she drew out her parasol. She did not mind freckles or a tan but as Fulton's guest she must attempt the occasional ladylike appearance. He had to live in the neighbourhood, after all. They had stopped by a field, but the gorge in the distance caught her eye as it was one of the details they had gleaned. Some luggage had been found there.

They walked around, each doing their own circuit. A dropped handkerchief sat damp in the grass. She picked it up, saw the initials and knew it belonged to Sylvia's maid. "Here."

Edward strode up with Fulton just behind. Her husband closed his eyes as if communing with spirits, only he was searching for magical residue. Jemima thought she should try that too. On closing her eyes, she inhaled deeply and could smell mud, grass, some horse leavings and rosemary. She opened her eyes and looked about her but there was no rosemary bush nearby. She inhaled again. "Can you smell that?"

Edward's eyes snapped open. "What do you smell?"

"Herbs ... rosemary to be precise, but I can see none around here."

"Ah ..."

Fulton sniffed and kicked a tuft of grass. "Care to enlighten me, either of you?"

Jemima furrowed her eyebrows. "I have no idea what it means." They both turned to Edward.

He lifted a shoulder. "I am supposing it is an aftertaste of a spell."

"So the blighter was a magician after all." Fulton hissed and shook his head. "Damn him."

Edward's lips pursed and he gave a slight shake of his head. "Not necessarily."

"Can you tell what the spell was?" Jemima asked.

Edward closed his eyes again. "It is complex. There is an aftertaste of coercion, a slight hint of riches on the tongue and an overlay of roast lamb."

Jemima blinked. "He went to get food?"

"Which way?" Fulton gave an impatient bark.

Edward turned abruptly. "Down that road there."

"But that is not the main road. The river is not far from here and if we continue on this road we should come along to Lower Heyford. I doubt they have an inn along that road."

Edward looked at them both. "Yes, the trail of the spell leads that way."

"Could it be a trap, do you suppose?" Jemima could not help but be sceptical. She met both their gazes.

"Obviously," Fulton said in sarcastic tones.

"Perhaps," Edward said with a hint of a smile and a shrug for good measure. "Makes no difference though, does it. We must find this chap to know more and I say the clue is this way."

The carriage had to take the road slowly as it was barely a track. They rolled and flumped in each other's laps despite holding onto the straps. Jemima was of the opinion that it would have been better to have walked instead.

They came upon a stand of five or so cottages, most in disrepair. The road beyond was a mere walking track. Jemima alighted the carriage to be met by a slight drizzle. Mist shrouded the trees and sank down thick around the cottage roofs. "Hello?" Fulton called out. "Is there anyone here?"

The air was strangely odour free. No livestock smells or animal sounds for that matter. No smoke from fires and none wafting from the chimneys.

"Driver?" Fulton said. "Turn the carriage while we investigate."

Jemima raised her eyebrows for there was not much room for the carriage to do anything. However, she left the coachman to his task and joined the others. The first cottage was little more than a shell. The second was a hovel that looked lived in, but there was no one about, nor had there been for some time. As they approached the third that was set back aways from the others, the smell hit her. Covering her nose with a handkerchief, she stood her ground. When Fulton banged on the door and it swung open, they all fell back a step. It was the smell of rot, of death, and of something else. Magic. It had to be. A deeper, richer scent that overlaid the rest. Jemima did not want to approach but did not wish to appear craven, so stepped up behind her husband, who followed Fulton.

The little one-room cottage with loft was clean and in good repair compared to the others they had seen. What furniture there was had been pushed against the wall, leaving a clear space in front of the hearth. Sprawled with arms and legs outstretched and completely naked were the remains of Bertrand Fulton Esquire. A dark red line from neck to navel gaped in his pale flesh and his innards were displayed around his torso. His eyes were burnt sockets and what was left of his tongue protruded. It was a sick mind that had done this. What was done to him was entirely unnecessary. Jemima felt the room spin and backed out, grabbing for the door frame to support her push for fresh air.

Fulton followed soon after, a handkerchief over his nose and mouth. Edward stayed longer but when he joined them asked, "Had you seen him before, Fulton?"

Jemima kept the handkerchief in place. Fulton had not met the fake heir when he had visited the King's Arms and Edward was asking if he had seen the man. She had not thought of that herself, that maybe the fake heir had met Fulton in the past, studied his habits.

It took a few moments before Fulton could answer. "No, yes, maybe."

"A relation then?"

"No. Not that. A salesman, I think. A few months back. 'Tis a bit vague now and in death, well, it changes one. He does resemble in body the man I sent on his way."

"A salesman. What kind?"

Fulton shrugged. "I cannot recall offhand. Come to think of it, I came upon him in the park. He was carrying a suitcase. A small one. I meant to ask my steward, Mr Allsworthy, about him because it looked like they had been chatting."

Edward rubbed his chin, thoughtfully. "Could he been checking the lay of the land, the approaches to the house and so forth?"

Fulton jerked his head. "Of course that is what he was doing, with the benefit of hindsight. What frightens me to my bones, though, is that this scheme has been in train for many months. My family have been in danger all this time and I did not know or even suspect. Do you think they planned the attack because you were arriving or was that just chance?"

Jemima bit her lip, moved by Fulton's distress. "I hope it was not by chance because the outcome would have been different if we had not arrived when we did."

Fulton's neck grew red and streaks of distress climbed into his cheeks. Jemima reached out and clasped his good shoulder. Fulton met her eye and nodded. He was in control of himself again.

"Since the destruction of the monastery, and the scattering of the remaining magicians, tales of Edward's talent and mine have spread. News of your strength and ability must have circulated widely too."

"It could have been any one of them or all of them," Fulton ground out. "I tried to save who I could but I am only one man and many had been killed before I arrived."

"It was not all of them, Fulton," Edward reminded. "Some are on our side and not envious of our abilities. Remember that."

Fulton scoffed. "I will try, my friend."

"Can we perhaps step away from this scene? The stench is trying to climb into my skin," Jemima said.

Fulton lowered his eyelids. "Yes, I agree. It is a scene I will not forget in a while."

Fulton and Jemima moved away and Edward joined them. "Nasty blood magic. Leaves a terrible aftertaste."

Fulton patted his friend on the back. "Do you think Mr White might know who he is?"

Edward's eyes widened. "Jemima please call Uncle Ferdy." He said this in a voice that imitated Jemima's and she snarled at him.

"Do not mock me. You know he has been an uncle to me since I was a small child. Just because he is not related by blood and a magician does not mean I cannot call him uncle. You find your family in this life. Not all of us are blessed with wonderful relatives." Edward's eyes widened, as if he feared she would bring up Aunt Prudence.

He raised his hands in surrender. "I do apologise. That was most uncalled-for."

Sending him a hard stare she turned aside. "Uncle Ferdy we need you." She fixed the place in her mind and sent a mind picture. "Come now. Just for a quick visit please."

There was a noise from inside where the corpse lay. "That did not take long," Edward said. However, when they entered, the room was empty except for the corpse.

"How strange? An animal?" Jemima ventured.

"No," Edward inhaled. "Him."

Fulton and Jemima whipped their heads around but could see nothing. Edward meant it was the villain they were following that had just popped in. A powerful magician if he could come and go so quickly. Uncle Ferdy said he needed to rest between jumps.

"Did he take something?" Fulton asked as he scanned the room.

Jemima shook her head as she had not taken note of things in the room and had completely missed if it had been important.

Edward gave up looking around the room and peered at the mutilated corpse instead. "The heart is missing," he said after bending over it with a hand over his nose.

Jemima recoiled. "Missing?" She bolted outside into the fresh air, and dug a handkerchief out of her pocket, and took deep breaths. Why steal a heart? Blood magic? She could not imagine that the body part would give them clues. And if it was the man himself, the magician behind all this who had popped in, so to speak, to steal the heart, then he knew they were on his trail. She tried not to entertain thoughts of what could have happened if he had popped in when they first encountered the poor deceased Bertrand Fulton Esquire.

Edward came up and put his arm around her shoulders and squeezed. "Are you all right? Blood and guts never used to make you queasy."

She lifted her gaze to meet his intense blue eyes. "Scientific endeavours are not the same as slaughter and blood magic."

"I fear you are right. It does not portend well that he came back to retrieve the heart and while we were here too. Very risky endeavour if you ask me."

This time there was a shout from Fulton inside and she followed Edward to return to the scene of the crime. The room was crowded now that Uncle Ferdy had joined them.

"Thank you for coming," Jemima said. "As you can see we have found the fake heir."

Uncle Ferdy swallowed a mouthful, and brushed crumbs from his fingertips. "Sorry for the delay. Morning tea, I believe it was."

Uncle Ferdy looked down at the corpse "Oh nasty, nasty and so unnecessary." He circled around the body and Jemima could not linger any longer. She did not care that the others might call her weak but the scene and the stench were making her feel ill.

Jemima left them to it, even though she thought she possessed more grit. The mist had begun to lift, and she explored the remaining abodes looking for signs of life, witnesses, anything. One of the small stone huts was definitely lived in, as there were twigs piled by the hearth and a mound of old potatoes in a basket. A bed was made, with a tatty grey blanket. She backed out, feeling her trespass. The other one looked recently abandoned. Everything had been stripped with just a few things left behind to give witness to their flight.

This little hamlet was good as place as any for a murder, she thought, as she took to walking in a wide circle. The grain in the meadows beyond looked untended, which was unusual for midsummer.

The jingle of the harness made her look up and she could see the carriage was almost in position for the return journey. Continuing her survey of the place, she continued walking in circles. She found the body after she tripped in the long grass and fell. Flies buzzed and formed a cloud as her foot had disturbed the corpse. The smell of decay wafted out of the rupture in the skin. She backed up on her behind to scurry away, only to put her hand on another cold, soft corpse. A scream left her mouth and Edward came running.

Scrambling to her feet, she stood still, glanced around her in case there were others. Breaths came in hard gasps and glancing at her hands she saw she was shaking. This was not like her to be so affected. It was not the first time she had seen corpses. Yet everything about these felt wrong. They had been dead longer than a couple of days.

"Are you all right? What happened?" Edward called on approach and then slowed when he saw the remains. An old woman and a younger man. The remaining hamlet inhabitants, she expected. They had merely had their throats cut and been left in the field.

Edward pulled Jemima into his arms and hugged her hard. "Mr White has identified Bertrand. He was in fact Brother Bertrand, an assistant to a magician. One Thaddeus Crompton."

"Oh … and do you think Thaddeus Crompton did this horrible deed?"

Uncle Ferdy came up and his face grew grave on seeing the bodies. He met her gaze and his eyes were dark with concern. "Brother Thaddeus was meant to have died in Geneck's attack."

Fulton walked carefully up to them, avoiding the bodies and their close surrounds. "Used it as cover I expect."

"Oh … was he one of the magicians who tried to take my heart?" Jemima watched Edward's face pale.

"I think so. It is not good news, for this Brother Thaddeus is knowledgeable and powerful with it. Not an easy foe."

"Would he really kill his assistant and these innocent people just to get Edward's designs?"

Uncle Ferry pursed his lips. "We cannot know until you find him with Fulton's arm. Then you would have proof. All this is supposition. You did not see who it was who claimed the heart from Bertrand's body?"

"No, just a sound. We thought you had arrived."

"At least we know what or who we are dealing with. That is one step closer." Fulton did not seem happy about this revelation.

"There is more. Crompton had a younger brother who was killed by Geneck."

Fulton's eyebrows lifted. "Really?"

"Yes, and now that I think I know who we are dealing with, I think I can develop a motive for the attack on your house."

Fulton swallowed. "I did not save his brother?"

Jemima sniffed and wiped her nose. "The Priory was terribly smashed up too."

"Yes, you three were both the cause and although Fulton, you came to aid us, it was too late for the young Brother Cromford."

"That makes little sense," Jemima began.

Uncle Ferdy lifted a hand. "You know, I think, that this magician is not of sound mind. Something has snapped. I offer only what I think is the reasoning behind these actions, why it feels personal."

Fulton jerked his chin down. "Good to have a theory. It does not cause me to pity him."

"No, of course it does not. He was with the people trying to take my heart, to kill me! I definitely do not pity him." Jemima folded her arms across her chest and gave a firm nod.

Uncle Ferdy looked around the space, closed his eyes. "I fear we are being watched." He turned slowly. "There, on that tree."

Edward strode up and stared at the bark and after a minute or two picked up a twig bound in cloth. He brought it over. There was a small green stone tied to it.

"An eye. Not sophisticated but useful."

"He has seen us then?" Fulton asked.

Uncle Ferdy squashed the charm in his hands and dropped the pieces to the ground.

"Yes, whoever it was has seen you enter here. My charms would have blurred your faces somewhat but he would know, I think, by your general outlines who you are. Do not be complacent. This could be Thaddeus's work but I could be mistaken, even though I have woven a possible motivation into my analysis. Until we know for sure, we need to keep an open mind. There could be others. There could be someone else pulling his strings. I will do some research into my magical brother and let you know.

"I suggest you follow that path back up the road and go to the next inn. Perhaps you can pick up the trail." He bowed to Jemima and inclined his head to Edward and Fulton. Then with a snap of his fingers he was gone.

"I wish he would stay," Fulton said. "I believe I trust him."

"Me too," Edward said. "We should go. The carriage is ready."

Jemima was filled with dismay. She put a hand over her heart. The pulse of the ruby driving her heartbeat was natural to her now. At that moment, she felt vulnerable. Thaddeus, or whoever it was, could snatch her life away without a care.

Edward cupped her chin. "You are so brave and clever. That rosemary scent you detected appears to be a way to trace this magician. You might smell it again if we hurry."

"And the bodies?" she asked, taking his hand. Fulton was already halfway to the carriage.

Edward turned back to the edifice where the body lay and frowned. "We will notify the authorities in the next village. They will send someone to retrieve them and investigate. I wonder if we are still in Sir Giles' jurisdiction. I cannot say I like the thought of that."

Fulton wiped his hands on a handkerchief as if he had been touching something revolting. She hoped he had not been because she did not want to share a carriage with someone who had been touching those defiled remains. She sniffed herself and inspected the hem of her dress. There was a slight aroma of decay and she hoped that she had not picked up any juices of the weeping dead flesh on her clothing. It was bad enough she had fallen over them.

She paused before entering the carriage to wipe her boots for they had definitely been in contact with dead bodies. As she stepped up into the carriage, she noticed something else. Cows lowing in the distance. The call of sheep and the barking of a dog. A bird cawed. Light broke through the clouds and gave the little hamlet a golden glow. The magic that had enveloped the place was broken. Perhaps that eye charm had more heft in it than just watching, perhaps it kept the animals at bay. As she took her seat, she bit her bottom lip. If that was the case, then Thaddeus wanted them to find the remains of those people. As a warning? An invitation? A dare?

At least the coachman and the footman had been busy turning the carriage and had not taken note of their discoveries. Having a hysterical driver would be a disaster. She hoped reporting their find did not embroil them in the investigation.

The journey up the track from the hamlet was even more uncomfortable than previously. "Please ask the coachman to pause, Edward. I fear I am queasy."

Also, Fulton's complexion was as grey as a washed-out sky after a storm. Once they were back on the road, the coach stopped and

Fulton and Jemima alighted, stretched their backs and walked about. "You look better," Fulton told Jemima.

Jemima smiled and wished she could return the compliment. Fulton's cheeks sagged.

"Are you feeling all right?"

"Of course, shipshape."

Jemima scoffed. "Really Fulton, you are a terrible liar."

He glared at her. "How dare you impugn my gentlemanly status. I do not lie."

Jemima quirked her head and nodded. "You do and often."

"Take that back," he said, and coughed at the effort of speaking. "I exaggerate. That is different."

Jemima breathed deep, the scent of decay no longer on the air. "If you say so, Fulton. As long as you do not deceive yourself. You are loved and wanted and I will not be part in aiding you to destroy yourself." She peered at the trees and the fields and then back at Fulton. "Is there anything I can do for you to relieve your suffering?"

"I am not suffering!" Fulton blustered and squeezed a hand into a fist.

Jemima just held his gaze, until Fulton blushed and looked at his feet. "Very well, I am suffering but I do not think there is anything you can do for my relief."

Jemima nodded once and walked up to the carriage door. Still in the carriage, Edward had his eyes shut. "Edward," she said softly. "Is there a chance you can make Fulton more comfortable? Whatever you did before has worn off."

Edward's eyes snapped open, his mouth formed an 'oh' of surprise. "Of course," he replied and was out of the carriage in an instant.

"Fulton!" Edward called as he assisted Jemima back into the carriage. She decided to give Fulton some privacy. Her husband and her friend walked out of sight into the trees. It was some ten minutes later when they returned. Fulton's complexion was pale, but no longer grey, and he moved more energetically. Edward smiled as he exchanged pleasantries with his companion.

The village of Lower Heyford did not amount to much. The subsidiary of the River Cherwood flowed in a stately manner and the bridge allowed them to continue on their way. The terrain was interesting with rising ground and they passed some ancient earthworks. It was significantly smaller than Kiddlington, where they were staying. In the square stood the Bell Inn and according to the innkeeper of the Kings Arms, a decent market was held there. The streets were mud and straw but the horse leavings had been recently scooped up.

At the Bell Inn, they requested a private room and a luncheon. While Jemima waited, Edward and Fulton went to see the local magistrate, who lived in the manor house down the lane, to report the murders they had discovered. Jemima washed her hands and face in the basin provided, relishing in the warm water. A small fire flickered in the grate. After she had refreshed herself and made herself comfortable, a young maid came in with a tea tray. "Your husband said you might need a little something before luncheon."

"What a dear he is."

As she watched the maid lay out the tea and small yellow-fleshed cakes with dark raisins in them, she wondered how to broach the subject of their magician-cum-murderer. "Do you get many strangers passing through here?"

"A few. Mostly people from the outlying properties and farms who come to bring their produce to sell or while they await the coach."

"Anyone travelling alone? I fear I could not travel on my own for obvious reasons. I am a lady, of course. But the boredom. All those hours alone in the carriage. The bouncing, the jolting and the discomfort. I cannot imagine how an older person might do it. Why they must be all bent over and cranky, demanding a bed and a large drink of port when they arrive."

The maid looked up, smiled. "Some are like that. It must be tedious. I have not travelled beyond Upper Heyford in all my life. And that was on the back of my father's hay cart. Very bumpy. My Da's been as far north as Banbury."

Jemima poured herself some tea. "This is excellent. I thank you." Her question had not elicited the information she wanted. "We were hoping to catch up with a relative of mine. He left his home in a great hurry. Possibly, yesterday or the day before."

The maid picked up her tray. "We have had no visitors at all for the last week."

"Truly? Oh, we must have mistaken our direction."

The maid shut the door, a quizzical expression on her brow. Jemima took another sip of tea and then walked to the window and opened it. She inhaled deeply and then coughed. Too much dust and the smell of horse manure. A waft from the stream sent the scents of animal slaughter to her nostrils. No hint of rosemary but an aftertaste of mint. Yet there was something in the maid's manner that made her suspicious.

Jemima was drowsing on the couch when Edward and Fulton returned. She had refrained from eating all the cakes but the tea was cold. That did not matter to them as they drank the tea cold while they ate the remainder of the cakes.

Jemima opened her eyes and sat up. "How did you get on?"

Edward glowered. "We were interrogated for two hours. What were we doing there? Did we know the victims? How can we explain how they died? Do we have any witnesses that we had not been there previously? Mr Coachman gave a good accounting of us. He does not miss much, I am afraid. He said he smelled death as soon as we entered the hamlet."

Fulton brushed crumbs from his lips. "As I was able to give him my direction and as I live in the neighbourhood, sort of, he let us go without further enquiry. Unfortunately, he knows Sir Giles and was writing off a missive to him while we were still there. Then he sent off a runner to call up men to help investigate and would send me word in due course, if I would be so kind as to remain at The Bell."

Edward harrumphed. "He said he would visit you to discuss the matter further, Fulton. Another delay."

"I see," Jemima replied.

"If you ask me, he was suspicious of us." Edward sat back in his seat and brushed cake crumbs from his lapels.

Fulton stood and went to the window. "Of course he was. It is not every day that a small rural hamlet has multiple bodies arrayed for the constabulary to investigate. If I were the magistrate, I would be put off my dinner and my breakfast at such news." He turned to face them.

"The worst of it is that we have lost the trail. The innkeeper says there have been no visitors in the last week."

"I do not think we have lost the trail," Jemima said.

"What do you know?" Edward asked, suddenly alert.

"Nothing more than what Fulton knows. The maid told me the same story but it cannot be true."

Edward jerked his head back in surprise. "How do you know that?"

"Look in the yard. There have been many horses here. The yard is rutted from carriage wheels. There is a delivery stacked in the corner."

"They do not consider them visitors?" Fulton suggested.

Edward shook his head. "There is a perfectly plausible reason why the staff report no visitors even though the inn is busy."

"Yes, they know all the people who visit here," Jemima said.

"Exactly." Edward nodded his head as if putting a nail in the argument.

"But that is not the only reason. Our quarry is a magician. Can magicians place spells on people? Can they make them say things that are not true? Can they give them a false memory?"

Edward stared at her. "Yes, of course but—"

"Or the person we are chasing is not a stranger to them," Fulton added.

"Possibly, but that is not where my thoughts are heading."

Fulton rolled his eyes. "Honestly, Jemima, I swear you will be the death of me. Here I was thinking we were done here and I could go back to the Kings Arms and spend time with my wife and child and now with a few observations, I am contemplating a number of actions and all them not so pleasing because either we need to continue on or I am to suspect a neighbour of trying to kill me."

"There is a simpler measure." She turned to Edward and lifted her eyebrows, waggling them.

He met her gaze, forehead furrowed. "Oh!" He said after a few minutes. He looked to Fulton. "She means I could remove the spell and find the truth."

"That does sound like a plan. Can we eat first?" Fulton said. "I am much more malleable on a full stomach and I suspect the innkeeper may be as well. I think we should secure rooms for the night too, if we need to investigate further."

"Indeed, after the meal is when I shall try to find the truth of things," Edward replied. "They will be distracted cleaning away the empty dishes."

Edward went off to order dinner and secure them rooms. Fulton paced around as if he was a caged, wild animal. "Fulton?"

He turned around suddenly. "Sorry, Jemima, I was deep in thought and if you must know, impatient."

After a delicious meal of roast ham, devilled eggs and celery and peas, they sat at table as the innkeeper's wife came to clear the plates. Jemima tried to follow the process by which her husband undid the spells on the staff. Edward frowned, played with his fork and then pointed it at the woman, who was at least forty.

Jemima felt a sensation, like a light breeze that swept past her ears. Edward inclined his head, giving her the signal. Leaning forward to catch the maid's eye, she spoke her thanks. "I believe all your guests must enjoy the food here. That ham was delicious."

"Thank you, ma'am. I believe they do. Just the other day a most impressive gentleman had a third serving. The suet pudding was his favourite though. Cook was most pleased."

"Were you able to give him directions to the next inn on his journey? Surely you can give the same hint to us as we must continue on."

The woman gaped at Jemima. "How did you know we gave a recommendation?"

"You are good innkeepers, and you care about your clientele."

The woman preened. "Indeed we do. We recommended him the Plough Inn of Satin Lane in Deddington. My cousin is the innkeeper. I also said he should see the castle. I've only seen it the once when we went for my cousin's wedding. I'll never forget the sight of it."

Deddington was a large town in this county, with a few holdings and nearby villages. Jemima grinned. They had a destination. It could be a false lead, of course. Then, again, maybe not. Why did Thaddeus spell the staff if he did not expect pursuit? Was he leading them on a merry chase or worse, leading them into a trap? Most likely they were being manipulated. He could translocate after all. All these thoughts dampened her enjoyment of the little apple tart with whipped cream that was her dessert.

Later, when they had retired to their room and readied for bed, Edward came up behind her and kissed her neck.

"Did I tell you how much I love you?" Edward said, as he drew her into his arms.

"Not recently," Jemima replied.

Edward kissed her directly and then matters took an interesting but enjoyable turn that left Edward snoring and Jemima smiling as she drifted off to sleep. She liked that her husband appreciated her and she liked the way he showed his appreciation. It was not nice to think that they were using marital relations to take their mind off darker matters. Her thoughts strayed to Fulton alone in his room. How he must be missing Milly and Aly. How profoundly this attack must have affected him. He lost his home, nearly lost his life and was nearly forever parted from his darling wife and son. Yet, he never complained. Actually, he did complain, to be honest. Talking to yourself is the first sign of madness. A smile lit her face and she drifted off to sleep.

CHAPTER 13

A banging at the door woke them before the cock crowed. "Yes," Edward said, throwing the bed covers off. "Who is it?"

"It is me," said the voice. However, they did not recognise the voice. Jemima climbed out of bed and endeavoured to light a candle in the embers in the fireplace. It flickered and took the flame.

In the warm yellow light, Edward readied a spell and then opened the door a crack. A hooded figure in a dark-coloured monk's robe stood there. Jemima held her breath and her heart hammered. Was this the evil magician come to kill them in their beds?

Edward lifted his arm, ready to cast his spell.

The stranger blurted, lifting his hands in surrender. "I had to warn you."

"Who are you?" Edward said, fingers twitching as he held his spell aloft.

"I am Francis, formerly of the Priory, cousin to Bertrand who you found murdered."

"Speak your warning then, sir, and begone."

Jemima tugged at Edward's elbow. "I think this is Frank."

"Frank?" Edward opened his mouth, closed it and narrowed his gaze.

Francis nodded his head vigorously. "Did I not say? Forgive me. I have only just found out from Brother Ferdinand that Bertrand was murdered. He told me he saw the body and I was already set to come and sometimes when I travel, I get nervous and anxious."

Edward lowered his arm. "Mr White sent you? I mean Ferdinand?"

"Yes." The lad was young, younger than Jemima, with some fluff on his upper lip that could not in all fairness call itself a moustache. He had dark, dishevelled hair, was thin to the point of starvation and had rounded shoulders. "He told me his theory of who is behind the attacks. If he is right then you cannot stop Thaddeus Cromford." The stranger sucked in a loud breath as if they had prepared a speech. "He is too powerful. You must understand that Bertrand was a good person, he worked with Thaddeus now and then. When he saw what he was about he tried to stop him and became ensorcelled, became Thaddeus's slave."

"Ensorcelled?" Jemima flicked her gaze to her husband. Had they both uttered the same word, at the same time.

"Yes, indeed. Ensorcelled."

Jemima's eyes widened. She flicked her gaze around the room. Not only did a draft threaten to quench the candle, their voices would disturb other guests, if the intruder had not done so already.

"Do come in before you wake the whole inn and keep your voices down both of you."

Acknowledging her point, Edward made way for their visitor and shut the door quietly after he stepped into the room. Jemima did not feel any prick of alarm from the newcomer, nor did she smell rosemary. Rather, Frank smelt of lilacs, and that scent was extremely nice.

Leaning in closer to Edward, she tried to catch his scent. But he just smelled of Edward, which was interesting. He did not have a perfume.

Jemima lit another candle so that they could see each other properly. The young man did not bear any resemblance to the erstwhile Bertrand. Bertrand had been short and compact, whereas the lanky youth was the opposite. He had pale skin, a pointed chin and cheeks red with acne. Jemima grabbed a robe and draped herself in it. Edward did not bother to cover up and stood there with a candle held aloft, and she was pretty sure a spell at the ready in the twitching fingers of his other hand. "Continue," Edward said.

"Yes. Thaddeus twisted his mind, made him believe things that were not true. Bade him do things that were questionable. Now he is dead." A sound like a sob caught in his throat.

Jemima lifted an eyebrow. What had the man done, other than impersonate Fulton's heir and abandon a young woman in his care. "Did you tell Uncle Ferdy about this?"

Frank gaped at her, mouthed 'uncle Ferdy' and then clarity erased his confusion. "Yes. That is why I delayed. I was meant to join your party sooner."

"And how are you involved in this?" Edward asked. "Why should we believe you are not working with this Thaddeus yourself?"

"By chance, I was not at the Priory when that monster attacked. I had contracted the measles and was in isolation." He turned to Jemima. "I was not involved in your kidnap, ma'am. I promise you. If you do not believe me, then apply to Brother Ferdinand for he would not have sent me if I could not be trusted." He rubbed the end of his nose with his thumb before continuing. "Afterwards, I met Thaddeus when we were called to help restore the Priory and introduced him to my cousin Bertrand, who was no great talent but liked to dabble. Sadly, I was mistaken in Thaddeus, despite his high rank, he was no good. I did not know the depths of his depravity. I did not suspect anything untoward until Bertrand left his home a month ago."

"But why are you here now and how did you find us?" Jemima asked, before Edward could open his mouth again. He had not relaxed his stance. Edward's readiness to strike gave Jemima comfort and courage to continue.

"I have come to help you. Not only for my cousin's sake, but because it is the right thing to do. Ferdinand told me where to find you."

"He did?" Jemima asked, shocked. "How did he know?"

Edward's eyes widened. "There is something you should know."

"What?"

"Mr White is able to track you and looks in on you from time to time."

"He told you this?" she asked, knowing the answer.

"Yes, when I awoke from the hex."

Jemima nodded. "So I am not so clever then. I called him but he was listening for me." She nodded again, decisively. "Thank you for telling me. At least now I can understand the limits of my ability."

Her gaze studied Frank. She could sense no ill in him but what would she know? It was instinct only, intuition, and that could be misleading. Uncle Ferdy would not betray them, of that she was sure. She was about to tell Edward to relax and lower his spell, when another knock on the door quelled further conversation. They all stiffened.

"Who is that?" Jemima whispered.

Edward shook his head.

Francis edged out of the way as the door swung open and Fulton entered, bristling with energy as if he was ready to hew down a pack of men readying their attack. He blanched at the sight of Francis, balled his fists and looked ready to leap, until Edward forestalled him. "This is Frank," Edward hissed. "Mr White sent him." He then let his spell dissipate, wiggling his fingers before lowering his hands.

The conservation with Francis was repeated as Fulton interrogated the visitor, asking the same things they had done.

Jemima sighed. There was only one way to be sure of this and put everyone's mind to rest. "Uncle Ferdy? Can you come here, please? We need you."

The room was now getting crowded so Jemima retreated to her side of the bed. Edward stood next to her and Fulton stood on Edward's side of the bed and Frank at the base of the bed between the bed and a wardrobe.

In the only available space by the door, Uncle Ferdy materialised, a slow fading into view. Jemima was impressed with the grace of his entry. Perhaps he could teach Edward that, or even herself. Edward's exits were jerky affairs and she herself had never tried.

Uncle Ferdy was dressed in a white linen nightgown, soft cap on his head and he yawned loudly. "Cannot a man get any sleep?" He blinked at the sight before him and covered a yawn with his hand.

Jemima smiled. "Thank you for coming and apologies for

disturbing your sleep. Uncle, do you happen to know this man?" He indicated Frank standing at the end of the bend.

Uncle Ferdy opened his eyes and focused on the newcomer. "Frank?"

The robed figure bowed his head. "Yes. It is me."

"What are you doing here?" This response caused both Edward and Fulton to stiffen as if readying to attack.

"Yes, what are you doing here?" Fulton said, shoulders bunching and fists clenching.

"You told me to help them and where they were so I have come."

"In the middle of the night?" He rolled his eyes. "No wonder there is an uproar." He turned to Edward. "Apologies. I did tell him where you were but I thought he had common sense and would wait until morning at least before coming here."

"I would have. My cousin was murdered and I was overwrought."

Jemima did not think this admission was a recommendation. "Why did you send him, uncle? Could you have not come yourself?"

Uncle Ferdy shrugged his shoulders. "I prefer to stay with the womenfolk. Despite Frank's bad timing, he will be a good resource for you. Besides Jemima, your aunt is persistent in her desire to entertain me and I am afraid that I cannot slip away at will without causing suspicion."

"Does that mean we should not call on you when we need you?" Jemima asked, her bottom lip pouting.

"Only when you really, really need me, pet," Uncle Ferdy replied. "Frank is capable and trustworthy, I assure you." He yawned loudly. "I am afraid I am very tired. May I go now?"

"Yes. Thank you Uncle," Jemima replied.

Fulton sagged, and then rolled his eyes. "We have to be on our way in an hour and a half. I am going back to bed." He made to move to the door, stopped, turned and poked a finger into Frank's chest. "You go away and come back then."

Frank nodded shakily. "I apologise. I can do that, of course."

Fulton brushed past him and left the door ajar. Edward coughed and Frank backed out, shutting the door behind him. That left Uncle

Ferdy, who was once again yawning. "Do not let us keep you, sir," Edward said.

"I need a minute to recover." They waited the allotted time.

Uncle Ferdy blew Jemima a kiss and faded away. Edward snuffed out the candle and they climbed back into bed but now they were awake they decided to snuggle instead.

Edward lay against her back, arms around her ribs. Jemima said softly, "I am so lucky to have found you, Edward."

"And I you."

"I worry for Fulton, though. He has fought so hard to get where he is and now this attack threatens all that he has gained. At least he still has Milly and the baby."

Edward kissed her neck. "I know. I feel for him. It reminds us how quickly life can change around us. None of us can predict the future and how easily circumstances can change. We must be grateful in the moment, hold it close to our heart so that we have the strength to continue."

Jemima turned and peered at him in the pale light of pre-dawn that filtered through the windows. "I do not think I could live on without you." The idea, that theory that she was immortal, loomed large in her mind. She half believed and half denied it. Contemplating life without Edward would cause her pain, unless he was immortal as well, then there was nothing to worry about.

Edward ran his forefinger along her cheek, gazed into her eyes tenderly. "Yet you must. You have a life to live, a destiny. All the uniqueness of you cannot come to an end, if I do. I would not wish that. Promise me that you would do your best to live on if I passed away."

Jemima shook her head. "Do not ask that of me. I wish to be free to follow the dictates of my own heart."

Edward shook his head. "Would you wish me to pine away unto death if you died?"

Jemima blinked. "If I was dead, I would have no say. I would want you to be happy and cared for. If that meant you must remarry, of course, I would not object." She pressed her face to his warm chest, the light smattering of hair tickling her nose. "How did we come to be talking of such morbid things after spending a wonderful evening together?"

"I have no idea. Circumstances, events, the turn of our minds, the way we feel about each other, perhaps. Fulton's situation is obviously weighing heavy on our minds as we did nearly lose him." Edward looked to the window. "Alas, we do not have time for more wallowing in our morose feelings as we must wash and dress and, perhaps, bespeak a basket for breakfast on the road."

Jemima threw back the bedcovers. "Indeed, we do. I shall call for warm water." She rang the bell to signal that they were awake. As they did not bring their own servants, they had to rely on the innkeeper to supply their needs. Hot water had been requested the evening before. A breakfast basket would need to be negotiated.

Edward unpacked his valise, bringing out a clean shirt and his shaving things. "You are still concerned for Fulton. He is your dear friend, I know."

Jemima went to hug him and once in the circle of his arms, looked up into his face, pressing herself against him, hot skin on warm. Light from her Ruby Heart leaked from its casing, giving his visage a pinkish cast. "He is dear to me, that is true. There is a steadfastness to him that I treasure and a sadness that I want to heal. Milly gave him love and a son. Yet, I fear he needs more."

"More?" Edward asked, his eyebrows descending to shadow his eyes.

"Yes, more. Validation perhaps. He needs to know he is worthy. That is what I think."

"But Fulton is worthy."

"Yes, of course he is. He does not believe though. I watch him, talk to him."

"You are perceptive. I see nothing lacking in Fulton or a chink in his armour that you have perceived."

"He suffered at the hands of his father, motherless from a young age and a bully of a brother. Nothing to give you a case of the self-doubts more, than it being drilled into you from childhood that you are not good enough."

Edward smoothed her hair and kissed the top of her head. "Time, perhaps, will heal his wounds. I think he has come a long way from that dreadful past. Stopping this Thaddeus from wreaking havoc on our lives will give him satisfaction and the knowledge that he will not come again."

"You are so wise. Yes, we must win through so that Fulton has a chance to be whole again."

A knock on the door heralded the arrival of their jug of hot water. Jemima went first and while she dressed, Edward shaved and made himself ready. The finishing touches to her dress were facilitated by her husband and then they quickly packed up their things.

CHAPTER 14

Fulton paced at the base of the stairs, waiting for Edward and Jemima to join him. A shadow passed over him and a tall, thin man appeared. He blinked twice before realising it was Frank, who was now dressed in a suit, having eschewed his monk's robe. If his prothesis had been working as it used to the young man might have been punched into next week. As it was, Fulton twitched, jumped back and then sighed.

"Good morning," Frank said. "Sorry to startle you."

Fulton nodded and ground his teeth. "You need to work on your entrances or you might be in danger of death."

"I beg your pardon?" Frank replied, eyes creased as if not seeing Fulton clearly.

"You surprised me. I could have lashed out, as we are all jumpy."

"Were you not expecting me?"

Fulton rolled his eyes as surely the lad was a simpleton. "Of course, I was but I supposed you would knock at the door and ask admittance not pop into existence next to me without warning."

The lad nodded vaguely, looking down his nose as if Fulton was the idiot and not himself. It was hard to believe he was a magician like Edward and Ferdinand. Yet, he must be.

Doubt lingered though. How could this callow youth help them find Thaddeus and stop him? Even with Ferdinand's endorsement, he found it hard to trust the young magician. In the back of his mind he tried to formulate a plan that would minimise harm if the lad did betray them, or failed them. Both were equally terrible prospects.

Fulton had suffered too much to go forth with an optimistic approach. He was not Jemima. He did not have her mental agility. He was firm, fixed and held to a purpose. A ghost of a smile lingered on his lips as he thought back to the shenanigans Jemima engaged in and how easily she had persuaded him to do the most outrageous things. Forged letters, lying to Aunt Prudence, spending Jemima's money and rescuing her from dangerous situations. However, he could not reproach her, for had they not recovered Edward, defeated the monster and he gained love and acceptance from Milly and even Aunt Prudence? Jemima was an instigator, an unraveller of lives and a marvel. He could not imagine life without her in it.

When Edward and Jemima joined them, Frank blurted out enthusiastically. "Is it true, Mr Huntington that you meld magic with machines? Brother Ferdinand told me."

Edward leaned forward and lowered his voice. "It is but you must not say so in a voice that people in the yard can hear you."

"I beg your pardon. Indeed, I should not. But it is so exciting. I do hope you will show me examples in action during this adventure."

Fulton hissed and balled his fist. The lad had no inkling of what he was asking. These were no toys but life-saving, life-affirming apparatuses. Frank jerked at the sound Fulton made. "You need to shut your mouth, you fool."

Frank blinked and took a step back from Fulton. A good idea, as Fulton's patience was wearing thin.

After taking a big breath, Frank continued as if there had been no interruption. "No wonder Brother Thaddeus is after your inventions, as he has always had a fascination for the mechanical. The applications are so numerous. The consequences so far-reaching."

Fulton sent a silent signal to Edward, hoping he would shut down the lad before he said more. Alas, Edward did not understand the signal and the boy went on. "I believe that your wife has such a device as well as Mr Fulton here."

Fulton growled. Edward twiddled his fingers in the air and Frank's mouth snapped shut and then his eyes bulged.

Jemima laughed to cover the situation as the server by the door looked on waiting for a command. "Please," she said to the server. "May we request a breakfast basket for the road. I fear we must make a move."

"Very well, ma'am, I will ask cook. I believe your breakfast is well in hand."

"There is a basket in the carriage."

The server bowed and presumably left to fetch their empty basket. It was not like Jemima to forget to organise things. But this delayed request appeared to be no bother to the inn.

Edward twiddled his fingers again and Frank slumped and exhaled.

"Why did you do that?" Frank asked. "I was only asking—"

"Shut up you fool," Fulton hissed out of the side of his mouth and lifted a fist in warning.

Luckily, Frank acquiesced before Fulton planted one on his pointy nose.

The four of them and their food basket gathered before the inn as their carriage was brought round. Fulton frowned and shook his head. "This will not do," he said to Edward.

"What is the matter" Edward replied.

"It is too crowded for such a long journey. Besides, it does not need the four of us to check the inn at Deddington. Perhaps our time is better spent splitting up and covering more ground."

Frank nodded and then changed his mind and shook his head. "Brother Thaddeus has estates on the outskirts of Banbury to the north. He could be in Deddington but he could have moved on and returned to his estates."

"We need to split up," Fulton said. "Edward, you and Jemima head to Deddington. Frank here will take me to a village close to Thaddeus's estates. If he is not at the inn and you have no clue as to his whereabouts, then meet us at the estate. "

"But how would we communicate?" Jemima asked. "The mail is

reliable but not timely. I do not wish to call Uncle Ferdy every five minutes and ask him to carry messages."

"Wait a minute," Frank said as he fished around in his pocket. "I might have a solution that does not involve calling Brother Ferdinand." He pulled out a gold locket and studied it. After a few moments, he lifted it up so all could see. "This trinket will allow you to contact me. Hold it, like this." He held the locket in his closed fist, closed his eyes. "And call out, Frank and what you want to say."

Frank passed the locket to Jemima, who frowned as she studied it. Fulton could see her mind working. "Can I call anyone else on this?"

His eyebrows formed a line across his eyes and he licked his lips. "'Fraid not. I made it and it is attuned to me."

Jemima nodded. "I see. Can we test this, Frank?" she asked the young magician.

"Surely we can." He looked about him. "How about we walk down the road and out of earshot?"

Fulton nodded and then asked Frank to lead the way. They walked a ways, still able to see Edward and Jemima although they had grown small to the eye. Frank came to a stop and Fulton joined him, casting his gaze across the fields, seeing sheep and the dry wall fences. He turned and surveyed the hedgerows. If anything untoward happened, they were screened from general view. They waited and then as if just remembering, Frank pulled an identical locket out of his pocket and put it around his neck. Meeting Fulton's eye, he nodded once and folded his arms.

"Frank. This is Jemima can you hear me?" The voice was so loud Fulton jumped.

"Crikey! Can you make it less loud?"

"Sorry," Frank replied and taking his locket in his hand, he answered. "We can hear you loud and clear."

"Oh this is wonderful. You must share this magic with Edward because it would be very handy. I could call Edward from anywhere in the house and grounds."

"Let's not get too carried away, Jemima," Edward said, and it sounded as if he was just standing there next to him. Fulton shivered at the uncanniness of it and then grinned as he pictured Edward trying to hide from Jemima while she called in from wherever she was. As much as they loved each other, Edward spent time alone with his thoughts, his devices and his magical study. He was sure there were secret places where Edward worked at Willow Park that Jemima had not yet uncovered.

Fulton and Frank headed back to the others. "How does it work?" Fulton asked. Despite his prostheses containing magic, he had no affinity with it.

Frank slowed his walk and faced him. "I have forged a link between the lockets, maintained by magic. As long as I live, it will keep working. I found it easy to embed magic into physical objects."

"Can you hear them by the same means?" he asked, wondering if they might be used to eavesdrop. Learning what your enemy is planning would be a big advantage.

Frank frowned. "I have not tried that, but I fear it might be an imposition. Impolite to listen in without permission."

Fulton shrugged, uncertain whether Frank not having a devious mind was an advantage or disadvantage.

"But if we need to call them, how do we do it?"

Frank nodded vigorously. "Ah ... you want to know if it works the other way. It does. Let me show you. Jemima?" he whispered, while his fist clenched on his locket. "Can you hear me?"

There was a pause before Jemima answered in a whisper. "Yes. Why are you whispering?"

Frank chuckled. "Just testing our connection. I can see you have company?"

They were closing in on Edward and Jemima and saw that there were ostlers and servants moving around them. With a sigh, he realised how difficult it might be to use such communication in normal company. On their own and with magicians it would be no cause for concern.

It was decided by Fulton that Jemima and Edward would take the carriage. "You would be more comfortable, Jemima."

"I am no fragile flower, but neither am I a horsewoman."

Fulton took himself off to enquire what could be had. There were no carriages or gigs available, particularly if they were not to be returned that day. Fulton had to hire horses to bear them on their northern journey.

When the two horses were drawn up before them on the stoop, Frank's mouth dropped open. "Cannot we hire a gig?"

Fulton drew his lips down and shook his head. "I sympathise young Frank, but this is all there is. Nothing else can be spared and we cannot wait for the mail coach."

They watched the carriage with Edward and Jemima bustle down the road.

"Do you know which direction we should take?" Fulton asked Frank.

"I do know it is near Banbury so we should take the main road and then circle round and take the northern road."

"We may need to stop before then and change horses. Perhaps secure a vehicle."

Frank's eyes lit up. "That would be most appreciated."

"I am glad you are pleased because we will be on horseback today at least." He managed to have his bag tied to the horse.

Fulton was given a boost into the saddle and the horse moved as it accommodated his weight. He held the reins with both hands, his real hand gripped for dear life and his not quite functional prosthesis held the rein loosely. He experimentally opened and closed his hand, noting that his control was improving.

Frank's face fell as his horse was drawn up in front of him. He needed a few tries of boosting him into the saddle before he gained his seat. Fulton had to look away as he did not wish to ridicule the lad, because once the boost near sent him over the horse entirely. Eventually, they were settled and on their way. Frank carried nothing with him and if the ostlers thought that was unusual they did not question it.

The ride was uncomfortable for the most part, and slow. Although mostly healed, Fulton had been abed a few days and while he rode generally well, he was not fit enough to canter or gallop and after a while the rising trot was most uncomfortable. In addition, Frank was a novice rider and getting him to trot at all was comical. They were both set for some serious saddle soreness.

Frank's frequent grimaces betrayed that he was not enjoying riding. Soon those silent facial expressions turned into vocal complaints. Moans, groans and requests to stop. Many times during that morning, Fulton wished he had not suggested the breakup of the group and wished himself squished into the carriage on his way to Deddington instead.

Hopefully they could hire equipage at the next posting house or inn. It would do them no good to arrive crippled by pain. The ride was quiet. Fulton did not care to speak much and the lad was in obvious discomfort.

On top of his discomfort, he missed Milly and Aly. Every time he pictured Milly's tears, his heart twisted. He felt so cruel to leave after what she had already endured but what was a man, a husband to do? He had to fight to make sure his family was safe and in that he had failed already. It had come to mind recently what would have happened if he had taken shelter with them in the safe room. Would the machine have tried to scoop him out like some pearl out of an oyster? Would it have been able to destroy the safe room with them inside? However, after witnessing that machine destroy his home, whoever had built that monstrosity was clever indeed and he feared what they intended. An image came to mind of indestructible magic-driven machines wreaking havoc on England, killing people, stealing from them, making them live in fear. It was like Geneck all over again, but instead of mindlessness, lust and desire for blood, this person was cold, calculated and unfeeling. The recollection of Bertrand's mutilated corpse made him shudder. The man had magic and a sick mind.

When they rebuilt Hatfield, he would need to reconsider the level of threat. Perhaps the safe room should be underground, hidden in the depths of the earth where none could get at them. Yet how long could they exist in such a place? He gave a shudder, realising he already lived in a world where such a threat existed. There had to be a balance of life and love and happiness, even though the world could be uncertain and cruel.

The machine took his arm. He supposed whoever sent it had his arm by now, as well. But whether they had by now divined Edward Huntington's secrets of manufacture was academic. A vague hope lingered that the mechanism could not be copied, that the techniques remained unfathomable. Yet, would that not then bring Edward Huntington into danger? Were Edward and Jemima riding into a trap?

He kicked his mount and said over his shoulder, "Keep up."

Frank moaned as his horse followed Fulton's lead. "We forgot to take our share of the breakfast. I am hungry."

Fulton nodded as his stomach grumbled. "I think there is an inn up ahead and we can eat there."

CHAPTER 15

Jemima missed having Fulton with them. The mood in the carriage was optimistically sombre and less crowded than it could have been. Still, after seeing Fulton so fragile, she harboured a tender feeling for him, a need to mother and nurse him, which was alien to her. How could she face Milly if anything happened to him? She could not.

The clouds overhead looked ominous and after a heavy shower, their pace slowed due to the road being soft. With a glance out the window she saw endless fields of grain and sighed, and hoped the others were faring well on the road. Perhaps the rain had passed them by.

After sharing the warm baps and cheese, she and Edward drank the ale the inn had provided and sat back and made themselves comfortable for the long ride. They stopped four times before they reached Deddington. Two breaks had been to make them comfortable in a field by the road. One was for luncheon. Jemima could not help that her stomach rumbled so much that Edward could not ignore it. The fourth stop was at the Plough Inn for the night. Jemima wished for more time to explore the town and the castle looming above them.

Tired and grumpy, they ate in a private room. For the evening meal, the inn had a thick pea and ham soup, fresh white bread and thick tasty butter. Not the finest of meals but tasty all the same. For dessert, there was creamed rice pudding and preserved plums. Simple fare that would keep them satisfied until morning.

"Our compliments to the cook," Jemima said before retiring to their room.

"Yes, thank you. Come wife, tomorrow is another day and we need to rest. Who knows what it will bring."

"I know we are tired but should we not seek answers here?"

"We will over breakfast and if there is nothing we shall begin our journey north."

"I would prefer not to delay," Jemima said and, yawning, covered her mouth.

"The answers will still be there in the morning, Jemima."

❧

Fulton and Frank made it to an inn, managed to secure rooms for the night and establish that there was a gig they could hire, at a rather high price, the next day. As they could both barely walk, although Frank was in a lot more pain, they did not care to haggle. Wet through, saddle sore and a lot worse for travel, they stopped earlier in the day than planned. Beggars as they were could not be choosers, and while he was by no means poor, Fulton agreed on the outrageous price to preserve his posterior and his dignity.

Sitting slumped in the taproom, nursing an ale and inhaling the aroma of a lamb stew, roast potatoes and bread, something occurred to Fulton. "You can travel by ..." he lowered his voice. "Magic. So why are you on the road with me?"

The barmaid was chatting noisily with a local, a farmer by the grimy smock he was wearing, who took his ale and joined his friends on a bench near the fire. It was warm in the room, slightly smoky and not well lit.

Frank lifted his head, eyelids drooping over shadowed eyes. "I cannot discharge my duty if I leave you behind. I must accompany you."

"Duty? What do you mean?" Fulton asked.

"Oh," Frank paused, licked his lips, and leaned in closer. "Brother Ferdinand required me to look out for you. I understand you are recovering from a terrible wound and have been weakened by it."

Fulton glowered. "I am not a babe in arms. You saw me today on the horse and I managed well."

Frank lifted his lips in a half-hearted smile, which quickly turned into a frown. "I did and a fine seat you have, sir. Your mood was tolerable until it rained. However, you are as miserable and sore as I am, no matter that you try to hide it."

Fulton was about to argue when the lad lifted his hand to halt his outburst. "Besides, one cannot just materialise at Thaddeus's estates. There will be wards, safeguards and hazards for the unwary. We could try and never materialise at all and end up shunted to some hell where we cease to exist as men."

"Heavens, does Huntington know this? What if he chooses to do just that?"

Frank narrowed his eyelids, his mouth pinched tight. "Quite right. We will speak with them directly and warn him against it. However, I cannot see him leaving his wife behind."

Fulton shook his head. "If I know Jemima, she is more likely to go haring off into danger or learning how to move as you do before they reach the north."

Frank nodded. "Brother Ferdinand did say she was extremely precocious." He took another sip of his ale and a spoon or two of soup. "Thaddeus might be expecting a swift response so us taking time on the road might make him relax, lower his guard."

"It is not making me relaxed. I have left my wife and child behind."

"Yes, you have and in the safe hands of Brother Ferdinand. Being unpredictable is the best way to force Brother Thaddeus into error. Taking our time will make him over-confident that we do not know who or where he is."

Fulton blinked. In that moment, he saw that Frank's outward appearance of youth hid a mature mind, a thinking mind. Digesting the younger man's words, he nodded. He did not know this Thaddeus, as a person, just the results of his work. He studied his stew. Almost too tired to eat, he forced himself to take a few spoonfuls as he needed the nourishment. It was tasty, with a surprising amount of rosemary mixed with the lamb. He took a few bites of the bread and chewed as his companion did the same.

Bread in hand, he gestured to Frank. "Thank you for coming with me and sharing the discomfort. I have to admit several times today I wished myself in the carriage with the Huntingtons."

Frank grinned. "Me too, constantly." Gingerly he moved on the bench and winced.

Fulton returned the grin. "Hopefully on the morrow we will have an easier time." He lifted his fork and finished off the remainder of his meal.

After a quick glance around the room, Frank did likewise. When the meal was finished, Fulton sat back and sipped some port, delivered by the server.

Frank did not partake, waving off the offering. When the server left, he said quietly. "I need a clear head and I already know I will sleep deeply."

Fulton lifted the glass. "After this I fear I will sleep as the dead."

Frank's eyes widened. "You should not say so. Do not tempt fate. Have you not just had a near-death experience?"

Fulton blinked, reconsidered his answer. "A log then. I am wearied unto my bones."

"Aye well, that is true for me too. I shall meet you at breakfast, around six."

"I shall be here. Pray inform Huntington of the danger of ... you know." He waved his hand like a butterfly wing.

With a nod, Frank stood, winced and wavered before he made for the door. Fulton sipped the remainder of his port, ignoring the tug of muscle in his lower back and the faint ache in his upper spine. He knew when he moved he would feel it more, and he allowed himself the weakness of postponing that sensation for as long as he could.

It was a bad decision. His muscles had seized up and he could barely straighten his back. It was an effort to stand and embarrassing to hobble toward the stairs. The barmaid narrowed her gaze at Fulton, one eyebrow lifting in query. Fulton nodded reassuringly and braved it up the stairs, suppressing the moans as he did so. When he made it to his room, he barely had the energy to undress, wash his face and clean his teeth. The bed beckoned and he toyed with the idea of sleeping in his clothes, but years of fastidious personal hygiene would not allow him to buckle. It was bad enough that he felt like dried-out horse dung, worse if he gave the appearance of it.

Dreams kept him from a restful sleep. The sound of Aly crying, the vision of Milly weeping, the echoes of Aunt Prudence chastising him. Jemima featured as well. He was chasing after her, fighting off hazards that she breezed through in a reckless manner, heedless of her own safety. Edward was not there. They were searching for him, seeking him in dark alleys, in abandoned dungeons haunted by ghosts and rattling chains. It was as if Jemima had led him into some gothic novel that he could not escape from. He sat up suddenly, winced at the movement and called out. "Edward!"

Dressing quickly, he slipped out the door and thumped three times on Frank's door before the young magician opened it. Bleary-eyed and candle in hand, Frank blinked at him. "What is it? 'Tis early yet."

Fulton barged in and Frank backpedalled. "I need to you to call Edward right now. I need to know he is safe."

"Why? Bad dream?" Frank forehead creased as if Fulton was a puzzle.

"Yes, a bad dream. A premonition. Call it what you will. I cannot rest until I know."

Nodding, Frank put his candle on the side table and drew out his locket. "Very well. It may take time to get through as they will be asleep."

Closing his eyes and clenching the locket, Frank called out in a low voice. "Mr Huntington? Can you hear me?"

There was a delay. Fulton's heart thumped, his breathing grew ragged. "Yes? What is it?" It was Edward's voice and he was annoyed. "Have you something to report?"

Frank met Fulton's glare. Fulton shrugged and inclined his head in acknowledgement. He had been wrong to call. "Ah, no," Frank replied.

"What the devil. Do you know what time it is?"

Jemima's voice murmured in the background as if she was still waking up.

"Apologies for the early hour," Frank said, diplomatically. "We wanted to check in with you as we are leaving in a few hours and we have acquired a gig to ease our way."

"And?" Huntington replied, no less irritated.

"And we need to warn you not to try transporting yourself into Brother Thaddeus's estates."

"Yes," Fulton interrupted. "There could be traps, snares, and you could end up nowhere until the end of time."

Edward scoffed. "That is a bit dramatic but thank you for the warning. We have not thought to take that route. We arrived in Deddington but are yet to question the staff for clues. We shall report in if we know anything."

Fulton nodded, relaxed, feeling his heart slow and his breathing ease. It had been just a dream, an anxiety-filled dream. With all that had happened, it was not a surprise, really. It was not like him to react that way to dreams. Circumstances were unusual, though, and he was confident he was not losing his mind. Better to know for sure.

"Apologies for disturbing you, Mr Huntington," Frank said, giving Fulton a long-suffering look.

"Yes, sorry to wake you," Fulton added.

Once Frank ended the connection, Fulton headed for the door, conscious that he owed the lad an apology but not able to form the words. "Thank you for humouring me. I will see you downstairs at breakfast."

Frank pursed his lips and then nodded. "Try to rest, Fulton."

"I will, thank you."

Frank snuffed the candle and Fulton slunk off back to his room. He had maybe an hour to rest before he needed to prepare for departure. While his immediate concerns were alleviated, there was an echo of fear in the back of his throat. Danger still stalked their steps, all the more terrifying because of its unknown source. He was no longer the confident monster slayer of the past. The giant machine that near killed him had taught him humility and fear. He hoped that it did not teach Jemima the same lesson. She would not bear it, he thought, as he drew up the bed covers.

Despite his early morning agitation, the morning passed off without incident and with a good breakfast under his belt, the peak of the pain in his muscles and limbs lessened. They headed on their way. The gig saved them saddle soreness but was by no means a luxury conveyance and very soon Fulton tired of it and grew grumpy. He was bone-weary and sick of being jostled.

They were bustling along a road. "That is the border of Thaddeus's estate."

A shot of excitement gave Fulton an increase in energy. He wanted to stop the gig, race across the road and leap the fence. Then he would hunt this Thaddeus down. Frank put his hand on Fulton's arm, drawing his gaze to the younger man. Frank shook his head. "We need a plan. We also need to hear from Mr Huntington. The map tells me there is a sizeable village a few miles hence. There we will plan."

Fulton grimaced, stared with undisguised need at the woods and fields hidden behind the perimeter wall, and then bit his bottom lip and nodded, letting that urge to act subside. His heart beat hard and fast and so did his breath. Frank was right. Fulton needed to sort out his feelings, order his thoughts and focus his anger.

"Will Edward and Jemima be able to meet us at the inn? Then we can plan."

Frank nodded. "When we have secured lodgings we can call the Huntingtons and see if they can meet us at the inn."

Fulton twitched the reins and started the horse again. "Sounds fair. If they can join us soon, it will be good. I thought they were yet to interrogate the staff at the Plough Inn. They can make better time in their carriage but can they make it all the way here from Deddington?"

At that moment, the horse shied and jerked against the traces. A wind blew up suddenly, shaking the trees, blowing leaves and branches and snatching their breaths. Branches creaked as if ready to fall and Fulton had to hold fast to the reins to keep the horse in check.

"What's that?" Fulton bellowed. Frank's eyes were wide. He moved his hands in a complicated pattern like he was weaving lace.

The wind increased and a boom echoed around them. A localised storm? Magic defences? Whatever the lad was doing was not helping. Fulton clung to his seat and tried to stop the horse from bolting. It began to scream and the sound gave Fulton's heart a start, for he had never heard such a noise before. The horse took off so fast the gig tilted and shifted. Fulton held on and tried to hold the young magician in his seat. Frank had to stop whatever spell he was casting and cling to the side of the gig lest he be tossed out.

Frank fell back and was holding on with one hand as the gig jolted along the road. The wind blew even harder and branches flew out from Thaddeus's property.

"Warding spell," Frank wheezed. "Powerful one. Reacting to my presence."

Fulton fought with the reins but the horse was spooked and all he could to was pray that a wheel did not break or that they would not be tossed in a ditch.

As it was a vast property, the warding spell arced up as they sped along the perimeter. Fulton did his best to control the horse and only the animal's desperate fatigue allowed Fulton to slow the gig. Why the wheels had not fallen off, Fulton did not know. Frank had tears and snot on his face when Fulton finally slowed them. The young man's clothing was torn and dirty. A glance behind and Fulton saw that he had lost his luggage. After what they had been through, he was not keen to fetch it back.

Climbing shakily from the gig, he inspected the wheels and went to the horse, murmuring comforting words. Sweat foamed its belly. "There, there," he said. The wind died down as the road angled away from the property. He gently led the horse by the bridle down the road, while Frank slumped in the gig. A small hamlet, not far from the village of Great Bourton, was less than an hour further along the road.

There was little to keep them there at the hamlet of Little Bourton, other than a drink and a quick meal at the Plough Inn. He lifted an eyebrow, as the name of the inn was the same as where the Huntingtons were staying. This part of Oxfordshire was a grain-growing district, so it made sense. The horse rested by a water trough and they sat around. "We need to move to Great Bourton. There is an inn there that should accommodate us all."

Glum-faced, Frank nodded. "That was surely a show of strength and I fear we have alerted our quarry to our presence."

"All the more reason to move along." Fulton let out an exhausted sigh.

Frank met his gaze. "It will not be far enough away, I fear."

"You think us in danger?" Fulton swallowed. As much as he wanted this confrontation, he wanted to be prepared and confident of success. At present, they were powerless and would likely die in the attempt.

The ride on to Great Bourton took twice as long as their horse was not able to do more than walk. Once more it was uphill, for the village sat on high ground. "Pity there was no other horse to be had in that little hamlet," Frank observed.

"It is better than using our own feet."

"Indeed it is."

It was near dark by the time they reached Great Bourton and the Red Lion Inn. Fulton had to explain his lack of luggage. Frank was able to materialise his. "I can lend you a nightshirt, Fulton."

"Thank you." He was able to request his shirt to be laundered while he was in his room.

As they were both so tired it was a toss-up whether to eat or sleep first. As it was, the hours at the inn meant that they had no choice. It was an early dinner and then to bed. Fulton also had to arrange for the return of the gig and the horse. His supply of cash was dwindling but at least it was in his pocket rather than in his missing bag.

"We can send someone to find your luggage, sir," the innkeeper said. "We should have it back around lunch time. Would that suit you?"

"Indeed it does. Thank you." Fulton followed Frank into the taproom to avail himself of an early dinner.

Later, in his room, Frank called the Huntingtons.

AT BREAKFAST THAT MORNING, JEMIMA HAD THE OPPORTUNITY TO question the maid who served them breakfast. "We did have a fellow here a few days back. Tallish fellow, dark hair. Strange thing is, he disappeared like."

"Did he leave without paying his due?"

"Oh I don't think so, ma'am. Like you, he had to pay up front like."

"So what do you mean he disappeared?"

"Well, he wasn't in his room when the maid went to bring in hot water. He never appeared for breakfast and no one saw him leave."

"How did he arrive then?" Jemima asked.

"He was dropped off, I collect. In a carriage, but the carriage did not stop here."

"He did not hire a horse or a gig or anything?"

"No, ma'am and that's what had us scratching our heads. He was gone. His luggage was gone but no one saw him leave. It was as if he disappeared into thin air."

"Mmm," Jemima said and took a sip of tea. "Thank you."

Edward joined her not long after. He had been talking to the ostlers and the grooms. "What did you find out?" he asked her, taking a cup of tea from her hand and snaffling hot rolls with the other.

"He disappeared as if into thin air." She snapped her fingers.

Edward buttered a roll and looked up. "Yes, that is what the lads in the yard told me too."

"Did he give a name?" Jemima asked, taking a roll onto her own plate.

"A Mr Cobb, apparently." Edward bit into the roll and his eyes crossed with delight.

"A false name, but otherwise fits our description. The use of magic to travel is a sure sign."

Edward swallowed and had his eye on another roll. Jemima scooped some bramble jam onto hers. "Or there is a portal hereabouts?" he said.

Jemima nearly choked. "A ppportal? I hesitate to ask what that is?"

"A permanent vortex in which to travel magically."

"I do not like the sound of that."

Edward was well in the way of disposing of his second bread roll, when the maid brought in a dish of scrambled eggs and side of sausages. The eating of these forestalled conversation.

Edward sat back and patted his stomach. "I shall grow big if I keep eating like that."

Jemima lowered her cup and it tinkled on the saucer. "Why have I not heard of these portals before?"

"Oh, I only just theorised their existence."

Jemima put her cup down and stared. "Theorised? Edward, I know you are clever and all that but what made you think of such a thing?"

Edward poured himself a cup and sighed. "Because I found the opening in the wardrobe in our room. It is not visible to the naked eye but I felt it."

"What? Where does it go? We cannot use it surely."

Edward rolled his eyes. "When we go to collect our belongings, I will show you. And I agree we cannot use it because we might end up in Thaddeus's lair and caught in a trap."

"Most definitely, for surely he knew he would be followed."

"That means you must spend more time in a carriage and on the road."

The trip back to the room was uneventful. Jemima closed her eyes and put out her hand to see if she could sense the portal. All she detected was a slight frisson on her extended fingertips. "What does it feel like to you?" she asked her husband.

"Like a throbbing maw of magic."

Jemima pouted. "I am not sensitive enough. I would not have known what it was had I encountered it. I feel so inferior."

"It takes time," Edward said, drawing her into his embrace. "You must have patience."

Jemima laughed and pulled away. "You know that is a virtue I do not have. Let us depart this place and head north. It will be good to see Fulton again."

They left the inn and headed north, keen to be on their companions' trail. "Banbury is not more than six miles but as we are bypassing it, we should arrive near the evening in the north. I hope Frank gives us their direction."

A broken wheel skewered their plans. Lucky it was in the village of Bodicote and they were able to get assistance from the inn.

"We'll have it fixed in no time, sir," said the innkeeper. "Perhaps you can rest inside while you wait."

Edward bit his lip. "I fear we must request a room for the night as we will be delayed and there is no moon tonight."

The innkeeper seemed pleased with that. "The best room for you, sir, and if you would like to step into the private sitting room, we will bring your things up shortly."

Jemima put her arm in the crook of Edward's elbow. "We are close now. Perhaps we should call Fulton and Frank to let them know we are delayed."

Edward ushered Jemima into the private room and assisted her to a seat. She was feeling around in her reticule when Frank's voice sounded. "Can you hear me?" Frank said in a whisper.

"Yes," Jemima responded. "We can hear you."

Frank told them of the freak storm on the edge of Thaddeus's estate and how he surmised it was a ward reacting to his presence. "And you are unharmed by this?" Jemima asked.

"Yes, quite well. The horse may never be the same again. It will be rested before returning to its owner."

"So you retreated to Great Bourton? We are not too far from you. We had an accident with the wheel of our carriage and are in a small, quaint village called Bodicote."

"I know it."

Edward told them of the suspected portal.

"I have never heard of such a thing," Frank exclaimed.

"You be careful, Huntington!" Fulton said. "This is one powerful character. Who knows what his next move will be and what he knows."

"Knows?" Jemima asked.

"Knows about our plans," Fulton explained. "You see, he must have noticed us there. We were nearly done away with during that brutal, magical storm."

Edward was stroking his chin with forefinger and thumb. "Mmm. We shall rendezvous with you tomorrow before noon. Then we shall plan our attack. Other than that, be watchful and alert us if anything untoward happens."

They agreed and Jemima pushed the locket back into the small fabric purse. "We should have asked Frank about the estate, entrances, the size of the buildings and so on."

"What makes you think he would know that?"

Jemima shrugged. "He seems to know a lot about Brother Thaddeus so I was wondering if he had ever been there."

Edward smiled and touched her chin. "My dear Jemima, I hear the suspicion in your voice. We shall ask Frank tomorrow face to face and you can get a feel for his honesty or not."

"That will have to do, I am afraid. And I will have to trust that Fulton can take care of himself."

The next morning after a hearty breakfast. Jemima left the room to make herself comfortable for the next leg of the journey. Edward was sitting on a settee, small notebook in hand and scribbling notes. Her carpet bag lay propped against his leg. She had what she needed in a drawstring bag. The ladies' retiring room was not spacious and her skirts were copious. However, after much fiddling about she was done. On entering the room, she found Edward gone. "Edward?"

She pushed her little bag into the cloth bag and picked up his notebook, which lay open on the settee. The pen was on the floor so she dipped to collect that too as she looked around the room. "Edward!"

With no answer, she poked her head through the internal doorways to catch sight of him. However, he was nowhere to be seen. She waved over the landlady. "Pray excuse me. Have you seen my husband? Tallish fellow, brown curls, blue eyes and fairly tall. He was wearing a brown coat and trousers."

The woman, somewhat shorter than Jemima, creased her brow and shook her head until her cheeks wobbled. "'Fraid not ma'am. He might be in the yard or already in your coach."

Jemima frowned. It was not like Edward to leave her behind or to wander off without announcing his intention. She took the landlady's advice and stepped into the yard.

The noise assaulted her ears. Horses tramping, blowing steam, whinnying. Ostlers calling to each other. Tackle jangling. Travellers issuing orders for their trunks, or a cup of ale. Children squealing as they played in the yard. She cocked her head and looked to all the possible places he could be. She then made enquiries. After twenty minutes it was apparent that Edward had not been in the yard, nor had he been seen at all. She reversed her steps to the room where she left him.

After staring at the spot where he had sat, she rubbed her chin. He would not have moved himself away by magical means without telling her. He would not leave her to shift for herself. He would not leave their belongings unattended. That meant he had been removed by magical means. She picked up the notebook and opened it. The last sentence was only half written and the last word had a great sprawl as if the pen had slipped, dashing ink everywhere. Edward had not left of his own accord.

The innkeeper came in. "May I help you ma'am?"

"Well, I ... did you see where my husband went?"

"Mr Huntington?" He looked around the room, which aside from a few furnishings was empty. "He was sitting right here last time I looked."

Jemima bit her lip. "Do you mind if I go in search of him?"

"Not at all. I shall search myself."

Some twenty minutes later, Jemima was back at the carriage, their luggage loaded and no Edward. Now it was time to panic. He would not have left her without a word and as he was not here that meant he was gone. Taken.

"Perhaps he has taken a walk. Wait another ten minutes," the innkeeper suggested.

Jemima consulted Mr Coachman. "Will the horses be all right?"

"I shall walk them, Mrs Huntington, and I will await your orders when I return."

Jemima wondered what she should do next. Obviously they were close. Otherwise why remove Edward. Why not take her? Drawing out her kerchief, she blew her nose and sniffed. What would happen to Edward if she was not there to protect him? All kinds of sinister thoughts pressed into her mind. There was nothing for it. She would have to drive herself to Great Bourton.

Mr Coachman returned. "Will not the master be joining us, Mrs Huntington?" he asked.

Jemima flashed a smile and tried to appear content. "He has gone on ahead and I am to meet up with him." She generously tipped the ostler and a footman handed her into the carriage. "When you are ready Mr Coachman. Next stop is Great Bourton to meet with my friends."

"Right you are, ma'am."

After some last minute tightening of the traces, the carriage lurched forward. Jemima tried to keep her mind calm and her worry at bay. Edward could look after himself. Edward will not come to harm. Indeed, it was Thaddeus who should be afraid of what Edward would do to him. She clutched the locket, wondering when was the best time to inform Fulton and Frank of the situation.

THE SOLO TRIP IN THE CARRIAGE SEEMED TO TAKE FOREVER. JEMIMA ruined several handkerchiefs, wracked with guilt at leaving Edward behind and full of anticipation in seeing Fulton and knowing he would help. Resting easy was out of the question as she hoped that Edward would just pop back in. Unfortunately he did not. The locket conversation with Fulton and Frank was garbled. She knew it, as she had been barely coherent. By the time she pulled up at the inn in Great Bourton, she was a mess. When Fulton snatched open the door, she fell on him in tears.

Fulton fell back. "Edward is missing? Tell me all."

In the background Frank lingered. "Oh, that's what she was saying."

Jemima shot Frank a withering look. "Yes, he just vanished. I went to the retiring room for a few minutes as we were ready to depart and he was not there. I had the whole inn searching. No one saw him walk out and the entrance had a watchman there the whole time." She twisted the damp handkerchief. "The inn was in an uproar. I was beside myself with worry." Wiping the tears from her eyes, she peered in Fulton's bright amber eyes. "I fear Brother Thaddeus must have him."

Fulton squeezed her shoulder and nodded to the footman so they could unpack her luggage. Turning on his heel, he faced Frank. "You did not tell me that Brother Thaddeus could transport himself and another?"

Frank back peddled in the face of Fulton's wrath. He held up his hands in defence. "I did not know. We know there was a portal in Deddington. Perhaps there is another in the last inn they were at."

Jemima glared at him and Frank lowered his gaze. "Are you telling us the truth? Can this Brother Thaddeus come here and snatch one of us at any time he chooses?"

Frank shook his head and shrugged. "Theoretically, yes. Obviously, Brother Thaddeus has what he wants now he has Mr Huntington."

Jemima narrowed her eyelids. "And I have delivered him. I have given him the very thing he craved."

CHAPTER 16

Jemima's statement was like a punch in the gut. Fulton drew her close, hoping to sooth her spirits. "We will get him back. Calm yourself. You need to think clearly. What do you mean delivered him?"

Jemima pulled back, lifted a handkerchief and blew her nose. He could see hers was barely fit for the task and handed his over. She took it with a nod and wiped her bloodshot eyes. He had never seen Jemima look so haggard. "Our renegade magician cannot learn the trick of Edward's devices from the device itself so he has abducted him and will probably torture him to get the secret."

Fulton clasped her by the shoulders, trying to appear strong and brave but was floored by Jemima's theory. He had lost an arm, with no heed to his life. What would this Brother Thaddeus do to Edward? He had murdered the fake heir and innocent bystanders. The fiend would not stop until he had what he wanted. Yet stand against him they must. Not just for Edward but for those who would be his victims. Hatfield had been destroyed. What was to stop the fellow crushing a village, annihilating a town, attacking the city? Just them. Jemima, Frank and himself, with the aid of Edward if they could recover him in time.

His gaze settled on Jemima. Dishevelled and worn from her journey, she looked fragile. Surely it would be best to send Jemima away, to where it was safe. He squashed that idea straight up. Futile to even think he could send Jemima anywhere or worse, tell her what to do. Despite his protective instincts toward her, she was their best weapon. There was so much magic stored in her that he would be a fool to ignore the potential. Combined with a good mind and courage, she was an asset. Their best asset.

He thought back to when they found Edward unconscious and hexed. Had they disturbed the plot in progress? Had the plan been then to take Edward? Had they been watched even then? A shiver of fright raced up his spine. Danger had been so close and he had not acted, had not even noticed. Sure he had just risen from his sick bed, but that was an excuse he would not accept.

The coachman drove the carriage to where the ostlers directed and saw to the care of the horses. By the odd looks in their direction, Mr Coachman was curious about what was going on. Fulton hoped he could rely on his discretion. Losing Mr Huntington was not easy to overlook and it seemed that Jemima had not even tried to fabricate a reason for Huntington's departure, leaving the coachman and the footman perplexed as to his whereabouts.

"Come," Fulton ordered Frank, who was clenching and unclenching his hands as if he was about to be caned by the schoolmaster. Jemima had been fierce in her accusations to be sure. Someone not used to her might take her the wrong way. This was the most distraught he had seen her. Edward had been snatched and she had no way of knowing how he was or the means to prevent him from coming to harm.

Guiding Jemima inside, he urged her to sit in the parlour they had hired. "Rest a bit. You are with friends now. We shall eat and we shall plan."

Jemima lifted her head. "Honestly, Fulton I do not think I could take a bite."

"Some broth then, some bread. Something light to fortify you, for you have had a long, tedious journey, full of anxiety."

She nodded her complacence and he turned to their companion. "Frank? What will you have?" Fulton said gruffly. The lad was young and it was difficult to blame him. Jemima had spoken to him harshly and it was up to Fulton to smooth the way, as there was no point in alienating him if they wanted information. It was up to them to ask better questions.

Frank looked between them. "Whatever is on offer."

"Right then." Fulton left the room to order their food.

When he returned, Jemima was wiping tears from her eyes and Frank was at the window staring into the yard.

"Dinner is likely to take an hour to arrive. I have ordered tea and scones. Enough to fortify us until then." He smiled down at Jemima and the grimace she supplied in return turned his belly to water.

"Frank, come and sit with us. We need to pick your brain."

Frank sat himself down and nodded to Fulton.

"So Frank. Brother Ferdinand," Fulton said. "Sent you to us for a reason. Now is the time to find out what that is."

Frank stared, open-mouthed. "Reason?"

"Yes, you were Brother Bertrand's cousin, nothing too sensational in that. You know Brother Thaddeus, worked with him perhaps?"

Frank nodded glumly. "Yes, on a few experiments. Just an extra pair of hands. I was not his confidant or close associate. He did not include me in discussions or his plans."

Fulton bowed his head and then lifted his eyes to the young brother. "Have you been to Brother Thaddeus's estate?"

Frank sat back, eyes wide. "Yes, on one occasion only."

Jemima dropped the handkerchief that she had screwed into a ball and shifted to the edge of the seat. "That is one more than either of us," she said.

Frank lifted a finger to halt their verbal assault. "There is one big problem."

Fulton tilted his head. "What problem is that?"

"Brother Thaddeus wiped my memory. He used a spell and while I recall being there, the details are smudged."

Fulton deflated. "You cannot remember any details?"

"I can remember some but I cannot trust what I do remember."

"Did Uncle Ferdy know this?" Jemima asked.

Frank turned to her. "I believe so."

Jemima faced Fulton, a quizzical gleam in her eyes. "So Brother Thaddeus knows we have Frank with us and knows that Frank can tell us nothing, other than where his estate is. Frank could have told us without accompanying us. I agree Uncle Ferdy sent him for a reason."

Fulton frowned and rubbed his head, which needed a shave. "We will have to ask him then."

Jemima nodded. "Indeed we do but not here in the parlour."

A knock at the door heralded the arrival of tea and scones. Fulton was so hungry he could have eaten a plateful. As it was he had to moderate his intake and share with Jemima and Frank. The young magician wolfed them down as if it was to be his last meal. Perhaps that was the right approach. It could well be their last meal.

"The ward detected you, did it not?" Jemima asked Frank when she poured her second cup.

"Yes, it reacted to me."

"Is that normal? Would it react that way to anyone? Or only to a magician? Or particular people?" She pointed to herself and then to Fulton.

Frank blinked. "Good question. I thought it was only to me because I am a magician. However, the ward could be attuned to anyone."

Fulton sat forward. "The man they sent to retrieve my bag on the road said nothing untoward happened so I am guessing the ward did not react to him."

Jemima nodded slowly. "Do you recall the layout of the house? How far from the perimeter is the house?"

Frank shook his head. "No."

A knock at the door and a servant came to retrieve the tea things and then another came to set the table as a preface to them being served, which meant all discussion about magic and breaking into Brother Thaddeus's manor house had to be suspended.

Jemima ate her soup and some bread and was eventually persuaded to have some fish and taste the side dishes of creamed fennel and roasted potatoes. Satisfied that she was not about to pass out from hunger, Fulton let her decide if she would eat some jellied fruits and whipped cream for dessert. These she passed on, leaving it to him and Frank to do justice to the dessert.

Just before the server left Jemima halted her. "Pray, do you know the Danverville estate at all?"

"Yes, ma'am. I was born there. My father was the coachman."

"Is it a long drive from the gates to the house? I thought we could seek to view the house while we are in the neighbourhood."

The woman frowned. "Not above half a mile, ma'am. But they don't take to visitors there. There's no housekeeper at all. Just the old butler now and a few manservants."

"Oh pity, I hear it is a good example of ironstone construction common to these parts."

""Tis, Ma'am, but in poor repair."

Jemima smiled and thanked the woman, who left promptly.

"Now then," Fulton said. "What is your plan Jemima? I can see it behind your eyes."

Jemima gave a small smile. "We need to retire to our rooms. I suggest we meet in yours, Fulton."

☙❧

FULTON'S ROOM WAS NOT BIG. JEMIMA SAT ON THE BED, HE IN THE corner and Frank leaned against the door. "We must call Uncle Ferdy," Jemima stated.

"What can he do?" Fulton asked.

"I cannot see how he can help," Frank said with a whine in his voice.

"Uncle Ferdy? Are you listening?"

Jemima kicked her feet as they waited. She tried once more and then the older magician appeared. He smiled at them, inclined his head to Frank and Fulton. To Jemima he bowed then took her hand. "I am sorry that Edward is no longer with you."

Jemima's eyes widened and then she bit her lip. "He is still in life, uncle. It would not serve Brother Thaddeus to kill him. Edward is the centre of this."

"I know, Jemima. I felt your distress but did not intrude until you called for me. How can I help?"

Jemima's eyes narrowed and Fulton would not be surprised if there had been a list written inside her eyelids. "Can you lift this spell that Thaddeus placed on Frank? Frank has been inside the Danverville Estate but cannot remember the details."

Frank nodded.

"I can try but I did not notice any spells on him." Uncle Ferdy gestured to Frank, urging him closer with his hand. Frank rolled his eyes but obeyed the silent summons. Uncle Ferdy took Frank's head in his hands. "Mmm I can detect no spell."

Jemima nodded. "Frank, try to remember the details of your visit with brother Thaddeus."

Frank grimaced and closed his eyes. Uncle Ferdy still had his hands on the lad's temples and had closed his eyes as well. After a moment, he nodded slowly. "Ah I see it now. Let me ..."

Frank jumped back as if slapped. "What did you do?"

Uncle Ferdy looked down at the ground and frowned. "Your memory was there, Frank. But there was a confundus on it, which means that the memory was scrambled. That is why you thought it was taken from you."

"Scrambled as in rearranged?" Frank asked.

Uncle Ferdy nodded. "Try to recollect your visit now, from your first arrival through the gates."

Frank closed his eyes again, forehead wrinkling in the effort. "We drove through the gates, down the drive. I remember the noise of the loose stones. It is not far to the front of the house. However, we drove to the back of the house." Frank's breathing ratcheted up a notch. "There was a door in the earth. Brother Thaddeus opened it with a word. I went down into the dark with him."

Frank opened his eyes. "I did not enter the main house at all. Just some ancient dungeon below the ground."

Uncle Ferdy nodded. "How did you leave?"

Frank blinked. "I do not know. I woke up in the carriage leaving through the gates." He looked between Jemima and Fulton. "I do not even know what I did there or for how long."

"When you returned to the Priory did you do an accounting then of the time?"

Frank nodded, and wiped at the sweat beading on his forehead. "Yes, I had been gone a week exactly. Two days for travel both ways, leaves three days that I do not remember."

Jemima glanced between the magicians. "But you said his memory was there but scrambled. Is that it?"

Uncle Ferdy sat on the bed next to her. "Part of his memory was scrambled. However beneath that, whatever Frank did once he was there is gone, taken from him and the rest disguised."

Jemima huffed out a breath and twisted a curl around a finger. "Well, we have something, we know we need to go underground." She turned to Uncle Ferdy. "There is a ward. Will it react to us?"

Her uncle frowned and pulled at his bottom lip. He looked to Frank and then back at Jemima. "I can only theorise that Thaddeus had placed recognition of Frank on the ward so that if he came back uninvited it would alert him and deter any ingress."

"So it was not reacting to Fulton?"

Uncle Ferdy shrugged. "Without vigorous study I cannot know for certain. It is obviously not a general ward because deliveries can be made and servants come and go. Frank had passed through the ward previously so the spell that maintains it would recognise him according to the instructions given it. A general repulsing ward would keep everyone out."

Jemima nodded. "So Fulton and I could enter without the ward reacting?"

"It seems so, yes."

"What about you Uncle Ferdy? Have you been to Danverville Estate before?"

Uncle Ferdy stilled, then let out a slow breath. Screwing up his face, his puzzlement was obvious. "Now that you ask, all I can say is I do not know."

Jemima cheek dimpled. "That is a 'yes' then. If you had not you could say so directly."

Fulton's frown deepened. "You mean both of them have been here before?"

Jemima nodded. "And both cannot come with us if the theory of the ward is correct."

⁂

FULTON SENSED JEMIMA WANTED TO SAY MORE AND HER thoughtful expression gave him the idea that she did not trust her magician friends. If she did not trust them, then Fulton certainly did not either. However, that left them under-resourced to attempt a rescue.

Brother Ferdinand still pulled at his bottom lip and then with a sigh he got up from the bed. "I must return to Kiddlington and continue my ..."

"No, you do not." Jemima said, grabbing a hold of the old magician's lapels. "You leave them alone."

"Alone? But Jemima I am looking after them. Aunt Prudence will be most disappointed if I do not return."

"I think not. Face it, Uncle Ferdy. You are compromised."

"Me, no. Not possible."

But Jemima shook her head, and Fulton's heart rate quickened. It was not like Jemima to accuse without reason, particularly her Uncle Ferdy. Had he left his wife and child vulnerable all this time?

"Entirely possible. I did wonder when Sir Giles offered them a house in the village. You were against it. I thought at first it was a rivalry. However, common sense prevailed and Sir Giles was able to move them into Frobisher Manor. I assume you are still staying at the inn."

Fulton's fist clenched. Surely, the old magician had not wanted to harm his family. Outrage was filling up his chest, making it hard to breathe.

"You cannot know what you are saying, Jemima. Yes, I am at the inn."

"Aunt Prudence invited to you join them, did she not?"

Brother Ferdinand's fist clenched. "She did, yes, but as I did not want to impose I remained at the inn."

"No, you are at the inn because that is how Brother Thaddeus can find you. He can get word to you easily. Letting the women move had set his plans awry."

"No!" Fulton exploded but one look from Jemima held him.

Brother Ferdinand shook his head, sweat beaded on his forehead. "No, I could never harm them."

"Frank would you be so kind as to check Brother Ferdinand's memory," Fulton said. "Perhaps you can shed light on this."

Frank nodded and moved closer to the older magician. Brother Ferdinand's body quivered once and Jemima put her hand on his shoulder as if holding him in place. "No, Uncle Ferdy. Stay."

She kept hold of him as Frank undertook an examination of Brother Ferdinand's mind. The boy's eyebrows lifted up and down and sideways and his lips moved as if he was chewing a very tough steak. "There."

Brother Ferdinand gaped at them. "No, I can be trusted."

"Frank?" Fulton asked.

"It is subtle, so faint I nearly missed it, which is why I checked again. There is a faint thread of compulsion in Brother Ferdinand's mind."

"Can you tell what it does?" Jemima asked.

Frank shook his head. "Just the flavour of it. It is like a coil of dark malice."

"And?" Fulton asked.

"Brother Thaddeus."

"Can you remove it?" Jemima asked Frank.

"Me? I have never tried." He studied Brother Ferdinand who was now writhing in Jemima's grip, tears bleeding down his weathered cheeks.

Jemima locked gazes with Fulton. "We cannot just let him go. We do not know what the compulsion is. What about another command."

Frank's head jerked back. "Like what exactly."

"How about sending him to sleep for, say, three days?" Jemima suggested.

Brother Ferdinand spluttered. "You cannot put me to sleep for three days. Fulton, what if harm comes to your wife, Fulton, your child? I will be powerless to protect them."

Fulton unclenched his hands. "Do not underestimate my wife or Aunt Prudence. I have seen them skewer felons with hat pins."

Brother Ferdinand gulped and tried to plead with Jemima. "Please, dear girl. You cannot do this. Am I not your Uncle Ferdy? Even if there is a light compulsion, he could not force me to harm anyone as my own inner moral code would not allow him."

Jemima eyed him. "We cannot risk it. I am sorry." To Frank she said. "Spell him to sleep for two days and let us hope we are finished with this business by then."

"Dear boy, I recommended you for this task. You cannot think that I ..."

Too late. Frank had actioned the spell and Ferdinand fell back on Fulton's bed. Fulton watched as Jemima and Frank made him comfortable. How he was going to explain a stranger in his bed, he did not know but he guessed he would think of something. He would just have to think like Jemima and pull whatever came to mind and make it sound plausible.

Jemima reached for Frank's hand. "Is there anyone you can trust to remove this compulsion thread?"

Frank glanced up surprised and swallowed. "Yes, but I can learn to do it myself given time."

Jemima blew out a breath making her lips vibrate. Very unladylike.

Fulton stood. "Jemima?" He knew that scheming look.

"I have an idea. Perhaps we should go to Frank's room."

Frank nodded. "Right oh then." With one last look at Brother Ferdinand, Frank led them to his room. After they entered and Frank shoved a shirt under the pillows, Jemima began. "Frank, we need you to create a diversion."

Fulton tilted his head, following where he thought her plan lay. "We need him with us."

Jemima met his eye and shook her head. "Compromised, he is no use to us. We know all that he knows but if he sets off the ward, say at the main gates, then that will distract Brother Thaddeus and allow us to enter by another gate."

Fulton pushed out his bottom lip as he considered this. "And if the ward reacts to us?"

Jemima pushed off the bed, took a step and turned. "If it does, Fulton, then we are stymied. We will not be able to enter, not with stealth at least."

Fulton blew out a breath. "It is a trap." He shrugged as there was not much they could do about that. Not with Huntington's life in the balance.

"Perhaps, because we have to leave our magical assistance behind. But he cannot know what I am capable of."

Fulton drew his head back. "What are you capable of?" He had not seen her in action since she absorbed the emerald fire from Geneck. Healing yes, fighting no.

Jemima shrugged. "I have no idea what my limits are. I have been learning to use the magic in me. I helped heal you. That was actually very hard and required a great deal of concentration. Uncle Ferdy helped me remove the hex from Edward. As to strength, I shifted roof beams and heavy furniture at your house."

Fulton drummed his fingers, like a fickle tempest beating on a window pane. "I take it your plan is for us to walk up to the manor house and ask to see Brother Thaddeus."

"That is too polite. No, I thought that while he is distracted by Frank trying to get through his ward, we would already be there by the back door to his dungeons or laboratories and take him by surprise."

"And if it is a trap?" Fulton asked.

"Then we spring it. Leaving Edward there is not an option."

Fulton nodded. He could think of nothing better. Using Frank worried him as the lad was young and he did not wish the boy ill. Brother Ferdinand, too, did not consent to being made to sleep but he could not fault Jemima's logic. If Brother Ferdinand were compromised then there was nothing for it.

What if this Thaddeus did something to his own mind? As he considered this possibility, he thought that it could not be much worse than having his arm ripped from his body, his house destroyed and him left bleeding out in the wreckage. He could not let Edward suffer, or for him to yield up his secrets. He doubted Edward had secrets as collaborating with others is what he had been doing at the Priory in the last six months. Obviously Thaddeus thought otherwise.

Often Fulton did wonder if Edward actually knew what his own secret was. While other magicians had built machines, none could be powered for as long as Edward's creations. Also, those that studied what Edward was doing were making standalone machines and not machines that were part of someone, like his arm, his leg and Jemima's Ruby Heart.

Letting his anxieties fade, he grew resolute and rubbed his hands together. "What are we waiting for?"

Jemima grinned. "I must change out of my travelling dress." She lifted the watch at her waist. "I think we need the cover of darkness and we will need supplies."

Fulton frowned. "What do you have in mind?"

"We are going into a dark hole in the ground. I think we need rope and um ..." she looked around the room as if for inspiration.

Fulton caught on. "A grappling hook, in case we need to climb out. Lights."

"I can possibly manage a light but we should bring a lantern as we do not want to give the game away too soon."

"What should I do?" Frank asked.

Fulton studied him. "Dress warmly."

"What about the locket?" Jemima asked, lifting it out of her bodice. "Do we need to make contact? I wonder if this could be used against us."

Fulton sighed. "You make a good point. Frank, what do you think?"

The lad straightened his spine. "If I am captured while I am triggering the ward, I might be forced to call out to you, or give you the wrong information."

Fulton nodded, and clenched his jaw.

"Can we not use a code?" Jemima asked.

Frank agreed enthusiastically.

"I have told you before you read too many novels, Jemima."

Jemima gave him a long-suffering look as if he said that to her every day for no purpose. "Code?" She prompted.

Frank rubbed his chin and licked his lips. "What about Uncle Ferdy is awake?"

Fulton mused over this. It was innocuous enough. "That would signify you have been captured?"

Frank lifted a shoulder. "I think so."

Fulton met Jemima's forthright look. "Well?"

"It is too long."

"Right then." Fulton tried thinking. "You may as well say Monkey!" He was out of ideas.

"Close, I think. What about a number. One that is not associated with any of this."

Frank nodded. "Eleven."

Jemima considered this. "Too many syllables. Ten is too obvious. One is too colloquial. Six is best I think."

Fulton wobbled his head, trying to think that through. Six was not that easily worked into conversation and random enough. It was not likely that Frank would use it otherwise.

"Right then, six it is. Six will tell us you have been captured or compromised."

Frank swallowed his Adam's apple bobbing with the effort. "Six."

"After you tell us 'six' we will ignore everything else you say."

"Really? But what if I am saying the truth?"

"Listen, Frank. You only say six if you are compromised. That means captured, or someone is about to spell you. After that we cannot rely on anything you say. It could be coerced out of you, or a spell that distorts your mind."

Frank sagged. "I do not like this plan. But as I cannot approach the estate without upsetting the ward, then I have no choice. Six it is."

"Can you make a hole in the ward for us to step through?" Jemima asked.

Frank did a double take. "Not easily. I thought you were going to sneak in while I distracted Thaddeus."

"Plan B, Frank. If we cannot get through the ward we will need help."

Fulton narrowed his gaze. "Do you have Edward's belongings?"

Jemima swung toward him. "Yes, of course." Her eyes widened.

"You mean his warding stones?" She grew silent. "I take it that we make our own ward using Edward's stones within the ward barrier and go through that."

Frank drew back, mouth agape. "That is not standard practice."

Jemima lifted her lips in a smile. "But it will work in theory."

Frank nodded. "Yes, a diabolical theory."

CHAPTER 17

Jemima and Fulton dropped Frank near the edge of the walls surrounding Thaddeus's estate. Not close enough to trigger the ward and not too far that Frank would be tired by the time he triggered the ward. Jemima held her breath in case their presence set off the ward. Nothing untoward happened. Fulton gave Frank a salute and drove them further along the road. They passed along the road as Fulton had done previously and all was quiet.

"Let us get into position, Fulton," Jemima said.

The gig they were riding in was excess to requirements at this stage. They could not leave the horse tied up with the gig attached.

"Shall I send it home, Jemima?"

She nodded. "If we get out of this, a walk to the inn will be the least of our worries. Besides, Frank can transport and so can Edward."

Fulton turned the gig, leading the horse by the bridle. Facing back the way they came, he slapped the horse and it bolted down the road. She suspected that once it was in familiar territory it would take itself to the yard. Jemima held a sack with their equipment in one hand and the lantern, low-lit in, the other.

A crack of thunder made her start. "The ward?"

"Yes," Fulton said. "We must hurry. Can you activate the stones?"

Jemima dug them out of the pocket of her leather coat as she walked closer to the wall. A tingle on her skin let her know she was next to the ward. "Fulton take that stone and place it there."

She pointed a few steps away. Fulton did as instructed. Then she took the one she held and rubbed it as she had seen Edward do and laid it on the ground. The tingling sensation intensified. "Can you feel that?"

Fulton shook his head. She must be attuned to the magic. With her hand outstretched, she put her hand through the ward she had created and touched the stone wall. A rush of relief washed out of her. "It worked." She tossed their bag of equipment over the wall and it landed with a thunk.

A flash of lighting drew their attention. A scream pierced the night. "Quickly," Jemima urged. Fulton put his hands together so she could get a leg up. She bounded up and caught the edge of the wall. Turning her body, she got her legs over and then reached down for him. Lantern in one hand, Fulton took it at a run, grabbed her hand with his spare and leaped. His leg propelled him over her head and their clasped hands meant he took her with him. He landed neatly, one leg in a kneeling position, dropped the lantern and caught Jemima as she fell.

They were in. Jemima theatrically wiped invisible debris from her arms and legs after Fulton caught her. His manoeuvre had not been anticipated and she had experienced a moment of panic.

Another scream and rumble of thunder let them know that Frank was still occupied. "Let us hurry. We do not have much time."

"Indeed," Fulton said. He snatched up the bag of equipment and bolted. Jemima snagged the lantern as she ran after him. Once Frank was caught, which there was no doubt he would be, they would have no time to get into position.

"What if Frank is caught and reveals our plans?"

"He has a spell that can prevent him talking. It cannot prevent him being coerced into doing something. Once he yells 'six' then we are on our own."

The path to the rear of the house was clear. They searched the ground for the doors that Frank had described. They were well disguised. A random footprint alerted her to its position. "Look Fulton, there."

Fulton switched directions, then hastily knelt in the dirt. He ran his fingers along the edge of the doors. "Here it is." He tried to rip them open with his hands and they did not budge.

"There must be a spell on them or they are jammed." Jemima knelt too and tried to see into the doors, see the magic. It was no use. She could see nothing. So she followed Uncle Ferdy's advice and tried to sense it. There it was, like a blanket over the door. She put her fingers along the edge of it. Not unlike the hex that had buried Edward in sleep. This was only a single layer. She managed to get a grip on it and tugged. It resisted at first and she bent her mind to it. Uncle Ferdy had said an incantation. She had no incantations. "Come away, my lovely," she said and then tugged. It worked.

"Quickly," Jemima hissed.

Fulton wrenched the doors open and then felt with his hands. "A metal ladder."

He turned and with the bag of equipment over his shoulder, he scrambled down. Jemima picked up the lantern, turned up the flame and followed him. The stink of stagnant water overwhelmed her. Her reaction was stronger that it normally would be. She had been in the sewers of London and not felt so nauseated.

Fulton grabbed the hand with the lantern and lifted it. It was a stone-lined tunnel, not too high but enough for them to navigate with ease.

The tunnel went in the direction of the house, so they were walking under it, rather than away. She suspected there was another entrance. Then out of the air above their heads, Frank's voice called, "Six!"

Fulton glanced back at her and shook his head. They were on their own. Jemima closed her eyes and prayed that Frank would be all right. Trying to communicate now would unravel all their plans so she bit her lip and continued on.

Another doorway loomed. Jemima put her ear to it. Nothing that she could hear, but the smell was different now. Like burnt metal. She sniffed and Fulton shook his head. He gripped the door and pulled it open.

A red glow swirled along the ceiling and as they walked further in, the floor changed from dirt to metal. Their boots clanked. As there was enough light to see, she turned down the lamp, wishing she could hide it for later, if there was a later.

The room was filled with long lengths of shiny metal interspersed with rusty scrap. Piles of it, some leaning in the corner, some big flat bits stacked on top of one another. A pulse of warm air snagged her attention.

"A furnace," Fulton whispered.

It made sense that a magician who made machines needed metal and the means to shape it. Perhaps he had assistants for that menial part.

They passed through the doorway into another part of the laboratory. Her eyes were eager to see Edward and only the chance of premature discovery prevented her calling out his name. Jemima walked through the next door, felt a tingle and whirled. Too late. The door snapped shut, leaving her on one side and Fulton on the other. They were discovered.

Jemima did not bother trying to get to Fulton. As she had sensed the magic too late, she kept walking.

Brother Thaddeus stood there up ahead, in a room that looked like a study complete with a Chesterfield settee. He was familiar in a vague way, dark straggly hair, goatee beard, narrow pale face and long nose with pale thin lips underscoring it. "Mrs Huntington, I presume," he said in a thin, nasal voice. It was so like a witch as described by Shakespeare, her eyes darted left and right looking for a cauldron.

She inclined her head. "You presume correctly. I appear to have misplaced my husband so I thought you might have stumbled across him."

Brother Thaddeus had the nerve to laugh at her. "Do you think me ignorant of your plans, your clumsy escapades across the country? I have followed you every step of the way."

"We expected as much," Jemima retorted. "We knew we were

walking into a trap. But are you powerful and smart enough to keep us here?"

A smirk on the man's face made her blood boil. If she was close enough she would have smacked it right off. "Your husband is the manufacturer of a technology I want to use. You bear some of that technology on your person."

"You have my husband and Fulton's arm. If you have not figured it all out yet, then you never will."

His fingers clenched and then he swiped his left arm through the air. Before she could move, metal curves surrounded her wrists and locked tight. Next she was lifted and her body pressed against a metal body. She looked up and over her shoulder. A metal monster had her held tight.

"Bring her," Brother Thaddeus said and walked out of the room. The metal contraption thunked and swayed in a path to follow.

The movement of the machine was clumsy and from what she could surmise, the machine was not animated as such, but rather a spell infused it with a semblance of life.

In the next room, she found Edward. Her mouth hung open. Her husband was unconscious and had been badly used. His chest lifted and hitched. He was injured but alive.

Brother Thaddeus moved both arms in an intricate gesture and then threw the spell. "Wake?"

Edward stirred, but his eyes only opened to slits. "I can tell you nothing," Edward said in a voice so thin, she wanted to weep.

"I have your wife here. You will tell me what I want to know or I shall rip the mechanical heart from her body and you can watch her die."

"No!"

"Do not listen to him, Edward. He cannot harm me. You know this."

Brother Thaddeus turned to her suddenly, eyebrows drawn into a line of puzzlement. "You think you can stop me?"

"Yes, I do." Jemima was not going to explain. She was not the helpless woman on an operating table at the Priory. Everything had changed. She had changed. For only now did she get the hint of recognition in that voice. He had been there in the background, watching while the other magicians nearly extinguished her life.

"If I cannot intimidate your harridan of a wife, I can use Fulton. I see you have replaced the arm with a newer, more improved version."

Jemima was not going to bite and hoped that Edward was sensible enough to his surroundings to recall that he had made it so that Fulton could live without the arm and that the loss of it would not also entail his loss of life.

The machine that held her captive shoved her into a chair. Before she could struggle out of it, a blanket of a spell landed on her. Panicked, she did not have time to fight it, or undo it before rope was used to secure her to the chair. At least she was with Edward. She had reached her goal.

Before she had done more than squirm, the machine's arm drove down and a blade pierced her thigh. She screamed. "Again," Brother Thaddeus said. And the blade descended with a machine's precision. No emotion to turn that blade. It bit into the flesh of her other thigh. Her scream rang out. It was unexpected and unnecessarily cruel. The blade had pierced her flesh and it had hurt. But she had power and she could feel it gathering, ready to respond to her will. Not yet. She whimpered at the pain. Let Thaddeus think her weak.

"Jemima?" Edward said, as if just realising she was actually there.

"Yes, Edward. I am here. I have come to save you."

Edward wailed and the sound of his despair chilled her heart. It was like he was already in hell and she had come to torment him. "Edward? Fulton is here too."

Edward wailed again and then broke into sobs. Jemima blinked. What had Thaddeus done to him? What threats had he made? She had never heard Edward sound as broken.

"Speak now for the next I shall mar her pretty breast by ripping out her heart."

"I have told you all that I know," he said while weeping. "There is nothing else to tell, no secret I retain."

"Oh Edward, what has he done to you?"

CHAPTER 18

In the dark Fulton stood alone. A thick door of metal blocked his path. Damp filled his nostrils and droplets glanced against his cheeks. Shafts of pale light filtered in through small grates along the edge of the ceiling. He had walked into a trap. He knew it was stupid and also deliberate. He tried to keep faith with Jemima's plan but a thick wad of fear filled his gut. Edward was at risk and now Jemima, oh Jemima—faced with an impossible choice. At least Milly was not here to witness his end.

Even though the steel door was impenetrable, he had to try. His replacement arm was not fully functional, but he still had his leg. Using his good arm, he steadied himself so he could lie on the flag stones. It had to be enough. Had to. What choice did he have? Walk away. Go back to his wife and child while Huntington and Jemima remained here to perish. No, he could not turn back. Shuffling on his rear and using his legs, he was able to position himself so that he could pull back his feet and then kick.

Thump! The sound echoed in the chamber and up the walls. He had to readjust because the force of his kick shoved him back. Using his good hand, he rolled up his trouser leg. There was a screw there that he could tighten. It was hard to see. But in the dark his fingers found it and wound. He was ready for another kick. *Thump!* The door rattled in the frame this time. The bolt jingled as well. Progress. He had moved away from the door and had to readjust, drawing himself along the ground. Again he kicked, and kicked. He had made an impression on the door. The bulk of it had twisted in the frame, a small bend in the metal. Not nearly enough to get through, but it was a start. His breathing sounded loud to his ears as if the bricks in the walls had taken up the whisper of it and amplified it. As if the ghosts of those who had passed had picked up a tune and were singing it with their ethereal voices, faint and thready, accumulating in the forgotten corners of this accursed house. Even with the flesh of his back rubbed raw, he shuffled down again and aimed his foot. *Thump. Thump. Thump!*

An exhalation of air from the other side wafted across his skin. It was warm. It was smoky. There was a fire here. A furnace. No, he shook his head, denying where his negative thoughts spiralled. No, he could not, would not. Edward was irreplaceable. Jemima?

❧

JEMIMA HATED BEING TIED UP AT THE BEST OF TIMES. BEING anchored with a spell, rope and chains and ugly slashes to her thighs was really annoying. She could break free, she supposed, but the time was not right. She needed Edward alert and ready to make their escape.

"Edward!" She hissed at him urgently. "Wake up!"

Her husband was in a sorry state. Beaten, battered, his clothes in shreds. Brother Thaddeus had tortured him to obtain the secret of his magical machines. Edward had nothing to say. Her husband did not really understand himself why his machines worked the way they did and their captor did not believe him.

Jemima surveyed the room again, hoping to find a way out of this predicament. Her own sufferings were considerable though she weathered them. The two wounds in her thigh throbbed and a copious amount of blood leaked out to make her skin stick to the seat. On several occasions, her tormentor had come close to testing the theory that Jemima was immortal and close to indestructible. He had made his machine bend her back, hoping to snap her spine, only it did not break. The strength in her kept her intact. He had the machine slap her in the side of her head. Other than blanking out, she suffered no ill effects. She peered at the wounds on her legs and saw that the blood had lessened. Using her magic, she asked the flesh to heal. If Thaddeus had noticed her use of magic he did not say anything.

Her resistance to torture only made him angrier. Jemima was not an automaton. She could not be coerced and would not do anything she did not agree with. Hence, she was totally useless for world domination, a lesson Brother Thaddeus was going to learn. If her own husband could not command her, what made that deranged magician think he could.

She would do anything to save her husband but not something that could directly harm others. The thought of his suffering brought tears to her eyes and anger to her heart. Glaring at her captor, she pictured what she wanted to do to him.

"I see the threat of ripping out your heart has no effect on either of you. Pity."

His dark eyes glittered in the light. "My magic is great you know. I used it to smash Fulton's home, to guide my machine to rip out his arm. I enjoyed his suffering as I do yours."

"Why though? How does that help you?"

Thaddeus licked his lips. "Fulton smashed his way through the Priory to save you. You brought Geneck to us and he killed indiscriminately. He took my brother and none of you lifted a hand to save him."

Jemima nodded, licked her lips. "You forget I was held prisoner by your friends who were busy trying to end my life. And we did all we could to stop Geneck."

He hissed, spittle flying. "They were stupid. I am not. I have other ways of getting what I want. If I cannot have Huntington's secret then I will remove it from this world."

The room suffused with heat as Thaddeus opened the door to a furnace. Another one of his machines lifted Edward's inert form and placed him on a conveyer belt. He was not tied to it but the machine hoisted a heavy weight onto Edward, effectively locking him in place.

"I must deal with your friend. Watch and learn, Mrs Huntington. The flames will tear the secret from his mouth or seal them forever."

"No, no. This is idiotic. The secret will die with him."

Thaddeus ignored her and headed to the door. "Wait!"

It was Fulton. Her heart leaped. While Fulton distracted him, she would free herself and save Edward.

Thaddeus paused in his exit and half turned, as if he did not care for Fulton's interruption at all. "What do you want? You have muscle but no brain. You are of little use to me."

"I know the secret of Edward's devices."

Swinging around, Thaddeus dropped his mouth open and then leaned forward, eyes narrowed. "What is it?" he said impatiently, as if he did not believe that Fulton had anything to say.

Fulton stepped forward. Jemima could barely pay attention as Edward was in danger and was not able to roll off the conveyer belt.

"Think about it. Huntington's devices are attached to people." He lifted his arm, then lifted a knee. He pointed to his chest and nodded towards Jemima.

"So what? That does not mean they cannot have a life of their own. He has the secret."

"Yes, Huntington does. The secret is him, his empathy, his love, a part of himself he embeds in the gems that power our devices. You cannot replicate that. You do not have it in you. He made these devices to improve life, give life. You want to take life and you cannot use Huntington's gift because you are empty. Nothing lives in you except hate and spite and envy."

Jemima was arrested by Fulton's words. She could see the anger build up in Thaddeus. He struck down his hand, in dismissal she thought.

"I will enjoy watching you suffer, Fulton. You survived the attack on your home but you will not leave this place alive. But first you will watch your friend die. If I cannot have the secret then no one can."

Time to move. Jemima bent her hand enough to grip a chain. It was an awkward angle, not a good place to tug so she gently brought her wrist back so that her hand was on the same level as the chain. There was no way to get her other hand on the same strand of chain so she had to use her hip as the anchor point. She tried and she flicked her gaze up toward Edward and back again. There was not enough leverage for her to break free. Her hip was not secure enough. Her other hand was behind her back. Carefully she wriggled and tried to grasp the length of chain she held in her right hand. Her shoulder hurt as she forced her arm into an impossible angle. Eyes closed she finger-crawled slowly, achingly until she closed on the link. Then she had to move her shoulder and adjust her hand so that she could tug hard enough to open the link. A whimper from Edward and she tried not to think of him sizzling as he headed closer to the flame.

With two hands on a section of the same chain, she pulled. She pulled harder. She brought all her strength to bear and then she threw in what magic she could muster. The chain had not broken, one link had opened a smidgen or was she imagining that. Jemima wriggled her wrists trying to get a hold of the chains that bound her. If she could grip them she could tug them and her strength should allow her to break free.

A cry split the air. Edward. Her head jerked. His coat was on fire. "Use your magic!" she called to Edward.

Her gaze flicked around the room. There was a bucket of water. Could she use magic to lift it? They had not even practiced such a thing. Closing her eyes she pictured it, pictured her hand around the handle, lifting it and throwing the contents. The sound of the bucket falling had her eyes opening. Steam rose off Edward's coat. "Move, damn it!"

"No!" Thaddeus roared.

Ignoring the crazed magician, she kept her gaze on her husband, while she hid her attempt at freedom. "Edward?" she queried in a whisper as she heard him moan.

His eyelids fluttered. "Jemima?" he rasped, his voice thin and used.

"Yes. I am here. Can you get yourself off that damned conveyer belt?" She signalled to Fulton. "Please help."

Fulton went to move but a creak and a moan of metal defeated him. A machine rose up to block his path. "No!" She heard him cry out, despair in his voice.

Jemima focussed on Edward. As Fulton could not provide immediate aid, it had to be her.

"Edward, listen." Edward mumbled a reply as his eyelids fluttered. Blood caked his curls and covered half his face. Yet, something must have sunk in, because Edward rocked his body back and forward. The weight impeded him.

"That is it! Use magic if you can. Move!"

It was so hot in the room that sweat stung her eyes, making it hard to see. Surely Edward could feel the heat from the smelter. If he did not get off that belt he was going in there head first.

Edward was rocking himself but not hard enough.

If he did not fall off the conveyer belt now, it would be too late. Jemima sucked in a breath, grabbed the chain and pulled. She clenched her jaw, forced everything into her muscles, pictured the link opening. With a cry of pain, she let go, and the chains loosened. Her stab injuries were numb spots on her muscles. She threw the chains to the ground and stood.

Thaddeus gaped at her. "How?"

"I bet you really want to know," Jemima replied.

Thaddeus drew a spell in the air, an elaborate pattern.

Jemima braced herself, concentrating hard. The spell hit and then rebounded, flung back with all her magical might. Thaddeus surged backward, landing hard.

"You ... cannot use ... magic..." he shrieked.

Jemima grinned. "Watch me."

Thaddeus crawled away, scurrying like a cockroach. His voice rose, hysterical. Strange commands issuing from his mouth. No time to deal with him now. The evil magician could barely stand and she doubted he would get far. Right now, Edward needed saving and she threw herself onto the conveyer belt.

The stink of burning flesh met her nostrils, but she could not think. Edward had to be alive. Had to live. She picked up Edward and threw him off the belt and away from the searing heat.

"Jemima!" It was Fulton calling out. "Ware!"

She stumbled and fell to her knees, but she knew that her coat was smouldering. She could feel the heat climbing up her back. With a breath, she brought all her magic forward, felt it ripple along her skin and tease her throat.

"Jump!" Fulton called. "Please."

Jemima met his horrified gaze. "Too late." The flames swallowed her.

"Jemimaaaaa!" Fulton screamed.

CHAPTER 19

With the machine punched into bite-sized pieces, Fulton flexed his arm, happy that it finally obeyed his commands. Then, looking up, he stood there struck dumb. Jemima had fallen into the furnace. She had not leaped to safety. She had not cried out. Just said "too late" as if she had missed a train.

His cry rang out. Snot and tears obscured his vision. The horror of what he just witnessed was too much to bear. Jemima? A whimper from Edward drew him to his friend's side. He hoisted Edward up, not able to assist him carefully and mind his burned flesh. Edward flinched, not really conscious and Fulton could see the damage from torture and the burns on top. They had to get out of there. Edward's back was burned and he was suffering. Fulton did not think he had registered that his wife had fallen into the fire.

Jemima!

The fire in the furnace erupted, flames lipping the opening as if it had too much fuel and too much fury. He gaped. It was going to explode. He had to get Edward out of there. If Thaddeus was killed by his own deadly fire then all well and good. The ground shook beneath his feet. The furnace rattled and the metal outer covering bulged.

There was no time to be gentle. Using his good shoulder and his arm, he lifted Edward and made for the door Thaddeus had used.

A fallen machine partially blocked the way. It looked as if Thaddeus had tried to launch it to attack but had faltered. A pair of legs stuck out beneath the heavy metal contraption. Thaddeus had met his end. Fulton eased around it, his heart finding no pity for the dead man.

Pipes threaded their way through the house, from the basement up through the floors to the house proper.

Up the stairs, Fulton made the ground floor and kicked the closest door to exit. Picking up speed, he unintentionally jolted Edward who moaned and cried out. The rumble grew stronger. Could Jemima be alive in that furnace? He thought not. But something was happening. He took loping strides to get as far away from the manor house as he could.

In the dark he stumbled, sending Edward skidding along the lawn. Something wet coated his trousers and when he turned around, he saw Frank's body, cut into four sections and spread out on the ground. Frank?

To own the truth he had never liked the lad. He had tolerated him but seeing him like this, ripped into pieces, he could not suppress the sob. "Frank?"

Edward moaned and Fulton dragged his gaze away from the dead magician and eased over to where Edward sprawled. "Come on my friend. Let us get you out of here."

"Jemima?" Edward mumbled. "I saw Jemima."

"I know." He lurched to his feet and eased Edward up so he could support him under the arms. Edward took most of his weight, sagging now and then as weakness overcame him.

From kitchen garden, Fulton saw flames, licking out of the basement windows. A rumble erupted, and the walls flexed and crumpled. Fulton dove to the ground, dumping Edward and then crawling over him as a concussive wave blew over them. The sound was deafening. Fulton screamed out his fear, his sorrow. In her dying throes, Jemima had won, destroying the magician and his evil machines.

He rolled onto his back, saw the wreck of the manor house. It brought back memories of Hatfield and the destruction there. House for a house. Life for a life. Was that an equal exchange? No, it was not.

Sobbing, he lay there next to Edward, hoping that his friend's wounds were not mortal. The heat from the fire grew intense and he slowly shuffled backwards, bringing Edward with him. Fulton had told the truth about Edward's inventions. It was a truth that Edward did not know himself, but Fulton felt it, knew it in his bones and in the throb of the gem that powered his devices, that part of Edward was inside him. And Jemima? His love had given her life. Her love for him had saved them all.

Tears leaked down his face as he watched the fire. He wiped his eyes, not sure what he was seeing. There was a human-shaped shadow there, growing bigger in the flames. He shook his head. "Edward? Can you see that?"

A green glow surrounded the figure as it stepped through the flames. "No." At first he thought it was the magician. Then he rubbed his eyes, blinked and opened his mouth. Heat and smoke dove in and left him retching. "Edward?"

His friend mumbled. Fulton helped him to sit. "Look."

Delirious, barely conscious from the assault, Edward's eyes were unfocussed. "Look," Fulton urged.

The figure moved closer, flame and green magic flowing around her naked form. Was she dead? Was he seeing her ghost? Was she some goddess come to life for she looked so beautiful, even with a green glow to her perfect white skin.

Tears fell and Edward gaped. "Jemima?"

A smile lit her face and she came up to them and knelt in the grass. "Can I have your coat, Fulton? I fear I have lost my clothes."

Fulton fumbled with his jacket, drawing it off and handing it over. She took it from his hand and draped it over her shoulders. "How is he?"

"Alive," Fulton said. "You are alive."

Jemima nodded slowly, a cheeky smile on her face. "An Amber Rose. That is what you look like, Fulton. Through the flames you guided me. A beacon in the dark. I followed you and found you. I have proved the theory, Fulton. I am immortal. I can be wounded but not even that furnace could destroy me. The light in your eyes guided me to you. Thank you for bringing Edward to safety."

The green halo faded, and her skin took on a normal hue, although her face had a greyish cast. It was hard to tell in the flame-lit night. "How are you feeling?" he said.

"Quite ill actually." Then she leaned over and vomited into the grass and then fainted dead away.

Fulton gaped but as she was breathing he relaxed and waited. He was spent. What had she been blathering about. Amber Rose. A beacon?

They did not have long to wait for the neighbours to see the flames, or the servants to break out the carriages and come to assist.

The innkeeper found them. "I thought something was amiss when Bestie came trotting back without ye. The earth tremor had me on my way as fast as I could."

Kneeling down, the innkeeper laid a blanket over Jemima. "I'll be fetching the doctor for your friend."

A doctor tended to Edward as they made their way back to the inn. It was a slow bumpy ride and Edward moaned and cried out while the doctor tsked. After Edward was carried to a room with the doctor in tow and Jemima deposited in another, Fulton went in search of a maid to help her into a nightgown and went to check on the old magician.

Brother Ferdinand woke after Fulton prodded him. "It is over."

Brother Ferdinand blinked and sat up. He took a few deep breaths. "He is dead." He locked gazes with Fulton to check his assertion. When Fulton did not respond, he closed his eyes for a few seconds. "Yes, his influence has gone." The old magician looked about him. "Frank?

"I am sorry. He was killed."

"Poor Frank. He was so keen to prove himself. It hurt him to know that Thaddeus had meddled with his mind."

"He helped us win," Fulton replied.

Brother Ferdinand smiled. "He would be proud to know that. He wanted revenge for Bertrand and he got it."

Fulton tugged the remains of his cravat off his neck and tugged off his boots. "Move over, Ferdinand. This is the last room at the inn."

Brother Ferdinand shuffled over and Fulton slumped onto the bed.
"Tell me what happened in detail. You smell like smoke."

He did.

"Will Jemima ever forgive me?"

"She will, Uncle Ferdy. She will."

EPILOGUE

They lingered in the inn for two weeks while Edward's wounds healed. Even with magic applied by Uncle Ferdy, movement hurt him. Jemima played cards with him, read him books and practiced magic. Ambrose wrote daily to Milly and she responded in kind. Uncle Ferdy had gathered up Frank's belongings, sniffling as he did so. From there he used magic to send them home.

Jemima bit her lip, thinking they had sacrificed the young magician. She could make the excuse that they did not know Thaddeus would kill him. But if they had not known, they should have strongly suspected because he had killed before without hesitation. They would never know if it was the evil magician or one of his automatons that had killed Frank, but was not that the same thing? The automatons had been driven by Thaddeus's magic and will. What they did was only an extension of himself.

They had yet to speak of what happened in the furnace. Of the secret that Fulton shared. Of her own burning and renewal in the flames. She was still Jemima, but that emerald fire she had siphoned from Geneck was now part of her, part of the fabric of her. It no longer sat around her like a cloak, or rippled under her skin. It was her.

When they arrived in Kiddlington, at the manor house the Fultons had leased, Jemima felt at ease. The tears were happy and the cries were of delight. Fulton hugged his wife close, hugged Aunt Prudence as if he treasured her and marvelled in the growth of his son, who now had chubby cheeks and fleshy arms and legs.

Edward stretched awkwardly and Jemima worried at the paleness of his complexion and the dark circles under his eyes. "We have a room prepared for my nephew," Aunt Prudence said. "Come this way."

Edward was grateful for the bed and was soon asleep. The trip had tired him out. He would mend. Jemima did not know what Thaddeus had done to him before she arrived. She did not know what threats he made. She could only imagine. When Edward was hale enough, he would tell her and somehow she would make it right.

Within the week, Edward was able to join in for afternoon tea. "Pass the scones, will you, Aunt Prudence. I am famished."

Jemima smiled indulgently at the return of her husband's famous appetite. Jemima passed him the jam and a big bowl of cream. She waggled her eyebrows because he had yet to notice the fresh sweet buns.

"And the buns, if you please," he said without looking up. "I can smell them."

Aunt Prudence laughed. "It is so good to see you well again, nephew. I could tell you a thing or two about my adventures. Not as dramatic as yours, but a worthy tale."

Jemima's ears perked up but before she could comment, Fulton spoke. "Are you writing a memoir, Aunt?"

Aunt Prudence looked up from pouring a cup of tea. "However did you know?"

Fulton shrugged. "A lucky guess."

Jemima locked gazes with Fulton. "A guess? I would never in a hundred years have guessed that."

Milly poured some milk into her tea. "What will you call this memoir?"

"A Prudential Light."

"Fascinating," Edward said after swallowing some sweet dough with lashings of butter. "Maybe I should write down ours."

Jemima snorted. "You are busy enough writing down..." She

coughed. "In your journals, if you started a memoir I would never see you."

Edward sat back and met them all eye to eye and then a grin popped up, making his eyes sparkle. "I do believe, my dear, that you have volunteered to write down our adventures."

Jemima rolled her eyes. "I would much prefer have a piece of that apple pie. Milly would you be so kind?"

Later as they nursed full stomachs and lounged around on the various settees and arm chairs, Milly came to sit by Jemima. "I have news," Milly said in a soft voice as she leaned in conspiratorially.

Jemima did her best to repress a burp. "What news is that?"

Milly leaned in to whisper. "I am expecting again."

Jemima laughed out loud. "Wonderful. You have been a pillar of strength in all this. You have managed everything so well. Congratulations."

"Are you really happy for me? I thought perhaps." She shrugged, and glanced sideways at Edward who was sitting in a distracted doze, an odd smile about his lips.

"Of course I am happy for you. Envy is not a trait I think I have. Besides," she said, leaning into Milly's ear. "I too am with child."

Milly drew back, an exclamation of surprise issuing from her lips. "But you said ..."

Jemima shrugged. "I know, and the theory was wrong." It explained her strange periods of queasiness.

"But you went into the furnace. Ambrose said you did. Does that mean the baby is ... like you?"

Jemima shrugged. "Like me? You mean charming and intelligent? Only time will tell."

Milly giggled, covering her mouth delicately. "No, I mean your strength and your power." Fulton did tell his wife everything.

Jemima nodded and sighed. "Edward has no theories at present, but I am sure he is working on one. The baby might arrive before he has settled his thinking."

Edward had roused himself and at once he discerned the topic of the conversation. "Yes, it is amazing to me and such a blessing. I could not be more proud, more happy."

Aunt Prudence, understanding Edward's awkward announcement, went into raptures and started to discuss with Fulton what baby clothes she wanted to make.

Once that discussion had died down, Milly narrowed her gaze. "What of this Amber Rose you told Fulton about?"

Jemima lay her head against the back of the settee. "I have a theory about that."

Edward came and sat on her other side, suddenly wide awake. "You do? I would like to hear it."

"It is simple really. Fulton has amber in his prostheses. Through the flames I could see him, my Ruby Heart saw his Amber Rose. That is what it looked like to me. It was not easy to see, through the smoke and the flames and I guess through the magic that surrounded me. And when I came upon you both on the lawn, Fulton's eyes were bright and glowing amber as well. If not for him, I would not have made my way out of the flames to your side. I may have gotten lost and who knows where I may have ended up." She grinned at her husband, her gentleman magician. "Am I close to your theory?"

"Very close. I did not intend for this connection between you both and I suppose it is a connection to me too. Fulton has talked to me long and often of his theories and what he told Brother Thaddeus."

Milly sighed. "You have a bond that I can only envy. Fulton is my heart and I am glad he has some love left for you two."

She hugged Jemima. "We will have babies together. I am so excited."

Jemima hugged her back. "Now I have walked through the fires of hell, what is a little childbirth on the scale of pain?"

Milly chuckled. "I will wager you will scream just as loudly as I do."

ACKNOWLEDGMENTS

I seem to say this a lot but this book was a long time coming. Sorry. However, when it did come together it did so very quickly.

Special thanks to Maxine McArthur who gave me feedback mid-drafting which really helped me get this over the line. For her efforts she got to edit the book as well. Poor Maxine! We have known each other since 2000 and she has been an inspiration, a mentor and good friend. I wish she would write again. Hear that Maxine?

I love Jemima Hardcastle Huntington. I wish I could thrive on chaos as she does. I also wish I could eat as many scones, baps, and buns that she does and be as trim as her. Alas, I would not get through the door if I did so.

Many thank you to readers as you inspire me to keep writing. I really love it when I get emails that say how much they liked the book, or positive reviews.

You can probably tell I had fun with this. If you had fun, please tell your friends.

Regards

Donna Maree Hanson
    April, 2025

ALSO BY DONNA MAREE HANSON

Cry Havoc Series (steampunk fantasy)

Ruby Heart, Cry Havoc Book One

Emerald Fire, Cry Havoc Book Two

Amber Rose, Cry Havoc Book Three

Silverlands Series (Epic Fantasy)

Argenterra: Silversands Book One

Oathbound:Silverlands Book Two

Ungiven Land: Silverlands Book Three

Dragon Wine Series (Dark Fantasy)

Shatterwing: Dragon Wine Part One

Skywatcher: Dragon Wine Part Two

Deathwings: Dragon Wine Part Three

Bloodstorm: Dragon Wine Part Four

Skyfire: Dragon Wine Part Five

Moonfall: Dragon Wine Part Six

Love and Space Pirates (Science Fiction Romance-Sweet level)

Rayessa and the Space Pirates

Rae and Essa's Space Adventures

Opi Battles the Space Pirates

Short story collections

Beneath the Floating City: Short science fiction stories

Through These Eyes: Tales of Magic Realism and Fantasy

Robots Hearts: Science Fiction Short Stories